CASHMERE AND CAMO

BILLIONAIRES IN BLUE JEANS BOOK THREE

ERIN NICHOLAS

ISBN: 978-0-9988947-7-5

Editor: Lindsey Faber

Copyeditor: Nanette Sipe

Cover artist: Lindee Robinson, *Lindee Robinson Photography*

Cover designer: Angela Waters

Cover models: Alexis Susalla, Dustin Oprisiu

❀ Created with Vellum

ABOUT CASHMERE AND CAMO

A friends to lovers romance...and then some.

Run a pie shop with her sisters for a year. Date for the first time at age twenty-nine. Don't be terrified.

Well, she's got the first thing under control at least. Mostly.

But this is exactly what a best friend is for. Advice, pep talks, matchmaking, sex education...

So what if her best friend is a guy? A very hot, tattooed, ex-Marine, mechanic guy? He's definitely well-versed in everything she needs to know. And she trusts him. Who better to teach her the man-woman stuff she's been missing out on?

But there could be one tiny problem. The only person causing her any butterflies...and dirty dreams...is her matchmaker himself.

PROLOGUE

1. Move to Bliss.
   1 year. Live in house together

2. Run pie shop. → profit by year end. $$

3. AVA- kitchen, baking, all products.
   NO business!
   Date a guy from Bliss. Give it
       6 mos. Have fun.
            No checklists!

4. BRYNN - customers/waitress.
   Time with people, get to know them.
   no kitchen, no business.
       Date a guys from Bliss.

5. CORI -books/accounting. no baking.
   leave customers to B.
   make a commitment. but NO DATING 1 year!
           6 mos

1

_____

Motor oil and tattoos.

Brynn Carmichael would never in a million years have guessed that motor oil and tattoos would make it onto her list of Top Ten Turn-Ons.

But it just so happened that they were number one and number two.

Okay, maybe it was the *sight* of motor oil streaked across the blue-jeaned ass of Noah Bradley that actually turned her on. Or maybe it was just the ass. Or Noah.

But whatever it was, Brynn Carmichael took a deep breath of the motor oil scented air around her, felt the hum of arousal ripple through her body, and settled back against the windshield of the baby blue 1953 Ford F-100 pickup—her favorite place in the entire town of Bliss, Kansas.

Granted, there wasn't a lot *of* Bliss, Kansas so her options for favorite places were more limited than they were back home in New York. Bliss was a tiny town smack-dab in the middle of the Midwest. But, truth be told, the hood of the pickup in Noah Bradley's garage was probably her favorite place anywhere.

It was the perfect reading spot. The windshield was a great

backrest and she could sit with her knees bent, her book or e-reader propped against her thighs. And being in the shop was strangely comforting.

Which had shocked her in the beginning. The first day she'd wandered to the garage on the walk, she'd taken to escape the close confines of the pie shop with her sisters, she'd stood in the doorway, watching Noah until he noticed her.

"You okay?" he'd asked, pulling the rag from his back pocket and wiping his hands as he'd come toward her.

"Can I just...*be* here?" she'd asked. "It's really loud at the pie shop."

She'd needed a place where she could get away from...everything. She wasn't used to dealing with people all day long. She definitely wasn't used to dealing with her *sisters* all day long. She loved Cori and Ava dearly. But they hadn't all lived together in eleven years. And they'd never worked together. Now it was Ava and Cori twenty-four-seven and well, Brynn just needed a break. She couldn't go to the house where her sisters might find her. There was no escape at the pie shop. She'd even realized that a walk in the park meant running into people and having to socialize.

But when she'd found herself in front of Noah's garage, something had made her step through the door. It wasn't quiet exactly, but he was the only one there, and he was hardly what anyone would call chatty. Plus, there was nothing here *she* needed to do. She had no idea what most of the machines and tools were that occupied the garage and there was no pressure here. It had seemed like a perfect hideout. Partly because no one would ever expect her to be here.

She'd always been very happy in the library or her lab. Places that were quiet and everyone just kept their heads down and did their thing. She'd never expected to find the same thing in a mechanic's shop in a little town in Kansas of all places.

The truck she'd claimed as "her spot" didn't run, but it sat inside the big doors of Noah's shop, out of the sun, with a perfect view of Main Street, Bliss, Kansas. And the perfect view of the hard, toned mechanic bent over an engine.

Brynn let her gaze travel over Noah's back and upper arms, his muscles bunching as he reached for something under the hood of the car he was working on. He wore a white T-shirt that was streaked with black and well-worn blue jeans with a hole by one back pocket and more black streaks. A red rag hung from his other back pocket that he used to wipe his hands when he wasn't absentmindedly wiping them on his thighs. The right sleeve of the shirt hid only a fourth of the tattoo that decorated that arm and shoulder, and Brynn found herself shift slightly so she could see more of the arm as he pulled on the wrench he held.

She'd been attracted to Noah from the first time she'd seen him in the kitchen of the pie shop she and her sisters now owned. But she hadn't expected him to become her friend. Or for his garage to become her oasis in the town that overwhelmed her with its friendliness and nosiness.

Interestingly, Noah's garage was even better than the library or the lab. It always smelled the same—a combination of motor oil, gasoline, rubber, and good old dirt. It always looked the same too. The vehicle in the bay changed, of course, but while it was cluttered with tools and parts back here, and stacks of papers, and invoices, and more parts all over the desk in the front, it had a nice...*feel* to it. It was unassuming. No one wore ties or heels or lab coats here. It was jeans and T-shirts and dirt and grease. And while it wasn't quiet, she found she preferred the sounds of metal tools against metal car parts, the occasional muttered curse from Noah, and the classic country music drifting from the ancient boom box that sat on his tool bench to the stark quiet of her lab.

Her lab was...sterile. Obviously. It was clean and polished, and everything was labeled and in its place and carefully controlled. But here, tools could be tossed into the toolbox without worry. Things were banged on, tires were kicked, hands and clothes got dirty. There were no delicate glass tubes or tiny microscope lenses. Here, things were big, and tough, and sweaty.

Brynn rolled her eyes at that last one. No, she didn't sweat in her lab, but she didn't really have a desire to sweat. The appeal of sweating had everything to do with the man she was now ogling.

The man she'd been ogling for about five months, two weeks, and six days. Ever since she'd started coming to his garage in the middle of the day.

If the tools and smells and sounds of this garage were a far cry from her sterile research lab in New York, the man in charge here was even more different from the men she typically spent time with. Scientists, researchers, scholars. Men who preferred lab coats and microscopes and thick textbooks. Noah not only worked on cars and had tattoos, he was an ex-Marine, wore denim and cotton almost exclusively, and read mystery novels.

She found that incredibly hot. Watching him prop a mystery novel on a denim clad thigh, while his big, calloused hand with grease under the nails wrapped around a bottle of beer got her going. It was probably very shallow to be so aware of all of Noah's physical attributes, but he was an anomaly in her world, and scientists *studied* anomalies. And hey, she hadn't been shallow up until now so she thought that could be forgiven.

She'd just never been as aware of a man as a *man* in her life, and she couldn't help but take note of everything from his reading preferences, to the way his jeans were slightly frayed at the bottom. She was thrilled with the attraction. Men were one thing she *hadn't* studied a lot and she'd admit it—she wanted to know more about *this* kind of chemistry. Noah was, in her opinion, the perfect subject. New, different, appealing, and *available*. He was always there for her, so getting to know him and observe —okay, ogle—him had been easy.

And then there was the most appealing thing about Noah— he didn't talk much.

He was quiet and thoughtful. Just like she was. He didn't need to fill the space with words. He didn't ask a lot of questions. Which, along with the view, and the no-Cori-and-Ava thing— and had she mentioned the view?—made his shop the best place in town for relaxing and reading.

"*Mer-ow.*"

Brynn looked over to find a large cat climbing out through the window of the pickup's cab and up onto the hood with her.

"Hey, Penn," she said, holding out her hand.

He bumped his nose against her fingers and then dipped his head so she could rub behind his ears.

Penn was named after Pennzoil brand motor oil because he was a sleek, solid black and looked like spilled oil when he sprawled on the floor of the shop. He slept on the front seat of the truck about sixty percent of the time. The other forty percent of his naps were taken either up on the top of some old boxes on the highest shelf of the garage or on the lowest shelf behind stacks of old invoices in the front office. He spent most of his time at the shop, though he did wander the town during the day, checking things out, as cats were wont to do.

Brynn shifted her tablet to the side as Penn climbed up onto her lap, his purring loud enough to be heard over the whirring of Noah's machines.

"How are you, baby?" she asked him, setting her tablet next to her so she had two hands for the rubbing and scratching Penn seemed to need. "Did you have a good nap?"

Penn started kneading his front paws into her thigh. He had claws, but he kept them carefully sheathed whenever they cuddled. Brynn was surprised by how much she liked Penn's once-a-day lap time. She'd never been a cat person. Then again, she'd never really been around cats. Or dogs. Or any other animals. She liked Penn though. He came and told her when he needed attention and then when he'd had enough, he'd jump down and go off to do whatever else he had on his agenda. Noah kept food and water out for him and the window in the truck rolled down so he could come and go. Otherwise, Penn seemed to take care of himself. In fact, Brynn suspected that if there wasn't food, water, and shelter provided, he'd make do on his own.

He did, however, seem to need help rubbing that spot behind his ear that made him close his eyes, arch his neck, and purr so loudly it vibrated Brynn like a massage chair.

She laughed as he settled his rump on her thighs as well, clearly ready to stay for the next several minutes. Running her hand over his silky fur, she glanced up. Noah was watching her and Penn, with a soft look on his face. It was a look she saw from time to time. It was clearly affectionate, but she wasn't entirely sure if he was feeling affectionate about her or the cat. Or both. She'd never seen him hold or pet Penn. In fact, that cat didn't get too close to Noah at all. He didn't shy away either. He just kind of did his thing while Noah did his. But Penn also didn't leave. He wandered from the garage from time to time, but he never stayed away. He always came back. And clearly Noah didn't dislike the cat. He fed him, made sure there was fresh water out, and never chased him out of the antique truck. He didn't fix the hole at the back of the garage where Penn slipped in and out. He even washed the blanket that Penn slept on in the truck every once in a while.

She opened her mouth, deciding it was time to find out what the deal was between man and cat, but before she could say anything, she heard, "Hey, Noah!" from just outside the garage doors.

Noah turned, his mouth stretching into a grin, and Brynn felt her heart trip. She loved his smile.

"Hey, Mitch."

A tall, good-looking man step into the garage. He was about their age—late twenties to early thirties—and had an easy smile.

Noah reached for the rag that was always in his back pocket. "What are you doing here?" he asked, as he reached to clasp Mitch's hand.

"I'm back," the other man told him.

"No shit."

"Yep. Seems none of us can stay away for long." Mitch chuckled.

Noah hitched a shoulder. "Does seem that way." But he wasn't laughing.

Brynn frowned. Noah loved it here in Bliss. Didn't he?

"So I was wondering if you could take a look at my car. Making a...clanking sound," Mitch said.

Now Noah chuckled. "Yep. Clanks are one of my specialties."

Brynn felt herself smiling.

"Great. I appreciate it. I can fix a lot of stuff, but cars are out of my league."

"Well, I appreciate that cars and stuff are out of your league," Noah said. "Makes paying my bills a lot easier."

Mitch chuckled again, and Brynn observed the interaction between the men with interest from her perch on the pickup. She was only a few yards away, but it was clear that Mitch hadn't noticed her yet.

Brynn watched Noah as he asked about Mitch's car problems. Noah could fix everything from leaky pipes to crooked floors. He kept the old house running she and her sisters had inherited from their dad. And the old car, Elvira, they'd inherited from their dad. And the pie shop that they'd inherited from their dad.

With all the old, worn-out stuff Rudy Carmichael had passed on to his daughters, there was no way they could have avoided getting to know Noah. Which she knew had been Rudy's intention. Noah had been one of Rudy's favorite people in Bliss during the five years he'd lived here. Probably one of his favorite people in the world, honestly. He and his friends, Evan and Parker, had been the sons Rudy never had.

But she wondered if her father had any idea how attractive a guy was when he could look at any problem, know exactly what needed done, and would step in and just do it.

Rudy might have. He really might have. Brynn just wondered if he knew that *she* would find that incredibly attractive.

She wouldn't have blamed him if he didn't. It was possible he believed she just wasn't into men. Not that she was *into* women. But she'd just never been that interested in dating. Men or women. And she was a twenty-nine-year-old virgin. Not that her dad had known *that* specifically. But considering that Brynn's last actual pick-her-up-at-the-door date had been when she was sixteen, and her dad had never lived with them so hadn't been there anyway, he might have suspected.

She didn't really want to date, honestly. She just never felt that need. Or desire. She worked with like-minded men who she could have dated. She hung out with her sisters—who would have gladly set her up with men, like-minded or otherwise. But she didn't need a man. And she'd never really wanted one.

Until Noah Bradley.

Maybe because she hadn't realized what she'd been missing. How it could feel to have a guy taking care of her. Not because she needed it. God knew her sisters took care of her—babied her actually. But with Noah it felt different. He was doing it just because he liked doing it. Liked being with her. No doubt about it, Noah Bradley's attention was addictive.

"So, I see you're taking over Jared's interest in old cars," Mitch commented, glancing out the garage doors.

Brynn knew he was referring to the 1937 370-D Cadillac that her father had left to her and her sisters. Elvira was parked out front because Noah had insisted it was time for an oil change.

"That belongs to a friend," Noah said of Elvira. "I'm just keeping her running from point A to point B. And that's the only one I work on."

A friend. He was referring to her. The car belonged to her sisters too and he considered them friends as well, but when he talked about them, he used their names. He always referred to Brynn as his friend. Besides, Brynn was the one who drove Elvira most. Because her sisters had boyfriends who would drive them places or would let them borrow their vehicles.

Of course, her *friend* Noah would gladly pick her up and drive her places. Or loan her a car. You didn't have to be in love to help someone with their transportation needs, and Noah was the most helpful person she knew

"That old truck of Jared's still not running?" Mitch asked.

Brynn straightened at the mention of her truck. Which wasn't her truck at all. But it was as familiar as the chair in her lab back in New York by now. And who was Jared?

"Nope," Noah said.

"You're not working on it?"

"Nope," Noah repeated.

"You looking to sell it, by chance?"

"Nope."

"You sure?" Mitch asked, stepping more fully into the garage again. He glanced over at the truck. Then straightened, noticing Brynn. "Oh."

She smiled and shifted to sit up away from the windshield. Penn made an annoyed noise at being moved and slipped off her lap, heading for the open window. He jumped down onto the truck's seat and she knew he'd be asleep in about two minutes.

"The truck is being used," Noah said. One corner of his mouth curled ever so slightly as he looked at Brynn.

"Yes, I see that." Mitch's grin was *not* ever so slight. It was wide and warm as he said, "Hi," to Brynn.

"Hi." She clutched her e-reader against her stomach and gave him a little smile.

Mitch was good-looking. He wasn't as...*alpha* as Noah, but still good-looking. She'd never used the word *alpha* to describe a man before coming to Bliss, but Cori and Ava had introduced her to the term, and it fit Noah. Really, really fit.

"You a mechanic?" Mitch asked, pulling her attention away

from Noah, who was now frowning as Mitch made his way across the garage toward the truck. And her.

"Um, no." She gave him a smile. "Just hanging out."

"You must be new here," Mitch said, stopping at the side of the truck. He tucked his hands into the front pockets of his jeans. "The place to hang out is the diner."

She gave a little laugh. "That's where most of the town spends most of its time," she agreed. "Which is why I take my breaks here."

"You like the smell of motor oil?" Mitch asked.

She did. She really did. She nodded. "And the quiet."

"Ah."

His gaze wandered over her, seemingly cataloguing details like her ponytail and her glasses and the black tank she wore with her khaki shorts. And her bare legs. He seemed to linger there. And suddenly she felt...jumpy. She wasn't used to men looking her over, and she wasn't used to thoughts like *well, I do have to date six guys by March.*

Her father's will had stipulated several kooky things. Like, that the girls move to Bliss for a year, and run his pie shop together, making it profitable by the end of twelve months. Something it had, apparently, never been when he'd been running it.

Even stranger, he'd put conditions on their love lives. Party girl Cori, who loved men almost as much as she loved baked goods, was not to date at all for six months. Powerhouse CEO Ava was to date one guy—one regular, raised-in-Bliss, non-CEO-type guy—for six months. And shy homebody Brynn was to date six different guys.

Cori was past her six months, and in love with Evan, and Ava had only two more months to go on her six-month timeline. Of course, the guy she was dating for those six months had turned out to be the guy she intended to date for the rest of her life, so... yeah, they were both doing well.

Brynn, on the other hand, hadn't even started. And she was

very aware that the last six months of their mandated stay in Bliss began in eight days.

She knew that Cori, Evan, Ava, Parker, and Noah, were aware of that too. Any minute she expected them to start asking about her plan. The plan she didn't have.

"There are other quiet places in town," Mitch finally said.

"Oh?"

"Like my back deck," he said with a nod. "I could arrange it so the only sound you hear is the sizzle of a steak on the grill and the top of a beer bottle popping open."

She couldn't help but smile. That was kind of smooth. And he'd just asked her out. And maybe now she did have a plan.

"But no smell of motor oil?" she asked. Huh, that might even be flirting.

His grin grew. "I'll buy you a can. You can sit and sniff it all night if you want to."

She laughed lightly. She was pretty sure this was definitely, maybe, flirting.

"I'm Mitch Anderson," he said, extending a hand.

Brynn wet her lips and held her hand out as well. "Brynn Carmichael."

Mitch didn't shake her hand. His hand engulfed hers and he just held it. "Carmichael? You're one of the triplets who own the pie shop?"

She nodded. She didn't want to pull her hand away, exactly. He wasn't squeezing, his palm wasn't sweaty, it wasn't unpleasant at all. But she kind of did want to pull away. It felt weird to be holding his hand.

Of course, that could have been because they had an audience. A glowering, *alpha* audience who was now stalking toward them.

"I hear you and your sisters have made some waves around here," Mitch said.

"Where did you hear that?" Noah asked, coming up beside Mitch.

Brynn slipped her hand from Mitch's and tucked her hands under her thighs. Yeah, it felt weird to be touching another guy with Noah right there. And that was not only confusing—she and Noah were friends and didn't do a lot of touching themselves—but it was going to be very inconvenient when she had to start dating. In eight days.

She'd just started really thinking about it. She'd been avoiding it. For six months. Telling herself that she should focus on the pie shop and her sisters first. But now...the shop was doing okay and her sisters were in love.

She was running out of excuses.

Mitch laughed at Noah's question. "Everywhere. My mom was telling me about the pie shop and everything before I even got back to town."

Noah shifted to wedge himself slightly between the side of the truck and Mitch. Mitch didn't comment on it, but he took a short step back.

"Heard that Evan and Parker are involved with two of the Carmichael girls." Mitch looked up at Brynn. "Didn't realize you were involved with the other one."

"We're just friends," Noah and Brynn said at the same time. They glanced at one another, then back to Mitch.

How many times had they said those three words? Individually and in harmony? Dozens and dozens.

Brynn swallowed and gave Mitch a smile. "Noah not only keeps Elvira running, he's helped us a ton at the pie shop."

Mitch looked over at Noah. "I'll bet he has."

Noah arched a brow. "I'm a pretty great guy. Love to help my friends out."

He hadn't specifically emphasized *friends*, but that's how Brynn heard it. Yeah, yeah, they were only friends. Fine.

"So really just hanging out?" Mitch asked. "That's great to know. Hate to think I'd asked your girlfriend to my back deck."

Had he said "back deck" with a strange tone? Brynn looked back and forth between the men who seemed to be having a stare down.

"Well, no worries," she said brightly. "I've never even seen Noah's back deck." She hadn't said it with a weird tone either, and yet it still sounded strange hanging in the air.

But it was true. She'd never been to Noah's house. And yes, it bugged her a little. But she saw him all the time. He was at Parker's diner a lot which was connected to Blissfully Baked, the pie shop. He was at the pie shop itself a lot as well. He really had helped them get it cleaned up and renovated. He'd painted walls with her and had redone most of the wood trim around the doors and windows. He'd even helped her with making the pillows that now decorated the seats of the wooden chairs throughout the shop. Noah, the big, tough, ex-Marine, mechanic had helped her make pillows. It was still one of her favorite things about him. He was also often over at her and her sisters' house. They had a near weekly game night that included Parker and Evan as well.

So she saw him a lot. She spent a ton of time with him even outside of hanging out at his garage. But she'd never been to his house. And while she considered him one of her best friends, she thought that was weird.

Too bad she wasn't the type to just show up on his doorstep. That was a Cori or Ava move. Brynn didn't...insinuate herself into situations or places. That just wasn't her style.

She sighed to herself. Nor was arguing her point or asking for favors or insisting on...anything her style. She had two sisters with very big personalities, and she'd learned early on that things were a lot easier if she just kept her mouth shut. It wasn't that she always went along with Cori and Ava. She did her own thing. She just didn't announce it or make a big deal out of it. She smiled and nodded and agreed, or kept quiet completely, and then did whatever she wanted when everyone's attention was elsewhere.

Though that had all gotten more difficult living and working with them 24/7. Time on her own was now an even more precious commodity.

"Then my back deck offer stands," Mitch said, giving her a slow smile.

Brynn felt her eyes widen as she felt a little flutter in her belly. Huh. That was a nice smile.

"I'm not much of a beer drinker," she said with a smile of her own.

"Anything you want, Brynn Carmichael," Mitch said. "You just say the word."

Yeah, there was another little flutter. *Anything you want.* Hmmm...those were three really nice words to hear. Especially from a good-looking guy who was watching her with clear interest.

If nothing else, Noah always paid attention to her, listening to her, watching her, often anticipating her needs before she even realized them. He was willing to help her out at all hours with anything she *needed*. But he was her friend. He wasn't romancing her.

Being romanced might be nice. She watched Mitch as the thought went through her mind. She'd been half anticipating, half dreading the dating thing. It would definitely be outside of her comfort zone, but she knew that was the point. Rudy Carmichael had demonstrated more insight into his daughters with his will than he ever had while alive. He'd put each of them into a position, both professionally with the pie shop and personally in their dating lives, that would make them step outside their usual, safe boxes and experience something new.

Brynn had initially realized it was a good thing. For her sisters. She'd even been the one to insist that they stop trying to get out of moving to Bliss and just do it. She'd actually agreed with Rudy that Cori needed some stability and Ava needed to learn to relax. Of course, Cori and Ava were pretty easy to figure out. Besides big personalities, neither shied away from letting their thoughts and feelings known.

Brynn was different from her sisters though. Rudy hadn't known her. Then again, she hadn't let him.

Still, considering he hadn't been an overly attentive father, getting two out of three right on what his daughters needed was not a bad percentage.

And the move to Bliss had been okay, even for Brynn. Temporarily anyway. She'd even gone so far as to appreciate the fact that, with Cori in one place for an extended period and Ava having to give less attention to Carmichael Enterprises, the sisters would all have more time together.

It had taken Brynn about a month of having Ava and Cori in the same space with her almost constantly for her to realize that, while she loved her sisters dearly, they were...a lot. Then her feelings of being overwhelmed and overstimulated had all really come to a head when they'd finally gotten the pie shop open and she'd had to wait on customers and interact with multiple people all day long. Along with her sisters. Constantly. Twenty-four-seven.

All of which had driven her to Noah's shop, seeking solace.

Now though, Mitch was making her think that maybe dating wouldn't be all bad. None of the other men in Bliss had paid her much more than friendly attention. They smiled, they held doors for her, they greeted her nicely when they came into the shop. But no one had asked her out.

Until now.

"How do you feel about margaritas?" she asked, swinging her legs around and over the side of the truck.

Mitch didn't step back as her feet swung past him. His eyes dropped to her bare legs. "I feel like I could become a big fan of margaritas," he said.

Noah let out a half-sigh, half-growl. "You probably need to get back to the shop," he said to Brynn.

She found herself staring at him. He looked like he was in pain. She frowned. "Are you—"

"The shop," he interrupted. "It's almost two."

They didn't have set breaks or lunch hours. The three sisters just took turns keeping the place open and running. They'd fallen into a comfortable pattern, each sister doing her part and filling in where needed. According to the will, Ava had to be in charge of the kitchen, Cori was in charge of the books and accounting, and Brynn covered the front of the shop, interacting with the customers. But that didn't mean that Brynn never helped peel apples or that Ava never boxed up to-go orders. Cori kept the books straight, but she was also their barista, keeping the coffeepot on and mixing up lattes and cappuccinos and her specialty, caramel macchiatos. She was actually the cook and baker of the trio, but she was supposed to have nothing to do with the pies they sold. At least until their first twelve months were up. Next March she would be taking the baking over with Parker, Ava's boyfriend, and from time to time even now she would experiment with new specialty pies and do taste-testings in the shop. It fit into a loophole in the will because they didn't *sell* those.

There were, fortunately, several loopholes they'd all found in their father's stipulations, and more than once Brynn had thought that Rudy had knowingly left them in there.

"Yeah, okay," she said. She did need to get back to the shop. She started to push herself off the hood of the truck, but both men stepped forward to help her down and ended up bumping into one another, Noah stepping on Mitch's foot, and Mitch banging his knee against the side panel.

They scowled at each other and Brynn slipped to the ground without assistance. She gave them both a wide-eyed look. "I'll see you later?" She wasn't sure who she was addressing that to. Probably both of them.

"Of course," Noah said, his expression softening slightly as he met her eyes.

"Definitely," Mitch said with promise.

She had no idea what else to say so she stepped around them. "'Bye, Penn," she called to the cat. Who likely didn't even lift an eyelid. Then she headed out into the September sunshine and turned toward the bakery. She felt a tingle on the back of her neck, as if she was being watched, but she resisted looking back. She did, however, feel an extra bounce in her step.

She liked the idea of two men standing there watching her go.

Huh. This was all very interesting.

She was hardly neglected. She wasn't *ignored* exactly. She worked to *not* call attention to herself so when people didn't pay her a lot of attention it was because that's how she liked it. But she was so not the one that people first thought of when they heard "The Carmichael triplets". She wasn't the one men tripped over trying to impress. She was not the one that people watched leave a room. Or a garage.

Until today.

And yeah, she liked it.

2

"So, that's Brynn Carmichael," Mitch said to Noah as Brynn rounded the corner at the end of the block.

Noah gritted his teeth. He turned back into the shop and to the car he'd been working on.

Cars. Those he understood. Those he could fix.

God, he loved cars.

Everything else in life less so.

He picked up a wrench and leaned in over the engine. He'd known Mitch Anderson all his life. He was hardly worried about hurting the guy's feelings or offending him by getting back to work in the midst of a conversation.

A conversation he did *not* want to have.

"Mom said that things have been interesting since the Carmichael girls came to town," Mitch commented, moving to lean against the front of the car.

Noah didn't respond.

"Now I can see why. Have there been a lot of injuries?"

Noah frowned. "Injuries?"

"From all the men in town tripping over their tongues?"

Noah rolled his eyes. Mitch was a dumbass. A handsome,

successful dumbass who had made Brynn blush. Noah gripped the wrench. "Everyone's been very nice to them."

"I'm sure," Mitch mused.

Noah tried to focus on the hoses he was supposed to be replacing. It wasn't working. "Of course, Cori's been involved with Evan from day one and Parker and Ava have been together for about three months now," Noah said. "So it's not like guys have been lining up or fighting over them." Mitch made a "huh" sound and Noah glanced up. "What?"

"Just that Evan and Parker are with Cori and Ava." He looked over. "No one's with Brynn." He paused. "Right?"

Noah clenched his jaw and straightened away from the car. He wiped his hands on a rag. No, technically no one was *with* Brynn. Except that *he* was with Brynn nearly every spare hour either of them had. They both worked a lot. Brynn spent her days at the pie shop and then at least an hour each evening on the phone or computer with people running her lab back in New York in her absence. Brynn also had her sisters and he had his mom and dad and Maggie, his buddy Jared's mom, to take care of. So they both had other things and people taking up their time, of course. But yeah, they seemed to spend a lot of time together too.

"She's not dating anyone," he finally said in answer to Mitch.

That much was true. What he and Brynn were doing wasn't dating. Because dating came with the expectation of things possibly progressing and becoming more over time. He and Brynn were exactly where and what they needed to be for each other. That wasn't going to change. No matter how much he wanted it to. She was here because her father had mandated it. And it was temporary. Thank God. Noah was looking out for her as her father had asked him to. But there was a *goal* here. An end point. Brynn was going back to New York in six months and he was never leaving Bliss. So yeah, they were just what and where they needed to be. For sure.

Mitch hadn't replied to the news of Brynn's single status.

"You're going to ask her out, aren't you?" Noah asked.

"Probably."

Noah sighed. Dammit. He had to get used to this. She *had to* date six men. It was in the will. If she didn't, she and her sisters didn't inherit Rudy's company, and his fortune. Noah didn't think the money, or the company for that matter, was that important to Brynn, but it was to her sisters, so she would do her part. For sure.

And her time was running out. In eight days, it would be exactly six months since the girls had arrived in Bliss. The pie shop was now fully renovated and open and doing fairly well. He didn't know the specifics of their finances, but business had definitely picked up. Her sisters had met their relationship conditions. So Brynn's dating mandate was all that was really left.

And Noah fucking hated even the thought of it.

He even hated that she'd smiled at Mitch with that sweet, almost surprised smile. As if she was trying to figure out if he was really flirting with her or not.

He wanted her sweet smiles. But it was that surprised part that jabbed him in the heart and made him tamp down the urge to punch Mitch right in his pretty face. Brynn should *not* be surprised when a man paid her attention. At least attention that had nothing to do with her being one of the foremost pharmaceutical researchers in the country. He was sure there were brilliant, geeky scientist guys all over the place that were impressed with and intimidated by Brynn.

But Mitch wasn't appreciating her brain. He was looking at her as the beautiful, subtly-sexy-without-even-knowing-it woman who blended into the background until you got a good look at her. Then you couldn't look away.

She'd been sitting on his truck, in his shop, hiding out in the shadows, literally. And Noah fucking hated that. Even while he loved it.

He felt divided in two. He loved that Brynn felt safe and

comfortable with him. They didn't talk much. They didn't really *do* anything a lot of the time. They'd painted and redecorated the pie shop. And she sat on the hood of the truck and read while he worked. But he loved that she felt like she could just *be* with him, and he wanted to keep her all to himself.

But he also hated that even here in his garage—maybe especially here—she was hiding out from the world. How could she figure out that she was special and amazing and that people wanted to get to know her and be close to her if she was never *with* people?

"There are some rules that you should be aware of before you ask her out," Noah finally said.

Mitch shrugged. "I already kind of asked her out."

"Rules," Noah said firmly. "Before you *take* her out."

Mitch turned to face him, looking amused. "Okay, like what?"

Noah sighed. He didn't love the idea of spilling the details of Rudy's will, but Bliss was a small town. Dating here was different. It was harder to date casually than it probably was in the bigger cities. Like New York. Or Kansas City where Mitch had been living. Here, everyone knew everyone else, knew their pasts, knew their relationship history, and paid attention to current relationships. It was also harder to date multiple people. The guys Brynn would be going out with knew one another. And their mothers were going to be upset if they only dated her once or twice and then she "moved on" to another guy. Everyone needed to understand what was really going on and not assume that this city girl was coming to sweet little Bliss to break as many hearts as she could.

That was one reason he'd held off for six months on insisting she get out there and date. He wanted the town to get to know her a little first.

And, of course, because it had taken about two hours for him to realize that he didn't want her dating anyone. Ever.

"It was important to Brynn's dad that she meet and date a

variety of guys. She's..." He sighed. This was coming out wrong. "Brynn's quiet. She's sweet. She's happiest with her nose in a book or calculating chemical formulas in her lab," he said, starting again. "She's not a social butterfly, she's not a flirt, she doesn't date much at all."

"She's inexperienced," Mitch filled in.

Noah had to nod. "Yeah. She's just had a lot of more important things to think about than relationships."

Mitch nodded.

"So when her dad decided she should live in Bliss for a year with her sisters and run his pie shop, he also made it clear that it was important to him that she go out and have some fun, but also get to know different types of guys. So she could maybe figure out what her type is."

Mitch nodded again. "That's pretty much what dating is, right? Looking for the perfect fit amongst all the options."

Noah had to admit he was surprised by Mitch's perspective. "Yeah, I guess so. It's just that with Brynn it's actually spelled out that she has to date six different guys. And she's only in town for six more months."

"So nothing serious or long-term. Just fun," Mitch said.

Noah nodded.

"Well, that takes a lot of pressure off," Mitch decided. "It'll be more fun if it's just about showing her a good time and knowing that no one's thinking marriage, right?"

"I guess." Noah supposed that was true. If the guys all knew that it was more of a project to introduce Brynn to the world of dating and that it was casual and short-term and just for fun, then no one would get their hearts broken. And no one would be buying diamond rings. Noah felt like scowling even thinking about that. He knew, firsthand, how easy it was to fall for Brynn. Even with the "casual and fun" rule firmly established, he couldn't guarantee that Brynn wouldn't be proposed to. Six times.

So far the guys in Bliss had been staying away from her. Evan and Parker maintained it was because Noah had made it clear that she was his. But she wasn't. He was simply her friend. Her guardian maybe. He'd promised Rudy he'd look out for her, and from day one he'd been determined to send her back to New York happier, more confident, and with her inheritance firmly intact. So he'd taken six months to help her adjust to small-town life, get her pie shop going, and get to know her so he could more effectively set her up with the right guys.

Not because he was a selfish, possessive asshole who had taken about one day to realize that he didn't want to share her.

He just needed to establish with all of the single guys in Bliss between ages twenty-five and thirty-five—that seemed like a good age range for the twenty-nine-year-old Brynn—that they were just a part of a larger project to show Brynn how fun dating could be. To help her practice for when she went back to New York and had to pick the nice guys out from the dickheads.

He could do that. He knew all the guys in town. He could easily spread the word that each date was a *one time* thing and that it better be fun for her and they'd better all be gentlemen.

Meaning no diamond rings.

And no sex.

He felt his chest tighten at that thought. Yeah, he could definitely spread that around.

He frowned at Mitch. "If you're going to ask her out, it's only one time and it's just for a fun, casual date."

Mitch didn't say anything.

"You *are* going to ask her out, right?" Noah asked. He supposed he couldn't scare all of the other guys off. But he could make sure they knew he was watching their every fucking move.

"Yeah. Eventually."

Noah felt his frown deepen. "Eventually?"

"Yeah, definitely. Eventually."

"What's that mean?" Noah asked.

Mitch pushed away from the car, gave Noah a grin, and

clapped him on the shoulder. "Just thinking, five other guys need to ask her out too, right?"

"Right."

"Well, with a woman like Brynn, you don't really want to be the first, knowing she's got to date these other guys. You kind of want to be number six, you know?"

Mitch started for the door. Noah scowled after him. "You want to be number six?"

"The last guy? The one that can stick around? The one that doesn't have to give her up to someone else? Um, yeah." Then he gave Noah a little wave and disappeared through the doorway.

―――――

K ahlua milkshakes and pedicures.

Brynn knew what this meant.

Her sisters were staging an intervention.

Thank God.

She took a deep breath. It didn't matter that Mitch hadn't called her or come by the pie shop in the last two days. It didn't matter that Noah hadn't said a word about Mitch's flirting the other day or that he didn't seem to care that it had happened.

Maybe they'd talked about her after she left. Maybe Noah had told Mitch that she was a nerd who preferred test tubes to people, and he'd decided not to bother with her.

It didn't matter. This was all just one big experiment, and she had two of the best resources for men and dating right here in this very house with her. Her sisters were both gorgeous and confident and dated a lot. Most of Ava's dates had doubled as business meetings, and Cori had been well-known for casual flings and nothing more. Still, they'd both had a lot more experience just being with and talking to men. Brynn was going to figure this thing out. Tonight. And drink a lot of Kahlua. Cori's adult milkshakes were second only to her macchiatos.

"Hi, hon," Cori said brightly from where she was sitting at the dining room table removing the bright pink nail polish from her toes.

"Hey." Brynn swung her bag from her shoulder and dropped it onto one of the chairs. "How was your day?"

"Good. We've got about half of the loan Ava took out paid off."

Brynn slid into a chair. That *was* good news. One of the most direct stipulations in Rudy's will was that they turn a profit with the pie shop by the end of twelve months and that everything they spent on the shop had to come *from* the shop, no using their own private accounts. Three months ago, just as they'd paid off the loan Rudy had for the shop, Ava had come to Brynn and Cori asking if she could take out another loan. She'd wanted to open up a doorway between Parker's diner and the pie shop and combine their two kitchens since Parker was going to be co-owner eventually. Cori and Brynn had trusted Ava to make that call. She was the business tycoon. She knew that you had to spend money to make money. And honestly, bringing Parker into the pie shop did seem to have increased business. The pies had improved—though Ava had finally figured out her own apple pie and it was amazing—and people apparently liked the idea that things were more stable and permanent with the shop now. Parker was a Bliss boy who had no intentions of ever leaving, and Cori was settling down with Evan. It seemed that knowledge had helped the town to start to invest more interest and money in the shop.

"So we've got six more months. If we pay that loan off, then everything becomes profit," Brynn said.

"Well, after expenses," Cori said. "Which have gone up a little. I had no idea how much more electricity that huge fridge and oven Ava put in would use."

Yeah, Brynn had no idea what a normal electric bill would be for a house, not to mention an entire restaurant. Cori even took care of the bills at the house. Brynn was pretty clueless about that stuff.

They were heiresses to a twelve-billion-dollar fortune. Clearly none of them had ever really worried about things like budgets or balancing loan payments with electric bills. They'd never had to differentiate between the things they wanted and the things they needed. Brynn hadn't really ever given a lot of thought to her finances. She had been given a monthly allowance from Carmichael Enterprises ever since she'd graduated high school. A lot of Brynn's work was funded by grants and by her own trust fund, but because she'd never needed a regular paycheck, she essentially worked for the lab for free.

"Oh good, you're here." Ava swept into the room with glasses that were rimmed with chocolate sprinkles.

Brynn almost laughed. Sprinkles and garnishes and details like decorating glasses were usually Cori's forte. But since Ava had been seeing Parker she'd become a lot more interested in food.

She accepted one of the hurricane glasses from Ava and held it out for Cori to fill. Ava dropped a piece of dark chocolate on top, slid a red and white striped straw into the drink, and then reached for her own glass.

Brynn sat back in her chair and brought the straw to her mouth, drawing a taste of the milkshake. It was delicious. And she was totally going to let her sisters lead this discussion. She had a few questions, for sure, but she was curious how they were going to approach this.

After they all had their milkshakes in hand and the scent of mocha overpowered the scent of nail polish remover, Ava said, "Brynn, we need to talk."

Brynn nodded and drew on her straw again.

"Tomorrow is six months we've been in Bliss," Ava said.

"I know," Brynn told her. She kicked her shoes off and

propped her feet on the chair beside her. She studied her toes. Yeah, she could use a touch-up.

"And that means there's only six months left to...get everything done," Cori said.

"I know." Maybe she'd let Cori and Ava pick the color of her toenail polish. Truthfully, she wasn't sure she knew what she was doing in any area other than her lab. She waited on people in a tiny pie shop in a tiny town in Kansas and still needed to escape for an hour or so once or twice a day. How was she going to handle dating?

"And there's really only one thing that we haven't even started on," Ava said. Almost carefully.

Brynn looked up and was alarmed to feel her eyes stinging.

Both of her sisters immediately sat forward. "Brynn?" Cori asked.

Brynn took a long drag of her milkshake and then sniffed and set her glass down. "I need to start dating."

They both nodded.

"And I have no idea how to do that."

"Oh," Ava said, glancing at Cori.

"Yeah, we were wondering about that," Cori admitted.

Brynn sniffed again. She was a brilliant scientist. She was an avid reader. She was well-informed and had a strong social conscience. But she had no idea about men. Her father hadn't even known what to do with her.

Sure, she'd tried to avoid him as much as possible so some of the lack of interaction had been her fault too. But it had really made her life so much easier.

It had made Ava happy to follow Rudy Carmichael's footsteps in business, and Cori had indignantly rebelled against just about everything that had been important to him from his company, to his money, to the importance he placed on social connections and making things "look good". Brynn hadn't taken either approach.

She wasn't gung ho about Carmichael Enterprises as a whole and had no desire to spend her life in an office and conference rooms. So she'd never faked any interest in her father's business or social life. But neither had she fought him. If he wanted his daughters at his birthday party, she showed up. If he wanted to take her and her sisters out for ice cream after their spelling bee, she went.

But that meant that she didn't spend much time with him and almost never one-on-one. He'd tried to spend some time with each girl on her own, but Brynn could still remember how awkward that first dinner between them had been. They had nothing in common other than her mother and sisters. And DNA she supposed. And Brynn never had understood the idea of small talk. She still didn't. And she was pretty sure that meant she was going to suck at dating.

"I guess we were kind of thinking that Noah was going to be the one setting you up with guys he thought you'd get along with," Cori said.

"He hasn't said anything about it," Brynn told her.

"Shocking," Ava said dryly.

Brynn frowned. "What's that mean?"

Ava gave her a small smile. "Noah doesn't want you to date anyone, honey."

"He doesn't?" Brynn felt her heart trip slightly. Then frowned. She couldn't let her heart get all worked up over Noah. Her libido, sure, but hearts were different. "Why not?"

"Because he's in love with you," Cori said. "Obviously that's going to make it hard to set you up with anyone else."

Crap. She sucked in a quick breath. "You think so?"

She had very little experience socializing with men, and she certainly had never had one in love with her before. Or vice versa. She didn't know the signs.

"You really don't know that he's in love with you?" Cori asked. She was looking at Brynn with a mix of wonder and affection.

"He tells everyone we're just friends."

"Sure. Because that's what he's telling himself too," Cori said.

"But you don't think it's true?"

"I think he wants it to be true," Ava said. "And I think you *are* friends. But yeah, there's more."

"And obviously that's a problem," Cori said.

Yeah, it was a problem. Because she was leaving in six months. And he was staying. Noah would never be happy in New York, and, as lovely and quaint as Bliss was, she couldn't be happy here long-term. She was a scientist. Her contribution to the world happened in beakers and test tubes. And there were so many *people* here. There weren't, really. Especially not compared to New York City. But it *seemed* like more here because in New York she did not have fourteen hundred and sixty-three people interested in her.

That's where Noah and his garage came in.

There were days she and Noah barely talked at all. She'd walk into his garage, say hi, he'd hand her a bottle of iced tea or root beer, she'd climb onto the truck, open her book and just stay there for an hour or more. It was the least pressure she'd ever felt around another human being.

She was very *aware* of him. She loved watching him. Loved being around him. But she didn't feel the need to talk to him. He was her haven. In the midst of a day full of Cori and Ava, in the middle of town that wanted to know every detail about her and her sisters, Noah just let her sit there and stare at his ass.

"It's definitely a problem," Ava agreed. "And you still have to date five other guys."

"Six," Brynn corrected her.

Cori lifted an eyebrow. "You're still maintaining that the time you've spent with Noah isn't dating?"

"It's not." Brynn shook her head. "We're friends." Cori started to protest, but Brynn said quickly, "Maybe it's become more." Like a pretty strong case of lust on her part. "But we've never formally decided to date."

"It doesn't have to be formal," Ava said.

"But don't you think for a relationship to actually get more serious and to progress, at *some* point the people involved have to acknowledge what it is and what they want?" Brynn asked. That was what was bugging her most about the idea of Noah being in love with her. He'd never said anything. So, even if that was how he felt, he didn't *want* to feel it.

"Yes, okay, at some point you do talk about what your relationship is and where you want it to go," Ava acknowledged. "But maybe that's what he's waiting for. He's waiting for you to get this dating thing over so that he can tell you how he really feels. I mean, maybe he wants to be guy number six. Right? The last one. The one that can keep seeing you and doesn't have to share you."

That made Brynn's heart feel like it had flipped over in her chest. She didn't want her heart feeling things, but for maybe the first time, her brain seemed to be the less strong of the two organs. Her head had talked her heart out of feeling hurt by her dad, but it was having a hard time tamping down what felt like excitement over Noah. Dammit. "If he wanted to get this over with, he'd be setting me up though, wouldn't he?"

Cori shook her head. "Even if he knows this is how it has to happen and he wants it over with, it's going to be really hard for him to see you with the other guys, not to mention actually setting those dates up." She glanced at Ava. "I know how much it pained me to see Evan and Ava together even though I knew they were only pretending to date. And you won't be pretending."

No, but she wasn't convinced it would feel very real either.

"Will Evan and Parker set me up then?" Brynn asked. "They know everyone around here and could pick nice guys."

"That might work," Cori agreed. "Though Evan's already said he's not looking forward to dealing with Noah if he's responsible for you being out with someone."

"So I just wait for someone to ask me out?" Brynn asked,

feeling frustration building. "I've been here six months and no one's even wanted to buy me a cup of coffee."

"I'm pretty sure that's not true at all," Ava said. "I'm thinking there are several that wanted to, but they think you're not available."

"I'm sure he's not telling them to stay away," Brynn said. He certainly hadn't said that to Mitch the other day.

"He doesn't have to *tell* them. It's pretty obvious how he feels and you're together a lot," Cori said.

"So I have to stop spending time with him?" Brynn felt her heart drop at the thought.

"Actually, I might have a better idea," Ava said.

Brynn sat up a little straighter. She loved when Ava had ideas. "Okay."

"*You* ask someone out."

Brynn blinked at her. "I don't know how to do that."

Ava laughed. "You just walk up to them and say 'would like to have dinner with me?'"

But Brynn was already shaking her head by the time Ava finished her thought. "I can't do that. I hate even trying to upsell people on à la mode at the pie shop."

Ava rolled her eyes. "I know. We need to work on that too. But, honey, any guy around here is going to be *thrilled* that you asked. You're not selling anything. You're asking another person to have a meal with you."

Brynn already felt sick at the idea. "I hate one-on-one dinners with people I don't know very well." Yes, dinner with her dad when she was a kid had scarred her. That wasn't a good thing, but it was true.

"So not dinner. Something else," Ava said.

"I don't even know who to ask."

No, she didn't want to go six more months without a date. But she wasn't sure how to start this whole process. Still, she'd actually been looking forward to getting more comfortable with dating and meeting new people. She knew that wasn't her strength. She'd planned to gain some confidence and experience to take back to New York with her. And now that her sisters were staying here and were up to their armpits in plans for the pie shop, Brynn could go back to New York and do a few things on her own.

She hadn't seen them daily of course, but Ava had dragged her to hot yoga twice a week and lunch at least once. Cori had dragged her out to clubs and crazy weekend getaways at least once a month. She loved her sisters, but she was looking forward to not being dragged anywhere.

It had made *them* happy for her to go along, so she did. But Evan, Parker and the pie shop were not taking a lot of their attention and Brynn felt the relief of that, she had to admit.

"Evan thinks that Sean Matthews might be a good guy to ask," Cori was saying. "He's the high school science teacher. Nice guy. Was engaged for a while, but she broke it off about a year ago and he hasn't been out much since."

"Maybe he wouldn't want to go out," Brynn said.

"Evan won't set you up directly," Cori said. "But he will talk to Sean if you want to ask him to dinner."

Brynn swallowed hard.

"Honey," Ava said, reaching out for her hand. "We're running out of time. I mean, you could date six guys in a week and meet that stipulation. So it's not *imperative* that you do it now. But I do think that the sooner you get started, the better you'll feel. You'll realize it's no big deal."

Cori glanced at Ava, then back to Brynn. "But Dad's intention was for you to get to know these guys at least a little. To give this a chance. I don't think you should go out with six guys in six days."

Brynn took a deep breath. "You're right. Let's get this thing going. Heck, it might be fun, right?"

"Of course it will be fun," Cori assured her. "You don't have to be in love or looking for a wedding ring to go out and have a good time with a guy. You deserve to be romanced and wined and dined, Brynn. You're amazing and I really think that this can help you see that there's more to you than your research lab."

That would be nice.

Brynn couldn't help the thought that tripped through her mind.

She was incredibly proud of the lab and the work they did there, but... it was all she really had. Being a researcher was all she'd ever been. And she'd ended up there because it was the easiest path. She'd been great at science and her sister had bought her a lab. When Ava had revealed the purchase to Brynn at dinner after she'd graduated with her PhD, Brynn hadn't been able to say anything but "thank you." That lab was how *she* took care of people, and that mattered to her.

But it had given her a place to hide. Plain and simple. That lab had been for her in New York what Noah's garage was for her in Bliss.

"Fine. Tell Evan to talk to Sean and get me his phone number."

3

———

Parker set a cheeseburger down in front of Noah and, in spite of his pissy mood that was going on six days now, he felt his frown ease.

And this was no ordinary cheeseburger. This one had fried Canadian bacon, grilled pineapple, and mozzarella on top, along with a teriyaki glaze. And it was *not* on Parker's diner menu.

Which meant something was up.

And Noah knew exactly what it was. This was an intervention.

Parker slid a cherry coke to him and then leaned onto the counter in front of where Evan was chowing down on a Hawaiian burger of his own. He was clearly relishing Parker's willingness to go off-menu for this. Parker *never* went off-menu.

Well, except for Ava. But that was another story.

It was past closing time, so they were the only three people in the diner. Blissfully Baked, right next door, was connected to the diner now with a huge doorway in the wall between them, thanks to Ava's huge I-love-you gesture to Parker, but the girls closed the shop before Parker closed the diner.

Noah didn't ask what was going on. He knew. And he wanted

to eat at least half of the burger before Parker and Evan told him a bunch of stuff he didn't want to hear.

Like how today was officially six months since the triplets had come to town. And officially six months from when their mandated year in Bliss would be over.

And how Brynn really needed to start dating.

He bit into the burger and concentrated on the amazing mix of flavors and textures. Parker had a gift. This burger was amazing. He should put it on the menu. Noah made a note to mention that to Ava. She was really the only way to get Parker to make any changes.

Evan picked up a fry and ran it through the drips of teriyaki sauce on his plate.

Noah just chewed.

Parker watched them both.

Evan picked up another fry and did the same thing.

Noah kept chewing.

"For fuck's sake," Parker finally muttered. "Tell him." He was clearly addressing Evan.

"You tell him."

"I'm not going to tell him. You're the one that... did it. You tell him."

Noah swallowed and eyed the rest of his burger, gauging if he could finish it off in the next two minutes. Probably. But his stomach was already knotting up over the conversation they were about to have. The last three days had been shit and this wasn't going to help.

After Mitch had made the comment about being number six on Brynn's list, Noah had tried to get back to work, but he'd had a hell of a time concentrating. Fucking Mitch. Who would have guessed he'd be so quick to figure all of that out? Or that he'd care.

That was really the last thing Noah needed. These guys *caring* about taking Brynn out. They were just supposed to be practice.

She was supposed to get more confident, get some experience going out with *nice* guys, so she could go back to New York and pick out the decent ones from the assholes.

She wasn't supposed to get serious about anyone here. And vice versa.

Noah had always disliked Mitch Anderson.

Thinking of what a dick Mitch had been in high school—starting quarterback, class President, Homecoming King, all of that cliché bullshit dickhead stuff—had Noah scraping his knuckles on the car engine and banging his head against the hood. He'd finally thrown his wrench across the room—earning him a glare and a hiss from Penn—and he'd given up on the car for the day and headed over to Maggie's place.

But Maggie had been home. Which meant he wasn't able to get the downspout fixed or the lawn mowed. She was supposed to be out of the house at that time every afternoon, but once in a while something happened with her schedule. He never knew what exactly. Because they didn't talk.

Yeah, he wasn't going to be able to finish this burger. He felt sick and pissed off in spite of the grilled pineapple. Dammit. He set it down, wiped his hands, and took a swig of Coke.

"I already know," he told Evan and Parker.

Evan looked over at him. "You do?"

Noah nodded. "It's six months today." He didn't need to specify what "it" was.

Parker shifted his weight behind the counter. "Yeah, it is."

"And Brynn needs to start dating," Noah said.

"Um." Evan glanced at Parker. "Right."

"And I should have encouraged it a long time ago." He'd really thought getting her settled and the shop going strong first had been a good plan. Because he hadn't planned on falling for her. That had definitely complicated everything.

"Well, that doesn't matter," Parker said. "It just has to get done."

"Why haven't you encouraged her?" Evan asked, in spite of Parker's words.

"I was concentrating on one thing at a time on Rudy's list," Noah said.

Rudy Carmichael's will specifically outlined what he wanted each daughter to do in order to inherit his fortune. The document, written by Evan himself, was pretty straightforward. Noah loved that. It was so easy to look at it and know what he had to do to keep his promise to Rudy to take care of the girls. Well, Brynn anyway. No one really needed to take care of Cori and Ava and, regardless, Evan and Parker had stepped into their lives pretty quickly.

Brynn was different. She didn't really do people. Or socialization. And Rudy had felt strongly that she needed that. But he'd also worried. So he'd asked Noah to look out for her.

Take care of her, Noah. Send her back to New York happier and more confident.

Those had been Rudy's words to Noah. *That* was what Noah ultimately had to do.

The last thing Noah had wanted in his life was someone he loved asking him to take care of someone *they* loved. Again. But who said no to a friend who was dying of cancer?

Besides, this time he'd had the checklist. Now that Cori and Ava were on track with Evan and Parker looking out for them, all Noah needed to do was make sure that each of Rudy's wishes for Brynn came true. And they were very specific. She had to waitress at the pie shop, spend time with people and really get to know them, and date six guys from Bliss. That was it. That list had actually seemed like a dream come true.

Noah really wanted to do something *right* for someone he cared about. He really wanted to be the guy people could count on to keep his promise. It hadn't worked out with Jared and Maggie. But he would, by God, keep his promise to Rudy.

Noah sighed. "Okay, I haven't brought it up to her before this because I'm a selfish bastard. I liked having her to myself. And I liked feeling like I was helping her—getting the shop fixed up and helping her get more comfortable socializing on a smaller scale, like when she waitresses and our game nights and stuff."

The six of them had game night at least twice a month, sometimes more, where they sat around the huge dining room table in the girls' house and played board or card games. It had started as a way for Evan and Ava to spend time together as they pretended to date without one-on-one time. But it was fun and they all enjoyed it enough to keep it up. And if sitting around with Evan and Cori and Ava and Parker felt like a big couples' date night... that had never bothered Noah and Brynn. They didn't call what they were doing dating, but they didn't mind being paired up either. In fact, when they were partners, they generally kicked the other couples' asses.

And yes, all of that—seeing her relaxing and laughing and comfortable with Evan and Parker—had made him feel like he was accomplishing the things on Rudy's list.

The girls were trying to make the shop profitable when it had never been that before. But they were on track now. And Noah liked to think he'd had a hand in that. Watching Brynn paint walls and put up curtains and weave between tables with a coffeepot in hand made him smile. It was a far cry from her research lab in New York, he knew, and yet she was just rolling with it. He admired that. She skyped with her co-workers regularly in the evenings, but, unlike Ava, who had continued to act like the CEO of Carmichael Enterprises even in the midst of trying to bake pies, Brynn focused on the pie shop while she was there. Sure, she needed a breather here and there—that she took in his garage—but she was in there, doing the job, smiling sweetly at the customers, and letting them grill her with questions and give her their opinions on everything from the crumb topping on the pie, to what the state legislature was doing.

Brynn wasn't what anyone would call talkative. She didn't flirt and tell jokes and laugh like Cori did. She didn't take charge like Ava did. She didn't talk much at the pie shop beyond, "What can I get you?" and "Would you like a refill?" but she got talked *to*. A lot. The older guys, Hank, Walter, Roger, and Ben, spent a few hours every day in the shop and loved to joke with her and give her advice. And it seemed that everyone else who frequented the shop—and that number was increasing all the time—also loved to talk to Brynn. Not *with* Brynn, exactly, but definitely *to* her.

Which, in spite of her smiles, drained her a little. But she was better at it than she gave herself credit for. He knew, because he saw the smiles she got in return.

"I know that I need to make sure she gets out there," Noah continued. "She'll need a little pep talk, but I can do that." He had no idea if he could do that. Could he actually encourage Brynn to go out with another man? "I'll talk to her tonight."

She didn't need to get serious about anyone. She didn't need to even see any of them more than once. In fact, that would be best. She needed to spend time with six different guys from Bliss. There were no other details included in the will. It didn't say how much time, how often, or what that time had to be like. Very technically, she could sit in a booth across from a guy for an hour for lunch and that could count. Noah had made sure to clarify that with Evan.

"You don't have to do that," Parker said.

"I don't have to talk to her?" Noah asked.

"Right."

Noah looked back and forth between his friends suspiciously. "What's going on?"

"We didn't set all of this up to get you to talk to her," Evan said. "We did it because we have something to tell you."

"Okay." Noah didn't like the sound of this.

"She's going out with someone. Tomorrow night," Evan said.

Noah felt his gut twist. "Who?" His voice had dropped to a low growl instantly.

"Sean Matthews," Parker answered.

Sean Matthews. Briefly, Noah wondered if there was any name they could have said that wouldn't have sent a hot shaft of jealousy through him. No way. It didn't matter who was taking Brynn out. He wouldn't be good enough.

Noah cleared his throat, then wadded his napkin up and tossed it on the counter. He pulled his wallet out, dug for a ten, and tossed it beside his plate. Then he got to his feet.

"Where are you going?" Evan asked.

Noah was pretty sure Evan already knew the answer to that question. "To talk to Sean Matthews," Noah said simply.

Parker handed his ten back to him. "No charge."

"Keep it," Noah told him. "If you keep babying me, I'll think that this is a big deal."

Parker paused, then gave him a single nod, and pocketed the bill. "You're right. No big deal."

Right. The woman he was in love with was about to start dating.

No big deal at all.

———

Well, that had completely sucked.

Brynn stood at the bottom of the porch steps leading up to the house she was sharing with her sisters. Evan and Parker were both here. Their trucks were in the driveway. Noah was very likely here too. They would all want to know how things had gone.

She blew out a short breath and then climbed the steps to the front door. She didn't want to admit that she was a dating failure —on date *one* no less—but she was pretty sure the people in her house were expecting this outcome anyway.

She stepped into the dining room a minute later. "Hey, guys."

Ava and Cori turned quickly, their eyes wide and curious, then they both, almost in unison, tamped their excitement down.

"Hey, you're just in time for the refills," Cori said. She gestured at the table where they were playing Settlers of Catan.

Cori had long ago taken it upon herself to make game nights into Events. With a capital E. There was always a theme and it tied the game and the snacks together. It was clear that she'd taken the "island" theme from Settlers and extended it to the food. There was coconut shrimp, mango salsa, and pina coladas.

Brynn wasn't going to point out that Catan was not a tropical island. She was sure Cori had figured that out by now—they were well into the game—and it didn't matter anyway. It was all just for fun.

She could let things go and just have fun.

Probably.

Besides, people didn't like being corrected. Tonight with Sean had given her further proof. But honestly, he couldn't be standing up in front of a classroom of sophomores and teaching them that there were only five senses and totally ignoring the other four proven senses. Sixteen-year-olds could understand and appreciate proprioception. Surely.

At least his refusal to admit that the science curriculum in most public schools was lacking, and the fact that he'd never even so much as written one of his Senators about better science funding made it easier for her to not want to go out with him again.

"I could definitely use a drink," Brynn told Cori, hooking the strap of her purse of the chair at the end of the table. She dropped into the chair with a sigh.

Cori rose and filled a glass for her, complete with a paper umbrella and an orange twisty straw.

After Brynn had taken a long drink, she looked around the table. Everyone was watching her and no one was saying anything. Her sisters both looked ready to bust, Evan and Parker looked mildly amused, and Noah—she met his eyes last—looked like he was nearly grinding his back teeth off.

"What?" she asked.

"Seriously?" Cori asked. "How was it?"

Brynn stirred her straw through the white cocktail. "It was..." She took a breath. "Terrible."

Out of the corner of her eye, she saw Noah visibly tense.

"What?" Cori asked, leaning in. "Terrible? How was it terrible?"

"I just..." Brynn shrugged. "It was awkward. We were talking about the only thing we have in common, but then we got into a debate about how important skepticism is in science and it basically devolved from there."

Cori snorted softly. "Isn't debate an important part of scientific discovery and research?"

"Sure." Brynn rolled her eyes. "We just didn't hit it off. Oh, but at least I did manage to convince him to tutor Mandie Marshall."

"Why does Mandie Marshall need a tutor?" Ava asked.

Mandie was twenty-eight and going back to college. She came in to study in the pie shop twice a week. "I noticed the she was really stressed out one day and that she was studying biology. I gave her a little help, but chemistry is my specialty. She came to mind tonight while Sean and I were talking about teaching theory. I mentioned it to him and he said to tell her to call him."

Ava looked impressed. "And isn't Mandie single too?"

Brynn shook her head. "I didn't bring it up as a setup."

"Still," Ava said with a shrug.

"Anyway," Brynn said. "Once I realized that there was no way he was going to kiss me at the end of the date, I decided to skip dessert and have him bring me home."

Noah made a choking sound and Brynn looked over at him. He was scowling at the game board, not even looking at her.

Evan laughed though. "It was all pointless if you weren't going to get kissed?"

She looked over at him. "I have several people I can talk science with any time of any day. I do not, however, have people I can kiss any time of any day. So, yeah, if I'm going to sit through a lame discussion about the former, I feel like I should at least have the latter to look forward to."

"Ah, right." Evan shot an amused glance at Noah who was gripping his pina colada glass tightly and still not looking at her.

"I could have been sitting *here* tonight, having a lot more fun with people I really like and a lot better food if that's all this was going to be."

"So you think the point of dating is kissing?" Parker asked.

She shook her head. "Not just that. I mean, not exactly that. But isn't that what's supposed to set guys, or girls, you date apart from the guys, or girls, you're just *friends* with?" she asked, unable to keep from emphasizing the word she and Noah had used over and over. "It's how Ava is different for you from me and Cori, right?"

Parker looked at Ava and a soft smile curled his lips. "Yeah, I guess that's true."

Brynn sat back in her chair and crossed her arms. "I dressed up, I did my hair, I put in my contacts. And I went out and dealt with mushy cheese balls and annoying conversation—I mean, I didn't even say anything when he first started talking about how he's teaching about electromagnetic fields, I just let *that* go—and then I didn't even get kissed! What a waste."

Evan gave a choking sound as if he was swallowing laughter.

"Evan," Cori said warningly. But she was fighting a smile too.

Brynn rolled her eyes. "I'm just saying that *kissing* is supposed to be a perk, right? I mean, you put up with a bad joke or two, or mushy cheese balls, because in the end, the kissing will be good."

"Man, I've had some mushy-cheese-ball kisses for sure," Ava said. "I think you're putting way too high of expectations on this."

Brynn slumped down further in her chair. That wasn't what she wanted to hear. She wanted to be kissing. She wanted to try all of this guy-girl stuff out. All of it. Bliss was kind of a controlled environment. She knew the guys were going to have similar backgrounds and lifestyles. So she could compare them to one another a lot more easily than she could the guys in New York. She hadn't dated since high school and if she was going to do it now, then she wanted the full experience. She wanted to go back to New York with all of her experiments done and some actual data to work from. And her working hypothesis was that kissing could be fun. And could make the nerves and the *talking* worth it.

"Yeah, I didn't realize you were thinking a lot about kissing," Cori said. "Or that you were thinking about that at all."

"I wasn't totally," Brynn said, honestly. She'd been focused more on just quelling the butterflies in her stomach and trying to not think about the fact that she hadn't even been able to successfully socialize with her own father. "Until I was halfway through the appetizers."

Cori snorted at that. "That wasn't very far in."

Brynn just shrugged.

The cheeseballs had sucked, and she had realized there had to be some payoff for everything she was putting into the date. So she'd started thinking about how the guys she was going to go out with would be different from Evan and Parker and the guys she knew in New York. The scientists and researchers that had never seen her as more than a brilliant mind.

The kissing was about it.

Yes, she knew that having men appreciating her for her brain rather than her boobs was a nice twist. But she was an identical triplet. Her sisters were gorgeous. Brynn was...okay. It was proof positive that personality had a lot to do with looks. But Ava and Cori were each high maintenance in their own ways. Ava more in the shoes-and-highlights way. The way she carried and presented herself as the CEO of Carmichael had been important. Cori more in the always-on-the-go-ready-for-adventure way. Cori was fun and daring. Which, frankly, made Brynn tired just thinking about it.

Her defining quality was her IQ and sinking into books, and the school laboratory that other students avoided as much as possible had made it easy to avoid challenges like bossing people around or being the life of the party. Being quietly, stoically nerdy had served her well, and she'd leaned hard on that differentiation from her sisters.

Brynn sighed. "It's just that I could have better company and food at home. The only thing the date gives me that I can't get here is the kissing."

Noah suddenly shoved his chair back and stood. "I need to go."

Brynn looked up at him. Go? Her heart knocked against her ribs and she felt her eyes widen. He looked...not angry exactly. But not happy.

"Where are you going?" Parker asked, clearly surprised.

"Something I have to do." Noah started for the front of the house.

Without thinking, Brynn scraped her chair back and went after him. "I'll be right back," she tossed over her shoulder.

Noah was already out the door and down the porch steps by the time she got outside. "Hey!" He didn't slow down. "Noah!" She ran down the steps and the front path. "Noah!"

He came to a sudden stop and she almost plowed into him. She came up short just in time. He swung to face her, his expression stormy.

"Are you okay?" she asked.

"No, Brynn, I'm not okay." He gave a short, humorless laugh. "I'm really not okay."

"Why? What's wrong?"

He shoved a hand through his hair. "I can't sit and listen to you talk about kissing other guys, okay?"

She paused. She had no idea how to read the emotion in his eyes. "I didn't kiss him."

"You wanted to."

"Well, yeah. Kind of. But...not *him*. Not exactly." Did he not like Sean? Was he jealous? Her chest felt a little tighter at that thought.

"It doesn't matter." He shook his head. "I can't listen to you talk about other guys at all."

"Even the bad dates?"

He ran a hand over his jaw. "Apparently not." He shook his head. "I thought I knew how I'd feel about this dating thing."

Her eyes widened. "How did you think you'd feel?"

He finally met her eyes directly. Intently. "I thought I wanted the dates to suck," he said bluntly. "I didn't want you to have any fun with any of the guys. I wanted them to be one and done."

"Oh." She had no idea what else to say.

"And he didn't kiss you because I told him not to. What I didn't tell him was to be sure that you had an amazing time. I guess I need to make that clear in the future."

She blinked at him. "Oh." Then she frowned. "That's..."

"A dick move," he filled in. "But I don't care." He shrugged. "I really don't. Even if you think I'm overstepping. Even if you think it's none of my business. I don't care. I *will* be sure these guys treat you right. I have to."

Her frowned deepened. "You have to?" There was something about the way he'd said it that made her pause. He was her friend. She was sure that Evan and Parker would want to be sure the guys she dated treated her well too. But there was something in Noah's eyes that made it seem like more than that.

Noah squared his stance and tucked his hands in his back pockets, clearly bracing for a fight. "I promised your dad. I told him I'd make sure everything he put on his list happened. The pie shop has to be profitable, you and your sisters have to get your relationships back on track, you have to date six guys, and you have to go back to New York happier and more confident than when you left. It's all working. But you have to get through these six dates yet and then you *have to* go back to New York. I have to be sure those dates go well and you get out of them what you need, but that there's nothing more there. So, I'm not sending you out on these dates without making my expectations really clear."

Brynn knew she was staring at him. But that was probably the most words Noah had ever said to her at one time. For one thing. The words themselves also took her off guard. "He actually told you all of that?"

"He did." Noah had a stubborn set to his jaw. "I will not let your dad down, Brynn."

Her eyes widened. The intensity in Noah's tone was not something she'd heard before.

"You're doing this because my dad asked you to. Not just because he put it in the trust, but *literally* asked you to?" she asked to clarify.

"Yes."

"What did he say *exactly*?" She wasn't sure why she felt defensive, but she definitely felt tension climbing her spine.

"Take care of her and send her back to New York happier and more confident. I want her better after being in Bliss."

Yeah, *that* was why she was feeling defensive.

Better. Implying that she wasn't as good as she could be before coming to Bliss.

The thing was, Rudy hadn't really known her so how could he know how she needed to be "better"? He thought she was an introvert. That was true. But he also thought she was shy and weird. Because that's what she'd let him see. And maybe it was a little weird to not want to be close to your father. But, well, then she was weird. But *Rudy* didn't know how to fix her. She was going along with all of this will stuff for her sisters. At first it had been because of the money, but now it was because Bliss and

Evan and Parker and the pie shop really were good for them. But *she* was fine. Which everyone would know if they ever, just once, *asked* her. But it was only for six more months. Then she could go back to New York and do her own thing and not worry about going along with things for everyone else's benefit.

She took a breath. "And here I was thinking I was pretty good to start with."

Noah sighed, as if this wasn't going as planned at all.

She knew the feeling.

"You are," he said. "But Rudy wanted—" Noah shrugged. "More for you."

Rudy's version of more anyway. "So you're basically stepping into the role of my dad since he's not here to do it."

He clenched his jaw, but then slowly nodded. "Yeah. Something like that."

Okay, *ew*. He didn't have to agree with her on that.

"And for six months it's been easy," Noah went on. "Get the pie shop running, help you settle in. But now..." He pulled in a deep breath. "Now I have to not only sit by while you date other guys, but it's clear that I'll have to set you up on these dates."

That was not what she'd been expecting. "You're going to set me up on the dates?"

He nodded, his mouth in a grim line. "I was hoping I wouldn't have to. But obviously, Cori and Ava didn't do a good job."

She couldn't argue with that. Though her sisters had had the best intentions. "Hey, Sean's the right age, lives here, teaches science. That seemed like a good fit on paper."

Noah scoffed. "Sean is also about as romantic as that light pole," he said nodding to the pole near the street.

"You would set me up with guys who were *romantic*?" That didn't sound bad. But it also didn't sound like Noah was feeling jealous or worried about these dates. She frowned.

"Brynn—" He blew out a breath. "You deserve to be adored. Romanced. Treated like a princess."

She blinked at him. "I do?"

He gave her a small smile. "You've been in your sisters' shadows for so long. You deserve the attention now. You deserve to spend some time with men who are with you because of *you*, not because you're one of the Carmichael triplets, or because Cori dragged you to a club and made you dance, or because you just made some big scientific breakthrough. You need to go out with regular guys who don't know shit about protons and neutrons and who have no idea what Carmichael Enterprises is and who haven't been doing tequila shots with your sister. Guys who just think you're beautiful and interesting and want to get to know you better."

Brynn knew her eyes were wide but she couldn't help it. How did he know that's how it all usually went down? "But I'll be spending time with men who are there because *you* told them to take me out."

His expression hardened. "I'll be finally giving them *permission* to take you out."

Yeah, that sounded a little dad-like. "Oh, really?"

"You haven't been asked out at all since you've been here."

"No."

"Do you really think that's because no one *wants* to ask you out?"

"You *have* been scaring them off?"

He lifted a shoulder, not looking a bit apologetic. "Not directly."

"But they haven't asked because of you."

"Yes."

Nope, not one ounce of apology in his tone or expression. Brynn crossed her arms. This was clearly important to him, so she'd do it. If he needed to feel like he was doing something good for her, and for her dad, she'd go along with it. But *he* wasn't her dad. And her real dad hadn't been all that protective. "My sisters don't keep me in the shadows. I stay there on purpose."

"I know." He looked at her with a mix of affection and exasperation. "They actually try to bring you out."

She nodded.

He wasn't done though. "But you stay in the shadows because then there's more spotlight for them."

Brynn felt her mouth open, but no words came out.

"And you stay quiet and shy because Ava and Cori *like* to encourage you and build you up and take you out. Like on game night when you let your sisters let you win."

She sucked in a quick breath. "I..." But she didn't know how to finish that.

"It's like when you let Hank and Walter and the guys give you advice. That you don't need. You just smile and nod. It makes *them* feel good to help you, so you let them."

"It doesn't hurt to let them talk."

"As long as *you* don't have to talk, right?"

She couldn't deny it.

"Your tendency to just stay under the radar and let everyone around you do whatever *they* needed to do started when you were young. With Rudy," Noah said. "You realized that he couldn't handle all three of you. Barely individually, but definitely not all together. So you tried to be easy. Quiet. Not needing any attention." Noah took a step closer to her. "And when you were older, you realized that your dad didn't really understand you. That you baffled him and made him a little uncomfortable. He could talk business with Ava and at least argue with Cori, but he didn't know what to do with you. So you played up being a super genius nerd so he could tell himself that you were too brilliant, too out of his league, and he'd be off the hook for not being able to relate to you or bond with you."

Brynn pressed her lips together. There was no way Noah would know all of that unless someone had told him. No, not someone. Rudy. Her throat felt tight. Whoa, she hadn't been expecting that.

"When did he figure that out?" she asked quietly.

"It wasn't until he was here and looking back." Noah took a final step that put him right in front of her. "He told me that you would bring textbooks to dinner."

"I only did that twice."

"Twice was enough."

She swallowed. "I just knew he thought I was weird and being weird just...worked."

"Did it work with other people too?" he asked.

She tipped her head. "What do you mean?" She totally knew what he meant.

"Come on," he said. "Did you use weirdness to keep other people away?"

"The lab in my high school was really quiet," she confessed. "Quieter than the library. No one came to the lab if they didn't have to. It was full of this intimidating stuff that people didn't want to mess with."

"So you hid out in there."

She nodded. "Everyone assumed that I loved science since I spent so much time in there. I was actually just reading and writing and drawing a lot of the time. I mean, sometimes it was about science, but not always."

"But you went into science."

She shrugged. "I did like it. And I *was* good at it." She paused, then continued, "And one of my science teachers nominated me for an award, that I won, that led to a fellowship and a scholarship."

"You didn't need a scholarship, Ms. Carmichael," Noah pointed out.

"No. But it made Mr. Calebus feel good to have gotten it for me."

Noah nodded. "Exactly. Brynn, you *let* people take care of you. You don't need it. But you let them do it because *they* need it."

She swallowed. It was true. It was a little pathetic too, and was something that would change when she went back to New York without her sisters. She lifted her shoulder. "It's an old habit."

"Yeah." He took another deep breath. "Well, I'm one of those people."

She knew that. He was a natural caretaker. Probably why she was going along with all of this. "And you want to take care of me because of Rudy."

"Yes."

Dammit. There was something about the idea of Noah taking care of her that made her feel warm and tingly. Until she remembered that the way he was going to do that was to set her up with other men. "Okay," she finally said.

"I will fix this," he told her, his voice dropping lower.

"This?"

"The bad date thing. That won't happen again."

"Noah, you can't mandate how my dates go."

"Yes, I can."

She gave a soft laugh. Actually, she believed that he could. He knew all of the guys here that would be eligible. And he was not only strong and built big, he was also well respected. She had the impression he didn't put his foot down often or get growly for no reason. If he started acting like that, the guys here would pay attention.

"You're going to tell them where to take me and what to do?" she asked.

He was studying her eyes. "Maybe."

"Write them a script?"

"Possibly."

On impulse, Brynn moved closer to him. "And will there be kissing at the end of these dates?"

His jaw clenched and his eyes flashed. "No."

She'd been expecting that answer. "But I want there to be kissing."

"I can't handle that part, B."

The use of B instead of her name made her start. He'd never used a nickname for her before. And she liked it. A lot. Parker called Ava Boss, and it always sounded affectionate and sexy when he did it.

"You're going to specifically tell them *not* to kiss me, aren't you?" she asked.

His eyes were swirling with emotion. "Yes."

She nodded, her mind working through the situation. "The idea of this dating thing was to help me experience it in a safe, controlled environment, right?" she asked. "My dad was worried that I was hiding away and not getting out and socializing and that I wouldn't know what I was getting into if I did decide to start dating."

"Right."

She drew herself straighter as she made her decision. Noah wanted to do what her father had asked of him. But she knew that he was going to have a very hard time saying no to *her*. And if it came down to choosing between protecting her for Rudy or making *her* happy, she needed to know which side he'd come down on.

"Then I want that." She said it firmly. "If I'm going to do this, then I might as well make it count. I need to experience *all* the parts of dating. When it's over, I want to feel confident that I really know what it's all about. I want to be prepared for anything."

He groaned and ran a hand over his face. "Dammit," he muttered.

"What?"

He took a deep breath and met her eyes again. "That's what I want," he said. "For you to feel confident. To know that people want you. To know that *you* are awesome even without your sisters or your money. And I want you to feel like you can handle anything."

Fine. That's what Noah needed. But she was getting inspired

to ask for a few things *she* needed too. "And I need kissing." *And more*, but she didn't add that part. She had a feeling he knew. "And I think there's really only one solution that will make sure you fulfill your promise to my dad, will make me happy, and will keep you from going crazy."

He looked at her for a long moment. Finally, he asked, "And what's that?"

His voice was gruff and it sent a shiver of pleasure and sense of rightness down her spine.

"*You're* going to have to be the one kissing me."

4

Yeah, that made sense.

Noah was ninety-six percent sure.

Sure, the endorphins and lust and jealousy coursing through his system might have been making it seem clearer than it really was, but it really did seem like a great solution.

Brynn needed to date other men and she wanted to experience kissing. But he wasn't going to survive her kissing other men. So he'd have to be the one kissing her.

Yep, that definitely made a ton of sense.

He was ninety-two percent sure.

"Do you *want* to kiss me?" Her voice was soft, her eyes wide. But she didn't look shocked. She looked excited.

This might kill him.

"I definitely want to kiss you, Brynn," he said sincerely. He was absolutely sure he'd never wanted anything more in his life. And that was a staggering thought. Because he knew a lot about wanting things—things to be different, to have made different choices, to be a better man.

"Right now?"

Heat flared through him and he had to clench his fists to keep from reaching for her. "No, not right now." He had to get his head straight about this. How it was going to work. What he was going to do. How he was going to survive it. How to make it everything she needed it to be. How to somehow also make it something they could both walk away from in the end.

"But you said you'd fix this bad date thing. And I did have a bad date. And I think I need a really great kiss to make it all better."

"I'm not..." *Prepared. What you need. Who you think I am. Good enough for you.* All of those thoughts tripped through his head as he trailed off.

But then Brynn reached out and grabbed his forearm, gave it a squeeze, and said, "Yes, you are."

He didn't know what exactly she thought she was reassuring him of, but those three words rocked through him. If he had been a better guy, he would have just turned and walked away.

But he wasn't.

He was selfish and stubborn, and he *really* wanted someone to fucking *want* him for something for a change. Not to need him. Lots of people needed his help and his expertise under the hood. Not to reluctantly put up with him like Maggie did. He needed someone to *want* him. He wanted someone to have a choice and to *choose* him.

Okay, Brynn wasn't really choosing him. He was manipulating this situation. But he didn't care.

Because she was looking up at him with big blue eyes filled with hope and anticipation, and pretty pink lips that hadn't been kissed in a really long time and probably never the way he was going to kiss them, and he *had* to be the one to do this. He had to.

"You're still going back to New York in March," he said. It wasn't a question. It was a reminder.

She nodded. "Yes."

"So this is...me taking care of you, helping you." That's what this had to be. No matter what else it felt like. Already.

"That's exactly what this is," she agreed.

Well, okay then.

He lifted a hand to her face, then slid it around to the back of her head, threading his fingers into her silky hair. He tugged her forward slightly and she came, nearly stepping on his toes, and bumping into his chest in an adorably awkward way that emphasized how uncommon it was for her to be this close to a man. And he fucking loved that. He loved that now that he could pick the guys and knew that he'd be the only one touching her, he wouldn't want to constantly hit someone.

"And you want me to show you how you should have been kissed tonight?" he asked her, his voice low.

"I do." She said it in a breathless way that shot an arrow of want straight to his cock.

Had a woman ever made him hard just looking up at him like he was the best thing since they'd made Reese's peanut butter cups into a cereal? No. Because no woman had ever looked at him like that.

"Okay, Brynn. This is definitely what should have happened tonight."

He leaned in and put his lips against her forehead, lingering there, breathing her in. God, he'd wanted to do that for months now. Then he dragged his lips over her temple slowly, feeling the silky, warmth of her skin against his mouth, her hair tickling his nose, her soft sigh against his neck. That warm puff of breath on his skin fired his blood, and he put his other hand on her hip and moved her up against him. They were touching chest to thigh. Barely. Layers of clothing between them. Yet he'd never been more turned on in his life.

He moved his lips down to her cheek, pressing a soft kiss there and feeling her hands curl into the front of his shirt. It felt better than any of the times other women had touched his chest. Even naked. Then he slid his lips along her jaw, his stubble rasping over her soft skin. He felt more than heard her little intake of air, and he smiled. And did it again. Then he continued to her ear where he said hoarsely, "This is how a guy who adores you kisses you on the first date." Then he nipped her earlobe gently. And stepped back.

Her fingers slowly uncurled from his shirt and she blinked up at him a few times, as if trying to focus. She was breathing rapidly and her pupils were dilated, and she looked dazed.

Noah fucking loved everything about it.

She pulled in a deep, shaky breath, and said, "Wow."

That one word was probably the best thing she could have said to him. He hadn't wowed anyone in a really long time. And he'd never wanted to wow someone like he did Brynn.

And that was from a kiss on the cheek.

Kind of.

It was definitely a hell of a lot more chaste than what he *wanted* to do to her tonight.

"I'll see you tomorrow," he told her, before his thoughts wandered too far in that direction.

She nodded, pressing her lips together. Lips he hadn't even touched. Yet.

"Brynn?" he asked, as she continued to stand there.

"Yes?"

"Go back inside."

She seemed to shake herself and glanced toward the porch. "Yeah. Okay."

But she didn't move. She looked back at him.

This was all really good for his ego. Really good. She needed to go inside before he rushed through the next several lessons of the physical side of dating all at once. Right now. On the front lawn of her house.

He stepped forward, put his hands on her shoulders, turned her to face the house, and gave her a little nudge. "Go."

She took one step. Then another. Then she turned around. He almost groaned out loud.

"When will you kiss me again?"

Yeah, this was going to kill him.

"After your next date, I'll show you how you should be kissed after a second date."

"When will that be?"

"Soon." He could promise her that. He needed to get this dating thing over with. He also couldn't wait to get his mouth on her again. But he needed to go over his list of candidates and have a few conversations first.

She nodded. "Okay. Goodnight."

"'Night."

He waited until the door had closed behind her to blow out a big breath and drop his chin to his chest. He'd kissed her *forehead* and *cheek* and was more wound up than he'd ever been over a woman.

This was the craziest damned situation he'd ever been in.

And he suddenly realized that it was possible Rudy hadn't chosen him to take care of Brynn because Noah needed a win in the Good Guy department. He might have chosen him to take care of Brynn because Noah needed a lesson in self-control.

———

B rynn shut the front door behind her and actually slumped back against it. She felt like every heroine in every cheesy romantic movie she'd ever seen. And he hadn't even kissed her. Not really. But just being that close to him, feeling his body heat, drawing in his scent, actually having his hand and mouth on her, no matter where it had been, had made her knees melt and her heart pound.

She could only imagine what having him actually kiss her would be like.

Yeah, this was a great plan. An amazing plan. A perfect plan.

This was what was known as having her cake and eating it too.

She made her way back into the dining room. She could feel the goofy smile on her face but could not hide it or even tone it down.

"Is everything okay?" Ava asked, looking up. Then she arched an eyebrow. "Oh, I guess so."

Everyone else looked too, and Brynn could see that they could see exactly what she was feeling. "Noah and I have a plan." She sat back down in her chair from earlier. "It's all going to work out great."

"Let me guess," Cori said. "Big Sexy found a loophole in the will."

Parker made a choking noise and Ava snorted. Brynn lifted a brow. "Big Sexy?"

Cori grinned. "That's my new nickname for Noah."

Well it fit.

"*Please*, I'm begging you, don't call him that," Evan said to Cori.

She shrugged. "Already a done deal." She leaned over and kissed Evan on the cheek. "You'll be okay."

Evan groaned and looked at Brynn. "Please at least tell me the loophole is easy. Tell me it's obvious."

"I'm going to be dating five more guys," Brynn told him.

He let out a breath. "Okay. "

"But Noah's going to help me with the kissing stuff."

Her sisters exchanged a look and Evan cleared his throat.

"That's awesome," Cori said.

"It is?" Evan asked her with a small frown.

"Of course. Who better to teach her about all of that than Noah?" Cori asked. "I already mentioned the *big* and *sexy* part, right?"

Evan narrowed his eyes.

Cori didn't seem a bit worried as she grinned. "She knows and trusts him," Cori went on. "He would never do anything to hurt her. He's really perfect for it."

Brynn agreed. One thousand percent. With all of it. The big and sexy part too. For sure. And now instead of nervous about the dating stuff, she was now looking forward to it. Almost enthusiastically. She could have dinner or whatever with the five guys. They were each taking her out on *one* date. It didn't matter how it went because she wasn't going to be thinking about a second date...or even what was going to happen at the end of the first date. The guy would be taking her home to Noah.

That sounded weird when she put it like that, but it was true. She had no doubt Noah would be there waiting for her. Especially if she asked him to be.

She'd eat a million mushy cheeseballs if she knew she'd get to kiss Noah at the end of the night.

And then some.

Her whole body broke out in goose bumps at *that* thought.

"So," Brynn said to Evan, "as long as I only have to go out with each guy once to count as a date and it doesn't matter who I end the night with, then we're fine."

Evan thought about it. "I guess that does meet the provisions," he said after a moment. "We all know that Rudy's *intention* was just to get you out socializing."

She nodded and then stood. "That's all I needed to hear."

But on her way up the steps she heard Even tell Cori, "You have no idea how glad I am that you weren't quadruplets."

"You can't orchestrate every single one of her dates," Evan told Noah the next morning at breakfast.

Noah pinned him with a look. "Are you saying that as a lawyer or a friend?"

If it was concern over what setting Brynn up on six dates with other men would do to his mental health, he could understand Evan's concern. If it was against the rules of the will, that was something else. The first he could blow off. The second not as much.

"A friend," Evan said. Then he sighed. "I guess it's not against the will for you to pick the guys, tell them what to do and say and what *not* to do and say, but, I really think you getting *more* involved in this is a recipe for disaster."

"It's the only way to be sure it all goes according to plan."

"You can't control every minute of this."

"The fuck if I can't," he said stubbornly. On the drive home last night, not only had he replayed every second of the kiss-that-hadn't-even-been-a-real-kiss, but he'd started feeling better and better about the plan as a whole.

He *did* need a win in the Good Guy department. He'd been racking up points by sewing pillows and unclogging drains and letting Brynn hang out at the garage. Now he was in the final quarter with time running out. He needed to make sure every bit of Brynn's dating life in Bliss went exactly according to plan from here on out. And now he was in control.

That had been what had bugged him before. He'd wanted to be in control, to insure it all went well, but he hadn't really had a plan. Now he did. Set up the dates, lay down some ground rules —like a curfew—and then end the date the way a guy who was crazy about her would. Brynn needed to practice the getting-to-know-you part of dating. Noah couldn't help her with that. They were past that. She needed to practice so many things about meeting and getting to know someone new. They couldn't do any of that. And he liked that. He liked that she was already fully comfortable with him. But he couldn't send her back to New York nervous and inexperienced. He just couldn't.

So the plan was flawless.

Because he got to keep kissing Brynn Carmichael.

And then some.

She hadn't said that she wanted to experience more than kissing, but he could read it in her face. And yeah, *no one* but him was going to be showing her any of that.

"And what happens if one of the dates still goes bad?"

"I'll make it better."

"How?"

"By showing her how a guy apologizes appropriately after screwing up."

"You mean by making the guy apologize in a way that you think is appropriate."

"Exactly."

Evan shook his head. "Yeah, nothing could go wrong with this."

"It's Brynn," Noah said simply. He didn't have a choice.

"So, have you picked the guys?"

"Yep." Of course he had. He wasn't fucking around with this.

"Okay, who's on the A list?"

"That A-list?" Noah repeated. "I've only got one list."

"What if they say no?"

Noah gave him a look. "They're not going to say no."

Evan laughed. "Okay, okay. Let's hear it."

Noah pulled a piece of paper from his back pocket. He, of course, had the list memorized. But he might want to take notes. Evan knew these guys as well as Noah did and he had to be *sure* they were right. "Caleb Holten."

Evan nodded. "Okay, I can see that."

Caleb was a farmer. Born and raised in Bliss. Nice guy. Never married. Would listen to Noah. "I figure he can take her to the football game on Saturday."

"Brynn likes football?"

"Does it matter? It's public so they won't be totally alone. There will be the game to watch so they won't have to really talk that much."

"And you'll be able to keep an eye on them."

Noah didn't deny it. "That will make her feel more comfortable."

"And Caleb feel more *uncomfortable*."

"I don't care how Caleb feels."

"And it will be over by nine," Evan pointed out.

Noah shifted. Yeah, it would be. "So?"

"So then you get her right after. Nine is better than midnight." Evan lifted his coffee cup and sipped in the really annoying, know-it-all way he had.

Noah shifted again. *You get her right after.* That sounded very possessive. And he really fucking liked that. "Then I was thinking Gage could take her to the barbecue."

"What barbecue?"

"The barbecue I'm having at my house."

"You're having a barbecue?"

"Yeah. You and Cori are invited."

"Gee, thanks."

Noah sighed. "What?"

"You don't have parties and barbecues at your house."

"I do now."

"And you are aware that I'm aware that you're having a barbecue so that you can set Brynn up on a date, so that you can keep an eye on her, and then keep her after Gage leaves."

Keep her. Yep, that also sounded possessive and he didn't feel even a little bad about it. "It's a big group thing—"

"So they're not alone and so they don't have to talk much," Evan filled in.

"Right." If Evan thought he was going to make Noah feel like he was overreacting to all of this, it wasn't going to work. He was very aware he was overreacting. And he didn't care. The end result was the only thing that mattered—that the stipulations of the will were all met and Brynn was happy.

Evan sighed. "What else?"

"I think then it might be time for her to ask someone out. Practice that too."

"Uh, huh. And who is it and what is she asking him to do?"

Noah got the impression that Evan wasn't fully in support of this plan. He narrowed his eyes, but said, "Sam Kent. And she can ask him over to game night."

Evan's eyebrows rose. "You're going to have her ask someone to come hang out with all of us?"

"Yes. Still a group, but smaller."

"And you'll be there, I assume?"

"Of course, I always come to game night."

"Yes, yes you do." Evan took another long draw of his coffee.

"And then, I think it will be time for a double date. Out to dinner and a movie. The whole thing."

"And the double date will Brynn and..."

"Someone." Noah wasn't sure yet.

"And will be with *you* and..."

Noah shrugged. "Someone."

Evan just looked at him.

"See what I'm doing? Going from bigger groups to smaller. Different guys. Different kinds of dates. Covering all the bases."

"Oh, I absolutely see what you're doing."

"Do you?"

Evan set his coffee cup down, folded his hands on the top of the counter, and said, "Noah."

"Yes?"

"What you're doing is dating Brynn."

"I'm going to be *around* while Brynn is dating."

"Noah."

"Evan," he said, mimicking Evan's tone.

"Listen, I get it. I get that you feel responsible for making sure this is all wonderful and perfect and happy. But, dude, you gotta give her a little space."

Noah folded the paper and tucked it back into his pocket. "No."

"No?"

"No." He knew he was being stubborn, but... this was Brynn. "I don't have to give her space. This is the perfect way to *not* give her space and still take care of everything."

"Noah," Evan said.

"The will says absolutely nothing about me not being there on these dates."

"Noah."

"And she wants me there." She did. He knew that much. She needed these dates to go well, and if he was there she'd be far more comfortable and herself. And the guys would really see how amazing and adorable she was, and the whole thing would be perfect.

"Noah."

"And the guys won't mind. They'll know that nothing's really going on." It wasn't totally crazy. It was *a little* crazy, but not totally.

"Noah."

"*What?*"

"Incoming."

Noah felt her the moment before he saw her. He turned to his right as Brynn slid up onto the stool next to him. "Hi." She gave him a big smile.

And he promptly forgot all about Evan.

"Hi." God, he wanted to kiss her again. He'd known this would happen. He'd wanted to kiss her, a lot, before last night, and he'd figured if he ever actually did it, he'd be addicted. But he had been unprepared for how strong his craving was. And he hadn't even gotten to her lips.

"How are you?" She sat sideways, propping her arm on the counter next to her.

"I'm great. How are you?" *You look amazing. You smell amazing. I want to lick you from head to toe.*

And then it got worse. Because her gaze dropped to his mouth as she said, "I'm a little sleep-deprived actually."

He cleared his throat. "Sleep-deprived?"

She met his eyes. "I tossed and turned before I could fall asleep last night."

Yeah. He knew the feeling. He wasn't sure she'd *handled* it the same way he had. But the thought that she might have, had his body heating and hardening. He cleared his throat. "What are you doing Saturday?" he asked.

"I'm going to Great Bend, actually."

He frowned. She couldn't go to Great Bend. The football game was Saturday. "What's in Great Bend?"

"Practice."

"For?"

"Dating."

He leaned in. "What are you talking about?"

She slapped a flyer down on the countertop between them. "I'm going to this."

He looked down. It was a speed dating event. They still did speed dating? He started shaking his head before he even looked back up at her. "No."

She put her hand on top of the flyer. "Yes. Cori brought it to me and it's perfect."

It wasn't perfect at all. It wasn't *here*. It wasn't...okay, it was *kind of* public, but she'd definitely have to talk. And he wouldn't be there. "Brynn, I told you I'd handle this."

She nodded. "I know. And I'll let you. But this can be a warm-up."

He arched a brow. He'd give her a warm-up. "What the hell do you need a warm-up for?"

"This is in public, so I won't be alone with anyone, and the chatting is timed, so I won't have to talk much."

Noah couldn't help but shoot Evan a quick I-told-you-so look over his shoulder. Evan snorted. Noah turned back to Brynn, but before he could say anything, she rushed ahead.

"This way I will talk to fifteen guys and it's only four minutes each."

"That's a lot of guys." A lot of guys. Fuck, he hated everything about that.

"But it's only four minutes each," she repeated. "Even I can do that."

Noah felt his expression soften. "You're not *that* bad at this."

"You actually have no idea." She tipped her head, a tiny wrinkle between her eyebrows. "I've never been awkward around you."

He shouldn't feel quite so triumphant about that. But he did. "You'll be okay. I've got this all worked out. The guys will be really nice, I promise."

Now *she* arched a brow. "I believe you. Because you'll tell them to be nice. And that's sweet. But I do really need to learn to talk to people I don't know. Male people I don't know. And this will force me to talk. But only for a few minutes each. And—" She leaned around and looked at Evan. "This can count as a date, right?"

"I suppose. The guys there will probably be enough like the guys in Bliss to count. But just one. No matter how many guys you talk to," Evan said.

She sat back and smiled up at Noah. And all he could think was *but will I still get to kiss you at the end of the night?*

"You're not going alone," he told her.

She tipped her head, still smiling. "I know." She laid two tickets on top of the flyer. One for a female and one for a male.

For some reason, that made his chest tight. She'd already known that he would go along with her. And this could count as a date, so she wouldn't need to go out with Caleb to the football game. That would work. Or he could set her up with Caleb for something else. And that would be six dates. And when Mitch came calling, she could tell him no.

"Okay, Saturday."

"It's a date." She gave him a conspiratorial grin and slipped off the stool.

He watched her go. Not correcting her about the date thing. Not trying to hide that he was watching her. Not sure that he had any idea what he was really getting into.

"Man, you are in so much trouble," Evan said.

Noah nodded. "Yep."

5

"Hi, MJ."

"It's so busy today." The older woman looked around the pie shop with a frown.

She was right. Every table in the pie shop was filled today. And Brynn was dying to get out of here.

Brynn made herself smile at the woman who came in about four times a week and sat at the corner table near the window and read a book. She didn't talk much, to Brynn or anyone else in the shop, and she always came in alone, but she was friendly enough and tipped well.

"It's busier than usual," she agreed. "But I was hoping you'd come in. I have a stool up at the counter for you." She led the way to the seat she'd saved for MJ.

They'd taken out the glass display case on this side of the shop and replaced it with a tall counter with more counter space and some cupboards behind it for the huge espresso machine and supplies Cori used to make her coffee creations. Actually, Noah had taken out the display case and replaced it with counters and cupboards. Evan had brought the two tall bar stools in so that he had a place to prop himself while he watched Cori work.

He'd even begun having client meetings at the "coffee bar" when the topics were things the client didn't mind discussing in public.

MJ didn't look thrilled with her new seat, but she climbed up without complaint and pulled her book from her bag.

"Your usual?" Brynn asked, moving behind the counter.

"Please."

MJ never changed her order, but Brynn asked every time. She set a cup down and filled it with coffee and caramel syrup. MJ thanked her quietly and opened her book. And that was that.

Brynn envied her. She looked around the shop. She wasn't sure when she was going to be able to escape over to Noah's garage today. Even if everyone cleared out soon to go back to work, she'd have a lot more dishes to help with than usual.

The pie shop had a few regulars. The older guys who always camped out in the shop—Hank, Walter, Ben and Roger—were there early so they already had their table. Evan's mom and her best friend had also slipped in just before the other tables had filled. But Brynn hadn't expected the surge of business right after the lunch rush at Parker's diner so she hadn't saved any seats for MJ or for Kayla, the young woman who'd been occupying a corner table near the window and scribbling in a notebook for an hour or so every day for the past two weeks and talking Brynn's ear off whenever she got close. Kayla was the new, very young stepmom to a five-year-old girl little who supposedly hated her. But Kayla was trying everything she could to win the girl over, including bringing her into town for gymnastics and dance class twice a week. Her stepdaughter didn't want Kayla to stay at the studio, and they lived a half an hour away, so Kayla came to the pie shop to kill time. She wasn't here yet, but Brynn expected her in the next ten minutes. If she didn't take one look at the packed shop and turn around.

The shop only had six small tables. There were four chairs at each, but they were most comfortable with only two people at a time. The tables and chairs were a mishmash of styles, collected from yard sales around town by Rudy. But the girls had painted them all white and put cushions in a variety of colors on the chairs. The centerpieces were small tartlet pans that held wax beads that smelled like various baked goods—apple pie, sugar cookies, gingerbread, and so on.

And the six men dressed in everything from jeans and T-shirts to suits who now each occupied the rest of the tables looked ridiculous sitting at them.

Parker's diner was now connected to the pie shop, and the men had drifted over to the shop after finishing their burgers and sandwiches for coffee and dessert today. And to talk to Brynn. Apparently. She'd been making small talk for the past forty minutes and she was about to scream. The speed dating thing was actually looking better and better. There a timer would go off and the guy she was talking to would have to move on.

Here, they could linger over pie and coffee refills indefinitely.

She assumed they all had jobs to get back to, but none of them seemed in a hurry. In fact, they seemed flirtatious. And competitive. She'd heard one asking another what he was doing here. One had mentioned a new restaurant in Great Bend while another bragged about some tickets to something he'd gotten, while still another scoffed and said "she" wouldn't be impressed by monster trucks. *He* had then mentioned tickets to a symphony.

If they were talking about her, they needed to know a couple of things—one, she had no idea what a monster truck was. Two, she didn't really like the symphony. And three, no way was she going to a restaurant one-on-one with anyone. That was her biggest phobia and she was going to avoid that like the plague.

But maybe they weren't here to ask her out. Maybe they were here for the pie.

Still, just in case, she was trying her best not to give any of them a real opportunity to have a conversation that would lead in that direction. She should probably just say yes to the first five and call her stipulation met. But, she didn't want to. She wanted to go speed dating. Mostly because Noah would be going with her. That insured that at least one of her four-minute "dates" would be with him. It also insured that she'd be with him the second her evening ended. So they could get on with the kissing. And stuff.

The same company that hosted the speed dating also did other singles events. She could take Noah along to one of those. Then she was thinking that she and her sisters could maybe host a barbecue at their house. She could invite someone over as her date for the afternoon, but they wouldn't have to be alone, which would make the talking easier, and Noah could be there. And he would stick around afterward and help clean up. And then they could do more kissing. And stuff.

She'd be up to date four by then. That all seemed easy enough. Surely there was a simple way to have two final dates that didn't involve one-on-one time with anyone either. Other than Noah of course.

They weren't going for a long-term thing, but she wasn't leaving Bliss a virgin, and she wasn't going to sleep with anyone but Noah. And that was that.

The bell over the front door jingled and Brynn looked up, half expecting to see another twenty-something guy walking in. But it was Kayla. Relieved, Brynn waved at her from across the room. Kayla met her eye and lifted a hand as well. Brynn pointed to the only other seat in the place—the stool next to MJ.

Kayla weaved her way between the tables to the counter. "Good grief," she said.

Brynn nodded. "I know."

Kayla glanced around. "I guess maybe I'll take my coffee to go today. I can go sit in the park."

Brynn shook her head. If nothing else, she could use a little more estrogen in the room. Cori had thought it was great that Brynn was the center of attention like this and had disappeared into the kitchen with Ava and Parker. "No, stay. Please. There's a stool right here."

Kayla glanced at MJ who was focused on her book. "Are you sure?"

Brynn nodded. If Kayla just sat with her notebook and MJ with her book, it would be as if they were at their own tables like usual. "Of course."

Kayla climbed up onto the tall stool. MJ barely spared her a glance.

"I'm going to grab Cori to make your latte," Brynn told Kayla. "Be right back."

A moment later, she stepped into the kitchen and breathed a huge sigh.

"You okay?" Cori asked, with a grin.

Brynn nodded. She looked around the kitchen. Ava had knocked down the wall between their side and Parker's side in the kitchen too. Which meant it was bigger and louder than it had been before. It wasn't as good a place to escape anymore. She eyed the storage closet near the back door.

Parker and Ava were over on his side at the moment. Ava waitressed and even helped with dishes so that Parker could concentrate on the cooking and actually get things done so that he had some free time outside of the diner. With Ava.

Cori was messing around in their kitchen with something chocolaty-looking. She wasn't allowed, per the will, to actually bake anything to be sold in the pie shop, but that didn't keep her from doing one of her favorite things—making amazing sweets that would make Evan fall even more in love with her. As if that was possible.

"It's just really busy," Brynn said.

"I noticed. So weird that we get overrun with handsome guys as soon as word gets out that you're able to start dating."

Brynn wanted to deny that it was anything but a coincidence, but she couldn't. "I guess Noah's been spreading it around."

And that was when she let it fully sink in that Noah was being very open about the fact that she was available to other guys now. Ugh. He didn't want her kissing other guys. He'd made that pretty clear. But he didn't mind that she was going to be spending time with them. And wasn't that a bigger deal? Getting to know someone and maybe like them? What if she started wanting to kiss one of *them*? Had he thought of that?

But she almost immediately sighed. That wasn't going to happen. She wasn't going to be spending enough time with anyone to get to really know them and like them enough to want to kiss them. These were going to be single dates. Dates that didn't include a lot of one-on-one time if she had her way. She was here to *practice* dating for when she went back to New York.

"I need a latte," she told Cori.

Cori turned fully and really looked at her. "Okay," she said, nodding. "I've got it. Why don't you take a break?"

"Oh my God, really?" Okay, that had been more enthusiastic than she'd intended.

"Really," Cori said, setting her whisk down and wiping her hands on her apron. "I've got things for a while."

Technically, in the will, waitressing and customer service was Brynn's responsibility. But they all knew that the idea behind the stipulation was to get Brynn out and interacting with people. She did that. A lot. She'd been doing it all day. Surely an hour off here and there was acceptable.

"Thank you."

"You got it." Cori passed her, the air around her smelling like sugar. "Oh, and you might want to go out the back door," Cori added. "If you want to avoid your fan club and all those symphony tickets."

"Those *are* for me then?" Brynn asked, untying her own apron and looping it over one of the hooks by the back door.

"Oh, definitely." Cori laughed. "And apparently everyone thinks that if you have money, you like stuff like that."

"Well, thank goodness there's no opera here."

"There is in Kansas City."

"That would be almost a four-hour car ride!" Brynn protested immediately. "I'm not doing that with someone." Even if it wasn't for the opera.

"Then you better avoid Dean Stevens." Cori gave her a wink and disappeared through the doorway and into the pie shop.

Brynn blew out a breath. She had been kind of hoping to keep the entire date to four hours. Or less. She stepped out of the backdoor, appreciating the quiet and lack of people for a moment. Then she automatically turned east, toward Noah's garage.

She walked along the alley behind the building that housed both the pie shop and the diner then rounded the corner to get to Main. Just as she stepped out onto the sidewalk, someone turned the corner and nearly plowed her over. She gasped and two big hands came out to grasp her upper arms, keeping them both upright and her toes out from underneath his.

His. She knew it was a man in the split second before she looked up. "Mitch!"

He grinned down at her. "Hey, Brynn." He held her just a few seconds longer, before letting go of her arms and stepping a half step back.

Brynn smoothed the front of her shirt and gave him a smile. She was dressed in a simple blue T-shirt and denim capris. She was usually covered in an apron so she didn't give much thought to what she put on in the morning. It was a lot like how she approached most of her work days in New York, where she was covered with a lab coat the majority of the time. But suddenly she was aware of the fact that her pink flip-flops didn't really match her outfit and that her hair was up in a...she had to think for a second, then she lifted her hand. A ponytail. Right. She hadn't remembered if she'd put it in a bun or a twist or what. She just didn't think about this stuff much.

Yet she suddenly felt like she wished she'd even *glanced* at a mirror sometime in the past four hours.

And why with Mitch? The pie shop was full of guys who were, evidently, thinking about asking her out, and yet she hadn't given a single thought to how she looked to them.

"How are you?" Mitch asked.

Frazzled. A little claustrophobic evidently. Pretty bad at flirting. Completely uninterested in the opera in Kansas City. "Fine. How about you?"

"Suddenly hungry for apple pie."

She felt her eyebrows rise. "What?"

His grin grew. "You smell like apple pie. Suddenly I have a craving."

Okay, so she wasn't very good at flirting, but she could recognize that that was what Mitch was doing with her right now. "Well, there's some pretty good apple pie right around that corner," she said, waving in the general direction of the pie shop. Which he hadn't come into once since they'd met. He was flirting with her right now, but he hadn't sought her out to repeat the invitation to his back deck. In spite of the fact that seemingly every single guy over the age of twenty-five and under forty had been told about her dating status.

"But you're not in there," Mitch pointed out. "No sense in going in now."

Uh, huh. She'd been in there almost all day every day since they'd met. Whatever. This was part of this whole dating/socialization/people thing that she dreaded. Figuring other people out. She didn't like small talk, she didn't like having to read between the lines, and she didn't like guessing.

"Well, I'll be back later on. Or tomorrow. Or...whenever," she said. "Maybe I'll see you." She started to turn away, feeling more and more desperate to get to Noah's.

"Brynn."

She turned back.

"Fiction or nonfiction?"

"What?"

"When you read, do you prefer fiction or nonfiction?"

She tipped her head. What was this about? "Fiction mostly."

He nodded. "Me too. I've read some great stuff recently. Maybe we can compare notes some time."

She narrowed her eyes. Was he asking her out? "That would be great. I'm always up for talking books." That was, in fact, one topic she had no trouble talking about.

"Have you read Paula Hawkins?"

"Don't tell me you only read the bestsellers?" she asked, almost disappointed.

He laughed. "Nope. But her recent one was great. And I do mix in some nonfiction. You might like some of it. We should definitely compare notes."

She nodded slowly. "I'd like that."

"Wonderful. Well, have a great rest of your day."

"You too."

He gave her a little smile and then stepped around her and continued up the side of the building. As he turned the corner into the alley in the opposite direction from the pie shop and diner, she realized that the hardware store at the end of the block was called Anderson Hardware. She assumed the owner was a family member.

And she also realized that he hadn't, actually, asked her out. Again. First the mention of his back deck, with no follow-up. No stopping in to the pie shop. And now a possible-maybe-future-book conversation? Would that be on his back deck too? Or would they meet somewhere else? Or would it just happen in front of the post office one day randomly? And if it was that, would it actually be a date?

Brynn rubbed the pads of her fingers over the middle of her forehead. Then stopped and dropped her hand. That was something both of her sisters did when they were frustrated.

She sighed.

She hated dating so far.

And she hadn't even really started.

———

On Saturday, Noah and Brynn drove to Great Bend without saying much.

Which was pretty much their MO. They had the radio on, they'd done the basic "how was your day" stuff. He'd told her that she looked nice without saying *you fucking look amazing and I don't want to share you for even four minutes with someone else.* He was proud of that.

Especially since he'd found out that the pie shop had been running over with guys the day before. Reportedly she hadn't talked to anyone specifically about anything more than pie and coffee. Until Mitch Anderson had caught her on the sidewalk outside and they'd chatted for a few minutes.

But Mitch hadn't asked her out. Because he was waiting to be guy number six.

Mitch was quickly becoming Noah's least favorite person.

It was a blessing and a curse that his two best friends were dating Brynn's sisters. He got to hear all the details, whether he wanted to or not.

He hadn't been at the diner when all of this had been going down. Which was likely why all the guys had suddenly had a craving for pie. Noah gripped the steering wheel tighter and frowned at the road.

He was never at the diner at that time of day because that was when Maggie usually left her house for a couple of hours, and he could get over there and take care of things like clogged pipes and loose shutters and oil changes for her car since the pie shop was within walking distance for her.

Not that she ever told him about those things. Even the oil

changes. She called other people. Like Stan Gallow, the local plumber. But then Stan told Noah about it and Noah took care of it. Along with giving Stan a discount on his next tire rotation or transmission flush.

And Maggie knew that those guys called Noah and that he took care of her issues. But she kept calling them anyway to make the point that she didn't want Noah to be the one doing things for her.

Thankfully, Stan, Mike, the local electrician, and Elliot, the heating/cooling guy, all understood where Noah was coming from, respected what he was trying to do, and let him in on the things Maggie called about.

Fortunately, he could see for himself how long her grass was getting or when her driveway needed cleared of snow or when her shrubs needed trimmed or when something was going on with the roof, and he could get there before she called someone or did it herself. When he'd first started asking the guys for these favors, he'd been afraid he was going to be taking care of all the cars in town for free.

But now, nearly six years later, they had a system. It wasn't a perfect system—a perfect system would be Maggie calling him directly for help—and every time someone told him that she needed something, he felt a jab in his gut. But she was being taken care of and that was the main goal. She didn't have to be happy about it.

"Are you okay?"

He glanced over to find Brynn watching him with clear concern. He made himself relax his expression. "Sure."

"I know you don't really want to do this tonight," she said.

"It's not that." He didn't want to do this, but that wasn't why he was tense and pissed off. "This is fine."

"Well, I was thinking," she said, shifting in her seat to face him. "Maybe we can arrange it so that you're my last guy."

Noah felt his heart jam in his throat and he had to clear it before replying, "What do you mean?"

"The way I understand it, the women all sit at a table by themselves. Then the guys are the ones who rotate through the room. I think we can figure out the pattern and arrange it so you can be the last one to talk to me."

"You want me to be last?" Of course he couldn't shake what Mitch had said about being last, the one who wouldn't have to give her up and watch her move on.

"Oh, definitely," she said. "I'll be able to look forward to it through all the other ones. And then, of course, we can leave together."

Heat and want flashed through him. Damn right they were leaving together. He didn't care who else talked to her, he knew who was taking her home.

And he wasn't kissing just her cheek tonight.

"Of course we're leaving together," he said. He wondered if she could hear the gruffness in his voice.

"But they can't know that we came together," she said. "We'll have to go in separately. And pretend we don't know each other."

Noah scowled. "Why?"

"Well, it's a little awkward to speed date someone who came with someone else."

"People never bring friends along to these things?"

Brynn shrugged. "I don't know. Yeah, I guess they probably do. But maybe not *guy* friends." She grinned. "Unless you want to be my gay best friend along for moral support."

"I'm *not* going to be your gay best friend."

She laughed. "Good. There would have been a lot of very disappointed girls in that bar tonight."

He didn't say anything to that. He didn't care about any of the other women that would be there tonight.

The event was being held at one of the trendy new bars downtown and he turned onto the street a minute later, spotting the place almost immediately halfway down the block.

"Go around the block," Brynn said as they took in the small crowd gathered on the sidewalk.

"Why?"

"They can't see us together. We have to pretend we don't know each other or people won't think we're taking it seriously."

"*Are* we taking it seriously?" he asked, glancing over at her. "I thought this was just practice."

"Well, yeah, but I have to *seriously* practice."

Whatever that meant. "Fine," he muttered. He pulled around the block, parking along a side street out of sight of the front of the bar.

"So no scaring anyone off or just watching me the whole time," she said. "You have to focus on your dates too. It's not fair to them if you half ass it."

"I'm not even sure how you would half ass a four-minute date." He put the truck into park and shut the engine off.

"You could be paying attention to me the whole time," she said. "I know that you want to be in control of the guys I see because Rudy asked you to be sure I was okay, but this is speed dating. And you'll be right there in the same room. So no scowling at the guys, no interrupting my conversations, and no ignoring the girls you're supposed to be talking to, okay?"

"Yes. Fine. Okay."

"I mean it, Noah."

He looked over again to find her frowning and looking far more anxious than she should have been, given the topic of conversation. "I said okay." He frowned. "What's going on?"

"I just..." She swallowed. "You're going in there because of me. But those girls are showing up hoping to have a nice night, if not to find Prince Charming. We'll be in a room full of people and stuff, but for those four minutes, the other person is there for you.

And vice versa. Just promise me that you'll pay attention and ask them questions and make them feel good."

He understood what she was saying and, honestly, it was probably not a bad reminder. He could be kind of an asshole and frankly, his entire focus here *was* Brynn. So yeah, she wasn't wrong to point out that he wasn't just her bodyguard tonight. He was supposed to be a four-minute date to fourteen other women. He needed to give the other girls the attention they deserved.

He ran a hand over his face as that thought sunk in. Fourteen other women. At least some of whom were coming here tonight with expectations for a love match. All of whom were coming with a minimum expectation of a nice time. God, he hated expectations. Maybe they didn't believe they were going to meet The One, but they at least believed that he would give their four minutes a fair shot.

Fine. He could do that. He knew the goal...and the time frame here. Be nice, even a little charming, for four minutes. As long as he knew exactly what he was supposed to do and there was an end point, he'd be fine.

Just like with Brynn.

He shook that off. "I promise," he said. "But—" He glanced over. "You want to tell me what this is really about?"

Because, the truth was, Brynn thought he was great. She didn't know about or see his asshole side. So for her to be doubting how he'd treat these women...well, it had to be coming from somewhere else.

She pulled in a breath. "I hate sitting across the table, one-on-one with someone and feeling like we have nothing to say to one another."

And understanding hit him—her dad. Rudy had told him about how awkward things had always felt between them. Obviously, even as a little girl, she'd noticed that same thing and it had stuck with her.

He reached over and covered her hand where it was resting

on her leg. She turned it over, linking her fingers with his as if it was the most natural thing in the world. "You'll be fine. It's four minutes and there's no long-term consequence to anything you say or do."

She nodded. "I know. But..."

"What?"

"It would be nice for them to *want* more than four minutes when it's over."

Noah felt an actual ache in his heart. "Brynn." He squeezed her hand and she looked up at him. "Anyone who doesn't want to be with you constantly is a dumbass."

She swallowed and looked back at their hands.

"And yes, your dad is on that list."

Her head came up quickly and she stared at him.

"I loved your dad," Noah said, his voice gruff. "And I know that he changed a lot after he came to Bliss. But I swear, every time I think about how he didn't really try to get to know you or even meet you halfway in your relationship, I wish I had the chance to...shake him."

"It wasn't all his fault," she said.

"It was." Noah took a breath. "This all started when you were a little girl. Your relationship with him was on him then. Little kids shouldn't have to try to make the adults around them comfortable and happy."

"Yeah, okay," she conceded. "But when I was older, I was very aware of the fact that I could try and I could figure out things for us to talk about and make it work. But I also realized that it was easier not to." She gave him a funny half smile that didn't look at all amused. "I kind of take the easy way out a lot."

"Come on."

"I do," she insisted. "It's *always* easier to just roll with whatever Cori and Ava want."

He had to snort at that. That was true even for gruff, his-way-or-the-highway Parker.

"And look at this speed dating thing. I'm knocking out one of my dates by spending *four minutes* with these guys. It's super low risk. And then, on top of that, I bring *you* along. Which pretty much ensures that everything will be great. This is way easier than actually spending an evening trying to talk to a guy and get to actually know him."

He loved that she thought him being there was a guarantee that things would be great. "The guy has to try too," Noah said. "It's still not all on you."

"I'm just not—" She blew out a breath.

"What?"

"I'm just not used to having someone's *full* attention on me, even for four minutes," she said. "When dad and I did go out, I brought a book and he had his phone. With Cori and Ava, it's always *both* Cori and Ava so they pay attention to one another too—and they're both very distracting, even to one another. In the lab or at conferences, there are other people around and work to talk about. I'm not used to talking to someone, one-on-one, their full attention on me with the *intention* of getting to know me."

She said it all in one big rush and Noah felt his chest tighten painfully again. Dammit. *He* didn't give her full, one-on-one attention either. If they were one-on-one it was at the garage where he was working and she was reading. Just like her and her dad. Fuck, he hated that. And when they weren't at the garage, there were always other people around whether they were at the diner, the pie shop, or the girls' house.

But that was all safer. If they didn't talk much, then she wouldn't tell him all the things she needed and wanted, and he wouldn't feel compelled to make it all happen. And if they didn't talk much, then they wouldn't get to know each other even better, and he wouldn't fall even harder.

At least, that had all made sense in the beginning.

"Brynn, I—"

"But it's a nice idea, isn't it? To think that someone is intentionally sitting down at the table across from you with the purpose of spending that time with you, nothing else going on, and learning something about you?" She smiled and this time it seemed more genuine. "I mean, sure, probably some of them are just looking to hook up for the night and half the time will be about them, but still, they're giving me two minutes to be me. It will feel weird, but it will be nice."

He wasn't sure what to say. That *was* nice. He supposed. Except for the hook up part, which he was sure she was right about. But these people were showing up tonight and putting other things aside for a couple of hours. Yeah, it was kind of nice when he thought about it that way.

He could honestly say that the most meaningful interactions in his life were ones that knotted his stomach when he thought about them. Maggie. And Brynn. And not necessarily in that order. The woman sitting next to him in his truck at that moment made him feel and do the things he didn't feel or do for anyone else. And he supposed the same was true of Maggie.

The idea that a guy would sit down across from Brynn and *not* give her his full attention made Noah's blood pressure spike.

Noah would, most definitely, now give all of his four-minute dates his full focus. Because there were at least three people he could think of that he'd love to have four minutes with again. Maggie, Jared, and Rudy. Hell, he'd even take four minutes of attention from Penn, the cat that hated him.

He shook his head, his chest tight. He hadn't told Brynn anything about Jared or Maggie. He didn't want her to know about his failings. But, with Maggie on his mind, he did say, "Just focus on the guys being here tonight. More than what they say. Remember that them being here means they *want* to be here. What they say might not come out exactly right."

That he definitely knew something about. He was a doer, not a talker. It had been that way since his best friend died in a car accident after Noah had said, "Sure, go ahead, I'll cover your shift and we can hang out tomorrow" instead of "don't go out with those assholes tonight" or "call me if you need a ride home". Words mattered. And he didn't always know which ones to use. So he used as few as possible.

He definitely never knew what to say to Maggie. There was really nothing he *could* say. She'd been a single mom to an only child who had died at age nineteen. The last two times they'd spoken had been at Jared's funeral and then, four years later, when Noah had come home from the Marines and shown up on her doorstep and informed her that he'd be taking care of the house and yard from that day on.

She'd told him to get the hell off her property and leave her alone.

He hadn't. But they hadn't talked again since then. Even when he showed up at her house twice a week. There was nothing Noah could say that would help her, so he'd committed himself to *doing* things.

And there had been nothing short of her calling the cops that would have kept him away after he'd seen the way she'd completely neglected the yard and house.

But she'd never called the cops. She'd never yelled at him again either. In fact, she'd started leaving the house when he came around. Which was good for her. He knew from his own mom that Maggie had become a recluse after Jared died.

It hurt that Maggie didn't want him around, but he knew he reminded her of Jared. However, it hurt more that she was so depressed and withdrawn. That she'd quit caring about her home and her life.

Being at the house where his best friend had grown up had been hard on Noah too, but he'd been determined to keep it in good repair and the way he remembered it. He'd been appalled when he'd finally gotten inside. They'd always hidden a key in the backyard, and it was still there when Noah went searching one day after Maggie left. But he hadn't needed it. She'd left the door unlocked, as if she didn't care if someone came in and took something. And once he'd stepped inside, he'd realized that no one would do any such thing. There was very little of value in the house, and what was there was buried under dust and junk. Maggie had turned into a hoarder and had a clear aversion to cleaning.

He suspected the hoarding came from wanting to hold onto anything and everything that might have even the smallest bit of meaning after losing her son. So, he hadn't thrown anything away, but he'd boxed things up, labeled them, and stored them in one of the spare bedrooms and the basement. He'd cleaned that house from top to bottom. And she'd never said a word about it.

They never said a word about anything.

Noah tamped down all of those thoughts and the emotions that still swirled through him even six years later.

Now he not only kept his fucking mouth shut, but he also never made promises he couldn't keep. Like telling Rudy that he'd look after Brynn. And like telling Brynn that he would be sure tonight was great. He wouldn't have said those things if he didn't know for a fact that he could make them true.

Brynn finally took a deep breath and reached for the door handle. "Okay, so we'll both focus on our dates. One at a time. Give them our attention. And then we'll be each other's last date and we'll meet back out here when it's over."

Sounded like something he could deliver on so he nodded. "Let's do this."

Brynn squeezed his hand and then slipped out of the truck.

Noah got out more slowly.

Wow, he really hated this dating thing. And *he* wasn't even the one technically doing it.

———

A fter eight four-minute dates, they took a break.

Brynn got a soda from the bartender and worked on breathing. It hadn't been bad. She could honestly say that all eight had been fine. For instance, she'd met Chad, a banker who was very into politics, and Dave, a chef who loved movies, Tom, an engineer who spent four months of the year in Hawaii, and Heath who was a freelance photographer and was into wine. All of them had been perfectly nice, relatively good-looking, and very attentive. And not a one of them had given her a single butterfly in her stomach or made any part of her tingle.

She had, however, introduced Colton, the real estate agent, to Greg, the guy looking for a condo downtown. Sure, the guys were here to meet girls, but that didn't mean that one of those girls couldn't help them make a business connection too.

She sipped her drink and surveyed the room. She had seven more dates. Well, six, if she didn't count Noah. But the problem was, she *definitely* counted Noah.

It was strange, but she was looking forward to those four minutes a lot.

She spent so many minutes with him almost every day. She spent almost as much time with him as she did with her sisters, honestly. But...not sitting across a table, talking and getting to know one another.

She wanted those four minutes of uninterrupted, full-focus time from him.

In fact, the *thought* of that made her stomach flip.

That was what she was looking for. Sure, tonight, the speed dating, these fourteen other guys were just as she'd said, practice. A way of dipping her toe into the talking, tell-me-about-yourself stuff. But ultimately, she was going to be out in the real world and talking to guys and *wanting* that flip, that tingle, the stuff she knew Evan and Parker did to her sisters.

The fact that so far, the tingles were only coming from Noah was a little concerning, but she'd figure that out. Or ignore it. Or something.

And where was he anyway? She scanned the room, wondering if he'd gotten cornered by one of his dates for a further conversation. But she didn't see him anywhere. She did, however, see Chad, the banker, headed in her direction.

Oh, no, she definitely needed a break to just not talk, not answer questions, not try to come up with questions of her own and not sound like an idiot. She deposited her glass on the bar, quickly ducked behind another guy, and made a beeline for the hallway with the restrooms. She just needed a little alone time in the midst of all of this *togetherness*.

Her hand had just touched the door to the ladies' room, when she felt an arm wrap around her waist and haul her in up against a hard chest.

"Hey—" But a second later, his scent hit her. Laundry detergent, a subtle cologne, and the faint scent of motor oil.

She relaxed against Noah as he pulled her behind a tall potted tree at the end of the hallway. He turned her so her back was in the corner and grinned down at her. "Do we need to go over some self-defense techniques?"

"Oh, I almost dropped you," she said, sincerely. "But then I realized it was you."

He seemed surprised, but she wasn't sure if it was about her "almost dropped you" comment or that she'd recognized him so quickly.

"I figured you could use a hiding spot," he said.

It wasn't like the tree totally covered them, but it was dark in this corner and with Noah's broad shoulders blocking her, she doubted anyone would recognize her. Besides, if someone did notice them, it was unlikely that they'd butt in. It would look very much like whoever was cuddled up behind this tree did *not* want to be interrupted.

"I could definitely use a hiding spot," she said, suddenly

acutely aware of *him*. His body, his heat, his scent. He was standing as close as he maybe ever had. Like the other night when he'd kissed her.

And with that memory, her entire body flooded with heat. And yes, tingles.

It's because being with him is so easy.

It's the tattoos.

It's the motor oil smell.

But then, unbidden, she flashed to the pleased look on his face when he'd made Parker belly laugh the other night. And the time he came storming into her office at the house, claiming she'd been working too long and practically dragged her down to game night. And the times when his eyes got soft when he talked about her dad. And just a little bit ago in the truck when he'd said that anyone who didn't want to be with her constantly was a dumbass.

It wasn't the tattoos or the smell of motor oil.

But before she could really get into what it *was*, he lifted a hand to her face.

"So in regards to the kissing and stuff that goes with dating," he said, his voice suddenly husky.

She nodded, pressing her lips together as they very specifically tingled.

"Well, there will be times when the guy you're with looks across the room and sees you smiling or laughing, and it will hit him in the gut how fucking beautiful you are when you laugh, and he might pull you into a private corner and kiss you for no other reason than that."

Brynn felt her breath escape on a soft *oh*, just before he lowered his head.

"And you really are fucking beautiful when you laugh," he murmured before his lips touched hers.

It was like he'd spilled warm water over her. In a wave that started at her mouth and swept over her body, her skin warmed and she felt her blood rushing, and she couldn't hold back the sigh of pleasure for anything. She leaned into him, her hands fisted the front of his shirt, and she opened her mouth without thinking.

Noah made a quiet growling noise that she felt against her hands as much as she heard it. She felt him open his mouth too, their breaths mingling, but before it went any further, he suddenly lifted his head. He stared down at her, his eyes dark. "Damn, Brynn."

She swallowed, not sure if that was a good damn or not. He looked almost pained, but, there was a heat in his eyes that she knew. She'd seen Evan and Parker look at Cori and Ava like that.

The tingles that erupted from that realization were enough to make her knees feel a little wobbly. She clutched his biceps and said, "Damn, Noah." Hers was a lot more breathless than his had been though.

"I should let you go," he said, even as his fingers flexed against her cheek and her hip where he held her.

"Please don't." And she curled her fingers into him as well.

He stared down at her, his breathing ragged. He gave a soft, muttered *fuck*, and then he kissed her again.

And this time her knees really did wobble. As his mouth opened over hers and his tongue licked along her bottom lip, she felt her nipples tighten and her deep pelvic muscles clench. She heard a little whimper and knew it was her. And she didn't care. She was helpless to control any of her reactions. Including going up on her tiptoes and arching against him and stroking her tongue along his lip the way he'd done to her.

She felt his hand squeeze her hip and then he was pressing her into the wall behind her, his hand slipping from her hip to her ass and lifting her against him, his leg wedged between her thighs.

God, that felt good. She needed pressure *right there*. It wasn't enough, but it helped. She wanted to take her clothes off. And to take *his* clothes off. She knew she wanted to be skin to skin. And she wanted to touch him. All over. Everywhere. And she desperately wanted his hand between her legs on that spot that *needed* pressure and friction and heat.

It was all instinctive. It was like her body knew exactly what it needed and didn't really intend to bother her brain about any of it. At least not the part that made decisions. The part that *felt* things and replayed every erotic romance scene she'd ever read was definitely working though.

She ran one hand over Noah's chest, reveling in the way the muscles were bunched because of how he held her. She stroked her palm down his side, over his ribs and those hard, gorgeous, drool-worthy abs. She hit the waistband of his jeans and started to follow it along to the center button.

And then a bell rang.

They both froze for a moment with their lips still pressed together. Then, slowly, Noah lifted his head. But he didn't move his hand. Or his leg. He looked down at her, breathing hard, his lips damp from hers.

She blinked rapidly, her hand resting on his waist, but itching to keep moving. He was big, and hard, and so unlike anything she'd ever run her hands over before, that she *had* to explore.

But she realized that the bell was signaling the end to their break.

"We don't have to go back in," she said as she felt him start to pull away. "I've had enough practice. With that part," she added. She needed *a lot* more practice on *this* stuff.

His gaze dropped to her mouth and she could see him thinking about ditching the rest of the event. But then he relaxed his hands and let her go. And stepped back. "We should go finish."

"But—"

"I can't drag you away from your other dates. No matter how much I want to. That would be a really bad habit to start."

So he wasn't talking about just tonight. She nodded. "Yeah, Okay." She couldn't drag him away either. There were other women in there waiting to meet him too, and they deserved their four minutes.

"Besides, I haven't gotten my four minutes of talking with you yet," he said with a small smile.

And that made her swallow hard. Because she'd been looking forward to that. Of course, the way they'd just spent the last few minutes was completely fine too.

"We can talk in the car," she said. "On the way back to Bliss. To your house."

His gaze grew hotter, but his mouth curled. "Yeah. But I want to be your last date here tonight."

Technically, he would be if they left right now. But...she wanted it to be official too. Or something. It was silly. This didn't really mean anything. She was going home with him either way —and that thought sent a little shiver down her back. But having him be her last four-minute date seemed symbolic somehow. Like even if all of the other dates had been fine, he was the one who could raise the bar to great. And it seemed that he intended to. Just like he was showing her how the kissing side of relationships should be, he could also show her how these dates *could* be.

"Fine. Let's go back in then."

He nodded, but it took him a second to actually move enough that she could squeeze out from behind the tree.

"I'll go in first?" she asked. They still needed to pretend like they were both available, right?

And they were. They were both available.

"Sure," he agreed.

"Okay. So..." Available or not, her body was still feeling the aftereffects of that kiss.

He ran his thumb over his bottom lip and she completely lost her train of thought.

"I'll see you in a few minutes," he said, his voice a little husky.

Right. She needed to...turn and go...do something. She took a breath, pivoted on her heel, and headed down the hallway. She felt him watching her go. Just like the other day when she'd left the garage and he and Mitch watched her walk away.

Except it felt nothing like that.

6

The other six dates were fine. As expected. There was nothing wrong with any of the guys, and she even found herself smiling and enjoying hearing about Jason's vintage record collection and Blake's two dogs.

But as each date stood up, all she could think was, "It's almost Noah's turn."

It was so strange. They talked every single day. Literally. Why did this feel so different?

Because it was a one-on-one across a table?

It was a stupid phobia, but she supposed the people who had a fear of crossing bridges or haunted houses realized on some level it wasn't rational. That didn't change the fact that they'd do whatever they could to avoid those situations. That was her and dinner with just one other person.

But maybe Noah could make her not hate it so much.

And then it was his turn.

He pulled the chair out with a grin that made her heart trip. She wasn't sure she'd ever seen that grin before.

"Hi, Brynn. I'm Noah."

Oh, they were going to do this like this? Okay. She smiled. "Hi.

It's nice to meet you."

"Since we've only got four minutes, I feel like I just want to jump in here, would that be okay?" he asked propping one of his forearms on the table and leaning in.

Brynn wet her lips and crossed her legs, also leaning in. "Of course. I appreciate the direct approach."

"I need to know what the worst-case scenario is, in your head, regarding a one-on-one dinner date."

She blinked at him. Well, this wasn't exactly the type of conversation she'd be having with a stranger. But she had wanted four minutes of Noah's attention and she was getting it. And it certainly wasn't small talk.

She took a breath. "Okay, I guess it's that we're sitting there, and I order my favorite dish and then, as we wait, we talk about the things we thought we had in common—people we both know, events we've both been to—but we quickly realize that we see those things completely differently and so we don't really have anything in common after all and it just gets progressively more awkward and I realize that he would probably pick at least a hundred other people to take to dinner over me and by the time my food arrives, my favorite dish is ruined forever."

Wow. That had just spilled out. She watched Noah process all of that. Then he gave a simple nod.

"What was your favorite dish?"

So he'd realized that her worst-case scenario had actually happened. He probably also knew it had been with Rudy. "Cheese ravioli."

"Damn." He nodded again. "That really is too bad."

She found herself smiling. "That restaurant had the best."

"After that, did you start ordering your least favorite thing on the menu?"

Her smile grew. "Yes."

"And what's that?"

"Grilled halibut."

He chuckled. "I love grilled halibut."

"Well—" She lifted a shoulder. "—it's not cheese ravioli, you know?"

"I get it."

"What's your favorite food to order in a restaurant?" she asked, realizing there were a lot of basics she didn't know about him.

"Steak."

She should have guessed. "And least favorite?"

He thought about that. "I really like most food," he finally said. "If I *had* to pick something, I'd probably say grilled chicken or something. Kind of boring. But there's not much I won't eat."

It was the dumbest thing, but she loved knowing that.

"Do you have any phobias?" she asked. "Like my dinner thing? Scared of heights or something?"

He gave a little frown. "I don't think your dinner thing is a phobia."

"No?"

"You have a legit reason for feeling the way you do. Phobias are irrational fears. Yours isn't irrational."

She felt a warmth in her chest at that. Which was different than the heat he sent through her body so easily. "What about you?" she prodded.

His expression tightened slightly, but he shook his head. "Not really."

"Nothing you're scared of?"

He met her eyes. "I didn't say that. Just not anything irrational."

She wanted to know all of his fears, secrets, stories. That was startling. She was certain she'd never felt that about anyone but her sisters before. "Noah—"

He glanced at his watch, then up at her and said, "You are the most beautiful woman in this room. Or any room that you're in. And this is the best four-minute date ever."

She felt pleasure ripple through her and she opened her mouth to reply when the bell that signaled the end of their four minutes rang.

For the first time all night, Brynn felt a sense of disappointment. Again, silly, considering she was going to be riding back to Bliss with him, and seeing him every day for the rest of her time in town. But she felt like *this* moment might be something that was hard to repeat.

Because this was kind of dating talk. And she and Noah weren't dating.

———

Now he wanted to make her cheese ravioli.

And he had no idea how to do that.

This was why he didn't ask people what they wanted and needed beyond their cars and trucks.

Noah shook hands, thanked their hostess, and even accepted numbers from three of the women he'd met tonight. They weren't supposed to do that. Each person was supposed to mark anyone they were interested in seeing again down on their info sheet, and if the other person felt the same way, the company that hosted the event would give out contact info. But he slid the cards into his pocket anyway. He wasn't going to call anyone from the evening, but Brynn's plea for him to be kind to the women still rang in his ears.

He and Brynn left the building separately. Noah actually went out to the truck before she did, so that it would be unlocked and she could get right in. But he kind of hated leaving her in that room with all of those guys. He was sure a few of them would be trying to slip her their numbers as well.

But she emerged only minutes after he'd started the truck. She climbed up and gave him a big smile. "Two down, four to go."

ERIN NICHOLAS

He eased the truck out of the parking spot and into traffic. "Yep. Only four to go."

Damn, four more dates seemed like a lot. Too many.

Then again that was four more opportunities to show her how good dates should end. He could only blame that thought on the kiss earlier. He hadn't meant to do that. He hadn't meant to back her up against the wall at all. He hadn't even really intended to touch her. But he'd figured she needed a breather and so he'd found a dark corner.

He, Brynn, her intoxicating body spray, the skirt she was wearing, and a dark corner were not a good combination.

Or they were an amazing combination, depending on how he looked at it.

That kiss. He'd been thinking about it nearly nonstop but had been able to force his mind onto other things while at the dating event. Now though, in the truck, alone with her, he couldn't think of anything else. But that kiss meant that he'd already kissed her tonight. Should he kiss her goodnight too back in Bliss?

He wanted to show her different kinds of dates, and he also wanted to give her a chance to experience the progression of a physical relationship. A slow progression. With plenty of build-up and her totally comfortable at every step. He wanted her to know that she was calling the shots. Because that's how it should go in the future with any *real* boyfriends. Slow. Very, very slow. Like maybe never actually getting to the sex stage until she met The Guy. Noah gripped the steering wheel tightly. He fucking hated The Guy.

"So, what's next?" she asked, tucking one foot under her butt on the truck seat.

He glanced over. "I don't know. Are you hungry?"

She shook her head. "No, I mean with the kissing."

Noah felt the wheel jerk and he forced his attention back on the road. "What?"

"You finally really kissed me. So what's next?"

Finally? *Finally?* Did that sound like she'd been thinking about it? Wanting it?

And what was next? *How about you against the wall again but with that little skirt bunched at your waist this time and you moaning my name.*

Noah ran a hand over his face. He needed to get a grip. And *not* a grip on Brynn. Up against the wall and thrusting deep was *not* the next step here. Probably.

"Well," he said, proud of how composed he sounded. "I did say that I'd be the one kissing you after each date. But we kind of already did that tonight, right?"

She pivoted quickly on her seat. "But that kiss was totally spontaneous. And surely people kiss more than once on a date sometimes."

Noah almost smiled. That naïve thing was pretty good. Very cute. But it was an act. Brynn Carmichael was brilliant. And she was twenty-nine. And she had two sisters who were not strangers to men, dating, and kissing. Just because she wasn't kissing many —or any—men, didn't mean she didn't know how this worked. She was messing with him. And maybe making sure he was prepared. He glanced at her. Maybe she had some expectations here. The kiss behind the plant had been spontaneous. And hot. But she was now making sure she was going to get more.

Brynn wanting him, no matter what it was for, made a shockingly powerful need rise up in him. The need to be there and give her anything and everything she wanted.

And he had a suspicion she knew that.

If she did, he was in trouble.

He nodded, as if he was taking her naiveté seriously. "Yes, sometimes people kiss more than once on a date. But you don't want to rush these things."

Out of the corner of his eye, he could see her arch a brow. "Right. Rushing. Wouldn't want that." She gave a soft snort.

"That's funny?"

"If that bell hadn't rung and interrupted us, I have a feeling I would have gotten way more than a kiss behind that plant."

Heat jabbed him in the gut, then slid lower. He cleared his throat. And said honestly, "You're right." She was *very* right. "You should probably avoid plants in dark hallways with other guys."

He knew she was smiling now even without looking.

"No way would I get behind a plant with anyone else."

Damn right. "Good," he said sincerely. And there was no way he wasn't kissing her again tonight. "But yeah, even if you're going *nice and slow*—" He emphasized those words carefully. "—you might find yourself kissed more than once on a date."

Unless she was dating dumbasses. Which he kind of hoped she would be. But not really.

This was making him nuts.

"Great." She sounded pretty damned enthusiastic about the idea of multiple kisses.

He frowned. "You might not *want* to be kissed again, you know."

"No, I *definitely* want to be."

He glanced over. "You don't know that. You need to really want to kiss the guy. You don't have to do it just because he took you out." And they were absolutely talking about when she went back to New York, not while she was in Bliss. Because she wasn't kissing anybody but him while she was in Bliss.

She met his eyes. "Oh, I thought you were talking about *you.* Yeah, I know I won't want to kiss every guy after every date."

The heat hit him hard again. Her wanting to kiss him, wanting him to kiss her, was nearly overwhelming. He could *not* push her up against the side of his truck and take her right there tonight. That was *not* going slow. And even though he felt as if he'd been freaking waiting—and waiting and waiting—for her, he couldn't keep her. He *had* to show her how all of this *should go* with The Guy.

The Guy who he *really* fucking hated.

"Okay," he said, focusing on this one night, this one lesson, and nothing more. Like when the lessons would be over. "So this is technically date two?"

"I guess so," she said. "If Sean was one and the kiss in front of my house was how a first date kiss goes, then this is number two." She nodded. "Yeah, this is two."

"Got it." Date two kissing. Okay. He could do this. Brynn deserved to have the best experiences with all of this. And he *would be* her best.

Did he kind of want to set the bar so damned high that she might never find someone else to ever satisfy her?

Yep.

But, as with all of this, he felt torn right down the middle. He did want that. He wanted her first experiences to be amazing. He wanted her to know how it *should* be, what she should be expecting from every guy. And no one would ever take care of her, care about her, and want to blow her mind as much as he did.

At the same time, he didn't want her to never find that again. He wanted her happy and fulfilled and taken care of for the rest of her life.

By someone else of course. Preferably far from Bliss so he wouldn't have to see it.

"So you have a plan then?" she asked.

Noah pulled in a breath. He had a plan alright. She was talking about the kiss he was going to lay on her later—and he *was* going to do that—but he couldn't forget his overall plan behind all of this: check off Rudy's list and send her back to New York happier and more confident. It was solid. It was good for them both.

He could get Brynn through all of this. Even with the wrench of being crazy about her while helping her date other guys. He had to remember that the *dating* stuff was easy. It was going out and having fun and enjoying the chemistry. The decisions were where to eat and what to get her for Valentine's Day and how to find out if she was into role playing without coming off creepy. The first six dates? Piece of cake. Even if it had been just him and her and not actually six first dates with six different guys. Six first dates were nothing.

But he was going to be around for her six dates. And he was involved, like it or not. He had wondered, more than once, if Rudy had somehow known that Noah started getting antsy after only five dates with the same woman and that he rarely—okay never—made it to date six. But there was no way the six-date stipulation for Brynn could have had anything to do with Noah. Right?

Rudy's intention was for Brynn to meet various guys and just "test drive" dating for when she got back to New York. It had nothing to do with Noah. Or the fact that he had an unspoken, mostly subconscious five date limit. After five, things started to get into more serious territory. The part that came with more promises and expectations.

That's when he was out.

Even with Brynn.

Especially with Brynn.

Of course, *these* six dates weren't between him and her.

Fuck.

He reached for the volume knob and turned Dierks Bentley up. The rest of the way to Bliss, the only sounds were the road and the radio.

In spite of the emotions twisting his gut, Noah felt the anticipation winding the muscles in his neck tighter and tighter. Brynn was fidgeting on her seat and he assumed it was for the same reason. He wanted to reach over and pull her up against his side. To reassure her. And because her wiggling was making him think about how her hips moved. Which was doing nothing good for his self-control and not-up-against-the-truck-tonight pledge to himself.

Finally, after what felt like a year, he pulled into the driveway of her house. Elvira was tucked into the garage and the porch light was on. No other vehicles were parked in the drive or by the curb. So Parker and Evan weren't here. Brynn wouldn't have to face the gang and recount the details of speed dating. But he wondered if her sisters were home. Not that it mattered. He was not going inside. Not tonight anyway.

He turned the truck off and looked at her. "I'll walk you to the door."

She nodded.

He opened his door, reached to shut off the overhead interior light, then got out and went around to her side, pulling the door open and offering his hand. His fingers wrapped around hers and as she turned to slide down, he was suddenly struck by how the truck seat put her at a really perfect height. Instead of stepping back to let her down, he stepped closer and her knees parted for him to move between them. Her free hand went to his shoulder. His settled on her hip. Then she slid closer. And he leaned in.

Their mouths met, and she gave a little sigh that made his gut tighten and his cock instantly harden. She ran her hand from his shoulder up the side of his neck to his head, her fingers gliding over his short hair and making a shiver shoot down his spine. Damn, how did that feel so good? His hand slid from her hip to her ass and he brought her forward. Instead of a sigh, this time she gave a little moan, and Noah felt a need unlike anything he'd ever felt before. She fit perfectly against him, her softness cradling his hardness. Which got even harder. Especially when she wiggled. He groaned. Yep, just like how she'd moved on the seat.

Her fingers tightened in his and he opened his mouth, needing to taste her. She followed his lead and their tongues were immediately stroking, hot and insistent. In fact, it was hard to tell who was more insistent at that moment.

Noah felt his fingers digging into her butt, not that she

seemed to mind, and he tried to gentle his hold, but she wiggled as he tried to let go, bumping the apex of her thighs against his fly. He tore his mouth from hers, looking into her eyes. Her pupils were dilated and she was breathing hard.

That was a decent second date kiss, right? It was more than the forehead and cheek from the first night. There was more tongue than behind the plant. He swallowed. Yeah, this was good. He could leave it here.

Then she said maybe the one thing that could have torn through his good intentions.

"More. Please, Noah."

Heat rocked through him. Jesus. That was the sexiest thing he'd ever heard. And, since it was Brynn, there was no denying her.

He leaned in to taste her where he'd been fantasizing about kissing her for months. The skin along her neck was silky soft and smelled amazing. He dragged his lips from her collarbone to her jaw and down again.

"You want more?" he asked huskily.

She tipped her head back. "Please."

With a little groan, he put both hands on her ass and pulled her firmly against him. He opened his mouth and gave her neck a lick and then sucked slightly. She gasped again and wiggled, pressing against him, seeking pressure.

He gave her pressure. He gripped her ass and pressed forward, rubbing the hard length of his cock against her.

"Oh my God, Noah," she breathed.

This was fucking addictive. He took her mouth in a hot, deep kiss, stroking along her tongue firmly.

Her hands were gripping his shoulders, then running down over his biceps, squeezing there, and then down to his waist, around to his back and up again. Damn, her hands felt good on him.

As did the hard points of her nipples pressing into his chest.

He was also acutely aware of the fact that her legs, not quite wrapped around his waist, but holding tight on either side of his hips, were completely bare from the sandals on her feet to whatever she was wearing under this short skirt.

God, he'd love to know what she was wearing under this short skirt.

Second date kiss. Just a second date kiss, a voice said in his head.

But in the next instant another voice said, *she said more. And please. Fuck the second date kiss.*

He ran his hands from her butt to her bare legs, stroking from her knees to just under the hem of her skirt where it was pulled up on her thighs. She gave a little whimper and, possibly subconsciously, moved her knees a little farther apart.

The rush of need that shot from his head to his cock made him a little dizzy. He moved his hands higher, stroking the soft, hot skin. Brynn's fingers dug into his back and she ran her tongue over his lower lip, then moved her mouth along his jaw and to his neck. Just as he'd done to her, she dragged her lips along the tendon that ran down from his jaw, along his collarbone, and when she got to the spot where his neck met his shoulder, she bit down gently.

Noah jerked. Then groaned. Did she know how fucking hot that was? No way did she know about biting. Or how sexy it felt for her to dig her nails into his back. Or how fucking good it felt to be pressed against her panties, even with denim in the way.

"Brynn," he said on a near growl.

She looked up at him, her lips a little swollen from his kisses. She made a cute little grimace. "Sorry."

"Don't fucking be sorry," he told her roughly. "But you need to realize what you're doing."

"What am I doing?"

"You're giving huge, bright green lights."

"Oh." She shrugged. "Well, good."

"Not good," he made himself say. "Date two doesn't end with your legs wrapped around the guy's hips."

She gave him a slow smile that, for all her inexperience, was incredibly, sexily, all-knowing. "I'm just going with what feels good."

He became all too aware that the truck seat height was absolutely perfect if he wanted to lay her back, lift her skirt, rip her panties off and make her feel better than she'd ever felt.

And he definitely wanted to do all of that.

"Date two isn't supposed to feel this good," he finally managed.

She laughed lightly at that. "I guess all of this isn't going to be an exact replica of how these real dates will go."

He pulled in a deep breath. "They can be. I just need to get my head on straight."

She shook her head. "With you it will never be how it will be with other guys."

He didn't want to hear this. Whatever she was about to say was going to make it impossible to take his hands off of her tonight. And yet, he still asked, "Why not?"

How fucking pathetic was it that he was prompting sweet words from her?

"Because I haven't been getting all worked up watching any other guy bending over cars for the past six months."

Noah stared at her. That was not what he'd expected her to say. At all. Even a little.

He cleared his throat. "You've been reading in the garage for the past six months."

"And ogling you. And wanting to run my hands over your back." She did just that as she spoke. "And eyeing this spot on your neck." She leaned in and kissed the spot where she'd bitten him. Then she ran her hands over his upper arms and shoulders. "And thinking about how it would feel to have these arms holding me up while you...kissed me."

Maybe, *maybe*, if she hadn't paused just before "kissed me", as if she could have filled something else in there, he might have let her go then. Maybe. But she had paused. And they'd both filled that blank in with something other than kissing.

He felt the groan rumble from his chest. Then he cupped the back of her head and brought her in for a long, deep, hot kiss. It wasn't a fast one. He took her mouth with long, easy strokes. But he made sure she felt it in every muscle. Especially the one pressed against his harder-than-ever cock. She wiggled against him, making needy sounds as he ran a hand up and down *her* back as she'd done to him before running it over her hip, then waist, up over her ribs, to cup her breast. One of the perfect, firm, hard-tipped breasts that had teased him over the past six months. She hooked her fingers in the belt loops of his jeans and just hung on. Which was fine with him. She'd been ogling him. He didn't consider himself a guy with a big ego, but that absolutely stroked what he did have and made it rear up and want to give her everything she might have even kind of fantasized about.

It would be damned near impossible to find someone who cared about her as much as he did. Who would want to make every single kiss, touch, and orgasm the best she'd ever have. Did that mean that he should leave her alone and not rock her world?

Probably.

Did that mean he was going to?

No fucking way.

He ran his thumb over her hard nipple, swallowing her moan of pleasure. He circled it, then tugged gently.

She ripped her mouth from his, sucking in air. She put her forehead against his, her eyes squeezed shut. "Oh my God."

"Pull your shirt up."

She hesitated. Noah knew she hadn't done this for a very long time, if ever, and he knew that the young guys in high school or college would have pulled her shirt up all on their own. But he wanted her with him. It was hotter than hell for a woman to undress herself, clearly wanting and needing to be naked as much as he needed her to be, and he wanted that from Brynn more than he'd ever wanted it before.

And, because she was fucking amazing, she didn't say a word or ask or even pause more than a few seconds, before she grabbed the bottom of her shirt, leaned back, and stripped it off.

He couldn't help his chuckle, even as he had to adjust his fly. "Or that will work."

"Oh, you did say pull it up. Sorry. I just... I don't know... I just wanted it off."

He shook his head. "Stop apologizing for going with how you feel. I mean it. Do whatever feels good. Do whatever you've thought about, anything you want to try." He lowered his voice and leaned closer, putting his nose nearly against hers. "Use me, Brynn. For all of the things you've ever wondered about. Or fantasized about."

She took a little breath. "It's a shockingly long list."

He gave a little groan.

"I mean the list of things I've wondered about," she said with a smile. "Though the fantasy list has grown a lot... lately."

She was going to kill him. Because if he didn't get her naked soon, he would die. And once he did get her naked, he'd never recover.

"I'm all yours," he said honestly.

She took another of those deep breaths. "That's really hot."

Well, good. Because it was absolutely true.

Then he could no longer ignore the fact that she was sitting in front of him with only a thin silky bra between him and her breasts. "Pull your bra down," he said gruffly. She started to move her hands and he added, "Not off. Just down."

This was a make-out session. And even though the truck seat height was damned near perfect for, well, everything except maybe three positions he had in mind, he was keeping this as a make-out session only. Clearly, they were on the path to more.

Clearly, he was going to teach her about more than kissing. But now that he knew she'd been ogling him and having some dirty thoughts of her own, he wanted to build this up. Teach her a little something about anticipation. And about the buildup, the slow burn, how good it could be when things finally exploded. And give her something to remember that would be very difficult to repeat. Because as much as he wanted her to be happy even after she left Bliss, he was still kind of an ass.

She tugged the front of her bra down, exposing her breasts, and Noah nearly swallowed his tongue. "Damn, Brynn."

She started to lift a hand and he grasped her wrist. He didn't know if she was intending to cover herself, or play with that pretty nipple, but he couldn't take either one. "Put your hands behind you on the seat," he told her, his tone low and firm.

Her eyes widened slightly, but he could see it was with excitement. She flattened both palms on the seat just behind her butt. The move pushed her breasts forward and Noah lifted a hand to cup one, brushing his thumb over the tip and reveling in how huge his hand was around the firm, perfect mound.

Brynn wiggled on the seat and her knees pressed into his hips. "God, that feels good," she said softly.

Considering she was easily the quietest woman he knew, Noah couldn't believe how much he loved that she seemed unable to keep from talking now.

"Just keep telling me how you feel, B," he said softly, before ducking his head and swirling his tongue around her nipple.

"Oh, wow, *wow*," was her response to that.

Then he sucked. And got a "Holy shit, Noah!"

He chuckled softly feeling triumphant. "And remember, no is also an option," he said.

"Why would I possibly say *no* to you?"

He paused. She hadn't said why would I possibly say no to *this*. She couldn't imagine saying no to *him*. That was dangerous stuff. That was the kind of stuff that should make him pull back,

ERIN NICHOLAS

quickly get her clothes back in place, and keep his damned hands to himself. For as long as she was in Bliss. Because that was the kind of power he loved. He loved being trusted implicitly, being the guy that people knew would take care of them.

It was the kind of power that had made him say "yes" when Rudy had asked for his help taking care of his girls and specifically looking out for Brynn. It was the power that had made him say "yes" when Jared had made him promise one night when they were sixteen and drunk on beers swiped from Noah's dad's garage fridge that Noah would take care of Maggie if anything ever happened to Jared.

Now he was on the precipice of letting that power, Brynn's faith and trust in him, push him into another no-return situation.

And because he was a little self-destructive and a lot selfish, he dove in.

He sucked again, while cupping her other breast. Her breathing was ragged, and she was gripping the back of his neck tightly as if to keep him in place. Her hips were wiggling against him and he couldn't stand it anymore. He took her ass in his hands, pulled her snuggly against him, and then rocked his pelvis against her, putting pressure and friction against her clit.

She ground against him, and he took her nipple between his teeth scraping them gently over the tip.

And the next instant, Brynn blew his mind. She gripped his neck, arched her back, and came with a soft cry.

Noah froze. He'd never given a woman an orgasm by just playing with her nipples. Okay, so there had been some grinding too, but no penetration. No direct attention on her clit. No hands or tongue between her legs. And she'd come.

He pulled back, lifting his head to look into her eyes.

She took a deep breath, and then grinned at him. "Date two kissing for the win."

He tried to come up with something to say to that. But one, he was still reeling from the realization that quiet, bookworm, Brynn

116

was a fucking firecracker. And two, he wholeheartedly agreed with her appreciation for date two kissing.

He lifted both hands, cupped her face between them, and brought her in for a kiss. "You're amazing," he said against her lips after he'd kissed her. "Thank you."

"Thank you?" She reached between them and pulled her bra back into place, then reached for her shirt. "Really? Thank *you*."

He suddenly wanted to know everything about every orgasm she'd ever had. She hadn't dated in a very, very long time, but had there been grinding and humping in her past? Surely she gave *herself* orgasms. With her fingers or toys or both? He needed to know if this amazingly fast, entirely hot orgasm was just how she was wired, or was it fueled by her fantasies? And were those fantasies all about him or were there others? And if it was something he'd specifically done right, he wanted to know so he could do it another three or four dozen times. Per night.

But no matter what, he fucking loved that quiet, reserved, in-the-shadows Brynn could find pleasure like that. So easily. So openly.

She was dressed again, but he was still standing between her knees. And frankly, between this woman's legs was exactly where he'd like to spend eternity.

"Can we go on another date soon?" she asked.

The smile she gave him was sweet with a little sexy around the edges, and she could get anything she wanted from him with that smile.

"Definitely," he told her.

"Great. When? And who's taking me out?"

When? As in when would he get to kiss her again? And progress their lessons? Tomorrow. Since later tonight was probably crazy.

But who? Fuck. She had just had an orgasm in his arms, and now they were going to talk about what other man she was going out with tomorrow? This had to be the craziest situation he'd ever been in.

Noah swallowed, cursed the could-drive-nails hard-on he was going to have to do something about when he got home, and stepped back. "I'm going to have a barbecue at my place," he told her. "Tomorrow afternoon."

He had no plans, no food, hadn't invited anyone, hell, hadn't even mowed his lawn. But he couldn't wait even a full day for date three.

"You're going to have a barbecue at your house?" She frowned. "You never have people over at your house."

"Tomorrow. Noon." Maybe then people would be out by three.

Who was he kidding? No one would leave until it was dark. That's how this stuff went. Especially on a Sunday afternoon. They'd sit around and drink beer and talk. Probably play volleyball. That's what they'd done in the past when he'd thrown parties. A long, long time ago. "But we'll do a pontoon party," he decided instead. They could gather at the river and float out on the water and have just as much fun. And then he could leave whenever he wanted to. Yeah, that was better.

"I've never been on a pontoon," Brynn said.

Of course, she'd never been to his house either. He stepped back and helped her out of the truck. Finally. "It will be fun. Swimming, a few beers, some burgers."

"Great." She smiled up at him. "Who's going to ask me?"

Yeah, who was going to bring this woman he was crazy about, who he'd just made come on the front seat of his truck, to the party he was throwing? Sure, this was a totally normal situation.

But he gave it some serious thought. It should be someone who would have to call it a night early so he could be up for work on Monday. Someone who wasn't a huge partier and might not want to stick around for a bonfire. "Tanner Greives." Tanner was a dairy farmer and had to be up at five a.m. to milk.

"Okay." Brynn bit her bottom lip and looked at his mouth. "I had a great time tonight."

He couldn't help his soft chuckle. "I know." He gave her a wink.

And she blushed.

He pulled her close, hugged her tight, and whispered into her ear. "Me too, B. You have no idea."

Then he walked her up to the porch, kissed her softly, and opened the door.

And then said the damnedest thing he'd ever said to anyone after a date. Or ever said to Brynn, period. "I'll have Tanner call you about the party tomorrow."

"Yeah. Okay."

Then she went inside and he went home.

As if everything was fine, normal, and on plan. When absolutely *none* of that was true.

7

Brynn floated through the pie shop the next morning, refilling coffee cups with a huge smile. And no clue what people were saying to her.

The shop was only open from nine to noon on Sundays, providing coffee and a place for some conversation to the after-church crowd and pies for Sunday dinners. Granted, it had only been recently that they'd seen an uptick in business on Sundays, and they all knew that Parker, and the fact that he now had some influence over the pie shop kitchen, had a lot to do with that. But that was fair. The pie shop was going to be Parker and Cori's in another six months or so.

Brynn didn't mind working Sunday mornings. She loved seeing the pie shop getting busier and people sitting around and enjoying the shop and each other. Sometimes she'd just stop and look around and wonder what her dad would think.

At first it had been hard for her to picture him here. But as she'd gotten to know his friends, Hank, Walter, Ben, and Roger, it had become easier to imagine. She was surprised by it. The Rudy she'd known was nothing like the friendly, warm, laid-back, involved-in-the-entire-town men who had essentially made the pie shop a clubhouse. But as she'd seen the effects of living in Bliss and running the pie shop on her sisters, she couldn't deny that her father had been right about bringing them here. Bliss had been very good for Cori and Ava. And she knew these men had been the ones to influence Rudy. She really loved them. So the fact that she had no idea what Ben had said to her two minutes ago and couldn't remember what Walter had told her about putting coffee grounds around plants was unusual. And probably rude. But she couldn't help it.

Noah. His kissing. His hand on her breast. His big, hard body against hers. That orgasm... She sighed. All of that was way more important to her than coffee grounds.

Sorry, Walter.

She was usually a fantastic listener. She preferred listening to talking, for sure. But today she wasn't really hearing anyone. She was far too caught up in her own thoughts. And memories. Last night with Noah had been...amazing. But that didn't feel like a strong enough word.

Yes, of course, the orgasm had been awesome. She hadn't ever had one of those with another person involved. She never would have believed she could have one with her panties still on and his hands, and other things, on the *outside* of those panties. And maybe best of all? Her sisters were completely jealous that she'd had one that easily.

But there was so much more than the orgasm that had her floating and grinning like an idiot today as she poured coffee and handed out pies. They'd talked, they'd flirted, they'd socialized and survived it. Both of them.

She hadn't fully realized it until Noah had mentioned throwing a party today, but he didn't go out much. He spent time with Evan and Parker, of course. Evan was a guy who could make any gathering into a party and prided himself on being able to help anyone have a good time. That included Noah. But she knew that without Evan, Noah would be almost as antisocial as she was without Cori. He came to game night, but she knew that had to do with her more than anything. Now he'd gone speed dating and was throwing a party. Also because of her.

More than anyone, she respected an introvert's desire to have alone time, but if she could bring Noah out of his shell a little too, she'd count that as a perk to her dad's crazy plan for her.

"Good morning."

She turned to find Mitch Anderson smiling down at her. Huh, he'd finally come into the pie shop.

"Hey, Mitch."

"How are you?"

"I'm great." She really was. "Can I get you some coffee?"

"I think I'll hold out for a beer."

She gave a little laugh. "Cori made some beer bread last week, but that's about as close as I can get." This crazy, quirky town didn't even have a bar.

"Oh, I'd much rather have it down on the river bank with you in a bikini later on," he said, giving her one of those slow grins that made her think flirting wasn't so bad.

But Mitch wasn't Noah.

"Actually, Tanner already asked me to the party," she said. He'd called her about an hour ago.

"Yeah, I know."

She looked at him in surprise. "You're asking me to go with you anyway?"

"I'm not asking you to go with me. I'll just see you there and we'll have a beer together."

Oh. He wasn't asking her to go with him to the party. But he planned to see her there and spend time with her? She really might prefer speed dating where she knew the rules going in. Or maybe a beer at the river had nothing to do with dating. She knew even less about river parties than she did about dating in general. "Okay. I guess I'll see you there."

Mitch gave her a little wink. "And I'm not saying that you might not wish you were there with me instead."

Flirting. That had to be flirting. Mitch was clearly confident, but he didn't come off as a jerk. So he was flirting. But he wasn't asking her out.

She sighed. She didn't know if she would ever totally figure out everything about dating. Maybe he was just taking the easy way out. It was easier to talk to a girl that someone else had invited, she supposed. She could appreciate that. She was a fan of the easy way out, after all. All of this was the easy way out for her. A barbecue at the river? Where there would be lots of other people, including her sisters and Noah? She might be going with Tanner, but there was very little to get anxious about.

"Well, I'm not going to make any decisions about you until I see what you put on your burgers," she told Mitch. "That says a lot about a person."

He seemed mildly surprised that she was flirting back. Heck, so was she.

"I'll bet you're an American cheese and pickles girl, aren't you, Brynn?" he asked.

She laughed. "I'm not giving you any hints."

"But you will be checking out my buns," he said with a grin.

She laughed again. "Yeah, I guess I will."

"That's only fair," he said with a nod. "I intend to take a nice, long look at yours after all."

She felt her cheeks flush, but she noted that there was no flipping in her stomach or tingles. Though in Mitch's defense, it would really take a lot more than some flirting, winking, and grinning to outdo what Noah had done last night.

"I guess I'll see you later then," she said, as the door opened and MJ came in. Brynn frowned. She never came in on Sundays. And Brynn instantly forgot all about Mitch's buns.

"Count on it," Mitch called after her as she headed to meet MJ at the counter where MJ had sat the other day with Kayla.

Brynn gave him a little wave over her shoulder.

"Hey, MJ," she greeted. "How are you?"

"Fine." The older woman frowned as she slid up onto the stool.

"Are you sure? I don't usually see you on Sundays."

"That's because Sunday is a day of *rest*," MJ said, plopping a book down.

Brynn wasn't sure that sitting in a pie shop, drinking coffee, and reading would count as *work* exactly, but MJ was clearly irritated about something. "What's different today?" Brynn asked.

"A bunch of guys are banging around my house."

"Guys you know, I hope?" Brynn reached for a cup and poured coffee for her.

"Oh, I know them. But I didn't think they'd be over *today*."

"What are they doing?"

"Replacing my toilet."

"Oh." Brynn slid the cup to her. "Well, that's nice." She frowned. "Did you hire them or are they friends?"

MJ's frown deepened. "I called to hire them."

"But you weren't expecting them today?"

"They never come."

Brynn set the coffeepot down and leaned onto the counter. "I'm not following."

"I call the guys to hire them. But then they always call this other guy—" MJ rolled her eyes. "And he comes instead. I figured he'd be there while I was at church and Bible study. He always comes when I'm not home. But he's got something going on today, so he called these guys back. But they couldn't do it until after church."

Brynn shook her head. She thought she was following. "But it's still getting done. That's good right?"

She shrugged. "Yes. I just...this guy who usually comes...I'm a little worried about him. He never doesn't come."

"Can you call him?"

MJ shook her head. "No. We don't talk."

Brynn frowned. "But what—"

"Hi, MJ."

They both looked up as Kayla slid up onto the stool next to MJ.

"Hi, honey," MJ greeted. Then she gave Kayla a big smile.

Brynn blinked. She'd never seen MJ smile like that. Or smile much at all. The older woman just seemed a little sad all the time. But it was clear she was happy to see Kayla.

"Hi, Kayla. What's going on? I don't see you on Sundays either," Brynn said.

"Hi, Brynn." Kayla grinned at her. "Well, the other day when MJ and I sat together we got to talking."

Brynn hid her smile at that. She was sure *Kayla* had gotten to talking anyway.

"And she suggested that I find something that Regan and I can do together," Kayla said of her stepdaughter. "Something that she'd be really into. So we came up with making tutus. MJ is going to teach me how to make them."

"You mean the little puffy, net skirt things?" Brynn asked. She looked at MJ. "You know how to make tutus?"

MJ nodded. "I know how to make a lot of things."

Okay, that might be. But tutus did *not* seem like MJ. For some reason. She was...gruff. She came into the shop in T-shirts and jeans. Her salt and pepper hair was cut short, and she wore no makeup or jewelry. Tutus just seemed a little girly for MJ.

MJ was watching her as if she knew the thoughts going through Brynn's head. The corner of her mouth curled. "I made some tutus for the school for their school play about two years ago. So, I know *how*. And I have the supplies. I thought Kayla could use them."

"You're a seamstress then?" Brynn asked, realizing she knew almost nothing about MJ.

"I can make almost anything if I have the right tools," MJ said. "I can fix most things too. Like toilets," she muttered.

"You could replace your toilet?" Brynn asked with a frown.

MJ shrugged. "Probably."

"Why do you call these guys to do it then?"

"Because they call the other guy. And he likes doing it."

But she didn't even talk to him. Brynn shook her head. She didn't understand this.

"Well, Regan is going to love it," Kayla said. "And maybe she'll think I'm not so bad. MJ, you're the best."

"Glad I can help."

"Brynn! Can I get some cream?"

Hank pulled Brynn's attention away from the two women. "Of course." She grabbed the cream pitcher, gave the two women at the counter another look, and moved off.

The fact that MJ and Kayla had struck up a friendship was amazing. And if they hadn't needed to sit at the coffee bar the other day, they might never have started talking. This was the most optimistic Brynn had seen Kayla about things with her step-daughter. Brynn didn't even know if MJ was a mom. But it was possible she had six daughters and had tons of advice for Kayla.

It was interesting that she'd seen Kayla and MJ both so often but didn't really know that much about them. She knew about Kayla's situation with Regan but not much else. She didn't ask questions. That was the thing. She now knew that MJ had some guy that fixed stuff around her house and that she knew how to make tutus. And now she wanted to know more about this guy and to see Regan in the tutus. Was the guy someone that was in love with MJ and this was his way of courting her? And did she love him too and that's why she let him do those things for her even though he apparently did it all when she wasn't home? Brynn really needed more details.

She was busy for the rest of the morning though, and every time she looked over, Kayla was talking and MJ was listening.

Brynn smiled. She didn't know Kayla's situation outside of the difficulties with Regan, again because she hadn't really asked, but she loved the fact that Kayla had clearly found a willing sounding board.

With that thought, Brynn grabbed the squeeze bottle of caramel and made another stop at Walter and Hank's table. They were also regulars—the most regular of the regulars—and they talked a lot too. But it occurred to her that she knew their opinions about a number of things and that she'd heard a lot of stories about her dad and that she'd gotten a lot of advice from them, yet she didn't know that much *about* them.

"Hey, how many granddaughters do you have, Walter?"

He brightened immediately. "Four."

"Any of them have tutus?" she asked.

"Tutus?"

"Little puffy skirts. Like ballerinas."

"Oh, sure, Paige is a dancer. She takes lessons here in town."

"How old is she?"

"Five."

She was probably in class with Regan. Suddenly, Brynn wanted to have an event in the pie shop geared toward little girl dancers. Cori had come up with an idea for kiddie pies—individual pies that were peanut butter and jelly or mac and cheese or other kid-classics—that they could do some Saturday. Make it a party. That might be something Kayla and Regan could do together. "Walter, you'd bring your granddaughters in here for a pie party some Saturday, wouldn't you?"

"Of course, sweetie. Would love to."

"Awesome." She gave him a smile and an extra swirl of caramel, then headed back to MJ and Kayla. "Kayla, what would you think of bringing Regan to a little party here at the pie shop next Saturday?"

Kayla shrugged. "Yeah, we could try."

Okay, that wasn't as enthusiastic as Brynn had hoped for. "We could do cupcakes or something other than pie if you think that would be better."

"Sure. I can ask her. Whatever you want. She'd probably think that cocoa with all the sprinkles and syrup and stuff you have for the coffee would be fun."

"Great. I'll definitely include that."

"Okay."

Brynn tipped her head. "I was hoping you'd be more excited about it."

Kayla smiled. "Sorry. It's really a nice idea and I would definitely try to bring her. But..."

"What?"

Kayla turned more fully on her stool. "Okay, you want to do an event here that I would be super excited to come to? Do a ladies' night out with wine and dessert. Women only. No kids."

That was interesting.

"Even better?" Kayla continued. "Set up some kind of babysitting for the evening in case women can't find sitters and their husbands aren't home."

Brynn felt her eyes widening as Kayla spoke.

"But off site," Kayla added. "And maybe have a few designated drivers to get us home."

Brynn waited a beat to be sure Kayla was done. Then she grinned. "Wow, Kayla, that's an amazing idea."

Kayla looked a little surprised. "Really?"

"Yes. Definitely. In fact, there are so many ways we could pair wine with *pie*." Her mind was whirling now. She was sure she could research pairings, but honestly, it wasn't rocket science. So many of the flavors in the wine and the pies would blend and complement each other.

"Okay, *that* I would show up for," Kayla said. "And instead of dragging Regan in here against her will, I could bring three or four friends who would *gladly* come."

"I'd come for that too," MJ said with a nod.

"Really? You're a wine drinker?" Brynn asked. She wouldn't have guessed that. But then the more she got to know MJ, the more she realized she'd been pretty far off on a lot of things.

"Oh, no. I'm thinking bourbon. But you'd have to have a chocolate pie to go with it."

Brynn smiled, feeling a streak of excitement go through her. "We could do that." Cori could make anything.

This was a really good idea. Her sisters had been doing so much for the pie shop. Cori was the mastermind behind the menu they were slowly expanding and some of the fun themes they were going to try like kiddie pies, sweetie pies for date nights, and a whole line of ice cream pies like root beer float and banana split. Ava was the one who'd brought Parker on board and knocked the wall down between the restaurants. Brynn had been doing her part, but she hadn't really added anything new. Now maybe she could. These were ideas that would cater to some new crowds. And as much as she really wanted to see these tutus, the ladies' night out idea was the one really taking root.

She couldn't wait to tell Ava and Cori that *she* was the one that thought they should make the pie shop even more social.

———

Noah watched Brynn across the stretch of sand and worked on just breathing.

It was Sunday, so she'd been at the shop and he'd been busy getting stuff ready for the party. He hadn't seen her until she showed up at the river with her sisters.

She'd met Tanner here, and Noah applauded her not riding with him. That meant she didn't have to leave with him. It might be a date, but that didn't mean the guy had to pick her up and drop her off.

Though Noah could already tell Tanner was going to try to change her mind about that. He hadn't left her side since she'd slid out of Elvira. Which was what a good date should do, of course. But Noah was sure it also had something to do with the short shorts and the bright green bikini top she was wearing.

"Damn, those Carmichael genes are something, huh?" Parker commented from where he was leaning against Noah's tailgate.

His eyes were on Ava, of course, but honestly, there was no way that anyone at this party—male, female, straight, single, or not—didn't notice that there was *a lot* of gorgeous, blonde sexiness going on at this party. The triplets were identical, and it seemed that extended right down to how they filled out short shorts, bikini tops, and flip-flops.

"Damn right," Evan agreed with appreciation in his tone as he watched Cori laughing and talking with a group a few feet away. He reached into the cooler on the back of Noah's truck and pulled out a beer. "Those billionaires look damn good in blue jeans, huh?"

They weren't really blue jeans. They *had been* blue jeans. But they had been cut off. Very short.

"I see Ava left her heels at home," Evan commented to Parker.

Parker swallowed his drink of beer and shook his head. "Only because I physically took them off of her. She didn't really understand the whole dirt and sand thing."

"She fight you on it?" Evan asked, waggling his brows.

Parker grinned. "Just enough."

Noah sighed. He was jealous of his friends. Very jealous. Super fucking jealous.

"Maybe we should have mentioned that they shouldn't *all* wear bikinis today," Parker said, his eyes on the girls again. "That's kind of...*a lot* all at once, isn't it?"

If he meant it was a lot of gorgeous skin and curves and distraction, then yeah, it really was.

Evan shrugged. "Just soak it up, my friend. Everyone here knows who those girls are going home with."

Noah felt a kick in his gut. Maybe he hadn't helped Brynn get dressed—or undressed—like Parker had with Ava, but yeah, she was going home with him. Even if that was kind of confusing and messed up since she was on a date with another guy.

"At least they all wore their hair differently and different colored bikinis." Mitch Anderson joined them and reached for a beer. "It'd be too bad if one of you took the wrong girl home." He popped the top.

"Yeah, I love Cori in red," Evan said, with a wink at Parker.

"Right. Ava's color is totally green," Parker agreed. "Or wait, is she the one in blue? Damn, this does get complicated."

Noah rolled his eyes. Ava almost always wore red and Cori was definitely the one in blue. Interestingly, when the sisters were together, it *was* easier to tell them apart. Ava was friendly, but was less exuberant than Cori, who was always smiling and laughing. Brynn hung back a little, always watching her sisters, it seemed. When she looked at them, she had an expression that was full of affection, but she didn't jump into conversations or activities until one of them pulled her in. Noah got it. He felt the same way around Evan and Parker. But he kind of hated it when he watched Brynn. He wanted her to feel wanted. Period. Rudy had fucked up big time with her when she was a little girl, and it was easy to see the effects were still there.

Mitch chuckled. "Feel really bad for you guys having to watch those girls so carefully all the time."

"Yeah, thanks, man. We appreciate the sympathy," Evan said.

"So Brynn's in green, I take it?" Mitch asked.

Noah looked over. "What do you mean?" Had he noticed how she smiled more shyly than her sisters? Or that she rolled her eyes adorably at some of the stuff Cori said?

"Well, she's the one you can't take your eyes off of, so I figured," Mitch said, lifting his beer can.

Okay, so he hadn't been as cool about that as he'd thought. He didn't care. "Yeah, she's the one rocking the green." *And who couldn't get enough of me last night on the front seat of my truck so fuck off Mitch*, he added silently. He tipped his own beer. She was on a date with another guy. Every male here, and possibly a female or two, were checking her out. And yet, she was going to *insist* on him kissing her goodnight. And more. So much more. He needed his hands really *on* her now.

He just needed to make it a couple more hours.

"So Tanner is number two?" Mitch asked, turning so he could watch Brynn fully.

Noah felt his hand tighten around his can. He should let Mitch think Tanner was number two. That meant it would be longer before Mitch asked her out himself. "Something like that."

"The speed dating doesn't count, then?" Mitch asked.

Noah looked at him. "You know about that?"

Mitch didn't quite grin, but Noah could tell he was amused. "Hank is a chatty guy and apparently Brynn learned something about planting lemongrass as a mosquito repellent from one of her dates. Hank came in to get some pots so he could put them out on his patio."

Noah just stared at Mitch.

"Sounds like she met some really interesting guys."

Noah kind of wanted to punch him. "She had a good time." That was for certain. *He'd* made sure of it.

Rudy wanted her happy? Noah was absolutely making her happy. At least at the end of her dates. And would do the same at the end of her date with Mitch too.

"Well, great. That means we're on date number three then," Mitch said.

We? We are on date number three? Noah scowled at him. "This is Tanner's date. Hope you're not thinking about making it awkward."

Mitch chuckled at that. "No chance." He pushed away from the truck and tossed his beer can into the tub where they were collecting the empties. "I don't like to share." Then he ambled off across the sand.

Fuck. Noah really hated that guy. Almost as much as The Guy that Brynn would eventually end up with.

Then a thought slammed him in the gut. Mitch Anderson could not be The Guy. The Guy needed to be from New York. He needed to be *in* New York. As did Brynn.

Stewing about Mitch, Noah didn't notice that Tanner had joined them, until he reached for a burger from the plate next to Noah and then into the cooler for a soda.

"Hey, Noah, thanks for setting things up with Brynn," Tanner said. "She's awesome."

Still irritated by the thought of Mitch and Brynn, Noah frowned at him. "Yeah, she is. She's also brilliant. Super smart. She's a scientist, you know." Okay, *he* didn't sound particularly brilliant or "super smart" at the moment. And no, Tanner hadn't said anything wrong. And being brilliant was certainly part of how awesome Brynn was.

Tanner lifted a brow and Parker and Evan turned toward their conversation.

"Well, I'm sure she is brilliant," Tanner said. "We haven't exactly gotten into the periodic table yet, but I'm looking forward to it."

"So what *have* you gotten into?" Noah asked, ignoring the *cool it* look he was getting from Parker.

But Tanner seemed more amused than anything. "Let's see. We talked about how she didn't have pets growing up but how much she loves your cat. We talked about new things we've recently done or learned, and she said that she thinks she can change a car tire just from watching you do it so much. We talked about what kind of music we like, and she said she didn't realize that she liked country until she started listening to it with you. Oh, and she told me that Helen Thompson needs some pumpkins for her kindergarten classroom." Tanner paused. "Yeah, so we've basically talked about *you* a lot. And pumpkins."

Noah wasn't sure what to say to that. *Fuck yeah* didn't seem appropriate, but he wasn't sure he could pull off saying something like "oh, well, that doesn't mean anything."

"Why would she tell you that Helen needed pumpkins for her kids?" Noah asked.

"Because I told her that I have a huge crop this year and wasn't sure what to do with them all," Tanner told him.

"And how does she know Helen needs them?" Brynn was now the local expert on all random trivia or something? But just before Tanner spoke, Noah realized that answer for himself. Brynn waited on people in the pie shop. She probably overheard just about everything about everyone.

"She heard Helen telling someone at the pie shop," Tanner confirmed.

Between the diner, the hair salon, and now the pie shop, there were no secrets in Bliss.

Noah cleared his throat and shifted his weight. Then he couldn't help it. "She didn't have any pets growing up?" he finally asked.

Tanner chuckled as if he'd been expecting more questions. "Nope. Guess not. I can find out anything else you want to know too."

Out of the blue, Noah wondered what her favorite vacation spot was, what her favorite ice cream was, and if she thought presents should be opened on Christmas Eve or Christmas morning. Did she get bad cramps with her period? Did she ever get migraines? Did she know when her transmission needed flushed?

All of those things tripped through his mind. He wanted to know it all. And he could honestly say that he'd *never* wondered about a woman's cramps before.

Brynn thought she could change a tire now? Just from watching him? He might have to quiz her on that. That was a great skill to have, and why hadn't he thought about teaching her some basic car care? Because she didn't seem the type? Because he wanted to be the one working on her car? Because he intended to send her back to New York where her car and its maintenance would be none of his concern?

Yes. To all of that.

"I can find the things out that I want to know," he told Tanner with a frown.

Tanner nodded. "Yeah. That should be pretty easy, I'd think."

It would. If he ever asked her any questions.

Noah's eyes flickered over Tanner's shoulder to Brynn. She was talking to her sisters, and Sarah Hanover. Then he noticed Mitch heading for her with two bottles of beer in hand. "You about done with your date?" he asked Tanner.

Tanner's eyebrows went up. "I don't think so, actually."

"You have to get up early in the morning," Noah said, meeting Tanner's eyes.

"Yeah. But some things are worth being tired for, you know?"

Noah sighed. He really didn't want to start hating Tanner too. "Well, you might be getting out-charmed," he said, nodding to where Mitch was handing Brynn a beer and gesturing away from the group of women. She looked at Cori, then back to Mitch, and nodded.

Tanner glanced over to where Mitch and Brynn were walking together toward the river. He laughed. "Mitch Anderson can out-charm anyone except maybe Evan."

Fuck. That was true.

"You're not worried about that?" Noah asked.

Tanner shrugged. "I was told that this was a one-time date and just to be sure she had a good time." He looked over to where she was laughing at something Mitch had said. "Looks like she is."

Noah frowned. *Damn*, this dating thing sucked.

8

Brynn looked over to where Noah was standing with Evan, Parker, and Tanner. How much longer did she have to stay? Did the couple of hours she'd been here, chatting with Tanner, drinking a couple of beers and eating a burger count as a date? There was nothing in the will about how *long* the dates had to be.

"How are things going with Tanner?" Mitch asked, tipping his beer bottle for a drink.

She watched him, eyes narrowed. "Great. I think he might be The One."

Mitch lowered his bottle and pinned her with a look. "He's not The One, Brynn."

She crossed her arms. "And how do you know that?"

"Because if he was, you wouldn't want to sleep with Noah."

Brynn dropped her arms and stared at him.

Mitch laughed. "Yeah, it's obvious."

"Noah and I are—" She glanced over at Noah. He was watching her. "Yeah, okay," she admitted as her stomach flipped just from the look he was giving her.

Mitch nodded. "You have good taste."

"Yeah?"

"Noah's one of the best."

"You've known him for a long time?"

"A very long time. Our whole lives."

She regarded Mitch. "So you didn't mean it when you invited me to your back deck?"

"Oh, I totally meant that." Mitch lifted his beer again.

"But you changed your mind after you realized how I feel about Noah?"

He gave her a slow smile. "No, Brynn, I didn't change my mind."

"But...I want Noah."

"Sure. While you're here with Tanner. And when you were out with Sean. And while you were speed dating."

She didn't ask how he knew about that. Hank knew so it was hardly a secret. She arched a brow. "But I wouldn't if I was here with you?"

Mitch turned to face her fully. "I don't think you would, no."

"And how can you be so sure?" It wasn't a stomach flip, but she didn't *hate* how she felt when she was flirting with Mitch. And it was more than what she felt talking to Tanner.

"Because I've got something Sean and Tanner and the speed dating guys don't," Mitch said.

There was something about his confidence that made her ask, "What's that?"

"I want you."

Okay, that was a little closer to the stomach flip. It wasn't quite there, but it wasn't nothing.

"You..." She cleared her throat. "You haven't asked me out."

"Nope. And I'm not going to until all this dating crap is over," Mitch said.

Her eyes widened. "Oh."

He gave her a nod. "Yeah. Oh. Because it's not going to be something you just check off your list, Brynn. It's going to be something you want to keep doing."

She wet her lips. Wow. There were a lot of things she wasn't used to, but confident men telling her exactly how they felt and what they wanted from her was maybe at the top of the list. "And they didn't? Don't want me?" she asked, glancing at Tanner.

"Sean and Tanner know that you're not really single," Mitch said. "And I think the guys at speed dating could probably tell too."

She wasn't. Sure, she was going through the motions of dating, but her heart wasn't in it. Not that it needed to be. The intention was just to go out, have fun, meet some guys and practice. But that didn't mean her heart wasn't involved at all. At least with one guy. Dammit. That all probably meant she *should* date Mitch. He was the only one who had come even a little bit close to making her tingle.

"I'm not?" she asked, even though she knew the answer.

"Not at the moment, no," Mitch said.

"But that doesn't matter to you?"

"I don't mind waiting."

"For what?"

"For you to get over Noah."

That made her straighten slightly. That sounded strange. Because she had just now admitted she had feelings for him? Or because getting over him didn't seem likely?

But she *had* to get over him. Noah wasn't coming with her to New York. And the last thing she needed was someone else taking care of her all the time anyway. Once she went home, she was going to be on her own. She was going to be able to eat wherever she wanted for lunch. Alone. But hey, she could take her book along. And she was never doing hot yoga again. Ever. In fact, she was going to completely quit her gym. And maybe she'd...get a cat.

Brynn pulled in a deep breath. Then nodded at Mitch and said, "Well, then, I hope you know a great place for seafood. I've been craving crab cakes." She hadn't really. But she knew they'd have to go out of town to get crab cakes, and that seemed like a great idea if she was going on a date with Mitch. She didn't think she could *actually* date another guy—as in a one-on-one date without Noah around—in Bliss.

Mitch looked surprised, then his face relaxed into a smile that *maybe* came close to making her stomach flip. "That's not easy in Kansas, but for you, I will do whatever I can."

Mitch moved in a little closer. "So only two more dates to go until you're on number six."

"And you're going to be number six?"

"And seven and eight and..." He trailed off, then reached up and ran his finger along her jaw. "As many as you'll let me be."

Dammit, that was sweet. Even a little sexy. But there were no tingles from his touch.

Wow, she hated this dating thing.

Mitch's eyes flickered to something over the top of her head, and he gave a little smile, but dropped his finger. "Looks like I poked the bear."

And Brynn knew it wasn't Tanner coming up behind her.

"Brynn, you ready to go?"

The much sought-after tingles came from Noah's deep voice. Damn, she was in trouble. She took a breath, then turned to face him. He tossed her a cardigan sweater, that was clearly hers, and she assumed that she'd left it in his truck, then crossed his arms.

It was also clear from his expression that he was interrupting on purpose. So he was jealous. Well, that was something. It wasn't true love forever, but at least he wasn't completely resistant to *everything* he might feel for her.

She pulled the sweater on and noted that it had the faint scent of the garage on it along with Noah's scent, just from being in his truck. She took a deep breath, feeling the flip in her tummy she'd been looking for.

"Yep, I'm ready," she said. She glanced at Mitch. "I'll see you around."

"You most definitely will," he said with promise.

She thought she heard Noah growl, but he simply grabbed her hand and started tugging her toward his truck.

"You can't leave. You have all the food and coolers," she said as she hurried to keep up with him. "It's your party."

"Don't care."

When they got to his truck, she found the coolers and portable grill had been transferred to Evan's truck. Noah boosted her up on the seat, slamming the door behind her without a word. They drove up the slight incline from the river without talking, and Brynn figured that was how it would go all the way to her house. As usual. Unless one of them changed the usual.

"That was fun," she commented.

"I'm glad."

Yeah, he didn't sound glad. Or like he'd had fun.

"Tanner is really nice. I hope you told him goodbye for me."

"Tanner's fine."

Uh, huh. She'd have to give Tanner a free piece of pie when he came into the shop next time.

"So you never had a pet growing up?"

She looked over at Noah in surprise. "Tanner told you that?"

"He also said that you love Penn."

"You know I love Penn."

She watched Noah squeeze the steering wheel. "I didn't know you didn't have any pets growing up."

She turned, tucking her foot underneath her. "Why would you have known that?"

"Tanner knew within two hours of knowing you." He looked over at her.

She shrugged. "He asked."

"Exactly," he muttered. "If you could have had any pet, what would it have been?"

Brynn didn't know what was going on but she answered,

"Anything, honestly. I love animals. I would have been happy with a cat or a dog or a guinea pig or...a ferret."

He nodded, focused on the road.

She draped her arm over the back of the seat. "What pets did you have?"

"Cats and dogs. Usually both at the same time."

"So you do like cats?"

"Of course."

"You don't like Penn."

He glanced at her sharply. "I like Penn."

"You don't pet him or hold him."

Noah blew out a breath. "Penn doesn't like *me*."

She watched him. She wasn't sure that was true. But that said a lot about Noah right there. He didn't think the cat liked him or appreciated him, but he kept feeding him, kept him safe. That made something twinge in her heart. "How long have you had him?"

"Ten years."

Brynn's brows rose. "Wow." He also stuck with it. He was there for Penn even if the cat never loved him back.

Noah nodded. "He showed up at the shop one day as a kitten and hasn't left."

"So he must not dislike you too much."

Noah gave a half smile. "Well, I have opposable thumbs and a can opener."

She laughed softly. They turned onto Main and then pulled up in front of the garage. She didn't mind at all that he wasn't dropping her off at home, but this was interesting. He looked over as if expecting her to ask what was going on. She just met his gaze.

She wanted this man in a way she'd never wanted anyone and, dammit, he was going to know that. Yes, she typically just went along with what the people she loved wanted, but if she was

ERIN NICHOLAS

going to be more independent back in New York, maybe she needed to practice going after what she wanted now.

Noah might not think Penn liked him, but he would believe that *she* did.

"I also hear you think you know how to change a tire from just watching me," he said, shutting the truck off.

"Am I getting quizzed?"

"Maybe."

"Okay."

"You're up for it?"

"For following you into the garage right now and doing whatever you want me to?" she asked. Because that was definitely what *she* wanted.

He arched a brow and she felt a little thrill. She was getting better at this flirtatious stuff. She fought a smile and just continued to meet his gaze directly.

"Is that right? You think that beautiful brain can handle anything I come up with?" His voice had dropped to a delicious, low, husky level.

She nodded. "And the rest of me too."

He stared at her for a few long seconds. Then he nodded. "Let's go."

She was out of the truck before he could get around to open it for her, and he took her hand without hesitation. He unlocked the door that led into the front office. Brynn took a deep breath of the motor oil scented air and felt equal portions of comfort and desire course through her.

Noah opened the door to the garage then stepped back to let her go first. She brushed past him, nice and close. She might have heard a soft intake of air from him, but when she glanced up at him, he was just watching her with a tight jaw.

She walked to the middle of the first bay. There was a car up on the lift and the second bay was empty. She looked over at her reading truck, wondering if Penn was sleeping inside. Then she felt Noah move up behind her and, as much as she loved the cat, she didn't care what he was up to at the moment.

She turned. "Well, this will definitely be easier since it's already up in the air."

"You know where the wrenches are."

Okay, then. She retrieved a lug wrench and went to the front tire on the passenger side. She eyed the lug nuts. Those had to come off. But the tire was so far above her that even if she could reach them, she wouldn't be able to lower the tire to the ground. She went to the button that would lower the car and let it down a couple of feet, then returned to the tire. She reached up to put the wrench over the first nut, then pulled. And it didn't budge. She pulled harder. Still nothing. Blowing out a breath, she pivoted so that her back was to the car. She pulled again, this time nearly hanging on the wrench to use her body weight. She felt a slight give and grinned. Turning back to the car she turned the wrench. The nut didn't come easily, but it did eventually turn fully and she was able to spin it off. She held it up to Noah.

He nodded. Then asked, "What's your favorite ice cream?"

"Lemon sherbet. Why?"

"Just wondering."

She lifted the wrench back overhead and fit it over the next lug nut. "What's yours?"

"Ben and Jerry's Cherry Garcia."

She looked at him. "Yeah?"

"Yep."

"Never had it."

"You're missing out."

She pulled on the nut, hanging on it like the first and it gave right away. She took it off and tossed it to him.

"Do you prefer to watch movies at home or in the theater?" he asked.

"Both. For different reasons. I love the huge screen and the sound and seeing a really highly anticipated movie with a bunch of other fans. But I also love to wear pajamas to watch, and Cori makes amazing popcorn you can't get anywhere else."

She reached to fit the wrench against another nut.

"Are you allergic to anything?"

It bothered him that she'd talked to Tanner about her pets. Or lack thereof. That made her feel strangely warm. "Nope. You?"

"No." Then he shrugged. "Maybe a little pollen in the spring."

She tossed the third lug nut to him.

"What did you want to be when you were little?"

She paused with her arms overhead. "You mean what job did I want?"

"Yeah. What did you think you'd grow up to be?"

"A piano teacher," she told him honestly. "I loved my piano teacher and I figured it was a great job because you got to listen to music all day."

"You can play the piano?"

She nodded.

And suddenly he shoved a hand through his hair and swore.

She dropped her arms. "*What* is going on?"

"Nothing." But he wasn't looking at her now.

"Well, what's with the third degree?"

"I just—" He blew out a frustrated breath. "Tanner knew stuff about you tonight that I didn't."

"Right. He asked me some questions that you never have. That's not a big deal."

He looked up, their gazes colliding, and Brynn felt something shift in the air between them.

"It felt like a big deal," he said.

"You can't know everything about me," she said softly.

"But I want to."

She thought about that. And she understood it. She felt the same way. This was messing with her, she had to admit.

But this man took care of a cat that needed him, even when he thought it didn't like him, when he didn't really get anything out of it, for ten years. And she suspected that maybe the cat wasn't the only thing that was like that.

She wanted to take care of *him* like that.

The thought seemed to hit her in the center of the forehead. But it was clear and nearly took her breath away.

Did anyone really take care of Noah? Did *she* really take care of anyone? She was the mediator between her sisters. She *let* people take care of her when she knew it was important to them. Maybe that was a little like taking care of them. But it wasn't direct. It wasn't active. The only place she took care of people was in her lab.

Her mom was a powerhouse philanthropist. Her sisters were, well, Cori and Ava. They didn't need her. Rudy had certainly never needed her. The only people who did were the people she was working to heal. And they were all strangers. People she would never meet.

But Noah... she wanted to be *active* with Noah. In so many ways.

"What did you want to be when you grew up?" she asked. She reached up to loosen the last two lug nuts.

"A mechanic," he said, watching her.

"Really? Always?"

"Fixing cars is easy," he said. "You can figure out exactly what's wrong with them, what you need to do, and then you do it. And everything is good again."

Brynn couldn't help but glance at him. Wow. There was a lot there. It sounded to her like he was more used to things *not* being easily fixed or staying fixed. "What was—"

"Dammit, Brynn." He suddenly stomped over to where she was standing.

She thought he was reaching for her, but instead his hands went to the tire over her head. He was nearly on top of her, his arms up, his big body stretched out right in front of her. He looked down at her with a frown.

"You have to watch what you're doing around cars. This could have come off right on top of you."

She didn't move back an inch. In fact, with his hands up balancing the tire, he was kind of stuck. Right there. Right in front of her. Almost against her.

She leaned in, pressing her body to his. "I never worry when you're around."

His brows slammed together, but his voice was husky when he said, "I won't always be around."

No, he wouldn't. So she had to enjoy every minute she had now.

She set her hands on his rib cage on either side. He sucked in a quick breath. She went up on tiptoe and put her lips against his jaw. "You're around right now. And I need you, Noah."

His abs tensed under her hands, as if he was holding himself still on purpose. She ran her hands up over his ribs to his chest. His hard, wide, hot chest.

"What's your favorite vacation spot?" he asked, his voice tight.

Still with the questions? "Italy," she said, moving her lips along his jaw to his chin. "Though I love San Francisco too, if we're staying in the US."

She trailed her lips down his neck and she felt, more than heard, his groan.

"What do you usually eat for breakfast?" It sounded like he had gravel in his throat.

"Yogurt," she said against the hot skin along his collarbone.

Then the skin to skin between her lips and his neck wasn't enough. She ran her hands down his torso to his waistband and snuck her fingers under the edge of his shirt. Her fingertips grazed over his abs and he sucked in a harsh breath.

"Brynn." There was a low warning in his voice.

She smiled without looking up. Yeah, like she was worried about upsetting him. This was Noah. And her. She knew that she had some kind of power over him. She knew that he wasn't this attentive to other women. He wouldn't follow someone else around on their dates to be sure they went well. He wouldn't notice when someone else needed a break from socializing and pull them behind a potted plant. He wouldn't care what pets someone else had grown up with. She was special to him. She knew it, and it gave her a rush unlike anything she'd ever experienced before.

She ran her hands higher under his shirt, stroking the skin, relishing the way his muscles bunched and his breathing grew ragged.

He tipped his head back, looking up at the car tire and swallowed hard. "What's your...what do...do you listen to music while you work usually?"

Yeah, she definitely loved having some power over this man. "Not usually, no," she said, running her hands up under his shirt to his chest. "But I've learned to really like listening to it here with you." Her palms brushed over his nipples.

Suddenly Noah's hands clasped around her wrists. He pivoted them, pushing her out of the way as the tire wobbled above them. He reached up, grasped the tire, and tossed it to the ground. It bounced and rolled until it thumped into the garage doors.

But he wasn't watching the tire. His eyes were hot on her.

"What was the best birthday party Cori ever set up for the three of you?"

Her eyes widened. They were still doing this?

"Come on, B," he said. "I know Cori was always in charge of your birthday celebrations, right?"

She nodded. He knew Cori. It didn't take long to know that Cori was always in charge of all parties, so it was a very educated guess. "I guess maybe the time she flew us to Orlando and we dressed up as princesses and took on a big, popular theme park."

"How old were you?"

"Twenty-five."

He actually grinned slightly at that. "And you got a lot of

attention, I'd guess? Gorgeous, twenty-five-year-old triplets traipsing around dressed up as Cinderella?"

She stared at him. "How did you know I was Cinderella?"

He just looked at her for a few seconds. Then slowly shook his head. "I'm not sure."

But she thought that he did know. He just didn't realize it. "Ava was Elsa from Frozen. And Cori was Rapunzel from Tangled."

"I don't know as much about Rapunzel."

"But you do know Elsa?"

"I haven't been living under a rock. And I have nieces."

"Well, Elsa—" She broke off and stared at him. "Wait, you have *nieces*?"

He nodded. "Two. My sister Lori's daughters."

"You have a *sister*?"

"Two of them too," he said, watching her as if he was concerned about her.

"I didn't... I didn't know that." How had she not known that? How had that *never* come up in conversation?

"They don't live here. They went off to college, fell in love, stayed where they were. Lori is in Manhattan. Kansas," he added. "And Kate is in Lawrence."

"But..." She was still staring at him, but this was a lot of new information. She had no idea why she was surprised he had sisters. She had just never heard him talk about them. "You're not close?"

"We're close," he said, lifting a shoulder. "They're not here every day and they've got their husbands now, so I don't need to do as much for them, but we're close."

"How old are they?"

"Lori's two years younger than me, so she's twenty-seven, and Kate is twenty-five."

"And they were into princesses?" Brynn asked.

"Definitely. So I know all about Cinderella."

Ah, right. Good old Cinderella. The classic princess. The one Cori had dressed her up as for their twenty-fifth birthday. Not their *fifth* birthday. Their twenty-fifth.

"Elsa is super independent. In charge. Does her own thing. Kind of takes over," she said. "I mean, yeah she basically tried to freeze everyone to death, but... she didn't really mean to." She frowned. She wasn't sure why she was explaining this to him, but it seemed important.

"Okay." He clearly didn't know why she was explaining this to him either. "Sounds a little like Ava. Maybe not the freezing everyone part." He lifted a shoulder. "Or maybe that a little too. Before Parker."

Yeah. Before Parker. And Bliss. And the pies. Brynn sighed. "And Rapunzel was all into adventure and trying new things. That's completely Cori."

"Okay," he said again.

"And then there was me and Cinderella."

"Right."

"The damsel in distress. The girl sitting around waiting for the prince to save her. She had to be practically forced to go to the ball!"

Brynn hadn't really thought of all of that before she blurted it out, but it was all true.

"I'm pretty sure she wanted to go to the ball," Noah said.

"She *wanted to*, but when it came time, she needed help with her dress and her hair and even *getting* there, for fuck's sake."

Noah's eyebrows rose. And the corner of his mouth curled. "I think walking all the way to the ball in glass slippers could be pretty uncomfortable. Even dangerous."

But Brynn wasn't in the mood to be placated. "Elsa and Rapunzel would never have worn *glass slippers*. I mean, that's practically screaming, 'I don't know what I'm doing and need help'."

Noah snorted. "Brynn, you're reading way too much into your costume."

She shook her head. "No. That is really me. I hole up in my lab, never going anywhere, until my Fairy Godmother, Cori, comes along and dresses me up and takes me out. Then I go home again and wait around for something else to happen. For my prince to come to me, I guess. What the hell is that?"

Noah shook his head. "Babe, I was asking about the birthday party thing just to get to know you better. I didn't mean to stir all of this up. I'm sorry."

"No, this is good," she insisted. "This *is* getting to know me better. That's who I've been, Noah. My *dad* had to force me to come here, to work in the pie shop, to *go out with men*. And then I get here and I sit around until *you* tell me what to do and that it's time to go out."

Noah took a breath. "Okay. So what do you want to do now?"

She thought about that seriously. What did she want? "I want to take myself to the ball."

His smile was full of affection. "Well, I can't let you go all alone. But I can follow along behind."

She studied his face. Then let her eyes wander over him from head to toe. She stepped forward and rested a hand on his chest. "You can come along," she said. "But you have to stop treating me like I'm wearing glass slippers."

He covered her hand with his, pressing it into his chest. "I can try. But you're pretty much a princess to me, Brynn."

Wow, that was sweet.

She didn't want sweet.

She opened her sweater. She saw him register what she was doing one second before she shrugged it off and tossed it on the ground. "How about we play prince and naughty servant girl for a while instead?" she asked.

Heat flared in his eyes and he sucked in a breath. "You sure?

Role playing is kind of a couple steps beyond where we've been so far."

She stepped in and ran her hands up to his shoulders. "You're right. We should keep it real and go with mechanic and naughty pie shop waitress." Then she lifted onto her tiptoes and put her mouth against his.

9

For a second, he did nothing. Just stood, letting her kiss him. But when her hand ran up the back of his neck and through his hair, he growled, wrapped his two big arms around her and picked her up. She pulled her legs up and linked her ankles at his lower back. As he walked toward her reading truck, he opened his mouth under hers. Their tongues tangled, stroking hot and firm, and Brynn felt her pelvic muscles clenching as tingles erupted everywhere.

Yes. This. This is what she wanted. Him. And that truck.

"God, I want to see you naughty, Brynn," Noah said roughly, putting her down on the hood of the truck and running his hands down her back to her butt then down her thighs.

"You won't be shocked?" she asked, feeling breathless already. The way he was looking at her made her heart pound and like her bones were melting.

He gave a short laugh. "Turned the fuck on. Not shocked."

She felt her eyes widen. "You don't even know what I'm going to do."

"Won't matter." He leaned in and kissed her, stroking over her lip and tongue, then pulling back. "Just you *breathing* turns me on."

That was also kind of sweet. But it was also very hot so she let it go. "Well, you know that I don't really know what I'm doing, right?" She bit her bottom lip. How pathetic on a scale from totally cool to omg-that's-so-sad was a twenty-nine-year-old virgin anyway? She'd never asked her sisters because she was a little afraid of the answer.

He met her gaze directly. "How inexperienced are we talking here?" he asked. "You're a virgin?"

She felt her cheeks flush. She figured that he'd known that for a while. If Evan and Parker hadn't told him, he'd probably guessed, simply from the fact that she didn't date. Ever.

He tipped her chin up with a finger before she even realized she'd looked down. "Brynn, I just gotta know. It doesn't change anything. If you want me to be the one—" He pulled in a shaky breath, "—then, babe, there's no getting rid of me."

Heat and something like gratitude, or relief, or just plain affection, flooded through her. She nodded. "Yes. A virgin." She grasped his hand and squeezed it. "And I definitely want you to be the one."

His eyes flickered with emotions. Including hot desire. He took another deep breath, then asked, "But you touch yourself? You've seen porn? You've read erotic romance? Something, right?"

"Yes, yes and yes."

He paused, then gave a soft laugh. "We are going to talk about all of that more. But right now..." He lifted her hands to his chest. "I just want you to do whatever you feel like doing."

A surge of power went through her. Whatever she wanted. She decided to be honest. "I feel like doing *everything*."

He swallowed hard but nodded. "I'm your guy."

God, he was. He really was. It hit her hard as he said it. He was her guy. For whatever she needed him for. And she wanted to be what he needed too. Not what he felt responsible for, not what he had been "assigned", but what he *needed*.

"First up, I'm going to need that shirt off," she told him. She leaned back, flattening her palms on the truck behind her.

He cocked an eyebrow. "Oh yeah?"

"Definitely."

"Your wish is my command."

Wow, she really hoped that was true. She had a list of wishes.

He stripped his shirt off and threw it over his shoulder. She quickly sat forward, already abandoning the whole I'm-in-control-here façade. She had no idea what she was doing, but she knew she needed to get her hands on him.

She spread her hands over his chest, marveling at how small she felt next to him. She brushed her hands under the dog tags that hung against his pecs. She stroked over the hard muscles that she'd barely felt and had only imagined until now. "God, you're huge," she said without thinking.

He chuckled, the sound rumbling up her arms. "You know just what to say."

Brynn ran her hands over his arms, tracing his tattoos, squeezing the muscles, and feeling her belly heat. Then she leaned in and kissed the center of his sternum just beside the dog tags. He let out a breath, and she ran her lips to one side, kissing his pec, and before she could think better of it, flicking her tongue out to taste his skin.

He pulled the chain from around his neck, tossing the dog tags over his shoulder too. She felt his hand come up to the back of her head, his fingers sliding into her hair. He pressed her closer and she assumed that meant she was doing okay.

But suddenly it was all not enough. She reached behind her and untied her bikini top, letting it fall to her lap. She shifted, putting her chest against his, the heat and hardness pressing into her breasts and making her nipples tighten and tingle. She sighed, her eyes sliding closed. "Ah, that feels good." She wiggled, dragging her nipples over his chest, and she heard air hiss out from between Noah's teeth.

She looked up at him. His jaw was tight, his fingers were curled into her scalp, and he was watching her with a hot look that made her nipples draw even tighter.

"You okay?" she asked.

"Just waiting for you to get done there and sit back so I can get a really good look at those gorgeous tits."

Brynn felt her eyes widen. *Tits*. No man had ever said that word to her before. And she was shocked how much she liked it. It was rough and raw and made heat pulse between her legs.

She slowly sat back, watching as his gaze dragged from her face to her breasts. The muscle along his jaw twitched as he drank her in. Brynn knew for a fact that she had *never* truly felt sexy and wanted and beautiful before that moment.

"Touch me, Noah." That was most definitely what she wanted. His big, hot, calloused hands with the grease under the fingernails, all over her body.

"Once I start, I'm not going to stop," he warned her.

She leaned back farther and parted her knees. He stepped between them, one hand moving to cup her right breast. She gave a little moan. "Good," she told him.

He squeezed gently, then ran his thumb over her nipple, watching it bead as if begging for more. And he gave it more. He rubbed and tugged, then finally bent his head and took it into his mouth, licking, then sucking.

Brynn gasped and arched closer. She gripped his bare shoulders, fingers digging into the muscles she'd been ogling for months in this very garage, from nearly this exact vantage point.

He moved to her other breast, teasing that nipple similarly and making her throb everywhere.

She hadn't needed much more than this the other night to come apart, but that wasn't happening this time. For one thing, she wanted more of *her* mouth on *him*. For another, she needed more than just some friction tonight. She wanted pressure and stretching and thrusting.

"Noah." She wiggled against him, but he seemed disinclined to let her go.

He did an extra-amazing sucking thing on her left nipple, while squeezing the right, and she felt her inner muscles clench. She blew out a breath. "Noah."

"You coming apart the other night with not much more than this might have been the hottest thing I've ever experienced," he said. "I know that you're a firecracker, Brynn, but I've been letting myself feel like a damned hero for that."

She grinned. "I want more tonight."

He lifted his head at that. "Oh, you're going to get more." He pressed against where she was wet and throbbing. Again, still wearing his jeans. She felt the sparks shooting out from that spot through her body, and she knew that it wouldn't take much to send her over the edge again just that easily.

"I want to be naked and spread out and have you deep inside me this time," she told him.

That made him stop moving for a moment.

"Noah?"

"Hang on." He cleared his throat.

"What's wrong?"

"Just making sure *I'm* not the one going all the way with my pants still on."

"Not sorry." She shifted against him, feeling a surge of sassiness that was unusual for her. But she could get used to it.

He pinched her ass. "Though I can promise, I'd still make you see stars."

She half laughed, half gasped. "Yes. Do that. Stars. For both of us."

"You got it." He reached up and undid the front button of her shorts. "I'm going to need to see what I'm doing here this time though."

Yes. She lifted her butt so he could pull her shorts down. He whisked them off her legs and dropped them next to him on the ground. He looked down at her panties. They were white, but they were bikini cut and were silk with some lace across the top. In other words, they weren't *entirely* boring, white underwear. "I have hot pink ones," she said, stupidly.

He gave her a slow smile. "Do you?"

"Yes. But..." She clamped her lips shut. *You don't have to call attention to the white panties. They're fine. They're feminine and hopefully going to be on the floor really soon anyway.*

"But?" he prompted.

He ran a hand up her thigh from knee to hip and she melted. It wasn't even her inner thigh and still, she felt... hungry. That was the only word that came to mind. She was hungry. She moved her leg to the side slightly, encouraging him to go more to the center.

"Brynn?" he coaxed, his voice low and rumbly. "Did you think about wearing them?"

She hadn't, actually. She bit her bottom lip.

"Brynn?" He squeezed her leg as if warning her not to think about not answering. "Did you think about wearing your hot pink panties for me?"

Finally, she shook her head. "No."

"Why not? I love pink."

"They ride up and give me a wedgie so I almost never wear them."

There. Talk about sexy.

But he just nodded solemnly. "Thank you," he said, looking her directly in the eyes.

"For?" She shifted her legs, aware that this was as naked as she'd ever been with a man. And loving it. While also feeling incredibly vulnerable.

But the next moment any awkwardness or self-consciousness fled because Noah said, "For realizing that it doesn't matter

ERIN NICHOLAS

what you wear. I want you more than I've ever wanted anything, no matter what. That the sexiest thing you will ever have on is the look on your face right now. The one that says you want me and that you will maybe die if I don't touch you. And, well, Brynn, the truth is," he said, his tone completely serious. "I would want to fuck your brains out even if you were wearing white cotton panties that went up to your chin and bagged in the back."

There was a beat of silence after that. The *fuck your brains out* part was really hard to ignore considering it made her toes curl. But she couldn't help it—laughter bubbled up and she couldn't hold it in. She giggled.

"That's funny?" But he was grinning as he asked it.

"I can honestly say I've never had underwear bag in the back," she told him.

"Well, even if you did, all I'd care about was doing this." He hooked his thumbs in the top of her panties and pulled.

They slid off and dropped to the floor, and Brynn realized that *now* she was the most vulnerable she'd ever been.

And the hood of this truck felt pretty damned great against her bare ass.

"Holy shit," Noah breathed, taking her in, fully naked.

"I did, however, go ahead and wax."

His eyes came up to hers and he said, "It wouldn't matter. *But* holy shit, Brynn."

She grinned. "Now you."

He skimmed his hands up both of her thighs. "I'm going to need to move you to the bed of the truck for that, babe."

"Okay." She started to slide forward.

"Hang on." He seemed to think her eagerness was funny. Or cute. Or something. Because he was watching her with a look in his eyes she hadn't seen before.

"What?" She ran her hand up his arm, needing to touch him. And hoping to tug his hand to where she was aching and hot.

He did let her move his hand. But he said, "This is your first time, B. I can't fuck you in the bed of this truck."

A shiver of pleasure danced over her at the word fuck. She'd had no idea that would be a turn-on. But it wasn't even dirty talk really. It was just Noah talking. She'd heard him swearing at engines and joking with his friends. This was just raw and unfiltered Noah. He wasn't talking to her like a princess in glass slippers. And she loved it.

"But you *have* to," she told him, again moving his hand higher. The pads of his middle fingers skimmed over her mound, and they both sucked in a breath. "I have fantasized about you and this truck so many times. I want it to be here."

He leaned in, putting his forehead against hers, one hand going to the back of her neck. He ran his hand up and down between her legs. It wasn't with enough pressure to really do anything. It was more like a promise. But Brynn found herself suddenly breathing hard.

"You didn't let me finish," he told her gruffly. "I can't fuck you in the bed of this truck until I make you come nice and hard right here on the hood. You have to be ready for me."

She groaned at that. "Noah."

"Yeah, practice my name. Just like that." Then he kissed her, as his fingers slid lower.

Brynn grasped his arm and kissed him back, parting her knees farther, and letting him take her mouth in a deep, erotic kiss.

He teased over her clit, then dipped lower. There was no way he'd miss how wet she was for him. She felt pretty damned ready right now.

Noah pulled back as he slid the tip of one finger inside of her, his thumb brushing over her clit. She pressed her hips forward, wanting more.

"So on date number three, you're going to learn a little something about oral sex, Brynn," he said.

ERIN NICHOLAS

When he said her name like that—low and deep and after something kind of dirty— she found herself willing to do just about anything he could ask of her.

No, not just about. She was willing to do *anything* he asked of her. "Okay," she managed.

"I want you to close your eyes and think about everything I'm doing to your mouth right now." He licked his tongue along her lower lip, back and forth, then sucked slightly.

Heat shot to where his hand was slowly sliding in and out. He was only going in to about his first knuckle, and she felt her entire lower body buzzing with anticipation.

"I want you to feel how I lick you and stroke you with my tongue." He slid his tongue in along hers firmly, then swirled around it before pulling back and again sucking on her bottom lip.

Brynn again tilted her hips, trying to get closer to his finger. To get *more*.

"And I want you to think about me doing all of that, right here." He thrust a little deeper and circled her clit at the same time.

She whimpered, throbbing, her hunger becoming more and more intense.

"And I'm going to stay down there, tonguing you until you come for me, Brynn," he promised darkly against her mouth. "I'm going to taste everything you've got." He stroked his tongue against hers again, and she swore she could feel it between her legs. "And *then* I'm going to take you to the back of the truck and fill you up."

She almost came right then and there.

Noah put a hand against her chest and pushed, urging her to lie back. She did, realizing that she would be spread out, exactly as she'd said she wanted. She tried to hook her legs over the front of the hood, to hold on...or something...but Noah was in control. He took her thighs in his big hands and spread her open. He

160

looked up at her, then down between her legs. And he gave her a very sexy, slow, *hungry* smile. "I really do love this old truck." Then he dipped his knees and put his mouth against her inner thigh.

Brynn jerked with the sensation of his hot mouth and scratchy jaw against that sensitive skin. She might have touched herself, but it was nothing like this. Already. It felt like every one of her nerves was drawn tight and that Noah was plucking them, making them vibrate.

She didn't know what to do, where to hold on, what to say. She had nothing. She was fully at his mercy.

He rubbed his jaw back and forth over her thigh, then pressed kisses, climbing higher. His hand cupped her, his thumb brushed over her clit, and again a single digit slid inside her heat. This time deeper.

"Damn, you're so tight," he muttered. "Fucking heaven."

She rolled her head back and forth. "Noah."

"Girl, give me some time," he scolded. "I've been waiting for this for months."

"You've thought about this?"

"Every day, Brynn. Every damned day." He slid his finger deeper and rubbed over her clit with more pressure.

"Noah!"

"Yeah, just like that," he said of her using his name. Then he *finally* leaned in and put his mouth where his fingers had been.

Brynn's hips bucked, but his big hand across her stomach held her down as he licked and sucked, swirling and stroking just as he'd done to her mouth.

And it took less than thirty seconds for her to come hard against his tongue.

Waves of pleasure washed over her, one on top of the other, and she fought to catch her breath. She felt Noah stroking her legs and up her sides until he hooked under her arms and pulled her up to sitting. He kissed her deeply, her flavor on his tongue, and then he scooped her into his arms.

He set her on the tailgate and then whisked off the plastic tarp that was always there. Underneath were some blankets, a sleeping bag, a rolled-up tent, and some fishing supplies.

"What are these?" she asked.

He climbed up into the truck. "A story for another time," he told her. He knelt and spread the blankets out first, then the sleeping bag. Then he gave her a smile. "You think you can scoot over here, or do you need help moving even that far?" He looked a little cocky.

She liked that look on him.

"Are you finally going to take your pants off?" she asked.

He undid the button and unzipped his jeans. "I am."

"Then I think I can muster up the strength to get over to where I need to be." She crawled over to the middle of the blankets, aware that he was watching every move.

She sat back on her heels, facing him squarely. "I'm ready."

His eyes darkened. "Damn right you are."

Her body throbbed with the memory of the orgasm, and she felt need gathering again as he stretched to his feet.

His eyes were on hers as he pulled the front of his jeans apart, his cock pressing insistently against the black boxers behind the denim. He shoved the jeans down over his hips and kicked them away. Then he hooked his thumbs in the top of his boxers and pushed them down.

He was...magnificent. Huge. Hard. Hot. She could feel the heat emanating from him even across the two feet between them.

She knee-walked toward him, her eyes on her first live cock. And she was already pretty sure that he'd ruined her for all others.

"Noah."

"Brynn," he said at the same time.

She looked up at him. And wet her lips.

His jaw tightened. "Not tonight."

Ah, so he did know what she had on her mind. "But you just—"

"I'm not coming down your pretty throat this time," he said gruffly, the graphic statement contrasted by the way he cupped her cheek. "I gotta have your pussy tonight, Brynn."

Said pussy clenched hard at that. "But—"

"And while I'd love to tell you that I have enough control for you to do all your exploring on my cock without losing it, I'm not gonna make it. Not this time."

She thought about that.

"You want me thrusting deep, filling you up," he said, his fingers holding her chin.

"Are you asking me?" She was completely breathless.

"No," he said simply.

Her eyes dropped to his cock again. "But I can do that some other time?" She looked up. "Soon?"

He groaned, dropped to his knees, and took her face in both his hands. He kissed her hard. When he pulled back he said, "I will insist on you doing that some other time."

Arrows of pleasure shot through her and she nodded. "Okay."

"Damn right, okay," he muttered. He kissed her again, laying her back as he did and moving over her. "It might be a little tough at first," he told her, kissing down her neck as she relaxed into the blankets. "We'll go slow."

"I'm not worried. I totally trust you."

She felt him tense against her and she looked down.

He met her eyes. "I don't want to hurt you."

She shook her head. "Then don't."

"It's not that—"

"Noah, that pain won't last. And then you'll make it all amazing. I won't even remember it."

He pulled in a breath and for just a split second she thought, for some reason, that he might change his mind. But that disappeared as he ran his hand up her leg to her core, slid a finger inside, then another, as he sucked on her nipples and talked dirty about how tight she was and how wet she was and how he couldn't wait to feel her milking his cock.

She was writhing against his hand, climbing toward another orgasm when she felt him shift. She looked down to watch him roll a condom on, his hand still working between her legs.

He slid his fingers from her and moved over her. One big hand grasped her knee, bringing it up and wrapping her leg around his waist. Then he flexed her other leg up, propping it over his shoulder. "Nice and slow. And deep," he told her.

The head of his cock pressed against her opening, and she felt the craving to have him thrust hard. "Yes, Noah," she gasped.

He had her spread open and he moved steadily, pressing deeper. His eyes were locked on hers, and she knew he was looking for any indication that she wasn't fine.

But she was fine. Very, very fine.

"God, you feel good," she panted. "So big. So full."

He groaned. "Killing me."

"More. You can go more. Faster. Harder."

"Brynn," he said tightly.

"Yeah?"

"Don't talk. For just a second, okay?"

She wasn't sure anyone had ever asked her *not* to talk before. She found that amusing. Even as Noah sunk a little deeper. She groaned. And decided that if she was going to become more chatty, this might be just the occasion.

"Noah," she said. "I want to be filled up. I want every inch."

"Brynn..." he said warningly.

She dug her fingers into his butt. "*Please.*"

He blew out a quick breath, then moved a hand under her ass, and tipped her pelvis. "Hang on, B."

He thrust, sinking deep, stretching her wide. She felt an intense pressure, then a sharpness, and she gasped. Noah's fingers dug into her butt. "Brynn," he said through gritted teeth. "Tell me you're okay."

"I'm—" She took a deep breath and just worked to relax. "I'm good." He started to pull back and she grabbed him. "No. Wait. I'm fine."

He gave her a half smile. "Yeah, well, this is how this works." He pulled back, then eased in again.

This time there was no sharpness. Just an incredible fullness. She felt her toes curling, literally. "Oh," she said softly. "Oh, yes."

He moved his hips again, dragging out of her slowly, deliciously, then filling her again, stretching her, stroking a spot she hadn't even been aware of. Pleasure streaked through her and she needed *more*.

Noah's muscles bunched as he moved, and Brynn flashed back to all the times she'd watched him working on cars and wondered what they would feel like under her hands. She gripped his upper arms, his triceps hard as he held himself up.

"Keep going," she gasped.

"No other option," Noah told her, his breathing ragged.

"You can go faster."

He chuckled though it sounded almost pained. "I'm barely holding on here, Brynn. You feel so fucking good."

"Good." She arched her back. "I want this to be good for you."

"Fuck," he muttered. "You have no idea."

"I want to come again. I want you to come."

He dropped his head to hers. "Killing. Me."

"Faster, Noah," she whispered. "Harder. No glass slippers."

He dragged in a breath. And then he started moving. Really moving. Hard, deep, fast. He lifted her up against him, and Brynn clung to his shoulders, gasping, trying to move with him. But Noah was truly in control. He hit the perfect spot every time, grinding against her clit, and winding the need deep in her pelvis tighter and tighter.

"Come for me, Brynn. Let me feel it. I need to feel it."

"Noah," she gasped.

Then he reached between them, put his thumb against her clit, and circled.

Her orgasm hit suddenly, everything in her clenching hard and then releasing as pleasure crashed over her.

Noah shouted her name, and she felt him pulse deep inside her as he came seconds later.

He immediately rolled to his back, taking her with him, still inside her. Her legs splayed over his hips, her arms flopped limply, and she rested her cheek against his chest.

She loved how hard he was breathing and the pounding of his heart under her ear.

Slowly he began stroking her back, and she stretched and considered purring. She totally got Penn in that moment.

And as if she'd conjured him, a minute later she heard a meow and the soft thump of a cat landing in the back of the truck. She laughed softly and pried one eye open.

Penn picked his way toward them. She stretched her hand out toward him and he sniffed her fingers. Then he pivoted slowly, stretching and rubbing against her hand.

"Hey, sweetheart," she said softly.

He made one more turn, then plopped down on the blanket next to them, and lifted a back foot and started cleaning his toes.

"Wow, jealous much?" Noah asked him dryly.

Brynn laughed. "He knows that I've been wanting this."

Noah rolled his head to look at her. "Yeah?"

"I've told him about how hot I think you are when we watch you work."

Noah's hands slid to her butt and he squeezed. "Is that right?"

"He's a really good listener."

Noah chuckled. "He's good at keeping secrets too. He hasn't said a thing to me."

Brynn nuzzled her face against his neck. And got another ass squeeze for it. "Well, now it doesn't have to be a secret. I'm hot for your body, Noah Bradley. And I want to do a lot of very dirty things to it."

"That can be arranged, Brynn Carmichael," he said, bringing her face up for a kiss.

She felt a wave of contentment wash over her even as her body began heating from his kiss and roaming hands. She started squirming against him, feeling him growing harder inside her again.

He pulled away from her mouth and looked up at her. "Okay, goddess, I need to go get cleaned up before we start over again."

She frowned then, though it probably had something to do with the condom. She really didn't know how *that* all went. She kissed him again and then he slid her up and off of his body, rolling her to the blanket. He kissed her yet again before pushing himself up.

"Don't go anywhere."

"No chance."

And she definitely peeked over the edge of the truck bed as he headed for the bathroom. Yeah, she got it. Watching someone walk away could be *really* nice.

10

Noah scrubbed a hand over his face and stared into the mirror over the bathroom sink.

He'd just made love to Brynn Carmichael.

He'd been her first. But he'd made it good for her, and he'd had a chance to pour all of his feelings for her into every kiss and touch.

And now she *really* had to go back to New York.

The fact that he was in love with her and was still committed to letting her go was a great way of proving that he was a good guy who could keep his promises, wasn't it?

He'd promised Rudy he'd take care of her.

Not that he wouldn't fall for her.

Cursing, he splashed water on his face, then stalked back to the truck, wondering if it was too soon for a very-recently-virgin to try a little cowgirl.

But when he rounded the back of the truck, he found his girl had already been claimed by another male.

Brynn had pulled the edge of the top blanket over her, and Penn was curled up in the crook of her arm. She was lazily stroking his head as she talked softly to him. The sight made something in Noah's chest tighten.

Penn had been a friendly, cuddly thing when he'd first shown up at the shop. Jared would sit on the hood of this truck, exactly like Brynn did, on his breaks, and Penn would climb into his lap immediately. Noah had considered the cat both his and Jared's, though Penn seemed to gravitate toward Jared. Of course, Jared sat still better than Noah did.

The first time Brynn had climbed up on the truck and settled back to read, Noah had struggled to take a deep breath. She hadn't known that he kept the truck there as his own tribute to his friend. If it wasn't for Jared, Noah wouldn't have this shop. And it had taken him almost four years to realize that it was okay to open the shop and make it work, just as they'd planned, even without his friend.

"Was I even across the garage before he settled into my spot?" Noah asked.

Brynn lifted her head and smiled at him. "He waited until you shut the bathroom door."

One of her legs was splayed to the side, the blanket covering her thigh and the pretty spot between her thighs that Noah needed to get his mouth back on really soon. But her bent knee and lower leg were all bare. He stroked a hand from the arch of her foot to her knee, and she gave a soft sigh.

"You're going to have to decide which one of us you want to cuddle with," Noah said, memorizing the silky feel of her skin.

"Yeah? Why can't I have you both?"

"Well, babe, I'm not into sharing," Noah told her with a small smile. "And more, if I get up there with you, Penn will get lost."

"You'll make him leave?" She gave him a little pout and scratched under Penn's chin.

"No. He'll just leave on his own."

She looked down at the cat. "You don't think he likes you."

"Not anymore."

Her gaze came back to his. "He used to?"

Shit. He hadn't meant to say that. He didn't want her to know about Jared. "When he was little," Noah said with a nod. "But he got pissed off when I went off to college and then the Marines."

"Ah." She rubbed behind Penn's ears. "Who took care of him then?"

"Hank."

Brynn's eyes widened in surprise. "Really?"

"He's the first house down," Noah said, pointing east in the direction of Hank's house. "And he's a softie. Penn went over even before we—I—left and so I asked if he'd take him in."

"So Penn lived with Hank until you came home? Then he came back?"

Noah felt his throat tighten. Which was stupid. It was a *cat*. "He never left. He slept here. He'd show up at Hank's if he got really hungry, but finally Hank just started coming over here to feed him."

Brynn shook her head. "Wow. Hank's the best."

Noah smiled. "Yeah. He is."

They were quiet for a moment, and Noah could hear Penn purring. Up against Brynn? He could relate.

"Come here," she said quietly, holding her other hand out to him.

"There's no way I'm not coming there," he said, crawling up on the tailgate and showing her just how excited he was to see her.

Her eyes dropped to his cock and her cheeks flushed. But this wasn't a blush of embarrassment. That was pure lust. And his cock responded in kind.

He slid up beside her, on the opposite side from Penn, and cuddled in close, resting his hand on her stomach and his erection against her hip.

The cat didn't move. He did look up at Noah with a "really" expression though. Noah actually chuckled. "You might have crawled on top of her first, P," he said. "But I can promise she likes how I snuggle more."

The cat put his head down, on Brynn's arm, and closed his eyes.

Really? He wasn't going to move? Just when Noah thought he and the animal had an understanding about personal space, they were going to have to share the woman Noah was pretty sure he was addicted to forever now?

Fine. He could wait. Lying up against her wasn't a bad way to spend a few minutes.

"You're not going to make him move?" she asked, after nearly a minute. She had an arm around Noah too, and her hand rested on his lower back.

"Nah," he said.

"You think Hank is soft? Look at you."

Noah just looked at Penn. "I don't blame him for being mad at me," he said after a second.

"Because you left?"

Noah nodded. "For a long time. Without really explaining it."

Okay, again, he'd said more than he'd meant to. Because he wasn't talking about explaining his absence to the cat. At least not just the cat.

"You should have explained that you were off to college and the Marines?" she asked. "You think that would have helped him forgive you when you got back?"

Noah felt a shiver of trepidation go through him. He was dangerously close to telling her some things he had no intention of talking about.

But he wasn't sure he could help himself suddenly. He hadn't just liked hearing that she liked lemon sherbet. He'd liked learning about how she didn't want to relate to Cinderella and how she feared she did anyway.

He not only wanted her to know that there was always a

carton of Cherry Garcia in his freezer, but that Penn had a good reason to hate him.

And so did Maggie.

"I could have told him *why* I was leaving," he finally said. "That might have helped."

"You served for four years?" Brynn asked, shifting slightly so she could look at him. Penn didn't move.

"Yeah." Noah's hand itched with the urge to reach out and pet the cat. But suddenly he was afraid that really might make Penn move. The cat had found someone he could cuddle with again. And she was a hell of a cuddler. He didn't want to take that away from the animal.

Noah wouldn't have been surprised if Hank had offered his lap to the cat while Noah had been away, but he also wouldn't have been surprised to find out that Penn would only cuddle on people when they were on or in his truck.

"So you didn't finish college then?" she asked.

He felt his neck tense. This was *really* close to the whole story. "I had it in my head that we needed business degrees so that we could open this shop and really kick ass," he said. "And, honestly, it was a great reason to get out of Bliss and let go a little."

"You needed a break?"

"Yeah. I—" He cleared his throat. Okay, this part she could know, he supposed. "My dad was a Marine. And when he deployed, he left me in charge. That whole you're-the-man-of-the-house thing. I was supposed to take care of my mom and sisters, the house, whatever came up."

"How old were you?"

"That probably started when I was about ten or eleven," he said.

"Wow."

He shrugged. "I didn't mind it. Or at least, I didn't realize I minded it. Until I got older. And Lori ended up in the hospital with a ruptured appendix when I was about fifteen. And Kate put a car in the ditch when I was sixteen. And my mom cheated on my dad when I was seventeen."

"Noah."

He felt Brynn's fingers curl into his lower back.

"It was just the one time and Mom and Dad worked it out."

"But, that wasn't on you," Brynn said fiercely.

"No, none of it was my fault," he told her. He knew that. He'd never really *blamed* himself. "But I was the one there to fix it and clean it all up."

"So you wanted to get away and have some time to yourself," she said. "I get that."

"Yeah. So I talked my buddy Jared into going with me. He wanted to just run this shop together, figured we could easily do it without a degree. And he was right, of course. But I talked him into going anyway. He got a scholarship and everything."

Brynn let the quiet stretch between them for several ticks. But finally, she said, "Mitch mentioned Jared the other day when he was here. Something about this truck."

That's right. He had. Fucking Mitch. Noah nodded. "This was his baby. Was determined to fix it up and get it running."

"And you've kept it to remember him by?"

Noah swallowed. "I kept it to remind myself that it's easier to fix things right away rather than waiting. When things are neglected for a while, it's a lot harder to get them...put back together." And yes, that was true of trucks and people. And relationships.

"What happened to Jared, Noah?" she asked softly.

He knew that she realized it was something bad.

"He was killed in a drunk driving accident just before Christmas break our freshman year."

Brynn sucked in a breath and he again felt her hand on his back, this time rubbing in little circles. "I'm so sorry."

He cleared his throat. "Me too. And that's why I took off to the Marines. I couldn't handle staying there, but I couldn't deal with coming back either. I couldn't look at this shop." *And his mom*, he thought silently.

"I get that." She took a breath. "So you went and served four years. But you did come back."

Leaving was the most selfish thing he'd ever done in his life, but then he'd come back and tried to put things back the way they'd been. But they would never be the way they'd been again. Almost worse, people admired his service. Thanked him for it. He cleared his throat. "I got my head on straight and realized that Jared would be pissed at me if I didn't come back and do what we'd dreamed of." *And if I left his mom all alone here.*

Again the quiet stretched between them, and Noah realized how much he loved that they could do that. They didn't feel the need to fill every second. Brynn didn't give him a bunch of platitudes. She just listened.

He spread his fingers wide on her stomach, rubbing over the soft skin.

Then he looked at the cat. He slowly slid his hand over Brynn toward Penn. The cat opened one eye. But he didn't lift his head. Didn't move. Noah reached for him, putting his hand gently on his head, then running it down his back.

He'd almost forgotten how silky the cat was. He felt like a plush stuffed animal. And he still didn't move. He didn't arch into Noah's hand. He didn't start purring. But he didn't pull away either.

Noah couldn't believe how good that felt. It was completely ridiculous to be that worked up over a cat. But, there it was.

He stroked over Penn's back as he asked Brynn, "The princess birthday in Orlando wasn't the best one, was it?"

She didn't respond immediately. "No," she finally said. "My favorite was when she rented out a bakery after hours, bought one of every single dessert they'd made that day, and we sat around, just the three of us, and stuffed our faces with fat and sugar."

"She didn't just bake for you?" Noah asked. "She loves that stuff."

"She does. But that wouldn't have been a big, elaborate, surprise event."

"Right." Noah chuckled lightly and Penn lifted his head. "*That's* Cori."

"It used to be," Brynn agreed. "Evan's given her... a foundation. A place to just *be*. She's a lot more relaxed and content now."

Noah moved his hand off of the cat, needing to stroke someone else for a moment. He ran his hand over her stomach and then up between her breasts. Her breath hitched.

"How did you know the one in Orlando wasn't my favorite?" she asked.

"Because it was big, and had lots of people, and involved sharing your sisters and their attention with an entire theme park," he said. "You have always shared them with all the other people and activities they've got in their lives. You love the moments when you have them to yourself. Or at least quieter times with them."

"Oh." The word was more of a sound.

He looked up. She looked like she had tears in her eyes.

She swallowed. "You might know me better than you think you do."

His heart squeezed so hard in his chest that he had to take a second before he could even nod. Yeah, maybe he did. "You're different on game nights than you are at the pie shop or other bigger occasions."

"How am I different?"

"You're happier. Softer. More at ease."

She nodded. "You're right. About all of that."

And that made him feel triumphant.

Just before the cold realization hit him. He was getting too close. He was letting her know how he felt. If she was falling for him and realized that he was in love with her, she might start rethinking her plans. Her sisters were staying in Bliss. She was happy at the pie shop. Surely she would miss her lab, but the woman was a brilliant billionaire. She could figure out how to make it all work if she wanted to.

He couldn't let her want to.

So, just after having sex with her for the first time—for her first time ever—he was going to lie in Jared's truck, holding her naked body, and set up her next date.

He swallowed hard. "So," he said. "I was thinking that your next date should be at game night. That's where you're more comfortable, and it would be good for you to practice being with someone in a smaller, more intimate setting."

He felt her stiffen.

Game night was almost sacred. It was the one thing the six of them did together. It would involve her sisters and their very-much-in-love boyfriends. It seemed almost sacrilegious to bring someone else in. Which made it the perfect thing to show her that he was still focused on the overall plan and goal first and foremost. Even if it hurt like a bitch.

"Will you be there?" she finally asked.

He looked up at her. "Of course."

"Will you be bringing a date?"

He frowned. "No."

"Because we'll have an odd number. And everyone else will be couples."

His frown grew deeper. There was no way she was dating some guy without him.

And yes, that sounded weird.

But it was true.

"There are plenty of games we can play with an odd number," he said, consciously working on not squeezing her as the tension ratcheted up in his body.

"Fine," she said, clearly trying to be nonchalant. "If you won't feel awkward."

His arm tightened around her anyway. "I won't feel awkward. Because there will only be *two* real couples."

Brynn pressed her lips together. Then finally nodded. "Fine." She moved her arm out from under Penn. The cat gave a soft *murr*, but then stood and stretched. Brynn started to sit up.

"Whoa, what are you doing?"

"Probably time to go home," she said.

She pulled the top blanket with her as she got to her feet. Penn gave a meow and she bent to stroke his back once more. Then he gracefully jumped up onto the edge of the truck bed, walked along it, then slipped through the open driver's side window. Brynn went to the end of the tailgate and jumped down without even looking back. Noah knew he should say something. *Do* something.

But he really couldn't. What would he say? *I'm sorry you have to bring another guy to game night*? Because he was, definitely. But that wouldn't do any good. She had to do it. He had to let her. Hell, he had to *make* her, if needed. And game night really would be the best choice. He'd be there. Her sisters would be there. It would be another type of date, but she would be more comfortable at home, doing something she enjoyed and...

Noah blew out a breath and ran a hand over his face. Truthfully, game night was the best way to remind them both that neither of them should get too attached to the things they did together.

No matter how much that might hurt.

And he knew he had hurt her.

He hadn't meant to. Well, he *had* meant to at that moment. A little. For her own good. To remind them both of the ultimate outcome here. But he hadn't meant for any of this relationship to get to the point where he could hurt her feelings at all. He had intended to keep his distance. Even while she'd dated. Which back at the beginning had seemed not only smart, but easy—at least, *easier*—than when it was really finally time. Yes, he'd been attracted to her the first moment he'd met her, but he met beautiful women all the time, and he didn't take them under his wing and become their personal not-at-all-an-angel guardian.

Noah gathered up his jeans and underwear and stepped into them. Brynn was getting dressed at the front of the truck, and he knew that she would feel too vulnerable if he joined her before she was covered up.

He hated the idea she'd feel that way. Hell, he wanted to keep her naked pretty much forever. With him. Under him. Over him. But he'd known going in that he'd have to give this—her—up.

He buttoned and zipped, then hopped down from the truck, taking time to refold the blankets and flip the tarp back over everything. His eyes landed on the tackle box that Jared had stored there the last weekend they'd fished together. Noah felt his throat and chest tighten. He hadn't fished since that weekend. It had been eleven years.

Giving things up didn't seem to be getting any easier.

He snapped the tarp, covering everything, and also signaling to Brynn he was almost done and would be coming around. The idea of her not wanting to talk to him was like a knife in his gut, but he wouldn't blame her. He'd give her space. But he wouldn't leave her alone entirely. Especially not when there were still more dates ahead.

He'd felt protective of Brynn from the beginning. Even before he met her. Because of Rudy. So he'd *intended* to treat her like another little sister. But all of his intentions to not notice her long legs, or her gorgeous lips, or her sweet smile had been shot to hell, oh, about the time he'd looked out the diner window and seen her leaning against a limo next to her sisters. He'd finally *admitted* it the first time she'd walked into his garage, asked if she could just *be* here, and climbed up onto his truck.

Now, however, he'd not only blown the she's-like-a-sister-to-me thing, he'd also completely fucked up the idea of keeping his hands to himself and his own heart uninvolved.

When he finally moved out from behind the truck, Brynn was dressed. He watched her cross to where she'd dropped her sweater. She bent and picked it up, turning to face him. As he came up to her, he saw that she was holding her sweater in one hand, and his dog tags in the other.

Cashmere and camo. They didn't really go together.

He took his chain from her without a word. She pulled her sweater on and then pivoted on her heel and walked out to his truck. His other truck. The one that was going to take her home.

But he steeled himself against all of the emotions. Including the regret that was lapping at the edges of his heart.

Whether she liked it or not, this whole thing was like Cinderella at the ball. She was going out for the first time, dancing with a bunch of guys, and trying to figure out which one fit best. Like her slippers.

And Noah was the commoner who was pulling her into dark corners of the ballroom for stolen kisses. Which was fine. As long as he sent her right back out there to the dance floor. It would be fun, it would ensure she felt like the sexy, powerful goddess that she was, and she'd eventually go on to bigger and better balls.

But it would also be a good reminder that this common guy wasn't going to be coming after her when she left this party. Even if she left a glass slipper behind.

———

"So we'll do apple pie and marsala wine, ice wine with cherry, bourbon with chocolate for MJ, and what else?" Brynn asked, scribbling notes from where she was perched on the kitchen counter.

Cori was finishing up the snacks and the "mystery punch" for game night, and Ava was washing eggs. Yes, chicken eggs. That she'd just gathered from Parker's farm.

That was by far the strangest thing Brynn had seen in a long time.

"We could do Irish coffee with a chocolate pecan for something else rich."

"And how about moscato and strawberry pie?" Ava asked.

Brynn rolled her eyes. Ava's new obsession with strawberries was because of Parker's greenhouse—and Parker himself— but she smiled and wrote it down. Ava being obsessed with something other than Carmichael Enterprises was really nice.

As was how much her sisters liked her idea of the Ladies' Night Out at the pie shop. They were coming up with a short menu of pies and liquors that would pair well with them for the evening.

"Or you know, a light ale could go with the apple pie too," Ava said.

Cori shook her head. "The only pie beer goes with is pizza." She turned to add a jar of something to the punch she was making, but she made sure that she blocked Ava and Brynn's view as she did it.

They were playing Guesstures tonight, and Cori was making everything a surprise...as in, they had to guess what they were eating and drinking.

The snacks were little dough pockets that had a variety of fillings but all looked alike, so you wouldn't know what you were getting until you bit into them. The punch was an interesting blue color and was a mixture of a bunch of undisclosed ingredients.

Brynn couldn't decide if she should stay far away from the punch... or drink a gallon of it. Ahead of time.

She shook her head, focusing on her task. As she'd been doing for days. One thing at a time. One focus at a time. No daydreaming. No letting her mind wander. And fantasize...

Frowning, Brynn added the ale to the list in spite of Cori's protest. She'd ask Parker about it. He was the other chef in the family and while Cori had plenty of beer drinking experience, Brynn thought maybe Parker would have good input about how tastes mixed and paired. "I was also thinking about doing some drinks that are pie themed all by themselves," she told her sisters. "Like the apple pie shots we've done here, or we could do a lemon meringue...kind of a lemon drop martini but with cream or something?"

Cori turned. "Ooh, I like that. We could make our own limoncello for it. Oh, and we could use some of that lemon sherbet you love so much."

Instantly, Brynn felt her cheeks heat. Talk of her favorite ice cream took her back to Noah's garage four days ago and everything that had happened there. Not that it took much to remind her of it. It hadn't been far from her mind for even a few minutes. But she'd been trying not to think about it in mixed company. Because she figured it was *very* obvious what she was thinking about when she started blushing and having a hard time concentrating.

It didn't help that she'd been trying to squelch her nerves about tonight. This would be the first time she'd seen Noah since they'd made love. Had sex. Fucked. Whatever it had been. She hadn't gone down to the shop for her afternoon break at all this week. For one, she had no idea how she could be with him and sit on that truck and not strip all of her clothes off and beg him to do it all over again.

For another, she'd been busy. The shop had been doing steady business lately. People were realizing that dessert really did complete a meal, and now that they could smell the scent of vanilla and cinnamon and apples wafting through the doorway between the pie shop and the restaurant, it was hard to resist.

And yes, there were still a larger-than-usual number of young, single men coming in.

That didn't mean she didn't miss seeing Noah. She missed

him almost too much. Which was the third thing that had kept her from the garage. The sheer *need* she felt to be there.

That was alarming actually.

Sex with him one time and she was completely smitten?

Then again, she'd been pretty smitten to start with…

"Hello? Brynn?"

She shook her head and focused on Ava. "Um, yeah?"

"So it was absolutely amazing? Big Sexy totally rocked your world? He was definitely the right one to lose your virginity to?" Cori asked.

Brynn looked over at Cori. "You were asking me about Noah?"

Ava grinned. "No. But that answers Cori's questions."

Brynn sighed. "Yes, yes and yes," she said. "Just to be clear."

"I'm so happy!" Cori exclaimed. "He's the best for you."

Brynn felt like Cori had just jabbed her right in the heart. "He was the best to be my first," she clarified. "But this is short-term. Just five more months.

"Right," Cori said.

"Of course," Ava agreed.

She looked at her sisters. They were… a lot. Especially together. But they loved her. They didn't let her make decisions or ask her opinion often, but they believed that's how she wanted it. She'd let them think that. Because it was easier than asserting herself. And now she had only five months until they wouldn't have to worry about her anymore.

That thought took her breath away.

Did Cori and Ava feel like Noah did about his sisters? Like she was an obligation?

Very possibly.

Coming to Bliss had brought them closer, as she'd hoped. But she was still letting them take care of her because it made them happy to do it. But did it? Or did it really just cause them to worry? And had she ever taken care of *them*?

Her thoughts spun.

Tonight was the first time she'd really contributed ideas to the pie shop other than...no, as she thought about it, she realized that all of the ideas from the pies to the cushions on the chairs, had come from her sisters. Yes, she and Noah had made the cushions, but it hadn't been her idea.

Until she'd brought up Ladies' Night Out. And Cori and Ava had listened and loved the ideas she had for the event. In all the time they'd talked about the shop, she'd just gone along, but it was fun being creative like this and pitching ideas and brainstorming with them on the details. Did they ever wonder why she didn't do more? Why she didn't try to get more involved? Did they ever wonder what they could do to make her want to be more involved? Did they think it was them? Because it really wasn't. It was all her. And she suddenly hated the idea that they might think she didn't care.

She looked at them both. She could tell them that she loved them and wanted to be a more integral part of everything, of course. But, that didn't seem quite enough. Instead, she needed to show them. Show them that she loved working with them, that she cared about the pie shop, and that she wanted to be a real part of things instead of just a tagalong.

And she had an idea about how she could do that.

It was really just an inkling of an idea right now, but it was taking shape, and she felt a little bubble of excitement rising up.

Having great sex and great ideas. Yeah, she thought she could get used to all of this.

11

Noah sat at the desk in his front office. Something he never did. He was always too busy in the garage. And he hated paperwork. His billing and ordering systems were computerized, and he did okay keeping up with them. If he got behind, his mom would come down and help.

Still, it amazed him how much freaking paper still came across this desk. But he wasn't sitting here because of any of that. He was icing his knuckles and thinking. The thinking had been going on for four days. He'd been trying to avoid it, tamping thoughts down as soon as he realized they were taking over. But today a few stray thoughts about Brynn and how gorgeous she was, and how amazing it was to be the guy she let so close, and that he'd been kind of an asshole to bring up her next date that way, had suddenly snuck up on him, and he'd whacked his knuckles against the engine he was working on.

After that, he couldn't stop the barrage of thoughts and emotions and memories.

Now he was getting nothing done and his hand hurt.

Apparently four days was the absolute limit to how long he could go without seeing her without going crazy. He'd missed her on day one, but had decided to give her some space when she didn't come to the garage. Day two, he'd gone to the diner for lunch but had stayed on Parker's side where he could see her but not be in her way.

Exactly where he probably should have stayed all along. On the side. Watching out for her, but not in her face. Or in her life.

Day three, he'd decided she was better off if he just stayed away entirely. His main goal was for her to be happy, and *he* had been the one to upset her the other night. In fact, he'd kind of ruined her first sexual experience. Out of self-preservation, he'd wanted to put a wall up. And he'd hurt her doing it. Brynn had put up her own walls for a long time. She'd stayed to herself, let her "weirdness" put a barrier between her and her dad and being hurt by his inability to relate to her. She'd extended that to pretty much everyone else as well. Then she'd come here and let *him* past those walls. And instead of just appreciating that and being grateful that a woman like her would even let him close enough to buy her a cup of coffee, not to mention all the delicious things she'd let him to do her, he'd gotten worried about how *he* felt. And he'd hurt her.

Now it was day four, and he was going to see her. Tonight. But not because he was awesome at reaching out and admitting when he was wrong and apologizing. Because he completely sucked at all of that. He was going to see her because it was game night. The time when he got together with five of his favorite people and just hung out.

Of course, tonight would also include Brynn's date.

Noah didn't have to be there. It was a date, but her sisters and Evan and Parker would be there. She didn't need Noah.

But Rudy hadn't asked him to be sure *someone* took care of her. He'd asked *Noah* to do it.

Just like Jared hadn't said, "Be sure you hire someone to take care of my mom if something ever happens to me." He'd said, "Take care of her, Noah. For me." Yeah, they'd been drunk, and young, and feeling sentimental and mushy. But Noah knew Jared had meant it. Noah had meant it when he'd asked Jared to take care of *his* family too.

So he had to go tonight. He had to be there for her. And he had to not be a dick about it.

"*Meow.*"

Startled out of his thoughts, Noah glanced toward the doorway between the garage and the office. Penn was rubbing himself along the doorframe.

"*Meow.*"

"Uh, hey, bud," Noah said. He turned the swivel seat to face the cat. Penn came the rest of the way through the door. He blinked his big green eyes at Noah.

"*Meow.*"

Noah sighed. "She's not here. Sorry." The cat hadn't had a warm lap in four days either. "It's totally on me. I'll get you some treats next time I'm at the store."

Penn came forward and sniffed the toe of Noah's boot. Noah held completely still. This was as close as the cat had been to him in months without Brynn. Once in a while, if Noah was a little late to fill his dish, he'd come trotting across the shop, but he stayed out of arm's reach.

He jumped up onto the desk and Noah watched him check over piles of papers and envelopes. Then he turned toward Noah. Noah reached out a caution hand, but the cat didn't move, and Noah rubbed the top of his head. Penn pressed a little closer and Noah rubbed again, coasting down the back of his neck. Penn turned slightly and Noah took the hint, petting his back and then returning to his head. After a few strokes, Penn looked over at him.

"Well, this is nice," Noah told him. Penn bumped his hand, and he stroked the soft black fur again before Penn turned a circle and laid down on the desk. "Okay." Noah looked around. For some reason he didn't want to get up and leave the cat in here. This was as close as Penn had gotten, and he seemed content to stay for a while. "Maybe I do need to catch up on some of this work," Noah said. He leaned forward and reached for one of the stacks. He pulled the top few pages from the pile but as he laid them on the desk, Penn got up. He started toward the edge of the desk. "Hey, hang on. You don't have to go." The cat looked back. On impulse, Noah sat back in the chair. "Am I supposed to just hang out? Not work then?"

Penn turned and came toward him again. But instead of reclaiming his spot on the desk, he put his front paws on Noah's thigh. Noah held still and Penn climbed down from the desk and into his lap. Then he crawled over Noah's stomach and up his chest until his front paws rested on Noah's shoulder, his face near Noah's.

And then he started purring.

Noah actually felt his throat tighten. The cat hadn't sat on him in...Noah couldn't remember a time. Jared had always been the one to hold him and pet him and talk to him. Noah would talk to him from time to time, a weird habit that just seemed to happen. But yeah, he'd rarely held him.

Now though...he understood the appeal. The gentle rumble of the purring, the soft, warm body, the trust. That was the thing that seemed to hit Noah hardest. The cat was totally trusting Noah, happy to just be there. He wasn't being fed, he wasn't being let in from the cold. Penn already had everything he *needed*. Technically. But he still wanted to be close to Noah.

Or maybe he was comforting Noah.

That made his chest tighten too, and Noah lifted a hand and stroked it down the cat's back.

He hadn't had a lot of downtime cuddling. He knew that. He hadn't *taken* that time. His sisters and mom had needed him *doing* things, not sitting around. At work, people needed him to be taking care of their cars. With Maggie...he didn't know how to just sit around with her. What would they talk about? Jared? That would be unnecessarily painful for them both. And with Brynn... well, once he started cuddling her he'd never want to stop.

And he had to stop. He had to be able to let her go.

But he couldn't shake the idea that the cuddling could really go both ways with her too. Maybe he was giving Penn some much-needed affection, but it was glaringly evident that it wasn't one-sided. This was nice, dammit. And it was a humbling, and somewhat scary thought that *he* might need some affection too. He was well-liked. His friends had his back. Lots of people, his friends and family, cared about him. He knew that. But he'd never put demands of his own on the people—or cats—he took care of. Not for doing things for him like errands or favors, and not for...well, fuck, not for hugs and cuddling.

They needed to be taken care of. How could he expect them to take care of him?

But as Penn purred against him, his paws kneading Noah's shoulder, he couldn't help but think about holding Brynn. And having her hold him back.

———

"The FDA approval came through on T-1587, and we're moving from preclinical trials to clinical trials next week on T-7143."

Brynn grinned at Jeffrey. "That's amazing. You guys are really moving."

They were doing their daily Skype session and she was thrilled with the news, but her mind was only half on what they were talking about.

As Jeffrey kept talking, she took a bite of the cherry pie she'd swiped from the pie shop kitchen. After she'd swallowed, she took a sip of one of the beers she'd picked up at the liquor store in the next town over.

She wrinkled her nose. "Ugh."

Jeffrey paused. "You don't think Shelly is ready to lead that development team?"

Brynn focused on him again. "Oh, no. I'm sorry. Shelly would be great."

He peered into his computer screen as if trying to see into her room. "What are you doing?"

She looked down at the pie and the four bottles of beer she had sitting on her desk. "Um...I'm eating pie and drinking beer."

"Oh." He nodded.

She tipped her head. "You don't think that sounds weird? Pie and beer?"

Jeffrey shrugged. "Depends on what kind of each. I've had some really great fruit beers so I can see why they could go together."

Brynn set her fork down. "You're a beer drinker?" There was so much she didn't know about the people around her. She had worked with Jeffrey for six years and she didn't know he drank beer? Wow. She really did need to become *a little* chattier.

"Love it. A friend of mine owns a microbrewery in fact," he said. "I've helped with some of it in fact. The process is fascinating and a lot of fun."

"Fascinating and fun?" Brynn asked. "Really?"

"Brewing beer is really just chemistry," Jeffrey said, lifting a shoulder. "When he first started dabbling in it, I helped him with experimenting with the yeasts and even gave him some equipment."

Brynn pushed her plate out of the way and leaned in closer to her computer. She felt a swirl of excitement in her stomach. She'd been taste testing liquors and different pies for the last few days, wanting to ensure the combinations they were putting together for Ladies' Night were perfect. But ever since she'd tasted the apple pie wine that she'd seen at the store, the niggle of an idea had been tickling the back of her mind. Or her imagination.

Pharmaceutical research was challenging and definitely took some creativity at times. They needed to make connections that weren't always obvious and had to be willing to try new things. And sometimes fail. She was used to that. In fact, she was quite comfortable with experimenting and working to perfect combinations. She was incredibly patient and could spend hours waiting for and observing reactions.

So this idea—the idea of combining tastes and scents, and even going beyond those basic senses—had been intriguing her ever since she'd started thinking about how to pair the different liquors and dessert flavors. She'd decided she definitely wanted to take the time for some taste testing. And, ironically, several times she'd flashed back to her first date with science teacher Sean and their conversation about teaching kids about their senses and how they worked together. Even the sheer complexity of the taste mechanism on the tongue was fascinating.

Brynn had gone on to research more about wine tasting and had spent hours reading about the process of growing the huge variety of grapes, combining flavors, and the many layers to tasting and sensing those flavors in the vast array of wines. It really was all amazing.

Now Jeffrey was telling her that the chemistry of brewing beer was interesting and fun.

Yeah, that swirl of excitement definitely intensified.

"Jeffrey, you are doing an amazing job with the lab. Thank you."

"Of course. You're welcome. You know how important this research is to me."

She did. Jeffrey's mother had Parkinson's disease and three of the medications their lab was working on, including T-1587 and T-7143 were for Parkinson's.

"I'm really excited about T-1587, and I think Shelly will do a fantastic job leading the team on T-7143."

"Great." Jeffrey gave her a big smile.

"And now," Brynn said. "Tell me all about brewing beer."

———

S am Kent was also a dumbass.

It seemed to be an epidemic in Bliss that Noah hadn't been aware of until Brynn started dating the entire town.

He lifted his beer, acknowledging that he was overreacting, but it didn't stop him from glaring at Sam across the dining room table.

Of course, Sam didn't notice. He was too busy looking at, smiling, and flirting with Brynn.

Obviously, *that* didn't make Sam a dumbass.

"Yes!" she gushed, giving Sam a high five. They had just won the most recent game of Guesstures.

Even though Sam hadn't been able to get "diving board". He hadn't gotten "painting" or "bottom" in the last game either. And Brynn had only gotten two of Sam's clues.

"Okay, Noah's in this time," Cori said, bringing the pitcher of punch around again.

Noah held his glass up. The stuff was potent. Making it perfect for sitting across the table from Brynn and her date for the evening. And watching her have fun.

Not that he didn't want her to have fun.

But he didn't really want her to have fun with Sam. Or anyone but her sisters. And Evan and Parker. And, yeah, *him*.

He motioned for Cori to keep going when she stopped pouring at half a glass. She arched a brow but topped it off. Then she gave his arm a little squeeze before turning to Sam. Great, so Cori was noticing that Noah wasn't handling this very well.

But even before he knew how her nipples tasted, how she sounded when he sucked on her clit and how she felt when he slid into her, he had been wound up and split in half about all of this. Now it was pretty much torture.

He wanted her happy. Period.

But it killed him a little to watch someone else make her happy.

That's definitely why she had to go back to New York.

"Who needs more food?" Cori asked.

Noah and Parker both raised their hands.

"You in this time?" Ava asked. "I can sit out."

"Nope, you guys go ahead," Cori said, already sweeping through the kitchen door.

Each game, someone had to sit out because they had an odd number of people. Because Noah was there being a seventh wheel. And he didn't fucking care. In fact, he'd happily sit there just watching. And drinking and scowling.

But he wasn't leaving. Brynn hadn't been at the garage all week and he'd been craving her. Not just her body—though damn right that was part of it—but just seeing her. Just having her sitting there like she usually did. Of course, if she climbed up on that truck now, he wouldn't be able to let her sit there just reading quietly. But after hanging out with Penn earlier today, he *really* needed to see her. He needed to...cuddle her. That sounded stupid even in his own head, but after reconnecting with the cat, he felt a sudden need to connect with others he'd let down.

Turned out he might be the biggest dumbass of all.

"Be my partner?"

He looked up and into Brynn's eyes. She was watching him closely.

All he could do was nod.

She'd said hello to him when he'd arrived. She'd even given him a sweet smile—that had jabbed him in the gut. They both talked throughout the course of the evening to the group. But they hadn't really spoken directly. And definitely not one-on-one. Now she was asking him to be her partner, and he couldn't help but feel it was an olive branch.

Except that *he* should be the one extending any branches.

"Great, I'll partner with Sam," Ava said, giving Brynn's date a smile.

"That leaves you and me, love," Evan said to Parker.

Parker lifted his middle finger at the "love". "Guess what this gesture means."

Evan chuckled and started shuffling cards.

Noah set his drink aside and leaned in to arrange his. There were four words he needed Brynn to guess before the time ran out. And they were going to kick ass. As usual.

Cori started the timer with a "Ready? Go!"

Noah began acting out what was on his cards, and Brynn easily got the first three.

With ten seconds left, Brynn yelled, "Peaches!"

"Yes!"

They high-fived as the timer ran out.

Cori was shaking her head. "Wow, you two are something."

Brynn caught Noah's eye. "Yeah, we are, aren't we?"

He couldn't argue. He just gave her a wink.

She looked at him for a beat longer. Then she turned to Sam. "So this has been really fun." She gave him smile.

He chuckled. "It has. Even if I'm not winning them all, I don't mind watching *you* win," he said. "You're pretty cute when you're trying to kick everyone's ass."

Noah had to cover the growl that escaped his chest with a cough. Sam wasn't wrong. But Noah didn't love Sam noticing...or commenting on it. "Hey, Cori, you have more food?" he asked.

"Of course." She got right up, surveyed the table to see what everyone needed, and headed into the kitchen.

"Well, I'm glad you had fun," Brynn said to Sam, scraping her chair back and standing. "Thanks for coming over."

There was a moment of hesitation, from everyone. Was Brynn following Cori into the kitchen or was she actually dismissing Sam?

"Uh, yeah, my pleasure," Sam said. He also stood. "Maybe we

can—" He glanced at Noah. Noah lifted an eyebrow. "—chat again some time," Sam finished.

Clearly Sam wasn't comfortable asking Brynn for another date with Noah sitting right there.

Good.

He shouldn't be comfortable asking her for another date at all. The guys in town, Sam included, knew that Brynn was dating *very* casually. That she wasn't looking for anything serious. That she was only staying in town a few more months. That she was, at the very least, a very good friend of Noah, Evan, and Parker's and, like three big brothers, they weren't going to let anyone get too close or serious if that wasn't what she wanted.

Noah hadn't specifically spoken to Sam about his date with Brynn, but he'd known about it almost immediately. She'd asked Sam as he was paying for a slice of peach pie. He'd practically gotten a medal of honor from the other guys who had been in the shop and witnessed it. But Noah hadn't felt the need to have a one-on-one with Sam. Because he knew how the date was going to go, and he didn't really care how Sam felt about it or what he tried to change about the plan. He was date number four. Period. That was it. And now that the night was almost over, he'd fulfilled his purpose and could move on.

It looked like Brynn was ready for him to go.

Cori brought a big plate of food in and set it in front of Noah.

"Are we playing again?" she asked, looking from Brynn to Sam—the only other two people standing—and then at Noah.

Noah just picked up one of the dough pockets and bit into it. This one was Philly cheesesteak. Nice.

"I was just going to walk Sam out," Brynn said. "I have an early morning tomorrow."

She was going to walk Sam out? Noah chewed, trying not to react to that. That was the nice and polite thing to do. She'd invited Sam over and now he was leaving. Big deal.

Noah reached for another dough pocket. This one was

buffalo chicken. Also very good. And there were at least five others on that plate. He was just fine right here for the next couple of minutes. The amount of time it should take Brynn to walk Sam to the door, say goodnight, and come back to the dining room.

Cori didn't say anything about Brynn's supposed early morning. She just nodded. "Okay. Well, Sam, thanks for coming."

"Thanks for having me. It was really fun. The food and everything was great."

"I'm glad." Cori gave him a smile.

Brynn started toward the front of the house, and Sam really had no choice but to follow. The dining room was quiet after they left. Noah reached for another dough pocket.

Barbecue beef. Awesome.

Cori propped a hand on her hip. "I don't know that I have enough supplies to support a big Marine eating his feelings."

"Shut up, Cori," Noah told her around a bit of beef and barbecue sauce.

She chuckled and took a seat across from him. "How long until you follow her out there?"

"Ten minutes."

"That long?"

"I'm sure Sam's coming up with some lame way to stall. I'll give him a chance to try before he's sent on his way."

"Makes the crash and burn more painful, right?" Evan asked, sounding amused.

Noah scowled at him. "Right." He reached for another dough ball, hoping for a pepperoni pizza one this time.

Evan shook his head. "These poor guys."

"Fuck that," Noah snapped. "They know the situation. If they want to get more out of it, they can try, but I'm not going to feel bad when it doesn't work." He bit into the pocket. Damn, teriyaki chicken. Still, it was good.

"What if it does work?" Parker asked. "Eventually she'll be

done with the six required dates and could go out with one of them again, right?"

Noah looked at Parker with narrowed eyes. Was he trying to piss him off? "She's going back to New York."

"She wouldn't have to," Ava said. "We could definitely figure out a way to make this work like I'm doing with Carmichael Enterprises."

Noah didn't respond to that. But the dough balls he'd been eating seemed to be forming a knot in his stomach. "She does have to. That's the plan."

"If you want her to stay, I think you'd just have to tell her," Ava said.

Her tone had softened and Noah fucking hated that. He didn't want them sympathizing or giving him pep talks...or tempting him.

New York was where her life was, and Rudy had pulled her out and put her in Bliss so that she could get closer to her sisters, maybe learn a few things about her father, learn to interact and even enjoy people outside of her lab, and *practice* dating. This was just her training ground. If Rudy had wanted Noah to be with Brynn, he wouldn't have set it up for her to date six men. He wouldn't have put a twelve-month stipulation on it. If Rudy had wanted Noah to be with Brynn he would have just said that.

And that realization seemed to hit Noah directly in the chest.

That was the bottom line. Rudy knew Noah. Noah had shared some things with Rudy he hadn't shared with anyone else. Rudy knew about Noah's father always putting him in charge of his sisters and mom and praising him when he came home. And the relief that Noah always felt when his dad was home again. How he'd felt free.

And Rudy knew about Jared asking Noah to take care of Maggie. And how Noah didn't feel free at all. Never would. There was no end point there, and he couldn't take his eye off the ball for even a second. The last time he'd done something for himself

—joining the Marines and getting the hell away from everything —Maggie had spiraled. He felt guilty as hell about that ever since. He should have come right home and stayed. *He* had needed the Marines. Maggie had needed *him*.

Rudy knew all of that. And he definitely hadn't asked Noah to take care of Brynn himself, personally, romantically, forever.

"I don't want her to stay," he said flatly, pushing his plate back. And that was absolutely true. If she stayed he'd have to watch some other guy make her happy—or try. And Jesus, if watching her find her fairy tale ending with some other guy sounded torturous, watching her *not* be ecstatically happy would kill him. And he'd have to kill the guy.

Speaking of the guys on that list, Sam and Brynn had now been outside together for ten minutes.

He wiped his mouth, tossed his napkin on the table, shoved his chair back and stood. "Curfew time."

No one said a thing to stop him.

Noah headed down the short hall and stepped into the foyer. He rounded the corner practically reaching for the door before he even saw it. Which meant he almost ran Brynn over.

She was standing in the alcove, leaning against the wall, reading on her phone.

He pulled up short. "What the hell are you doing?"

She looked up at him. "Finally." She turned her phone screen off and tucked it into her pocket.

"Finally?" he frowned. "What's going on? Where's Sam? Are you okay?"

"I'm fine. Sam said he'd had a nice time, I asked him if he knew his ex was going to be in town for a wedding this weekend, he said he'd been considering skipping the wedding because of that, I told him that I thought he should show up anyway, he thought about it, agreed, and said goodnight."

Noah was just watching her, feeling a little...flummoxed. "So you just encouraged your date to maybe get back together with his ex?"

Brynn nodded. "I heard her mom talking with the mother of the bride and she said that her daughter never got over Sam. I especially paid attention once they said his name. I asked Hank if it was the same Sam and he said yes." She pushed away from the wall. "So, that's all done."

"And you're fine?" Noah didn't really care about Sam and his ex. The woman in front of him was all that mattered.

"I'm fine." She stepped toward him. "But I want to be great."

"Wha—"

Brynn grabbed the front of his shirt in her hand and pulled him toward her. She went on tiptoe as he stumbled forward and pressed her lips to his.

He wasn't sure what exactly was going on, but Brynn was kissing him, so he didn't care. And it felt a little like...forgiveness.

He kissed her for a long moment, relishing the feel of her under his hands, the taste of her, the smell of her. But eventually he pulled back. "I'm sorry," he said against her lips.

He'd been an ass the other night. But she had been waiting in the foyer for him and was now kissing him so maybe things weren't so bad.

"I know," she told him.

And just like that he felt some of the tightness in his chest ease.

"I've been trying to keep you safe and happy and then I'm the one that fucks it up."

She pulled back and looked up at him. "Noah?"

"Yeah."

She reached up and put her hands on either side of his face. "I know you would do anything for me. And that *makes* me safe and happy. Bottom line. No matter what else you say or do or don't do. I know that you will be there. But—" she went on before he could respond. "—you're not the only one in charge of my happiness. *I* can make myself happy. So when you screw up, because you're human and not perfect and torn between what you want and what my dad wanted, I'll be okay. Because I *know* how you feel about me. And because I'm very capable of thinking that through and remembering the *whole* picture, not just that one moment. And I know myself. I know that if I talk to my sisters, or go for a walk, or get lost in a book, or go to the pie shop, I'll feel better. So you are not fully in charge of making me happy every single second of every single day. You can mess up and I'll still be okay."

She moved forward and he backed up a little, dazed and amazed. *You can mess up and I'll still be okay.* He wondered if she had any idea how much that mattered, how much that helped him.

Brynn turned them, putting his back against the wall, then leaned in and said softly, "And right now, nothing would make me happier than putting you up against this wall and touching you. All over. A lot."

His entire body, and hell, his *soul*, reacted to that. The whole speech really. He lifted his hands and cupped her face, the way she'd done to him. He stared down at her. She met his gaze directly and gave him a smile that he couldn't even describe. Except that he knew she really was okay. Better than okay. She was...confident. Yeah, one of those Rudy words that had been so important to him. She knew herself and what she wanted. That was one of the things they were going for here. And it was there. In her eyes. In the way she was standing with him. In her words. Most especially, in *his* gut. He felt it.

"You're pretty fucking incredible Brynn Carmichael, you know that?"

"Thank you for noticing." She gave him a little smile.

But he shook his head seriously. "I've been noticing for a while now. Like since I met you."

"Then trust me," she said, also solemn. "Trust me to know

when I'm happy."

He nodded. "I'll...try."

"Good enough for now," she said. Then she pulled his head down for a kiss.

He needed to figure this all out. But then her tongue stroked along his lower lip and... yeah, he'd figure it out. But later.

Much later.

He should *not* feel like he needed to claim her or brand her or erase all memory of any other guy, like the one she'd just been on a date with, but he did. He so did.

Still, this whole thing with her backing *him* up against the wall was pretty great. She was taking some control, going for what she wanted. And she wanted *him*.

That was more than pretty great.

She slid her hands up under his shirt, her hands against his sides, and he groaned. She ran them up and down, sending shocks of desire through him. His body tightened and he had the need to press into her. But he couldn't from this position. She was in charge. For now, anyway.

"Brynn—" He now knew how those little needy pleas he got from her actually felt. He needed her to touch him, to press closer, to relieve some of the pressure he felt building.

Her hands stroked over his chest, then around to his back. Her fingers dug into the muscles on either side of his spine, and she pulled herself closer to him. She bumped against the hard ridge behind his zipper and she gave a little moan.

He was going to let her do this. He was going to let her lead this. He was.

He hoped.

Noah grit his teeth as she arched closer, grinding against him, then slipping her hands lower to his ass and gripping there as she pressed closer.

Okay, he could let her lead, but that didn't mean he couldn't get his hands on some skin too. Noah slid his hand up under her shirt and relished her little gasp as he deepened the kiss as he stroked up her sides to cup a breast with one hand. Her nipple pebbled and he ran his thumb back and forth across the sweet tip. His other hand slid low to her ass and he brought her up against him more firmly.

"Yes," she breathed against his mouth.

Yes. That seemed to sum everything up so perfectly.

He held her tight against him, letting her grind and rub. He squeezed her nipple and she whimpered. Then her hand was sliding between them and down over his cock. Denim between them or not, he felt like his whole body was on fire, and she was the sweet, cool water he needed to put it out. He pressed into her hand, letting her feel how much he wanted her, nearly begging her for more. More touching, more pressure.

He felt the button on the top of his hands give and the zipper slip down. He knew he should stop her, but he also knew no one from the other room would be coming out here, and he honestly wasn't sure he'd care if they did. He had to have Brynn's hands on him. Now.

Her hand slipped between his stomach and the top of his jeans and into his boxers, and then she was stroking his length. Skin on skin. Hot, greedy skin on hot, needy skin.

She ran her palm up and down over his aching cock and then she wrapped her hand around him.

He tore his mouth from hers, needing to breathe. "Brynn," he choked out.

"God, I love touching you," she told him, almost panting.

"I fucking love it too, Beautiful."

"So you don't want me to stop."

He rested his forehead against hers and chuckled gruffly. "Never."

"Seriously? Because I want to do this. A lot. Like—"

He pressed into her hand. "Seriously. Keep going, Brynn."

She gave a little shiver and he knew it was pleasure and

excitement, and he felt something that felt a hell of a lot like humble. She *wanted* to touch him. She wanted to pleasure him. This goddess who he would do anything for wanted him. So fuck yes, she could have him.

"Tell me what to do," she whispered as she ran her hand up and down.

He squeezed his eyes shut. "You're doing just fine."

"But I want to *really* do it. Teach me."

She was all about him, and he wasn't sure anything in his life had ever been hotter.

"Curl your fingers around," he managed, the idea of it nearly enough to do him in. Her doing any of this was heaven. Wanting him to coach her? Pure ecstasy.

She did as he instructed, gripping him lightly.

"Squeeze harder." He was having a hard time pulling air into his lungs.

"Really? How hard?" she asked.

They were safe in this little alcove. Their friends would no way come out here now. Noah had to let go of her to push his jeans to his knees. Brynn actually pulled back slightly so she could look down. He chuckled even as he felt his heart try to stop beating.

"Hard," he told her. "You're not going to hurt me." Her hand was small and he was, well, pretty good-sized if he did say so himself, and there was no way she was going to do him any damage.

Her hand was still inside his boxers and he let her just *feel* now, but she had a lot more room to work without the denim in the way. She gripped him, squeezing harder, and he worked on keeping his lungs working. "Now up and down," he told her.

Brynn moved her hand along his shaft, squeezing and milking him, going up and down in a near perfect rhythm. She was a natural.

"You know what makes hand jobs even better?" he asked

huskily.

"What?"

"Getting to touch you back." He moved a hand up under her shirt again, pulling the cup of her bra down, and taking her nipple between his thumb and finger.

She sucked in a shaky breath. "I never knew that could feel that good."

He rolled the hard tip, moving his hips slightly as he thrust into her hand. "It's all good with us, B," he told her. "It's all good."

She nodded and looked up at him. "Yeah. It really is."

Not that she would know. The thought hit him unexpectedly. She didn't even know how great it was because she had nothing to compare it to. But he shook that off quickly. He didn't fucking care that she didn't know. This was amazing. *He* knew it. And she trusted him. He didn't need to prove to her that this was different than it would be with anyone else.

He slid his other hand into the back of her shorts and panties and over the bare, smooth, firm curve of her ass.

She kept stroking him, squeezing, then letting go slightly, then squeezing again as she went from tip to base.

Noah slipped his hand lower, feeling the heat and dampness before he even got to her center.

"Oh, *yes*," she hissed.

His middle finger moved lower, sliding through her wetness. He pressed into her, just slightly, and her hand stopped moving on his cock.

He laughed softly. "You stop moving, I stop moving, B."

She quickly resumed the stroking and he moved up to her clit, circling and swirling over the sweet spot. A shiver went through her and she gripped him harder.

"That's right, sweetheart," he coached. "Just keep moving. Just like if I was buried here and stroking you deep." He slid his thick middle finger into her, amazed all over again at how tight and hot she was.

She arched her back instinctively. "Noah."

Damn he loved his name on her lips. "Right here. I'm not going anywhere." He added a second finger and thrust deep. "Just like this." He pulled out, then slid home again. "Stroke my cock like your pussy is stroking my fingers."

Her inner muscles squeezed him in response, and she gave a little moan as he curled his finger against her G-spot and rubbed before sliding out again. Her hand tightened and she moved up and down a little faster.

"That's my girl," he told her without thinking.

At his words, her muscles again squeezed. She liked that? There was a lot more sweet talk where that came from.

"I fucking love knowing that no one has touched you like this, Brynn," he told her honestly. "The idea that my fingers, my tongue, my cock are the first to give you pleasure like this."

She whimpered and her pussy clamped onto his fingers.

"The idea that these muscles have never stretched for anyone else. That no one else has made this sweet body get all hot and wet—" He stroked in and out, increasing his speed.

He felt the effect in the way her breathing increased and the way she was stroking him, now on instinct rather than because of coaching. She ran her thumb over his head and he felt his knees wobble. At the base, she brushed her finger tips over his balls, and he felt everything get harder and tighter.

"I fucking *love* the idea that no one knows how sweet you taste and sound. That I'm the only one who's heard you come. That I'm the only one that knows how your hand feels around his cock."

And she came just like that. Without warning. She gasped his name, her whole body arched, and he felt the sweet heat against his hand.

"You really are perfect," he told her gruffly.

She let out a long breath. "Now you."

He started to pull back. "No, I—"

"I know I'm not the first," she said, stopping him. "But I want to know what this is like with you. I want this connection of being *one* of them."

He felt like his heart was actually twisting in his chest. She might not be the first or the only one, but he wanted her to be the last. That he knew to his bones. She was the only one that he wanted to know him. Not just because her hand on his cock was heaven itself, but because she was the only one that mattered.

He pressed his hand against hers on his cock. "You're *the* one, B."

Then she kissed him. She put one hand behind his head, her lips against his and *kissed* him, nearly knocking him to his knees. As her tongue stroked hungrily against his, her hand moved again, and this time Noah let himself get lost. He'd been holding back. In so many ways with her. Afraid of going too far. Getting in too deep. And now he just let it all go.

He arched into her hand, he curled her fingers even tighter around him, and he thrust into their combined grip. And with her breathing heavily against him, her sweetness still on his hand, her scent rising up around them, he felt his orgasm rushing at him, coursing up his spine, his entire body hardening and straining.

"I'm going to come, B," he told her hoarsely.

"Yes, please," she answered.

And then he let it go.

They stood together, panting, their hands in each other's clothes, for several long moments. Then Brynn took a big, satis-fied-sounding breath and leaned back. "I totally get the appeal to being the one putting the other one against the wall."

Noah couldn't believe how good he felt. Orgasms were always good, of course. But with this woman, it was so much more.

And he was screwed for ever being happy with anyone else again.

But he still felt fucking amazing.

He gave a little growl and quickly twisted, so she was between him and the wall this time. "Yeah. It's pretty great." He kissed her long and hot.

When he finally lifted his head, her eyes were dilated again and she licked her lips. "So, I was wondering..."

He lifted a brow. "Yeah?"

"Well, I mean, after a hand job, what happens? Everyone just goes home until another time?"

Noah felt his heart thump hard. Were they talking about a sleepover here? Were they ready? Did he care? All night in Brynn's bed? He was trying to be a better guy, but he was still a selfish bastard at times and yeah...he wasn't passing that up.

"It can depend," he said. "But showers are pretty close to the top of the list."

"Oh, showers." She nodded as if really giving that some thought. "That makes sense."

He leaned in and put his mouth against her ear. "You wanna learn about shower sex, B?"

"I do," she said softly.

"Just so you know, it really works best if *you're* the one against the shower wall."

She tipped her head as he dragged his lips down the side of her neck. "Am I facing away from the wall or toward it?"

Heat slammed into him and he pulled his jeans up, scooped under her butt, and picked her up. "Yes," he answered, and started for the steps.

She giggled, wrapping her arms and legs around him. "Which do you like better?"

"Buried deep inside you," he told her honestly. "Nothing else about it really matters." He started up the stairs.

She squeezed him tightly. "I intend to make you too tired to drive home. You should stay."

He lived about three minutes away. He nodded. "I should definitely stay."

12
___

"You might have a future as a party planner." Cori bumped Brynn's hip with hers, giving her a huge grin.

Brynn looked around the pie shop and took a big contented breath. "It's going really well. *But* I'm going to leave the party planning to you and Evan." Her sister was a natural. For Brynn it wasn't about the party, it was about giving these women a place to go and relax and talk and connect with other women.

So many of them needed this. Not just Kayla. Sure, the young moms deserved a break, some time that wasn't about their jobs or their kids. But the older women with kids who were teens and young adults and more self-sufficient had just as much stress. They worried about their kids too. They worried about their husbands, their parents, their friends. It was nice for them to have a place to come and share some of that stress with people who would understand. And have a few drinks. And maybe forget about those worries for a little bit.

Brynn focused on MJ. This was not a Moms' Night Out. It was Ladies' Night Out and she was glad to see the woman here. She was sitting with a couple of other women her age, but Brynn had seen her chatting with Kayla earlier, that soft half-affectionate-half-exasperated smile on her face. Brynn didn't really know MJ's family situation. She'd never asked. But she never heard the woman talking about a husband or children. It did, however, seem that she had some friends. And she had the guy who came over and took care of her house. Brynn wanted to know more about her, but it would take time. MJ didn't share easily, like Kayla did, and Brynn wasn't a pusher. But MJ was definitely on her radar. She'd figure her out eventually.

"Well, I think this is awesome," Cori said. "And I got the little china tea sets in the mail yesterday so we can start doing some Mom-Daughter teas and birthday parties. I love that you've come up with all of this, Brynn."

Brynn shook her head. "But I didn't. I heard other people say it."

Cori lifted a brow. "You heard someone say that they wished we had little tea sets and would host teas and birthday parties?"

"No." Brynn lifted a shoulder. "I heard them say there wasn't a great place for a birthday party for her daughter who didn't want to go to the park, and that the woman thought her house was too small to host a really nice party. And, by the way, it can't be a Mother-Daughter tea. Some of the girls don't have moms. And some of them would have a grandfather who would love to bring them."

Cori gave her a look that reminded Brynn of the way MJ looked at Kayla. "Which grandfather?"

"Walter. He's the one who pays for and takes his grand-daughter to dance class. It's so sweet."

Cori shook her head. "Well, honey, I think *you're* sweet. You might have overheard the conversations, but you took what they needed and wanted and told me to order tea sets and came up with pie and liquor pairings. That's a pretty great thing."

"It will be good for business, I think," Brynn said with a nod.

Cori nudged her and gestured with her chin toward the room. "It's good for *them*."

Brynn looked around again. Everyone was smiling, including her sisters, the conversation was loud and friendly. She felt herself smile too. "I'm glad."

"I love that the least social one of us is the one turning this place into a social hub."

Brynn felt her smile spread. That was pretty cool. "If I'd known socializing could be like this, I might have tried it a long time ago," she teased.

Cori laughed. "Well, I hate to break it to you, but socializing is *not* like this just anywhere. At least, it's not the same. There's something about this town."

Brynn felt her heart squeeze at that. She nodded. She'd kind of been afraid of that.

"Oh, I've got a couple of coffee customers," Cori said, waving at the two women standing at the counter. They were the women who had been sitting with MJ. "Talk to you later. You did good."

Brynn was touched by the look of pride and affection in her sister's gaze. "Thanks. Nobody I'd rather do it with than you and Ava."

And that pang in her heart intensified. When she went back to New York, Cori would stay in Bliss and run the shop with Parker. Ava would be living in Bliss almost full-time, taking trips to New York only as needed for her position as Carmichael Enterprises' CEO. Brynn would be in New York alone.

Which had seemed like a good thing a few weeks ago. And for the past seven months. Now...she wasn't as sure.

Putting this Ladies' Night Out together with her sisters had been fun. She'd contributed on every level from the food and drinks, to the decorations and the invitations. Instead of just letting her sisters lead, she'd been a real part of it. And it had been fun. Strangely, her sisters had seemed less overwhelming when she wasn't just sitting back, observing and listening. They stopped talking and listened when she talked, and it had been fun putting it all together.

Maybe things like twice a week workouts and lunch and shopping and weekend trips would have felt less overwhelming if she'd given her input and not just let them always take the lead. Maybe she wouldn't have felt dragged along then.

Maybe being alone wasn't what she wanted so much as she wanted to just be a real part of things. And maybe she shouldn't have been waiting for them to ask her what she wanted or for her opinions. She should have been just giving them all along.

Seeing all of this come together and actually happening in front of her now gave her a thrill she'd never had before. When things came together in the lab and clinical trials went well and they got FDA approvals, she was always happy and proud. But she didn't get to actually see their products at work. This was different. It might not seem as big as the pharmaceutical work, but, it felt like it was at this moment.

With a smile and a sense of contentment she hadn't had in a while, she started for MJ who was now sitting alone, at least temporarily. "Hey, MJ." Brynn pulled out one of the chairs at the table. "How are you?"

"Great." MJ lifted a shoulder.

Brynn noticed that MJ had eaten all of her pie, but had only sipped down her drink down a little ways. "You don't like the bourbon with the pie?"

"Oh, it's good," MJ told her. "And it goes perfectly. Just like I figured."

"You're not drinking much."

"Honestly, I'm more of a beer and potato chips girl." She gave Brynn a smile. "Simple. But this is good."

"You don't seem to be having as much fun as I'd hoped," Brynn told her. She wasn't typically this direct with people. She learned things about them over time, just by listening. She didn't pry. But this was MJ. She'd fascinated Brynn from the beginning, and she had a feeling that MJ would be okay with direct.

"I'm a little...ticked off," MJ admitted. "Just some things on my mind."

"Want to talk about it?"

MJ looked up, seeming a little surprised. Heck, Brynn was a little too. "Okay," MJ said with a nod. "I'll tell you about it."

Brynn felt a flip in her stomach. She wasn't sure if it was happiness or dread. What did she know about talking like this? But she settled back in her chair. "Hit me," she said.

"Remember the guy who comes over and takes care of my house for me?"

Brynn nodded. "You call other people, they call him, and he comes instead. But the other day he couldn't make it."

"Right." MJ dragged her fork around her pie plate. "And after that, I started thinking about how it annoys the shit out of me that he does that. Not the not showing up. I was actually glad. I mean, the guy needs to do his own stuff, you know? But he's always over taking care of me."

Brynn frowned and crossed her arms over her stomach. "Why's that annoy you?"

"Because he's doing it out of a sense of obligation," MJ said. She shrugged. "It just doesn't feel as good when someone *has to* do something for you. If he just did it because he cared or because he liked me, that would be one thing."

Brynn couldn't say why, but she felt tension tightening around her spine. "He doesn't like you?"

"He used to," MJ said, almost sadly. "He was my son's best friend growing up. He was at my house a lot."

"And now?" Brynn wasn't sure why, but she steeled herself for MJ's answer.

"Jared was killed in a car accident his freshman year of college," MJ said, her voice catching. "Noah was his best friend. After Jared died, Noah took off for the Marines. When he came home, he came back determined to take care of me the way Jared would have. The way Jared asked him to."

Brynn's stomach roiled and she gripped her hands tighter. MJ's son was Jared, Noah's friend. The one he'd lost. "Jared asked him to take care of you?" Brynn asked. "You're sure?"

MJ nodded. "Noah told me the first day he showed up on my porch, banging on my front door, telling me he was home now and *he* was going to be taking care of things from then on."

Yeah, that sounded like Noah. "And you let him?"

MJ scowled and sat up straighter. "Hell, no. I took one look at that angry boy that was missing my son and feeling guilty for going off and not coming straight home and nearly bent over under the pressure of all of that and the responsibility to right all the wrongs, even though he never really could, and I told him to get the hell off my porch and not dare touch anything on my house."

Brynn felt her eyes widen. "Wow," she said softly.

MJ sighed and slumped in her chair again, her expression now sad. "It wasn't the best way to handle it, I'll admit. And I was a mess. A big mess. I just...let everything go. I didn't care about anything. And yes, when Noah first got home, he brought with him a bunch of memories of Jared and a horrible sense of loss all over again. I lost Jared, I lost Noah for four years, and then he was suddenly back, and I realized I'd stuffed a whole lot of feelings down deep. They all came roaring back seeing him again."

"But he kept coming over anyway," Brynn said. "Right? He didn't stay away?" But she knew the answer.

MJ gave a short chuckle. "No, no he didn't. He kept coming. And honestly—this sounds weird—but even feeling angry, helped. It was something other than numb." She looked up. "I'd felt numb for four years. Nothing mattered. But once Noah was back, he stirred up feelings and—" She sighed. "It was good to feel things."

"And he made a deal with the other guys in town to call him if you ever called them needing work done?" Brynn asked.

"Yeah. I don't know what he said to them exactly, but I know he gives them all discounts on their vehicle repairs in exchange."

Brynn swallowed hard. She was torn between running to Noah and hugging him tight and telling him he didn't have to try so damned hard to be a good guy and shaking him and then still telling him that he didn't have to try so damned hard to be a good guy. Either way, she really wanted to see him.

"And now you're annoyed with him for it?" Brynn asked, feeling a little annoyed herself. Though she wasn't sure if it was at Noah or MJ. Or both. Did Noah have to *insist* on taking care of MJ even if she didn't want it, just because Jared had asked him to? And damn that seemed familiar. He was taking care of her because of Rudy. Sure, she hadn't known that at first. She'd just gone along, because that's what she always did. She'd let him take care of her because it made *him* happy to do so.

Until it didn't. Her going out with other guys wasn't making him happy. Sure, they'd found a loophole. None of her dates had really been dates. At least, there had been no intention of them turning into anything more than the simple outing. But as she and Noah had gotten closer, and more intimate, it had obviously been less and less satisfying for her to be out with other people. For both of them. Rudy's wishes or not.

Yet, she knew that he would insist on date number six happening.

But she was also annoyed at MJ. Why didn't she release Noah from this feeling of responsibility? Tell him she was okay. Tell him he didn't have to keep doing something that made him unhappy. And why didn't *she* do that same thing?

"Do you think he's happy doing these things for you?" Brynn asked MJ.

"That's why I let it go for a very long time," MJ said. "I thought it would help him work through some of the stuff over losing Jared. And honestly? I wasn't leaving the house much for a long time after Jared died. But I'd leave when Noah came over because...I just thought we were reminding each other too much of him, and I felt bad that he kept doing things for me, but he wouldn't stop. So, he did help get me out of the house." She gave Brynn a rueful smile. "Leaving the house to get away from him maybe doesn't sound positive, but it probably was in that it made me actually get dressed and interact with people. And then it felt like it had all gone on *too* long to change things. I don't know if it helps him or not, but I just try to leave him alone."

Brynn caught her breath as she thought back to what Noah had said about taking care of things—like the old blue truck— sooner rather than later. That things that had been neglected for a long time were harder to put back together.

He'd been talking about MJ and their relationship as much as the truck.

Brynn's heart was aching. For both Noah and MJ. But, of course, he'd kept going to MJ's house. Just like he kept taking care of Penn even when the cat didn't seem to want him or need him. Noah was just *there*. Solid, unmoving, stubborn, but in a way that made those around him feel secure. Even if they were annoyed.

"Why are you mad at him *now*?" Brynn asked. She wasn't about to tell MJ that she'd handled it wrong or that she shouldn't have let Noah keep doing these things. She had no idea about grieving a son, or a best friend, or MJ and Noah's relationship in the past. Or what Jared had said to Noah.

And honestly? She wanted to. And it hurt a little that he hadn't shared all of that with her. He knew about her past with her dad, the awkward dinners, her weirdness, the ways Rudy had failed as a dad. He knew about her past, most painful relationship, but she didn't really know about his. Because they didn't really talk about that stuff much. It felt like they'd gotten closer to some of that. Closer to each other. But Noah wouldn't voluntarily share any of this. Because it was painful and sad. And he didn't want her to feel those things.

She frowned. That wasn't good. You couldn't have a relationship with someone if they didn't share the good *and* the bad. He couldn't spend a lifetime only giving her the good, shielding her from the bad. That would be exhausting for him. Frustrating even, because there was always some bad in life. There just was. And not only could he not save her from all of it, but he wouldn't allow *her* to help him with his bad stuff? That wouldn't be a relationship. That would be...what they'd had since they'd met.

"I'm mad because, I walked into my bathroom yesterday, and realized that I didn't need anyone doing any of this for me. Not Noah. Not the other guys. I can take care of this stuff myself. I didn't for a long time, I'll admit that. But—" She sighed. "I want to do it now. It's *good* for me to do it. I want to take it away from Noah to show him that he doesn't have to feel this obligation. I want to show him, somehow, that I'm okay."

Brynn sucked in a breath. She knew exactly what MJ was talking about. She'd just experienced it with her sisters. She'd shown them that they didn't have to always lead the way, and it had been so great. There was more to do, but it was a great start. Now she needed to do the same thing with Noah. She wanted to be happy. Now. Not in five months. And she wanted Cori, Ava, and, most especially Noah, to see it. Up close and personal.

"I s there something he could do that *would* make you happy?" she asked MJ. "That might make him happy too?" She knew how amazing it had felt the other night to just be there for Noah and make him feel good. Sure, it was physical but...no, it had been more than that. She was sure of it.

MJ looked at her for a long moment. Then she nodded. "Yeah. He could just be there. And talk to me."

Brynn sat forward in her chair. "Really? That's what you want?"

"No one knew or loved Jared as much as Noah and I did. For a long time, Noah reminded me of Jared and it hurt. But now...I'd like to remember him with someone who knew him too. I'm sure there are stories I haven't heard that Noah knows. There are stories I know that I could tell him."

Brynn nodded.

"I don't need my vanity put in," MJ said. "I can do that myself actually. I *want* to do it myself. But I can't talk about Jared with myself. And I haven't had a big guy who loves my meatloaf over for dinner in..." Her voice caught again. "In very long time."

Brynn reached out and grabbed MJ's hand. "You have to tell him."

MJ shook her head.

Brynn squeezed her hand. "Yes. You do. I know exactly what you're feeling. Noah needs to realize that people *want* him, not that they only *need* him for the things he can do." Her mind was suddenly whirling ,and she realized that she'd let Noah take care of her for too long. Had it made him happy? Yes. For a while. But following that checklist, doing Rudy's bidding, completing all of that like a work order at the shop, wasn't what he really needed. He needed to be happy. For once, he needed to put *his* happiness in front of what someone asked of him.

And she did too.

She'd let her sisters guide the way. She'd taken the path of least resistance. She'd put her head down and just gone with everything.

But now she wanted to be happy. She'd always thought she was. She'd been content. But now she'd been given a taste of what more she could have. She could be *happy*. Ecstatic. Joyful. Fulfilled. If she opened herself up. If she took a couple of chances.

"MJ, I never give people advice," Brynn said. "I stay out of things. I listen, I don't talk. But I'm going to make an exception here."

MJ gave her a small smile. "Okay."

"You need to put that vanity in yourself. And then when Noah comes over to do it, you need to invite him for meatloaf."

The other woman didn't respond for nearly a minute. Then she said, "Will you be offended if I make a pie too?"

Brynn felt her eyes stinging. "You make pie?"

"Really good pie," MJ said with a nod. "Noah loves my key lime."

"I wouldn't be offended at all," Brynn said, sniffing. "And I just won't tell Cori."

MJ laughed and squeezed her hand back. "You should consider giving advice more often."

Brynn just smiled. She didn't know about that. But she could give *herself* some more good advice.

"You said you're a beer drinker, right?" Brynn asked.

"Sure. Love it."

"Would you be willing to taste test something for me?"

MJ looked intrigued. "Of course. What are you up to?"

"Pie themed hard ciders and beer."

"Pie themed?"

Brynn couldn't help but grin. "This whole liquor and pie thing started me thinking, and now I'm experimenting with apple cider, of course, then cherry and peach too. It's actually pretty fun and—" She shrugged. "Well, I'm a science nerd. This is all basically chemistry." Jeffrey had been right about that.

"And you're doing beer too?"

Brynn nodded. "Trying it. I'm not a beer drinker so it will take some playing around. But beer takes longer than cider so I'm not sure how it's going to turn out. But if you wanted to taste the cider, I'd love to know your thoughts."

"Sure. Is it here?"

Brynn looked around. Her sisters were occupied, so she nodded. "Ava and Cori don't know I've been making it here, but I've got it stored back in the storeroom and they don't go in there much."

MJ laughed. "Bring it on."

Brynn got up, excited to be sharing this with someone other than Jeffrey. He'd given her some pointers on how to get started and then they'd brainstormed a few tweaks. But she really wanted people *here* to be in on it with her.

"I'll be right back." She could easily fill a glass and pass it off as one of the liquors or the wines they were using tonight.

She felt a flutter of butterflies as she let herself into the store room. They'd barely used this room even before Ava had connected the pie shop and the diner, and now they shared Parker's store room for the most part so it was easy for Brynn to stash her equipment and supplies in here without Ava and Cori knowing about it.

She hadn't wanted to tell her sisters in case they thought she was getting ahead of herself. Or ahead of all of them. They needed the pie shop to be running well, and turning a profit and the kitchen duties were supposed to be all Ava's. There was a good argument to be made for them focusing on the pies alone at this point. But Brynn couldn't help but feel excited about this. For one, it was a very fun application of everything she knew about chemistry and lab work. She didn't miss the lab actually, but she kind of missed the science. For another, if they could make a cider, beer, and wine that was pie themed and carried their name, it would be another income source and further their brand. And well, if nothing else, Brynn definitely saw the value for the town in turning Blissfully Baked into a bar at night. Did it seem strange to have a pie shop/bar? Maybe. But this was just extending the hours and putting their pie in a different form.

She really thought it was a good idea. In fact, she already had a name and logo in the works.

Was she getting ahead of herself? Maybe. But she'd never done that before. She'd never done anything like this before. Something creative, something a little crazy, and a little outside the box—her box anyway. She'd let Cori be the outside-the-box sister, the slightly crazy sister, the sister that didn't worry about if things made sense, but went with her gut, and her heart. Ava, too, had pushed boundaries and gone outside the box in growing Carmichael Enterprises, and Brynn knew her sister got a thrill from taking a risk and coming out on top.

Brynn, on the other hand, had just followed the path that had been laid out in front of her. She'd never done anything that wasn't someone else's idea first. Yes, Mitch had mentioned that Bliss needed a bar. But everyone knew that. And yes, Kayla had said a ladies' night would be a big hit. But Brynn had taken those comments and made them into something real.

It was what Noah did, wasn't it? People had to tell him there was a problem with their car before he fixed it. She felt a ripple of excitement and nerves go through her. What would Noah think of her plan? He was the most supportive of her being appreciated and involved. She didn't think all of that came from Rudy. Maybe before they'd met, but now, she felt like Noah really wanted her to be happy.

But what if he's not happy? Rudy told him to send you back to New York. And will it matter if he's not happy?

It would. She wanted him to be happy as much as he wanted it for her. But... Brynn took a deep breath. She was going to do this anyway. And that was a huge change for her. She was the easy one for the people around her. Her going back to New York would be easier for Noah. It would be easier for her too.

But she wasn't going to do that.

The butterflies swooped and dipped in her stomach, and she had to take another big breath. She could do this. And more, she *wanted* to do this.

She was excited about the idea of doing something for the community that was fun and would bring people together. She needed to focus on that. That *was* definitely outside of her box. As Cori had said, the least social one was suddenly the one hosting parties?

Wait until they all found out she wanted to be a bartender.

She knew that the idea of opening a bar as a community service might seem like a stretch to some, but she loved the way the pie shop would fill up and people would chat and laugh together, exchange stories, even give advice and find ways to help each other out. Yes, she'd facilitated some of that, but some of it just happened naturally too. She loved it. Being a hub, a place for people to gather, made her feel warm and... a part of something.

There was no debate that what she and her lab did was important and she would, for the rest of her life, support the lab with funding and use her last name however she could to advance the research they were doing. But she didn't want to go back to the lab.

She wanted to open a bar in a pie shop instead.

And how she felt and what she wanted mattered. It mattered the most. She needed to remember that.

She squatted in front of the shelving unit in the storeroom and leaned to reach to the back where her mason jars of cider were hidden. She grabbed the first she could touch, deciding that it didn't matter which MJ tried first. But as she was stretching back up, her eyes caught sight of the mason jars on the third shelf down.

She paused. They were the jars of pie filling their dad had made and stored here. Each jar had a hand-written label that said *apple*, *cherry*, or *peach*.

Brynn reached out and ran a finger over one of the cherry labels and felt a sudden sting in her eyes. Her dad had picked the fruit, made the pie fillings, and canned them. Right here in this kitchen. He had been a billionaire. Billion with a B. He'd had three houses. Knew CEOs and world leaders. He'd dined with politicians and princes. And then he'd come to Bliss, Kansas and started making pies. And canning his own pie filling.

"Wow," she whispered out loud as she studied his handwriting on the jars in front of her. "We finally have something in common, Dad."

In the strangest twist yet, Brynn realized that of all the people in her life, her father would have understood her wanting to make cider and beer in Bliss better than anyone.

13

"What's this?" Noah reached hesitantly for the paper bag Parker had just slid across the Carmichael triplets' dining room table. The guys were settled in for game night—sans any other dates for Brynn—while the girls got the food and drinks ready in the kitchen.

"That, my friend, is a thank-you gift," Parker said.

Noah opened the bag and peered inside. It was a jar. He pulled it out. It looked like salsa or jelly. He lifted it up and looked at Parker questioningly.

"Jalapeno, raspberry jam," Parker told him. "Homemade. Of course."

Which meant, homemade by Parker. "And...why?" Noah asked.

"It goes great on turkey sandwiches," Parker said.

Evan nodded. "It really does. Spread some cream cheese on there too. And we should definitely try it on a peanut butter sandwich."

Parker nodded. "I might glaze chicken with it. But I was really thinking a grilled brie with this as a spread would be amazing."

"Oh, let's do that."

"What the *hell* are you two talking about?" Noah broke in.

"Trying some new things," Parker said. "When you get the right blend of sweet and spicy, you kind of want it all the time, you know."

Noah stared at his friend. Was Parker making an analogy with *jam*? "So you're changing up the menu at the diner because of Ava, and somehow you're getting around to telling me that I need to change something too?" Noah asked.

"Oh, hell no," Parker said shaking his head. "You bring that stuff into my diner, and I see it, I'll confiscate it."

Noah rolled his eyes. "What if I sneak it in?"

"I fully expect you to sneak it in," Parker said. "That stuff's amazing."

"So do you have a point here, or am I going to get lucky and find out that this is really just jam and you like me enough to share it with me?"

"I told you, it's a thank-you gift," Parker said.

"For?"

"Well, since you've been sleeping over here with Brynn *every night* for the past three weeks, Ava's been at my house *every night* for the past three weeks. And I really appreciate that."

Noah couldn't help his smile at that. He had, in fact, just come down from showering upstairs after work. The past three weeks had been amazing. They'd spent the time exploring lots of sexual firsts for Brynn, but they'd also spent it getting to really know one another. They'd talked about favorite childhood memories, their grandparents, foods and movies and songs they loved and hated. He'd told her all about Jared. They'd talked more about Rudy. And they'd dated. They'd gone to two movies, a concert, and a football game. And they'd eaten dinners, one-on-one, sitting across the table from one another. Noah had made a couple of those dinners at his house, in fact. Just two nights ago, they'd eaten steaks on his back deck.

"Happy to help. And glad Ava knows Brynn's safe and sound with me."

"Well, that, and the fact that apparently the quietest of the triplets is also the loudest in bed," Parker said, giving Noah an atta-boy grin.

Noah didn't even try to deny it. Brynn was definitely gaining confidence in the bedroom and she was surprisingly, and amazingly, vocal about it.

"But I'm also trying to make a point," Parker said.

Noah's smile died and he sighed. He supposed that he deserved this. He'd given unsolicited advice to both Parker and Evan when they'd been figuring things out with their girls. But man, they'd been such dumbasses.

"So, let's hear it," Noah told him.

Parker looked at Evan, then back to Noah, and Noah knew that whatever was coming was from both of them.

"This raspberry jalapeno jam is amazing. But it's also kind of different. Not your typical mayo and mustard, you know?"

Noah lifted a brow.

"So if you start putting it on *everything*, that must mean you really love it."

Jesus. The metaphor definitely wasn't subtle. Noah motioned with his hand for Parker to keep going.

"It would be pretty hard to go back to just grape jelly without noticing the huge difference," Evan decided to add.

"I'm sure you're right," Noah said. "But maybe you just decide to go without any jam or jelly. Maybe you just resign yourself to plain peanut butter."

Both of Evan's brows went up. "You're just going to be done with... jam, entirely after this...jam, is gone?"

Noah almost smiled at Evan's attempts to stick with the analogy instead of just coming out and talking about Brynn. But he was talking about Brynn. And that eventually she was going to be gone.

He nodded. "Can't imagine anything else ever measuring up."
Was he resigning himself to a life without women? Without ever
settling down? With just making a couple of trips here and there
to New York when his craving got too strong?

Yeah. He thought maybe he was.

"You're actually telling me that you still think Brynn should
go back to New York?" Parker asked, sitting forward and finally,
thankfully, abandoning the metaphor.

Noah scowled at him. "Yes. Dammit. Nothing's changed that.
Everything is on track. She's almost done with everything in the
will and she's definitely come out of her shell, gained confidence,
learned to socialize. Hell, she even *likes* it. I've done a *hell* of a
good job here. She's in the perfect position to go back exactly the
way Rudy wanted."

Parker sighed and looked at Evan. "You try."

Evan sat forward now. "You're sleeping with her *every night*."

"Yeah. I'm very aware."

"Do you really think that's the best way to do this?"
Evan asked.

"So you're *thanking* me for being here every night, but now
you're lecturing me about it?" he asked.

"Actually, the jam was a lot more about making our point than
a thank-you gift," Parker told him.

"No kidding," Noah said dryly.

"We're concerned about Brynn," Parker said.

"I've been taking care of Brynn since she first set foot in this
town," Noah said. "You don't need to be concerned about her." In
fact, it irked him that anyone would think they needed to worry
about her. He had this. It was all good.

"But now you've changed... grape jelly...for her too," Evan
said. "Is that fair? I guess if you're okay being a miserable monk
after she leaves—though if you turn into an asshole, you can't
hang out with us anymore—that's one thing, but are you doing
her any favors?"

"I'm fucking showing her what it's like to have a great, healthy, happy relationship with someone who—" He broke off and swore.

"Someone who loves her," Evan filled in. He shook his head. "You're showing her what it's like to be with someone who's in love with her. And then you're going to take that away from her?"

Noah felt a knot in his stomach. He'd never pretended to *not* be a selfish bastard. That's all this was really. He wanted her. As much of her as he could have. So he was taking it. Every day and night that he could get. "If you find really amazing jam, but you know that eventually it's going to run out and you'll never be able to have it again, of course you're going to have it on everything," he said, turning their stupid analogy back on them. "You're going to gorge yourself and be happy that you at least got that much."

Did they really expect him to leave her alone now that he'd gotten this close to her? Yes, she was leaving. But that was even more reason to be here every damned day until that time ran out.

He told himself it wasn't all selfish though. From the start, he'd wanted to show her what it was like to be involved with a man who was with her for the right reasons, who would treat her well and appreciate her. He'd been showing her how it should be, so that she'd look for that. So she wouldn't settle. So she wouldn't get duped by some dickhead in New York who only wanted her money, or only saw her amazing, long legs. She needed to know what it felt like to be loved...so she could find it again.

"We just—"

Whatever Evan had been about to say was interrupted by the girls coming into the room. Cori and Ava carried plates of food—all fruit themed. They set down the plates of grilled fruit kabobs, chicken and beef kabobs with fruit dipping sauces, and tiny fruit tarts. Tonight, they were playing Fabled Fruit. It was technically for players ages 8 and up, but Cori had a way of making even the kids' games they played more adult. Sometimes she added extra rules. Always she added liquor.

Which was where Brynn came in. She was carrying the tray of drinks.

He caught her eye and his heart gave a stupid thump when she smiled at him.

Was he being selfish playing the full-time, serious boyfriend? Probably. But he really did want her to know what it was like to be romanced and adored so she would expect it, even demand it, in the future.

Or maybe so that when she went back to New York she'd miss him and would come back to visit often. Ava would be flying back and forth. They had a private jet after all.

Yeah, okay, he was being selfish.

But when Brynn brushed against him, setting a glass down in front of him, and he caught her scent and felt the heat from her body, he just didn't care. She was his for now. For as long as they could make it work. And if he had to eventually let her go, then he'd do it knowing that he'd shown her what it was like to be in the spotlight of at least one guy's life and how great that felt.

That thought made him freeze in reaching for his glass.

Rudy had wanted her to be in the spotlight. He'd said those very words. He'd wanted her to be the center of attention for a change. It seemed that she was more comfortable in the midst of everyone and everything at the pie shop now. She didn't shy away from attention now. She didn't come seeking refuge from it all in the garage every single day now. But no matter what else she was feeling or how else she'd grown, Noah could honestly say he'd done at least part of what Rudy had wanted. He'd made her the center of *his* attention.

"Damn, what is this?" Parker asked, peering into the glass Brynn had set in front of him.

"You like it?" Brynn asked. The glasses on her tray had all been distributed and she was holding one, standing at the end of the table.

"I do."

ERIN NICHOLAS

"It's cherry cider," she said. "Actually, it's hard cider." She glanced around the table. "I made it."

She looked a little excited and a little nervous. Noah frowned, not sure why he felt a niggle of trepidation, but sensing that something was going on. He picked up his glass and took a sip.

"That's a beer."

He looked up at her as he swallowed. "Yeah." He couldn't help but notice the flavors on his tongue. There was the familiar malt taste, but there was also some apple, a hint of cinnamon, and it had a creamier taste than his typical ales. "It's good."

"I made that too."

He felt his eyebrows rise. "You *made* this beer?"

She nodded, her smile growing. "It's apple pie beer. Did you get the hint of nutmeg?"

"Apple pie beer? Hard cherry cider? What's going on?" he asked.

"This is peach, right?" Cori asked Brynn, holding her glass up to the light.

Brynn grinned. "It is. I've got a peach cider and a peach pie beer."

Noah frowned, setting his glass down. "What are you talking about?"

She shrugged, but she was almost bouncing on the balls of her feet now. "I've been playing around after I was tasting beers for Ladies' Night. I started reading up on everything, and my friend Jeffrey and I were talking about the process of making beer and ciders and wine. It's all basically just chemistry."

Jeffrey. Her buddy in New York. Another brilliant genius scientist. Noah didn't like Jeffrey. He'd never met him, of course, but he didn't like him. Jeffrey had a ton in common with Brynn. He was probably the first guy she should date when she went back to the city and her lab.

Yeah, he didn't like Jeffrey at all.

Cori laughed. "Well, chemistry is definitely your forte."

Brynn nodded. "I was thinking about it all when we were at the river and people were talking about how Bliss really needed a bar. And then we had the ladies' night and it was so successful. Everyone loved the pairings and even the pie themed drinks. So... I thought..." She trailed off, suddenly looking nervous. She reached under one of the placemats at the table and pulled out a sheet of paper. She looked at it, took a deep breath, then set it in the middle of the table. "I was thinking that we could expand our business. Pie themed ciders and beer. The *brewed* could also apply to the coffee drinks we make."

Everyone around the table leaned in simultaneously. They stared at the paper. Ava was the one to finally reach for it.

"Blissfully Baked and Brewed?" she asked, looking up at Brynn. "You want to turn the pie shop into a bar?"

The sheet of paper was emblazoned with a new logo. Or really just a logo, since the pie shop under Rudy's direction hadn't had anything official like that. In fact, most of the businesses in Bliss didn't have a logo. Some of them, like Parker's diner was just "the diner". It was probably legally called something, but Noah wouldn't have been surprised to find that it was something basic like "the Bliss Diner". And his own shop was simply JN Motors, for Jared and Noah. They just didn't get fancy around here.

But then again, they were talking about the Carmichael triplets here.

"Well, it would still be a pie shop too," Brynn said. "Say until 4 or 5 p.m. Or maybe just after Parker closes at six. Then we'd switch over to a bar. People could come in for dessert and wine after community events. They could come in for a beer after work. We could do a regular ladies' night. And," she continued, "we could also maybe distribute our ciders and beer. Jeffrey has a friend who runs a microbrewery that is willing to sit down and talk with me. We'll need capital, of course, so we'll have to wait until our profit margin is a lot bigger and we have some extra money to play with, but it will be a fun way to brand our business and expand."

"How about frozen pies and canned pie filling?" Parker asked. He looked at Ava. "I know you've been thinking about that stuff too."

Ava just gave him a little shrug. Parker rolled his eyes.

Brynn looked like she didn't know if she should take him seriously or not. But she lifted her chin. "Yeah, maybe all of that too. Why not? There are lots of ways to extend the pie business and brand of Blissfully Baked and Brewed."

Noah felt his gut knotting. He should be getting used to feeling torn right down the middle, but he still couldn't believe how one half of him loved seeing her excited and how the other half only felt anxious. This didn't sound like something she was planning to dabble in temporarily. And that was going to be trouble.

Evan was nodding. "You might get to the point of needing to hire some more people. That would be really good for the town. Rudy would have loved that."

Brynn's smile brightened and Noah felt his heart expand. Damn, he loved that look of excitement and happiness on her.

Then a thought occurred to him. "You'd be setting up a facility to make the ciders and beer here in Bliss?" he asked.

She turned her full attention on him. "Yeah. I mean, maybe. I hope so. If we get big enough. But for now, I can easily keep doing it in the kitchen at the shop. I've been doing it in there anyway. There's plenty of space in there for a little while."

"You've been doing this in the pie shop kitchen?" Cori asked. She looked at Ava. "How did we not notice this?"

Ava shook her head. "I've been going over to Parker's side to help with clean up and next day prep so I'm not in the pie shop after three."

"And doing God knows what in Parker's kitchen," Evan said. "I try not to think about it when I'm eating over there."

"Feel free to take your business elsewhere," Parker told him.

He said that often. And it was an empty offer. There was nowhere else to go. Even if Parker's food wasn't outstanding—which it was—and Parker wasn't one of Evan's best friends—which he was.

"I guess she's been sneaking behind our backs," Ava said, watching Brynn.

Yeah, that was kind of Noah's thoughts. Why hadn't she mentioned any of this to them? To him?

Brynn laughed. "You're both completely distracted by being in love. I could be raising a baby elephant in that kitchen and you wouldn't notice a thing as long as I get you talking about Parker and Evan."

The guys gave each other cocky grins, and Ava and Cori said nothing to dispute Brynn's statement.

But they were getting off on a tangent. Away from the subject of Brynn making hard ciders and brewing beer in the pie shop and wanting to turn it into a bar.

"You really think this is a good idea?" Noah asked. His tone was short and he didn't mean it to be. But he wasn't feeling good about all of this.

"Well it would require expanding our hours, which means more staff," Ava, ever the businesswoman—and not the woman Noah had been talking to—said. "That or we stagger when we're all at the shop. Which could work, but we all already have stuff we need to be doing."

"I could easily work later a night or two a week," Cori said.

"You could?" Evan gave her a wide-eyed look.

She laughed. "I could. You could work with me. We could mess up the kitchen in the pie shop like Ava and Parker mess his kitchen up."

"Well, when you put it that way..." Evan wiggled his brows.

"I could work a night, I guess," Ava said, shooting Parker a look. "But Parker gets up too early as it is."

"I'm fine, Boss," Parker said. "We'll do whatever we have to do to make it work."

Noah gritted his teeth. They were already to the "whatever we have to do" stage? Brynn had *just* brought the idea up.

Ava shook her head. "You can't work until one in the morning—"

"Two," Evan broke in.

"Two what?" Ava asked.

"The bar can sell alcohol until two."

Ava nodded and looked at Parker. "Yeah, you're not doing that."

"Well, we could hire someone," Cori said. "Profits are up and this would be bringing in more money. We could afford someone I think. At least some of the time."

"Yeah," Ava agreed. "We'll probably have to."

"So we'll need glassware," Parker said. He reached for the pad of paper that they were going to use for keeping score and started a list. "And we'll have to—"

Suddenly a shrill whistle split the air.

Everyone pivoted toward Brynn. She was still standing at the head of the table, now with her arms crossed. "Excuse me. But I believe this whole thing was *my* idea," she said.

"Oh, it was. And I think it's great," Ava said.

Brynn shook her head. "What I mean is, *I* will be running the bar part of the business. I appreciate your offers to help, but you all have plenty to do. *I* will be taking care of the bar. I will be the one ordering glasses and doing any hiring that needs done."

Ava's brow creased but she nodded. "That's great. You can definitely get it kicked off and going before you leave. But we'll need a long-term plan."

Brynn blew out a breath and dropped her arms. "*I* am the long-term plan. *This* is the long-term plan. We keep going with the pie shop, Cori takes it over with Parker, and we add the bar. That I will manage."

Cori frowned and turned more fully on her chair. "You are the long-term plan? You mean, you want to stay in Bliss? And be a bartender?"

"I want to stay in Bliss and be a business owner and provide a service to this community and do something that's fun and different and..." She paused, then nodded. "Yeah, I want to be a bartender."

"But," Ava started, looking surprised. "You're a research scientist. You work in a pharmaceutical research lab. You...make drugs." She looked at Cori and Parker as if for help. They evidently had none to give. Ava looked at Brynn again. "Why do you want to be a bartender?"

"Because I like it here. And I like making beer." Brynn shrugged. "I know it sounds strange, but it's no weirder than our billionaire father leaving New York to come to Kansas and make pies."

"Okay," Cori acknowledged. "But..." She stopped and looked at Evan. "I've got nothing. She's right. It's weird but, then again, maybe it's not."

Noah ran a hand over his face. He had no idea what to do or say here, really. He should have seen this coming. He probably had. Brynn wanted to stay in Bliss because it was now her safe place. She'd come out of the shadows a little, had found that it wasn't so bad, and now felt comfortable here. And her sisters were here. And, yeah, he was part of it too. As Evan and Parker had *just* pointed out. He'd been playing long-term, committed boyfriend. And she was starting to feel long-term about Bliss.

"But you...*save lives*," Ava finally said. "The work you do is hugely important."

"The work the lab does is hugely important," Brynn agreed. "But I hardly need to be the one doing it. They've been doing fine without me."

"But your talents, your brain, I mean...you have to do something meaningful with all of that," Ava said. She looked at Cori. "Right?"

Cori shrugged. "I don't know, Boss," she said, using Parker's nickname for Ava with a touch of sarcasm. "You're a big tough CEO who runs the company that owns the lab that makes those medications. And yet, you're here, waitressing in Parker's diner."

Ava opened her mouth, then shut it. Then opened it again. "But other people can take care of the company too. And I still oversee what I need to."

Cori nodded. "Exactly. No one knows Carmichael or has the experience with the company that you do, and yet someone else *is* able to run it. And do it well. It's the same for Brynn."

Cori gave her sister a smile and Noah felt frustration settle in. So he was going to be the one to tell Brynn she couldn't stay, and he wouldn't even have the backup of her sisters.

"Brynn is brilliant and dedicated, but that doesn't mean she can only do one thing with her talents. She doesn't have to be the one overseeing the lab. And I think meaningful things can happen anywhere," Cori said. "Definitely here in Bliss."

Brynn's expression softened at that and Noah felt a breath lodge in his lungs.

Ava took a deep breath. "Yeah, you're right. Being a part of this town has been meaningful to all of us."

Brynn's mouth curled into a smile, and Noah felt his heart try to flip behind the band that was constricting his chest.

"The lab's work has to continue," Brynn said. "But Jeffrey can definitely take over. And this bar will be like the pie shop and the diner—a place for people to gather and interact and be welcomed. That's no small thing. I think that's meaningful."

Dammit. Noah couldn't avoid the thought. She was right. He fixed cars. That seemed like a pretty basic, not-life-changing thing. But he knew that it meant a lot to the person he was fixing it for. Fixing a carburetor was nothing for him, but having a car that would get them to their grandmother's birthday party or to a big job interview or to their son's baseball game reliably meant the world to the car's owner.

Running a bar might not seem like something that was on par with developing new medications, but medicine couldn't heal everything. Friendship, laughter, and a feeling of community could fix a lot of pains.

Noah shoved a hand through his hair. Brynn, the quiet, shy, let-everyone-else-have-center-stage, was going to start a bar in Bliss and become a bartender.

Yeah, he hadn't seen that coming.

And it was partly his fault. Or maybe mostly his fault. He'd wanted her to get to know people and open up a little. He just hadn't expected her to be so good at it.

"You're right," Ava finally said. "My choice to be a waitress and dishwasher in a diner is a pretty big leap from my regular life and yeah, it's meaningful. To me anyway."

"To me too, Boss," Parker said, his voice low.

Ava gave him a smile that punched Noah in the gut. *That* look, that one right there, was what every man ultimately wanted from the woman he loved.

Cori nodded. "I get it too. Right now, I'm pretty much pouring coffee and making lattes and I'll fight anyone who tells me it's not meaningful."

That was really nice. And that really sucked. Noah was going to have no backup at all. He was going to be the sole voice urging Brynn to go back to New York. And she wasn't going to buy it. He'd never seen Brynn stand up for herself like this. He knew that she rarely, if ever, argued with her sisters. And there was no way he was going to pull her back now.

Noah shoved his chair back and stood. "I'm going to get going."

Brynn looked like he'd just slapped her. "What? You're leaving?"

"Yeah." He nodded and swallowed. "Some stuff I have to do."

Like start trying to get over you. Like start figuring out how in the hell I'm going to live in the same town with you and not be with you.

"But..." She clearly was at a total loss for words.

"I'll...see you." He avoided looking at Evan and Parker as he turned to leave the room, knowing exactly what he'd see on their faces. That he was an ass. And an idiot. And that it was all his fault he'd let it go this far.

He'd known that he couldn't have her. Couldn't really *have* her, and yet he'd gone ahead and fallen for her anyway. Worse, he'd let her fall for him. He knew she had. Or that she thought she had anyway. And he hadn't done one thing to try and stop it or dissuade her.

He yanked the front door open and stomped down the steps, digging in his pocket for his keys.

"Noah!"

Of course she'd come after him. He'd known she would. And he whirled on her as she came down the porch steps, his emotions swirling in his chest. "I told you, from day one, that the plan was for you to go back to New York," he told her. "You knew that. I never changed my mind on that."

She stopped at the end of the walk and planted her hands on her hips. For a moment, Noah was distracted by how great she looked when she was a little defiant. She never looked like that.

Until now. Until the plan was *almost* complete. Until he'd *almost* done everything right. Of course.

"Well, that was my plan too. But I changed my mind," she told him. "I want to stay."

"And that's not about me at all?"

"Of course it's partly about you. *Partly.* But it's mostly about me." She lifted her chin. "And that's not only okay, it's also good."

"So what I think doesn't matter? The plan doesn't matter? You've been convinced that your dad was right about a lot of things—bringing you here, you and your sisters working together, the pie shop—but now suddenly you don't care about the rest of it?"

"My dad wanted me to go back to New York happier and more confident, right?" Brynn asked.

"Right."

"Don't you think the *happier* and *more confident* part of that is most important?"

It was. Of course it was. "But you moving your whole life to Bliss is kind of a big deal."

"It is." She pressed her lips together. "I was kind of hoping that you would think it was a *good* big deal."

"Yeah, well, it doesn't matter what I think."

She took a step forward. "That's not true."

"It clearly is. But worse, it doesn't matter what your dad thinks. Anymore."

Brynn tipped her head, looking concerned. "I'm not sure that's ever mattered to me as much as it does to you."

"He's been *right*," Noah said, his voice gruff suddenly. He cleared his throat. "He's been right. Bringing you all here was the right move. Wanting you to come out of your shell. Having you go on those six dates. All of that was *right*."

"Do you really think we did that the way he intended for us to?" she asked.

"Even if not, it worked out. Dating, socializing, interacting—it all showed you that you're *good* at that. That you even like it. And we wouldn't have done any of it if he hadn't mandated it."

She wet her lips and nodded. "Okay, I'll give you that."

"So you also have to admit that he made some good calls. And that New York could be one of those."

Brynn crossed her arms. "Fine. He's been right about some things. But he didn't really *know* me, Noah. He didn't know all the things I want and need. You know he wasn't that attentive."

"You and your sisters all have to admit that he knew more than you thought he did."

"He did," she conceded. "And he would be happy we were together, wouldn't he?"

Noah's heart sank to his toes and he shook his head. "No. That's the thing, Brynn. Of all the things he wanted for you, the very specific things he laid out, I wasn't one of them." Noah felt like his gut was never going to unclench, like he was never going to be able to take a deep breath again.

She frowned. "What are you talking about? He loved you."

"He did. And he knew me well. And he loved you. And he had several very specific ideas about what you needed and what he wanted for you." He tucked his hands into his front pockets. "And I wasn't one of those things."

Brynn's lips parted and her arms dropped. But she didn't say anything.

"He was very specific about you dating six guys. For whatever reason. And that they be from Bliss. And hell, everything else about your time here. If he wanted me to be a part of it, he would have said that."

"He didn't say that Cori should be with Evan or that Ava should be with Parker either," Brynn said, her voice soft.

"No. But he wasn't worried about them. Not the way he was about you," Noah said. "Yeah, he wanted them to handle their relationships differently, but he wasn't *worried* about them. He didn't ask anyone to look out for them. But he wanted *me* to take care of *you*. And he never once suggested that I should be one of the six."

Brynn looked at him for a long moment. Not saying anything. Pressing her lips together. Thinking about what he'd just said.

Finally, she said, "And you think, because he was right about so many of the things he mandated, that he's right about the things he *didn't* mandate?" she asked.

He lifted a shoulder. "I can't *not* think about that, Brynn."

She took a deep breath. "And what's that all got to do with New York?"

"That he was right about you going back too."

"I want Bliss," she said, a stubborn set to her jaw.

"Or are you just feeling confident and spreading your wings? Because I get that. You've felt the thrill of finally standing up and putting your foot down. I get that too. But eventually you'll want the familiar and comfortable, right? Because this stubborn, feisty side isn't really you."

She looked completely offended. Which was great. If he pissed her off, she'd stop looking like she felt sorry for him.

"You mean, you want to keep me in the shop, on the truck, where you know I'm fine."

Those were the good old days. "Yes," he said solemnly.

"I can be good like this."

"What if you're not?"

"You mean, what if I stay and then end up regretting it?"

He nodded. "I've been torn, practically in half, the entire you've been here. Half of me wants you to stay and be incredibly happy and loves the idea that Bliss can be everything you want and need. The other half..." He blew out a breath and shook his head. "The other half of me is completely scared that you might stay and Bliss *won't* be that. That this town, my town, can't be enough."

"So you want me to go back to New York because there's no risk there."

"There's definitely less risk there. It's what you know."

"Which means, you want me to just go along with what my father wanted."

"Yes. And I want to actually do what he asked *me* to do. You've always followed what other people thought you should do, why do you have to change it *now*?"

She flinched. She actually flinched. And so did he. Noah wasn't sure he'd ever felt like a bigger asshole in his life. He sucked in a breath.

She'd changed because of him. In part, anyway. All the

dating, all the getting to know people, all the *Bliss*. That's what had changed her.

"I just want you to be happy."

"If I'm with you, I will be happy."

"We don't know that."

"Because my father—who never made me happy himself—didn't say you would make me happy?"

Noah frowned and steeled himself. "Yes."

Brynn seemed to realize they were at an impasse. And she wasn't a fighter. Not really. She drew herself straight. "So if I stay, we won't be together."

His entire body went taut and he felt sick. "Right."

"Okay." She nodded. "But you need to know that I know the truth."

"The truth?"

"That it's not because you don't think you can make me happy. It's because it would make *you* happy, and you have never felt like your own happiness is important. Everyone around you gets to be happy first. Even dead guys."

He sucked in a breath. He'd hurt her, he knew that. And she had the right to lash out. But damn.

"Brynn—"

She held up a hand. "Unless you're going to say you're sorry and you love me and you want to be with me, there's nothing else I want to hear."

She paused, as if giving him a chance to say any one of those things. Then she gave him a nod, turned on her heel, and went back inside.

And Noah watched her go, ironically appreciating the fact that sweet, shy, never-rattle-a-cage Brynn Carmichael had, more or less, in her own way, just told him to fuck off.

He was glad she'd learned to do that.

Even if he had to be the first one she practiced on.

14

Brynn stepped into the dining room, adrenaline coursing. Had she really just told Noah to not talk to her unless he was going to apologize and tell her he loved her? What kind of gauntlet was that to throw down? And what did she do now that he hadn't picked it up? All of her inexperience in dating absolutely included fighting with a boyfriend. She didn't know what to expect next.

"What happens when you've had a fight with the guy you're in love with and you kind of just broke up?" she asked her sisters.

They both stared at her for a moment before Cori seemed to kind of shake herself and said, "Ice cream or liquor."

Brynn appreciated them not asking what exactly they'd fought about. Because she wasn't completely sure she could explain it. Noah did want her to be happy. He wanted everyone around him to be happy. And he was now having to choose between two people he cared about being happy. Her and Rudy.

And she wasn't quite important enough to be picked outright.

"Or ice cream *and* liquor," Ava said. She looked concerned. "Seriously."

Ice cream and liquor. Huh. Okay. She could go with that. At

least part of that. An idea started to form quickly. "Liquor it is." She pulled out her phone and began sending texts. To all the men she'd dated over the past few weeks. *Blissfully Baked and Brewed is OPEN tonight! Bring your friends!*

"You guys coming?" she asked, looking up.

"To wh—" But Cori broke off as her phone pinged with a text. Evan's, Parker's, and Ava's did as well.

"We're opening the bar tonight?" Cori asked, grinning at Brynn.

"That's where the best drinks in town are," she said.

Then she headed to the kitchen to gather up the beer and cider she'd brought home from the pie shop.

Twenty minutes later, she was pouring drinks from the behind the counter of the pie shop.

All of the guys were there with friends, brothers, even new girlfriends, and already a few people had walked in when they'd seen the cars in front and the lights on.

"Brynn."

She looked up from setting glasses on a tray. And she smiled. "Hi, Mitch."

"This is..." He looked around. "Interesting."

She nodded as she placed the last two glasses on the tray and motioned to Cori who was playing waitress, and of course loving every bit of it. "Thanks." She wiped her hands on her apron. "What can I get you?" Then she grinned. "I love saying that. Isn't that stupid?"

"I think it's amazing."

"You do?"

Mitch gave her a smile. "I do. You're beautiful when you're here, helping people, watching them have a good time."

Brynn just looked at him. Mitch saw it. Why couldn't Noah? She tucked her hair behind her ear and shook her head. "Dammit."

"Dammit?" He arched a brow.

"That's really sweet."

He nodded. "I mean it."

"I know you do. That makes this even worse."

"Worse?"

"Why can't *you* give me butterflies? Full-on, real butterflies?"

He took that in. Then sighed. "Not even one little one?"

She'd actually felt more attraction to Mitch than she had any of the other guys she'd "dated". Mitch had given her attention that wasn't Noah-directed, had made her feel he was truly interested, that he wanted to get to know her, regardless of the will. His flirting had been new and fun and a little exciting, if also a bit confusing. Mitch had shown her that even guys who weren't doing Noah a favor could be interested in her. And yet...he wasn't Noah. No matter what he had going for him, there was that simple truth that kept the butterflies quiet.

She shook her head. "I wish."

"Well, then, I agree with the dammit." He tucked a hand into his pocket.

He really was good-looking. But, clearly, that wasn't enough. Dammit, indeed.

"So any chance you'll let me be date number five then?" he asked.

She laughed. "You've been keeping track?"

"Of course."

"Right. And you'd want to do that even knowing about the no-butterflies thing?"

He shrugged. "I'd still like to buy you flowers and make you laugh for one night."

"Argh!" Brynn groaned. "*Seriously*. Why can't it be you?"

Mitch laughed. He set down a ten dollar bill and took one of the glasses from her tray. He held it up and waited.

She picked up a glass and clinked it against his.

"To date number five."

"To date number five."

They both drank and then smiled at one another.

Then she shook her head. "I'm sorry. I really am."

"I know." He gave her a smile. "And I'm not promising to stop flirting when I see you."

"Thanks," she said. "I actually think I might need that once in a while."

"Yeah?"

She nodded. "How do you feel about me stopping in to see you just for the flirting?"

"Kind of like a flirting booty call? Friends with flirting?" Mitch asked. He laughed. "I could go for that. Until, of course, I find Miss The One."

"Of course." Brynn felt a warmth in her chest. She didn't care what her dad and Noah thought. Staying in Bliss was the right thing to do.

Except, she thought a second later, she *did* care what Noah thought.

The door to the shop opened and she looked over, hoping that maybe it would be him. She was mad at him. He'd hurt her. He was being stubborn and ridiculous. He was keeping himself from being happy. But she still wanted to see him.

She still wanted him. Period.

But it wasn't Noah.

It was Hank. And Don Trimbull, the town cop.

"I'll, um, let you go," Mitch said, also looking at their mayor and cop. "Let me know if you need bail money."

That made her pause. "You'd really give me bail money, wouldn't you?" she said. "Even after saying no to more than date five."

Mitch looked at her like that was a silly thing to say. "Of course, I would."

She took a deep breath. Yeah, this was where she wanted to be.

She stepped out from behind the counter and met Hank and

Don halfway across the shop where Ava and Cori were already talking with them. "What's up?"

"We don't have a liquor license," Ava said. "We have to shut things down or we could face big fines."

"Hey, I don't want to do this," Don said. "Just have everyone go home. Make sure anyone who needs a ride has one. And then get your paperwork together before you do this again."

Brynn looked around the room. People were drinking, yes, but they were also talking and laughing and relaxing. This was night one and it was already exactly what she'd pictured. She wasn't shutting it down, and she wasn't waiting to open up after some stupid paperwork was done. This bar, *her* bar, was now open. For good.

"But you only need a license if you're *selling* liquor," she said. "Right, Don?"

"You're *not* selling liquor?" He looked, understandably, skeptical.

"I'm not." She hadn't collected even a dollar so far. "This is all beer and cider I've made. Or wine and stuff we already had. It's all our personal stuff. And we've haven't charged anyone anything."

Don looked around. "So it's really just a party?"

"Exactly," Brynn said. "Just a celebration."

"What are you celebrating?"

"Brynn's decided to stay in Bliss even after our year is up," Cori said, looping an arm around Brynn's waist.

"Yep. We're all going to be here for good," Ava said, putting her arm around Brynn's shoulders.

Don paused, then took a breath. "Well, God help us," he said. Then grinned. "Okay, keep the noise level down and make sure everyone gets home safe."

"Of course," Brynn assured him.

"Have a good night." And he headed out.

But Hank stuck around.

"So, Mr. Mayor, you going to stay and keep an eye on us?" Cori asked.

"Actually," Brynn said, extricating herself from her sisters and stepping forward to loop her arm through Hank's. "Hank is here to be my date. My sixth date."

Hank looked mildly surprised, but he nodded. "Best offer I've had in a long time."

And she could really use his advice. Next to Evan and Parker — who were pissed at Noah—and her father—who was, obviously, not available—she guessed Hank would be the next person in Bliss to have some insight into Noah and what was going through his head.

But she didn't need to know what Noah was thinking. She needed to know what *Rudy* had been thinking. And Hank was the best one to ask.

"Okay, well you two have fun," Cori said to them.

"And be a doll and bring us a couple of ciders," Brynn told her over her shoulder as she led Hank to a table.

Cori rolled her eyes and Brynn grinned. She kind of saw why Ava liked being the boss.

And then it hit her. She was the boss here. She was going to be running the bar. She was going to be in charge, taking the lead, the face of the business. And she felt what could have been panic at that. But Hank pulled out a chair for her and she slid into it, took a deep breath, and looked around again.

She wanted this. It was unexpected. It was a risk. Not necessarily financially. It was the only bar in town, for one thing. For another, she was still a billionaire. She could run a nonprofit bar if she wanted to. But it was a risk to her comfort, what was familiar to her, to who she thought she was. At least, who she'd been before coming to Bliss.

And she was ready.

"I'm...amazed," Hank said, taking in the shop around them and then picking up the glass of hard apple cider Cori had set down. He sipped. Then nodded with a sound of approval. "Nice."

Brynn smiled. "I'm guessing Rudy wouldn't have expected this."

Hank set his glass down. "I wondered when we were going to talk."

Brynn arched a brow. "You knew I'd want to talk?"

"Eventually."

"But I always go along with everything," she said. She knew he could hear the note of bitterness in her voice. "If my dad told you all about me, surely you couldn't have expected that I'd veer off the path and go against the plan."

Hank folded his hands on top of the table and leaned in. "Maybe not *expected*, but *hoped*, Brynn."

She looked up. "You hoped that I'd finally learn to go against the grain?"

"Not me. Your dad."

Brynn felt a little wave of shock go through her. "My dad *hoped* I'd go against the grain?"

Hank nodded. "He'd hoped that you'd find something in Bliss, or maybe just Bliss itself, worth doing that. You've never had something that really tempted you to go against the status quo."

She started to respond, but then sat quietly. That was true. She hadn't thought about quitting the lab because she hadn't had anything that mattered more, that made her feel...more...than it did. She'd been dedicated to the lab and the work. It had been easy to feel like it was worth committing to. Because it was. Until something else, something *more*, came along.

"He knew that?" she asked Hank.

"He did." Hank took a breath. "He also knew that *he* was never enough to make you want to...try, I guess," he said, finishing with a shrug. "It was easier for you to keep the walls up between you because he didn't make getting closer to him worth trying to tear them down."

She frowned. "He never tried either."

"No." Hank shook his head. "I know he didn't."

She breathed deeply. "He wanted me to go back to New York. After everything he found here, after all the happiness he felt here, he told Noah that he wanted me to go back. He didn't say that about Cori or Ava."

That was what had been bugging her about what Rudy had said to Noah. Why would Rudy specifically say that he wanted *her* to go back to the city? As Noah had pointed out, Rudy had been very particular about the things he'd laid out as instructions. All of them had reasons. Why would he feel the need to push her back to New York?

Hank reached out and took her hand. "If your dad wanted you to go back to New York for sure, no questions, he would have put it in the trust. He wouldn't have just told Noah."

That was a good point. "So why'd he do it?"

"What did he say to Noah exactly?"

"That he wanted Noah to send me back to New York happier and more confident."

Hank nodded. "Do you feel happier and more confident?"

"I do."

"Then go back to New York."

"But...I don't want to be in New York."

Hank smiled and squeezed her hand. "It says you need to go back, not that you have to *stay*."

And suddenly, it all made sense.

She had to go back, with the option of staying in New York, of the easier path, or coming back to Bliss. She had a choice. There was a path laid out for her, if she wanted that. But if she really was happier and more confident, then she could choose another path. One that she could make her own.

"I have to help Noah understand this," she said, squeezing Hank back. "He has to understand that Rudy didn't mean for me to follow any certain path. And that's why he didn't pick any guys out for me. Including Noah. That all has to be *my* choice."

Hank nodded, but he was clearly hesitating.

"What?" Brynn asked.

"Noah needs to make a choice too, Brynn," he said gently. "Noah is self-sacrificing to a fault. Rudy knew that. He knew Noah would take great care of you, but Rudy couldn't tell him that he wanted you to end up together because Noah would have just...done it. He would have been with you because Rudy wanted it. But he should make a choice too. He should decide what *he* wants, what makes *him* happy."

Brynn felt her heart tightening in her chest. Hank was right. Rudy was right. But... "Will he do that?" she asked softly, scared of the answer.

"Well," Hank said, not nearly as confidently as Brynn would have liked. "He's never been in love before, so I think there's hope in that."

Yeah. Maybe. But, Brynn realized, that Noah's choice wasn't between *her* happiness and Rudy's happiness.

It was between what he thought would make Rudy happy and what would make *Noah* happy. And Noah never worried about his own happiness.

———

"Alex, it's Noah. Hey, did you guys put the new vanity in at Maggie's place?"

"No, man, we just got the toilet done."

"So you only came over that one Sunday?" Noah clarified. He'd hated calling them in to bail him out, but he'd had to prepare for the river party and, well, Maggie needed her bathroom done. It had killed him a little to not be the one doing the work, but he'd chosen to do what he needed to do for Brynn instead.

"Yep. Just the one time. Why?"

"Because I'm staring at a brand new vanity in her bathroom," Noah said. "And I didn't put it in."

"Huh."

Huh? That was all Alex had to offer? "You didn't hear from anyone else? No one said anything about doing it? Maybe someone on your crew?"

"Nope. Nobody's said anything."

"Can you ask around?" Noah asked, gripping his phone tightly.

He realized he was overreacting to the situation, but he'd kept all of his other emotions under a tight lid since he'd let Brynn walk away three nights ago. Something was going to have to give. And it might be his cell phone. Or this fucking brand-new vanity in Maggie's bathroom.

"Sure thing," Alex agreed. "I'll let you know."

"Thanks." Noah disconnected. What the hell? Maggie had called somebody else and they hadn't told him. There was no one in Bliss or for at least a twenty-mile radius that didn't know the rule about calling Noah when they heard from Maggie. And she knew it. He was sure she did. It was a weird balance but it worked. Kind of. They both got what they needed anyway—he got to take care of her and she got stuff done. For free even.

He turned on the faucet. Which worked perfectly. He looked underneath the sink. Everything was hooked up correctly. He wiggled the vanity. It was solid. Well...fuck.

She must have called someone farther out. Which meant he was going to have to do some digging to find out who it was and make a deal with them too. It meant more discounted work on his part in exchange for them letting him know when Maggie called. And more people thinking he was a little crazy.

He slapped the countertop and then pulled his phone out. He could start with the contractors over in Gerrison, he supposed.

But before he could dial anything, he heard someone behind him.

He swung around. And came face-to-face with Maggie. For the first time in well over a year. Probably more like two.

"I put the vanity in myself," she said.

Of all the things he'd thought she might say to him, that wasn't even on the list of remote possibilities. He glanced back at the vanity, stupidly. "*You* did it?"

She propped her shoulder against the doorjamb to the bathroom and crossed her arms. "I did. I know how to do a lot of things. Jared taught me a lot."

Noah felt like she'd reached in and sucked all the air out of his lungs. They hadn't spoken in so long that it seemed almost surreal now. And they hadn't said Jared's name to one another in nearly six years.

Long, heavy seconds ticked by between them and finally Noah forced himself to speak. "I wanted to do it for you."

"I know."

He blew out a breath and tucked his hands in his back pockets. "But you did it anyway."

"Yes. Because I don't want you doing this stuff for me."

On top of losing Brynn—okay, pushing Brynn away—Noah felt the pain of that more acutely than he probably would have otherwise. She'd always felt this way. This wasn't new. But hearing it out loud, now, sucked.

"Maggie, Jared asked—"

"This isn't what he meant," Maggie broke in.

Noah stopped, a knot in his gut. "What do you mean?"

"Jared asked you to take care of me," she said. "If he was ever not here to do it himself."

Noah nodded. The plan had always been for Jared to come home, run the garage, and take care of his mom. "Right."

"But he taught me to do stuff like mow the lawn and air up my tires and—" She gestured toward the vanity. "—lots of stuff. That's not the kind of taking care I needed."

Noah frowned. "But you weren't taking care of yourself, or the house, when I got back."

She leveled him with a look. "And you think that's because I didn't know *how* to mow the lawn?" She shook her head. "It was because I didn't care. I didn't have anyone coming home. I didn't have anyone but myself to keep the house clean for."

He shifted his weight and looked at the floor. He felt like shit about running off to the Marines the way he had and not being here. "You have friends." He looked up. "Right?" *Please God, say yes.*

Maggie was his friend's mom. Noah had come over here to camp out in their backyard and to eat cookies after school and to play catch with the football and to play video games. He'd made out with his first girlfriend in Maggie's basement. He'd tried spinach for the first time at her dinner table. He'd slept on her bedroom floor with Jared after they'd stupidly watched horror movies after dark. She was someone who'd always made him smile, who said that she was proud of him, who he liked. But he'd never given much thought to Maggie as a person. She and the house and the yard were all part of one big...*impression* on his life. He came here to be a guy. In a house full of women—women he'd been put in charge of taking care of—he came to Jared's to just be a guy who could watch football in peace, eat pizza rolls until he felt sick, and where he didn't have to worry about anyone or take care of anything.

Until Jared had died. Then it seemed like this house and this woman were loaded on top of Noah's shoulders too. And yes, he'd mourned the loss of the carefree feelings he'd always had here.

Maggie nodded. "I had friends. But I didn't want to go out or have people over and slowly, over time, they got frustrated with trying and quit calling and coming over."

Noah swallowed again, hard. Fuck. "I'm sorry I wasn't here."

She tipped her head. "When?"

"After...when I enlisted."

She sighed. "You haven't been here even since you've been home."

He frowned. "I've been here. I've done everything I could do. Even stuff you wouldn't *let* me do."

"But, like I said, I didn't need someone to clean my house." She paused and straightened from the doorway. "I needed someone to make me care about having my house clean."

"I—" But Noah had no idea what to say to that.

"It's not your fault," she said. "I didn't realize it at first either. But, because you were coming over anyway, even when I told you to stay away, I started leaving. And then coming back home. And I guess I had to walk out of the house to walk back in, knowing you'd been here, to really see it." She sighed. "You did help me. You did take care of me that way."

He didn't feel placated exactly, but he'd take it. "I'm glad."

"But recently I've realized that I don't want to leave the house when you come over anymore," she said. She met his gaze. "I would really like to stay. And spend time with you."

Noah started. "You would?"

"Someone gave me some advice recently. Advice about being happy. And that doing things to make other people happy is great, but if it makes *you* unhappy there's something wrong."

That sounded strangely familiar.

"And I realized that leaving when you come over might kind of make you happy because you can do your thing around here and feel like you're helping. But it doesn't make me happy. I want to be here. With you. And I think maybe, deep down, it doesn't make you happy either."

"I don't mind doing any of this, Maggie," Noah said firmly. "I'm happy to do it."

"Happy to *do* something and *happy* are not the same thing," she said. She stepped forward, into the bathroom. "And I would really like to know that you're *happy*."

He felt his throat tighten unexpectedly. "I'm—" But he couldn't finish the sentence. Because he wasn't sure what he was.

"I watched you grow up," Maggie reminded him. "I knew you before your dad started deploying again. You would come over and be loud and boisterous and make a mess with Jared. I'd have cookie crumbs and muddy footprints all over this house. And I'd have to tell you both to slow down and quiet down." She smiled. "And I loved it. And I remember distinctly the change that happened when your dad started leaving again and put you in charge at your house. You got so serious. You were so much more careful and conscientious."

Noah gave a soft laugh, though he didn't feel amused. "That's not a good thing?"

"Not in a kid," Maggie said, shaking her head. "Not in you. I was so happy that you could still come over here and let go a little. It wasn't the same. It would take almost an hour before you'd relax. But it was good to see."

"And then Jared and I left," he said, his voice hoarse.

She nodded. "I was upset. I didn't want either of you to go. It was totally selfish, I admit that. But that's really how I felt. And…" She trailed off and took a breath. "And then after he died, I was in a bad place for a long time. You did remind me of him and that was hard. You were like a second son to me, but having you around right after did remind me of what I'd lost. And that was… it was just the way it was. I wish I'd felt or acted differently, but I can't change that."

Noah nodded. He didn't blame her. "I know. Me too. I wish I'd come back right away."

"I know you do," Maggie said. She gave him a small smile. "And I know how you found me made you feel even worse. But —" She straightened. "I'm better now. And I want to get even better. And my friend gave me some really good advice."

"So you do have a friend now?" he asked. He was kind of teasing her. But he also really wanted to hear that she had a friend.

"I do. A few of them," Maggie said. "Some from before. They didn't all leave me. And then Kayla, this young gal who seems to think I'm kind of interesting."

He gave another soft laugh, this time feeling it more than before. "I'm glad."

"And, of course, Brynn," Maggie said.

Hearing her name was like a knife to his heart. He was going to have to get used to that. If she was staying in town, he knew he'd be hearing her name a lot. But the hurt was fresh, and he couldn't help the wave of *want* he felt when he heard it now.

"You and Brynn are friends?"

"I hang out at the pie shop while you mess around here," she told him with a wry smile.

"And Brynn gave you some advice about me?" He couldn't help it—he wanted to know.

"She did. She said to invite you for meatloaf and key lime pie."

He blinked at her. "Invite me for..." He trailed off.

Maggie nodded. "Dinner. Just to spend time together. And talk."

"Brynn thought we needed to talk." That didn't sound like her. Except...it did. This was the Brynn that listened to people, saw what they needed, and helped make it happen. Did he need to sit in the kitchen where his best friend had grown up, where he'd shared happy meals where he didn't have to worry about anything, where his friend's mom had let him just be a kid? Yep. He really did. He took a deep breath. Then gave Maggie a nod. "Okay. Let's talk."

She seemed relieved. She smiled. "Dinner will be done in about forty-five minutes."

"Great."

"I don't suppose you could sharpen my lawn mower blade while you wait?" she asked, turning on her heel. "I'd like to mow tomorrow, but I think it's a little dull." She shot him a smile over her shoulder.

Noah felt like he was fifty pounds lighter as he laughed and followed her down the stairs. "Yeah, Maggie, I could do that."

"Call me MJ," she said, turning into her kitchen. "All my friends do."

He paused in the doorway leading out back. Friends. He and Maggie had moved or were *moving* at least—to friends. "What's that stand for?" he asked.

"Margaret Jean."

"I didn't know your first name was Margaret." Because he'd never thought about it. She'd been "Jared's mom" or "Maggie" as long as he'd known her.

"There was no reason for you to know that about me," she said with a smile.

He gave her a nod. "Yeah, I guess not." Because little kids didn't really need to know their friend's mom's full first or middle name. But people did know that stuff about their friends. "Until now," he added.

Her smile grew. "Right. Until now. Noah Michael."

And two hours later, while chatting with Maggie, he ate the best key lime pie of his life.

Not that he would ever tell Cori or Parker that.

15

"Brynn!" Noah banged into the pie shop six minutes after leaving Maggie's house. "Brynn!" He got everyone's attention...and none of them were Brynn.

In fact, the person coming toward him in an apron was about as opposite of Brynn as Noah could get.

"Something wrong, Noah?" Hank asked.

Noah was distracted by Hank's ruffles for a moment. Then he shook his head and focused. "Where's Brynn?"

"New York."

"Okay." Noah turned on his heel. Then froze. He swung back. "*What*?"

Hank grasped Noah's upper arm and pulled him off to the side, closer to the coffee bar where Cori was shining her cappuccino machine. "She's in New York. Left yesterday."

"But...I... but..." Noah's heart was racing and his mind was spinning. She'd gone to New York? After telling him she was definitely staying and making beer *here*?

But he'd said that horrible thing about her always going along with things. And she hadn't actually said she was staying. Not after he'd said those things anyway.

He shoved a hand through his hair. Then he sucked in a deep breath. "Okay. I'll go to New York," he said.

Hank looked surprised. "You're going to New York?"

Noah nodded, the spinning in his head suddenly stopping, the answer clear. "I'm going to be wherever she is."

"To stay?"

Noah sighed. "Yeah. I'll have to."

"You'd have to leave your shop and your friends," Hank said.

"Yep. But Brynn makes me happy. And I want to be happy, Hank. So I need to be with her."

Hank gave him a smile that looked almost proud. "You deserve to be happy, Noah."

Noah felt his heart swell a little at that. Had everyone realized that he was less than completely happy over the past few years?

"You'll also have to leave Maggie behind though," Hank said, moving in closer, mild concern in his eyes. "Are you okay with that?"

That one took Noah just a little longer to answer. But he nodded slowly. "I think she'll be okay. There are other people who can look out for her and help her."

Hank smiled. "There are. People who will gladly do that if *you'll* let them."

Noah felt himself return the smile. "She doesn't really need my *physical* help. At least not all the time. Not with the basic stuff. And I think I can give her what she does need with phone calls and Skype and regular visits."

Hank clapped him on the shoulder. "Good. That's all really good, Noah. So you're really not going to just go to New York and bring Brynn back here?"

Noah considered that for a second. He'd love to do that. He really did want Brynn *here*.

Because this was where she was happy.

The thought seemed to slap him across the face. He'd known it, of course. Even if she hadn't said it, it had been completely obvious. Brynn was happy in Bliss. Happier than she'd ever been. Happier than she'd been in New York.

"I don't think Rudy knew what he was talking about," Noah said to Hank. He knew that seemed out of context, but he couldn't not say it. "He wanted her to go back to New York to be happy, but *this* is where she should be."

Hank didn't say anything at first. Then he shook his head. "Maybe we should have a seat."

Noah didn't have a better idea at the moment, so he slid up onto the stool at the coffee bar next to Hank. He sighed and ran a hand over his face. Then he looked at Hank, aware that Cori wasn't far away. "I just...I don't think Rudy was right on this one, Hank."

"I don't know. I think Brynn definitely went back to New York happier and more confident." He swiveled on his stool and pinned Noah with a serious look. "So you did what you said you would. Mission accomplished."

Noah swallowed. "Yeah. I guess so."

"That's a good thing, right?" Hank asked. "She's dated six guys—"

"Who was number six?" Noah asked with a frown.

"Well, me," Hank said. "We sat right at that table over three nights ago and talked about her going to New York."

"*You* told her to go to New York?"

"No. I encouraged her to go." He leaned onto his elbow on the counter next to them. "To get that last thing checked off Rudy's list."

Noah felt himself nodding. "Yeah. I guess she did have to go back."

"And now anything can happen."

"But Rudy—"

"Never said when she had to go back. Or what she had to do while she was there," Hank said. "Maybe it was just to go out to the restaurants she loves without worrying about where everyone else wants to go. Or see a show that she's never seen because no one else wanted to see it. Or maybe it's just to go shopping with her mom and be able to put her foot down and buy the dress she wanted to instead of the one her mom liked best."

"Yeah. I'll definitely encourage all of that," Noah said. "We all love sweet Brynn, but she deserves to do things her way. She deserves people who ask her what her way is."

Hank nodded. "Definitely. But you won't have to encourage any of that. She's already done it."

"What do you mean?"

"I mean, she texted me a little bit ago to tell me that she's done all of those things. That's why those were my examples." The older man grinned.

"You and Brynn text?" Noah asked.

"Sure." Hank shrugged. "She needs progress reports."

"About the pie shop?" Noah looked around. It looked like business-as-usual. With the exception of the seventy-something-year-old man wearing a ruffled apron.

"And you."

Noah sat up straighter. "Me?"

"She asked me to take care of you while she was gone." Hank gave him a smile.

"Really?"

"Really."

Noah felt his chest get warm. "And what have you told her?"

"That you and Penn have made up. That MJ installed her vanity and was inviting you for dinner. And that I thought you looked like hell."

Noah just stared at him for a long minute. "How did you know about the cat and MJ?" The looking like hell thing was pretty obvious. And accurate.

"The cat hasn't been coming around my house as much," Hank said. "I assumed he was getting attention elsewhere. And since Brynn isn't here, figured it was you."

Noah couldn't help but nod. "Yeah." He cleared his throat. "I guess...I've been taking a break in the afternoons." And Penn had been crawling into his lap just like he did with Brynn. It was almost as if Penn had just been waiting for Noah to slow down and just *be* instead of doing all the time. But then Noah frowned. "Wait. He hasn't been coming around your house as much?"

Hank chuckled. "He usually comes by around two in the afternoon. We nap in my recliner. Then he comes back after you close up the shop and has dinner and spends the night."

Noah's eyebrows rose. "He doesn't sleep at the shop?"

"Not when you're not there. And I figure two o'clock is about the time Brynn goes back to the pie shop and you run over to Maggie's, right?"

Noah nodded, a little stunned. "He needs that much attention? He can't be alone?"

"Oh." Hank shook his head. "I don't think he comes around for *him*. I think he comes around for me. And then goes back for Brynn. And for you."

Noah felt his throat tighten. Stupid. It was a cat. But he could admit that there had been a lot of afternoons when he'd first come back to Bliss, when it was only him and Penn in the garage, that it had felt nice knowing the cat was there. Sure, he'd told himself that he was taking care of the cat, but now, looking back, he saw how Penn had kept him company too. And he was now looking forward to the afternoon lap sitting that had become a habit.

"So you'll look after him for me when I go to New York?" Noah asked.

"Or he'll look after me," Hank said. "Either way, we'll be okay."

That did, actually, make Noah feel good. Everything was going to be taken care of.

"I can do this, right?" Noah asked. "Move to New York to be with her. Or bring her back here. Or whatever works out."

"Of course."

"It's a disruption in Rudy's plan," he pointed out.

"Are you willing to do that?" Hank asked. "Are you willing to put what you want in front of what Rudy wanted?"

Noah took a deep breath and blew it out. "I know Rudy was your friend. He was mine too," he said. "But dammit, Hank, I don't care if he didn't want me with Brynn. He was wrong about that. So yeah, I'm going to put what I want first. I did everything else he asked of me, I respected those wishes. But now...*I* want to make Brynn happy. I don't need a list from anyone else telling me how to do that."

Hank was watching him closely when Noah looked up. Slowly, his mouth spread into a grin. "That's my boy." He clapped him on the shoulder.

Noah's eyes narrowed. "Yeah?"

"Yeah. You've got this." Hank sighed and sat back on his stool, looking very satisfied. "And now I've got *my* checklist finished too."

"Your checklist?"

"The things that Rudy wanted *me* to do."

"What things?"

"Things to take care of you kids."

Noah didn't understand. "Us kids? Me and Brynn?"

"And Cori and Evan and Ava and Parker," Hank said with a nod.

Rudy had asked Hank to take care of *all* of them?

"What things were on that list?" Noah asked.

"Oh, you'll find out." Hank got to his feet.

"When?"

"Eventually." He smoothed the front of his apron. "And now, I have some customers to wait on."

"But—when will we find out about your list?" Noah asked.

Hank looked back at him. "Does it *really* matter what's on the list?" he asked.

Noah thought about that. About Brynn. Cori and Evan. Ava and Parker. The pie shop, the sisters' relationship, Evan's mini-golf course, Parker's diner, him and Maggie. And he shook his head. "No. It doesn't matter. No matter what Rudy thought or wanted, it's all worked out perfectly."

Hank nodded. "I agree." Then he headed for the table of women that had just sat down, pulling out a pencil and a pad of paper to take their order.

Noah pivoted back to the counter, lost in thought. Until Cori came and leaned on the counter across from him.

She just arched an eyebrow.

Shit. She was probably pissed at him.

He leaned in, deciding he'd rather be on offense than defense here.

"Okay, I know. I was a dumbass. It's in the water here, I think." He paused. Nope, not even a small smile at his quip. Okay, then. He took a deep breath. "My dad asked me to take care of my sisters and my mom when he was gone. So I did. I was a kid so in my head I thought that meant *doing* things. Fixing things. So I did everything I could for them. And I did a good job. At least, their cars always ran and the roof never leaked and the guys all knew they had to treat them well. But, I didn't listen to them. I didn't talk to them. I just did what I thought was best, without ever asking them what they really needed or wanted. And then my dad would come home and tell me I did a great job, because that's all exactly what he would have done, so I felt good about it. And then, when they left for college and met their husbands and my dad finally came home and retired, I felt *relieved*. I was off the hook. It wasn't my job anymore."

Cori didn't say anything, but she was listening.

But then it got worse. Ava came out of the kitchen.

"Oh, Noah." Ava's tone was icy and she barely gave him more than a passing glance as she grabbed a cup and poured herself some coffee.

"Hey, Ava," Noah greeted. He deserved this. He'd hurt Brynn. He'd rejected Brynn. He'd chosen Rudy over Brynn.

He really was a dumbass.

But sitting at the table in Maggie's kitchen, remembering what it had been like to just be happy and carefree, where someone was giving *him* stuff and waiting on him and asking him about his life and how he was had felt so damned good. More so because it had obviously made Maggie happy too. He didn't expect to have someone catering to his every wish and need. He intended to argue with her about who was going to be doing the bulk of the mowing at her house. But being there had reminded him that it was possible to make someone happy and be happy at the same time. And he knew he and Brynn could do that. Because they'd been doing it for six months before she'd started dating other men.

Yeah, that still sounded crazy.

"I was just telling Cori that I'm really sorry about how I messed up with Brynn," he said to Ava.

She studied her nails.

Parker came out from the kitchen just then and took in the gathering at the counter. He sighed and met Noah's eyes. "It's about time you get here."

Noah nodded. "Yeah."

"Go on with what you were saying," Cori said.

"Okay." He cleared his throat. "My buddy Jared asked me to take care of his mom. I, of course, said yes. But I was still a dumb kid. Older, but not really any smarter. I messed all of that up too. I didn't take care of her the way she needed me to. And I felt it. I knew it deep down. But I had no idea how to change it. And then Rudy came along." Noah felt his voice wobble. He cleared his throat again. "Rudy came along and gave me another chance. I thought that he'd asked me to look out for Brynn because she needed a guardian or something. But she didn't." He shook his head, his heart expanding as he thought about Brynn.

"All of the ways Brynn has grown and gained, isn't anything I've done. Rudy made her step out of her comfort zone and as soon as she did, she blossomed. She tuned in to the people around her and she let her big brain, and her even bigger heart, loose on them. That wasn't me. Hell, I would have kept her in the shadows, hidden away, all mine if it had been up to me."

He sat back on the stool and looked at Brynn's sisters, the only people who loved her as much as he did. He met their gazes directly. "Brynn and I have a lot in common. It's always been easier to just put our heads down and do what was right in front of us. But once we look up, and actually take it all in, we want to be a part of it. The chance to be with her is the only thing strong enough to make me break out of *my* comfort zone." He took a deep breath. "She doesn't need me. I need *her*. I thought Rudy sent Brynn here so I could take care of her but the truth is, he brought her here to save me."

There was a long beat of silence and then someone sniffed.

It was Ava.

"Damn," she said. "That was *really* good."

Cori nodded. "It was. Brynn deserves to have *that*."

Noah blew out a breath. Relief coursed through him. Brynn was way sweeter than these two. If he could convince them, he could convince her.

Evan came through the doorway between the pie shop and the diner just then. "Hey everybody." He looked from Cori to Noah to Parker to Ava. "What's going on?"

"Noah is here regaining our approval," Cori said.

"Oh, good. Damn that was a long three days." Evan headed around behind the counter, kissed Cori, and then poured coffee for himself.

He thought it had been a long three days?

Noah focused on Cori. "Where is she?" he asked. "I mean, I know she's in New York, but I'm going to need an address."

Cori looked at Ava. Ava gave her a little nod. He didn't know what all of that meant, but he did know that he was going to New York. Soon. But—his mind spun—not tonight. Not yet. There was something he needed to do first.

"We'll give you the address. But you should know, she's planning to come back tomorrow," Cori said. "She just went to officially resign from the lab and check into selling her apartment."

"And enjoy the city her way for a change," Noah added.

Cori blew out a breath, nodding. "Yeah. That too. We—" She glanced at Ava. "We're learning that we sometimes made it hard for her to be herself. We were really trying to make it so she could be whoever she wanted to be, but sometimes we might have..."

"Drowned her out?" Noah supplied.

"Yeah, okay," Cori agreed, a bit sheepishly. "But we promise that we're going to work on that."

Noah gave them both a look. "Yeah. You will."

Ava didn't look overly impressed with his firm tone, but she did nod. "Yeah. We will."

"So, then, I need a favor," Noah said.

"What's that?" Ava asked.

"Stall her."

"Stall her? You mean, make her stay in New York?" Cori asked.

"Yes."

"Why?"

"I have a plan," he said. "It's something I really want to do, but it's going to take a couple of days. And I really want to go to her. To go after her."

That got a smile from Cori, and Ava's shoulders at least relaxed a little. "Okay," Cori agreed. "We can stall her."

"Great," Noah said, anticipation and a feeling of *rightness* coursing through him. He was going to *do* something, but it was something that *he* needed, something that would make *him* happy. And Brynn too, of course. "And hey, Evan?"

"Yeah, man?"

"I'm going to be cashing in those three hours of manual labor you owe me."

Evan's groan was just one more thing to love about this whole situation.

———

B rynn had tears in her eyes and she was holding her breath. For what she wasn't sure, but she couldn't make her lungs expand.

She heard some shuffling and footsteps and then the door shutting and then Cori's voice come back over the phone line, "Did you hear all of that?"

Brynn nodded, then realized Cori couldn't see that. "Yeah," she croaked out.

She and Cori had been talking when Noah had come stomping into the pie shop. She'd heard everything thanks to Cori hitting the speaker button and Noah, apparently, not noticing the phone lying on the counter where he and Hank were sitting.

She'd been sitting with her heart in her throat throughout Noah and Hank's conversation and then everything Noah said to her sisters.

I thought Rudy sent Brynn here so I could take care of her. But the truth is, he brought her here to save me.

Wow.

"Why didn't you let me talk to him?" she asked. She was now physically aching to talk to him.

"Because he needs to come to New York after you," Cori said.

"But I had this whole big thing planned for when I got back to Bliss," Brynn protested. "I was going to show up on his porch with flowers and ask him to be my only date forever."

"That's nice," Cori told her.

"Definitely," Ava agreed. "*But* he needs to grovel and while groveling and apologizing to *us* was pretty great, he absolutely needs to do it to you. In person."

"I would have been okay with it over the phone," Brynn said, her heart actually hurting. God, she'd missed him. She'd been thankful for the excuse to head to New York because it had kept her from going to find him. She'd hoped he'd come around. She'd hoped he'd realize...well, all of the things he'd realized. But it had been a really long three days, and she had planned to show up and tell him that she was going to treat him like he'd treated Penn for these past few years—even if Penn didn't give a lot of love back, Noah hadn't stopped taking care of him and being there. She was going to do that for Noah.

"But you can't have make-up sex if he's apologizing over the phone," Ava said.

Brynn grinned at that. "Well, that *is* on the list of kinds of sex I haven't had."

"Have you had phone sex?" Cori asked. "Because that can be pretty great."

"I haven't." Brynn almost felt like she should start a list.

"Hey, *we* haven't had phone sex," Evan said.

Brynn giggled as Cori said something quietly that Brynn couldn't make out. She did hear Evan clear his throat though, and she could only imagine how Cori had placated him.

"Anyway," Ava said. "He'll be there in a few hours and you can have New York sex. And *not* tell us about it."

"Is New York sex really good?" Brynn asked, grinning.

"Hey, we've never had New York sex either," Evan protested.

"Oh, Ava wouldn't really know the difference," Parker said. "Ava's having *Parker* sex. It's always good."

"Well, I didn't only have New York sex with *you*, you know," Ava said.

The next thing Brynn heard was Ava's shriek and Parker's low voice and the sound of footsteps.

Cori was laughing when she said, "Okay, so they're gone."

Brynn rolled her eyes but laughed. It was amazing to hear her sisters so happy.

"So... how long do I need to stay here and wait for him?" she asked. "What's he doing?" She just wanted him to *get here* if he was going to.

"I don't know," Cori said.

"Me either," Evan added. "But I guess I'm going to find out. I'd really hoped he would have forgotten about that."

"Why do you owe him manual labor?" Cori asked.

"From all the work he did on the golf course," Evan told her.

"You didn't pay him?"

"I tried! But then he said he'd just take payment in the form of services. I thought he meant legal services," Evan said. "But *after* I agreed and the course was done, he informed me that he never intended to need a lawyer and he'd rather have three hours of manual labor."

"Well, I can't wait to see you all sweaty and working shirtless," Cori told him.

"I'll be working shirtless?"

"If I have any say in it."

"Oh, you can have all the say you want..."

Brynn sighed, then put her fingers to her lips and gave a shrill whistle to get their attention again.

"Sorry," Cori said, with a laugh.

"How about we get *my* love life back on track before you guys keep rubbing yours in my face?" Brynn asked.

"Well, just hang out. Go to lunch with Mom. Talk to your realtor in more detail. Go to Carmichael and pretend to be Ava." Cori laughed.

Brynn rolled her eyes, but she couldn't help her grin. "Maybe I'll just sit in my quiet apartment and read for hours and hours without being interrupted or distracted."

"Hmm," Cori said. "I give that about five hours."

"What?"

"I bet you're bored and wishing for some noise within five hours."

No, Cori was totally wrong.

It would be more like three hours.

———

I t had been four days.

Four of the longest days of his life.

But he was almost there.

Noah slammed on the brakes and stared at the car in front of him.

Holy shit, there were a lot of cars here. A lot of fucking cars. And people. And noise. How had Brynn stood this for twenty-nine years? The woman who loved quiet and being alone?

But she hadn't really known any different. She'd found the solitude in her lab and had kept herself inside that bubble. It wasn't until she'd come to Bliss that she realized that peacefulness could extend for acres.

Unless of course someone had some gossip to share.

A horn blared behind him and Noah looked up into the rearview mirror. The guy behind him was glaring at him. Noah gestured to the lineup of cars in front of the truck. Where did the guy think he was going to go? But the guy couldn't see the gesture, and Noah didn't think giving him the *other* gesture he was thinking of would be a good idea. The truck had a Kansas plate on it. It was already drawing enough I'm-not-from-here attention.

Please, God, don't let Brynn want to live here again. Please let her want to come back to Bliss. He'd stay here for her, but damn, *that* would be a grand gesture for sure.

He patted the dashboard of the truck. Actually, as far as grand gestures went, he thought he was doing pretty well.

Finally, after what felt like fourteen years, he pulled up in front of Brynn's building. But there was nowhere to park. Because of course there wasn't. Because he was driving a truck in New York City.

He dialed Cori's number. "There's nowhere to park," he said as soon as she picked up.

"Just have the doorman do valet."

He sighed into the phone. "So the valet—" Good lord, he was in love with a woman who had a doorman and a valet, "—will put it in a parking garage or something?"

"Right."

"That kind of defeats the whole purpose," he told her, starting to feel the hours on the road and the manual work he'd done before hitting that road. He was tired. So tired. Not just physically, but in his heart too.

He'd been going on adrenaline and caffeine for four days now and it was all starting to wear off. He'd been at the garage, just him and Penn, every day for almost six years and had been fine. He'd gone to the diner for lunch, to Maggie's to work, even to Rudy's pie shop once in a while. And he'd been fine.

Then Brynn had shown up. And everything changed. Maybe not immediately. It had taken time to change the pie shop. It had taken until a few days ago to really change things between him and Maggie. But everything, absolutely *everything*, in his life had been destined to change the moment Brynn Carmichael smiled at him.

And now she'd been gone, away from the garage, the pie shop, his life, and he was definitely not fine. Not just because everything felt empty without her, but because he'd realized that being *fine* wasn't enough.

"Well, if you stay in the truck and double-park, they might come yell at you, but at least you won't get towed," Cori said. "Just call and tell her to come down."

Noah sighed again. Dammit. He'd been so intent on just

getting here that he hadn't really planned all of this out. "Okay, fi—"

"Hey! Move your ass!"

He looked into his mirror. And sighed *again*. This guy was leaning out of his window and yelling. Noah waved what he hoped was a "sorry" wave, but he didn't move his ass. And frankly, if the guy wanted to make something of it, Noah was fast approaching that mood himself. The tall buildings were giving him claustrophobia. The place smelled like a weird mix of exhaust, rubber, and tacos. And he hadn't seen Brynn in a week. *Fine* wasn't even on his emotional radar at the moment.

"What the hell, Iowa! Go back to the farm!" The guy laid on the horn.

Noah rolled his eyes. His license plate clearly said Kansas. What an idiot.

The car behind him blasted its horn too. A taxi swerved around them all, nearly scraping the side of the truck, then had to slam on its brakes almost immediately just past Noah's front bumper.

"Why didn't you talk me out of this plan?" Noah asked Cori. "What kind of idiot drives a truck into New York City?"

"This plan is amazing," Cori assured him. "Just ignore them. If they're not yelling at you, they'd be yelling at someone else."

Yeah, he really didn't want to live here.

"I just wanted to—" But he stopped midsentence.

In the midst of the honking and the yelling and the taco-exhaust smell and the fatigue and the emptiness, everything was suddenly very, very fine. In fact, it was *right*.

Brynn Carmichael stood on the sidewalk in front of her building. She was looking right at him. And she was smiling. And crying.

"I'll talk to you later." He disconnected with Cori abruptly and threw the truck into park.

He didn't love noise and chaos any more than Brynn did,

honestly. But at the moment, the entire city could start honking and yelling—nothing mattered but getting to his girl. The girl who made everything in his life better. Who quieted the noise and calmed the chaos. Who also stirred things up and made him care and get involved.

Noah shoved his door open, leaving it hanging wide as he stalked to where she stood.

"Noah, I—"

He wrapped his arms around her, picking her up, and covering her mouth with his before she could complete the sentence. He kissed her deeply, his arms around her waist, her feet dangling above the New York sidewalk.

And not *all* of the noise from the street quieted. But that was because the guy in the car behind the truck was suddenly shouting, "Yeah, buddy! Show her how the cowboys do it!"

Noah lifted his head, chuckling in spite of himself. But he wasn't going to correct the guy. There were cowboys in Kansas. Somewhere.

Brynn grinned up at him. "Hi," she said softly, putting her hand against his cheek.

"Hi."

"You're *finally* here."

Yeah, he wasn't surprised that her sisters had told her he was on his way. "It's a bit of a drive."

Her eyes sparkled with tears as she looked at the baby blue Ford behind him. "You drove twenty-one hours in the truck that doesn't even run."

Noah set her down on the sidewalk and glanced back at the truck too. He also noted that the two cars behind him were, well, still behind him. The drivers were both out of their cars and were now watching him and Brynn. Suddenly, they didn't have to get going after all.

"The truck that does run. Now."

"You fixed it."

"I did."

"How did you get the parts so fast?"

Noah turned to look at the truck, keeping one arm around Brynn, and her tucked securely up against his side. "I already had the only part it needed."

She looked up at him. "But you never put it in?"

"Jared had the part. It took him weeks to track it down and then the price was astronomical. But he'd finally gotten it. He just didn't have time to put it in. It was supposed to be a weekend project for us when we came home to visit from college."

He felt Brynn tighten her hold on him.

"I'm sorry," she said quietly. Then she asked, "So why now?"

He cleared his throat and turned to face her. "I kept that truck around as a reminder that it's easier to fix things right away rather than wait. The older something gets, the harder it is to repair." He moved his hands to her upper arms and looked directly into her eyes. "But you showed me that it's still worth it. It takes more work, it might cost you more—emotionally, if not financially—but it's still worth fixing."

One tear spilled over her bottom lashes, and Noah wiped it from her cheek with the pad of his thumb.

"As much as I've loved having you sitting on this truck in my garage, I realized that it needs to be out on the road, in the sun. I'm not going to let it sit in the shadows and feel like I'm protecting it or saving it for Jared anymore." Noah heard how gruff his voice was, but he didn't even try to cover up the emotion. "Jared's gone. And I miss him like hell. But I'm still here and I want to take road trips in that truck and load the back up with picnic supplies, or jars of Blissfully Brewed beer and cider. I just want to...enjoy it." He paused. "If you'll let me."

Brynn sniffed and frowned. "If I'll let you?"

"Well, the truck is yours," he said. "You're the reason I want to get out there and do more and be more and be happy. And I'm done keeping you to myself in the shadows too. I'm not protecting you for Rudy, anymore, Brynn. I'm just going to love you and enjoy you and make you happy. Not because Rudy asked me to, but because making you happy makes *me* happy."

He stood looking down at her as several seconds ticked by. She looked overwhelmed. And a little dazed. But mostly happy.

"That's a kick-ass truck!" the guy from the street called out. "Tell him thank you and kiss him for fuck's sake!"

Brynn and Noah laughed. Then she went up on tiptoe, wrapped her arms around his neck, and said, "Thank you."

Then she kissed him with so much feeling that Noah's heart swelled in his chest. He gripped her hips and brought her as close as they could get on the city street with an audience. Of course, this was New York...

He lifted his head. "Any chance we could go inside and talk about your plans for Blissfully Brewed and I can tell you about my dinner with Maggie and about how Penn spends the night with Hank?"

Brynn settled back on her heels. And shook her head. "No."

"No?" He lifted his eyebrows. "You don't care about Maggie and Penn and Hank?"

"Maggie already told me about your dinner—though I do want to hear your side— and Hank already told me about Penn," she said.

Noah rolled his eyes and smiled. "Of course they did."

"And I can tell you all about Blissfully Brewed on the twenty-one-hour drive home," she said.

That sunk in and he pulled her in for another kiss. But it wasn't nearly as long and deep as he wanted.

She finally pulled back. "So right now, let's have Tom put the truck in the garage." She moved in closer and dropped her voice. "And you can teach me all about make-up sex."

Heat, want, joy, and love surged through him and he gave a little growl, bent, swept her up into his arms, and started for the door. She laughed and looked over his shoulder.

"Hey! Keep an eye on that truck until the doorman comes out, okay?" she called. "I'll give you five hundred bucks to keep it safe!"

The guy on the street yelled back, "You got it!"

"You know him?" Noah asked.

"No."

"You talk to strangers on the street all the time? And offer them money and trust them with your stuff?"

They got to the door and the man Noah assumed was Tom opened it for them with a formal, "Miss Carmichael."

"Will you put my truck in the garage?" she asked sweetly from Noah's arms. "The keys are in it. And please pay the gentleman watching it five hundred."

"Of course, Miss Carmichael," Tom said with a little tip of his head.

But Noah caught the man's smile as he turned away.

"In answer to your question," Brynn said as Noah strode to the elevators. "I never used to talk to anyone on the streets, but since I've been back, I've been doing more of it. People can be so nice and interesting."

Noah shook his head as he stepped onto the elevator. "You can't just go around talking to strangers, Brynn." He wasn't going to smother her and keep her in the shadows, but he sure as hell was going to keep her safe.

She leaned to push the button for the penthouse. Because, of course she lived in the penthouse. He was ninety-nine percent sure that Ava had picked the place out and moved Brynn into the place without even really asking her.

"I thought one of the goals was to get me to open up and interact with people more," she said.

He was still holding her in his arms and he gave her a little squeeze. "The goal was for you to see that you have a lot to offer the world and people around you."

"Right. I've been giving money to people on the street too."

He squeezed her harder. "We've created a monster."

She laughed and shook her head. "I'm just looking around more, thinking about what makes me smile, and trying to do more of that."

This time when he squeezed her, it was with love and a desire that was almost painful. "I love you, Brynn."

She looked up quickly. "You do?"

God, it killed him that she didn't know that down to the very marrow of her bones. But that was a very good lifelong project to start working on. Right. Now. "I do. With everything in me. Everything I am."

"I love you too."

The sincerity and emotion in her eyes was enough to convince him without anything further. He lowered his head and kissed her, tasting her until the elevator arrived at the penthouse and the doors swished open. He lifted his head and looked into her eyes. "You need to get undressed."

Her eyes widened for a moment, then she wiggled for him to let her down, a sweetly seductive smile on her lips. "Well, I probably should warn you," she told him, starting on her buttons as she stepped out of the elevator and into her apartment.

For a second, Noah was a little distracted. The penthouse had floor to ceiling windows along two sides of the living room, and the view of New York was breathtaking. He had to admit that Ava had great taste.

But he quickly focused back on the woman who was already down to her panties. Her very tiny, electric blue panties. He started for her. "You should warn me about what?" he asked, moving until he almost stood on top of her.

"That thing you said, about creating a monster?" she said, pushing her panties to the floor. "I think you might be right about that—in the bedroom, anyway."

He couldn't help grinning at that. "Huh." He reached for her, drawing her up against his body, his hands roaming over her bare skin. "Then, I guess it's a good thing I'm going to keep you right here in this living room. Bent over that couch."

Her eyes flared with heat and she took a deep breath. "That might be safest. For now."

Then Noah proceeded to teach her all about make-up sex. And New York sex. And living room furniture sex.

And then road-trip sex. And fancy-hotel-room sex. And dive-hotel-room sex.

And, most of all, madly-in-love-with-your-partner-forever sex.

And, on the last night of the road trip back to Bliss, that had taken them five days to complete, he taught her about we-just-got-engaged sex.

EPILOGUE

March...

Ava Carmichael was worth twelve and a half billion dollars. Billion. With a B.

It was official.

It was the year anniversary of the triplets arriving in Bliss, and they were in another meeting with their father's lawyer. But this was no conference room in Manhattan, and Evan was here as Cori's fiancé, not an attorney. They were in the pie shop on Main Street in Bliss, Kansas and Parker, Noah, Ben, Walter, Roger and Hank were with them.

"Thank you all for being here," Hank started.

The sign they'd hung on the door read *Blissfully Brewed will be closed tonight for a special private event.*

They were done. The stipulations in the will had been completed. Their time was up.

Cori looked around the room, her heart full. The truth was, their time was just beginning. They were just getting started.

"I've brought you here together at Rudy's request," Hank said.

Hearing his name, Rudy, the St. Bernard, yapped at Hank from where he was sitting at Cori's feet.

Hank laughed. "Not you, Rudy."

The dog yapped again and wiggled his butt, clearly excited, but he stayed by Cori. The months of puppy school were starting to pay off. She laughed and leaned forward, her hand on his head. "Good boy," she praised. He turned his head and licked her cheek.

"You father," Hank said, clearly trying to avoid using the R word, "wanted to commemorate the one-year anniversary of you coming to Bliss. And he had a few things he wanted to say."

Cori focused on Hank, her heart suddenly pounding. Her fingers curled into the puppy's fur and felt Evan's hand on her knee and the little squeeze he gave her. "Breathe, Cori," he said softly.

God, she loved him. He knew exactly what she was feeling without her having to say a word.

She looked at her sisters. Ava and Brynn both met her gaze, then glanced at each other. They looked equally nervous. Or maybe it wasn't nerves. It was...something that was hard to name. They'd thought the last words they would hear from their father were in the trust he'd drawn up, mandating they come to Bliss, run the pie shop, and mind their love lives. Now there was more? And was that good or bad?

Cori watched as Parker slipped an arm around Ava, and Noah threaded his fingers through Brynn's, lifting her hand to his lips for a kiss.

And just like that, Cori felt a calmness settle over her. It was going to be okay. Whatever this was, whatever Rudy said next, they were going to be okay. Together.

"Okay, let's hear it," Ava, ever the leader, said.

Hank pulled a piece of paper from his back pocket. Then

looked at the other older men in the room, the men who had been Rudy Carmichael's first true friends.

Hank unfolded the paper and read.

"Dear Ava, Brynn, and Cori," Hank started. "If you're hearing this it means your year is complete. You've been in Bliss for twelve months and you have some decisions to make. I hope that you aren't too upset with me anymore. Perhaps the stipulations were a little bit of an overreaction, but I was trying to put years of fatherly mistakes right and, frankly, *I* was angry when I wrote the thing. At the cancer. It didn't give me time and that meant I had to act a bit drastically. It didn't give me time, but it did give me clarity. So, overreaction or not, I'm not sorry about making you come to Bliss and try new things. I'm not sorry about making you bake pies and figure out the accounting and wait on the customers. If you're angry, after doing all of that for the past year, then that just means I was wrong. But I'm not sorry."

Cori didn't know how to feel. He wasn't sorry for turning their lives upside down, for exerting this final bit of control, for manipulating them into coming to Bliss.

But she wasn't sure she wanted him to be sorry. He'd been right. About everything. She and her sisters had needed this, and it had all turned out perfectly.

No one said anything, so after a glance around, Hank continued.

"Ava," he said, turning to face the oldest triplet more fully.

Ava sat up straighter in her chair and Parker ran his palm up and down her upper arm. "You have always known exactly what you wanted and who you were. I hope that, by now, you've realized that the only thing, the only person, you really need to be the boss of, is yourself. If you're happy and fulfilled, you'll be someone people *want* to follow naturally."

Parker leaned over and said something softly in Ava's ear that made her smile. Cori could only imagine what it was—surely something about Ava bossing *him*—but Cori loved him for being able to make her uptight, type-A sister smile and relax. Her *previously* uptight sister, Cori corrected mentally. Though Ava was still very type-A, she'd definitely softened up and learned to enjoy life.

"I hope," Hank continued reading to Ava, "that you've learned that mistakes and failures and trials can help you as much, or more than, successes, and that when you go back to New York, you'll remember that there are a lot of different ways to accomplish a goal. You need to find *your* way. You don't need to follow in anyone's footsteps, Ava. Make your own footprints with those amazing shoes you love so much. Don't let my recipe be the only one you ever try."

Cori felt her eyes sting as she watched Ava swallow hard and sniff. Parker pulled her in and kissed the top of her head.

"Brynn," Hank said, turning to the next sister.

Brynn met Cori's eyes. Cori gave her a quick smile. Brynn nodded at Hank, indicating she was ready. Or as ready as she was going to be.

"This town is full of wonderful people who see others for who they are, not for who they want them to be, or worse who they think they need them to be. And I hope that by being here, amongst them, that you've learned that not everyone is like me. Not everyone will fail to appreciate you."

Cori frowned and felt the urge to grab Brynn's hand, but Noah was there, hugging her against his side and Cori took a deep breath.

"You have nothing to prove to anyone, Brynn. You have no one to impress. In making you get out and interact, I wanted to show you that you are already perfectly perfect just how you are, and that the rest of the world is better than me at seeing and encouraging that. When you go back to New York, I hope it's with confidence and a sense of your place in the world—which is wherever you want it to be. Don't hide away just because I was too dumb to really see you."

Brynn swiped a finger under one eye and put her head against Noah's chest.

And Cori felt a sense of trepidation go through her. She was next.

"Cori." Hank turned to face her and Evan leaned in closer, squeezing her hand.

"Ready," she said, giving Hank a smile.

He returned it. "I know, honey." Then he looked down at the paper. "Cori, you and I had a hard time seeing eye to eye on nearly everything."

She swallowed hard.

"And I think it was partly because I was jealous of you."

Cori felt a shaft of surprise arc through her.

"I was envious of the way you refused to let anyone else tell you what your life should be about, what *you* should be about. Even me. Especially me. I never fought the mold and I have often wondered what else I could have been or done. You won't ever have to wonder about that. But I hope that you've learned that when you're with the right people, in the right place, like with your sisters, that some routines are worth repeating over and over. And when you leave Bliss, I hope you take that with you. Don't let my failure to appreciate the things you did, keep you from *repeatedly* making everything around you bigger and better."

Her throat was tight and her eyes were stinging. She looked up at Evan and he met her eyes and smiled. That was all he did. That was all he had to do. She'd found exactly what her dad had hoped she would.

But she wasn't leaving Bliss.

"And as for you boys," Hank said before anyone responded.

"There's stuff in there about us too?" Parker asked.

Hank nodded. "Of course. This is for all of his kids."

The guys all exchanged looks, and Cori realized they were

now feeling the anxiety she and her sisters had felt. She squeezed Evan. "Breathe," she reminded him.

He smiled down at her. "Right. It doesn't matter what he says."

"Right." They were all exactly where they needed to be. Nothing would change that.

"Evan," Hank began.

Cori felt him tense beside her anyway.

"Thank you. Thank you for making my trust what I wanted it to be, thank you for dealing with the girls—I'm sure that was no easy task."

Everyone chuckled softly at that.

"I know you thought I was crazy. And maybe I was. But you were my friend first and foremost and you made it happen. I know for sure that you did whatever you could to make the girls' transition to Bliss easier. Because that's who you are. You make the people around you feel good, you make them happier, you make sure that no one loses sight of what's really important. And I'm sure the girls needed that. So, for all the things I know you did for them, thank you."

Cori frowned slightly. That was it? No "I hope you learned" stuff for Evan? She looked up at him. "I guess you don't need advice."

Evan looked puzzled too. "Well, that's definitely not true."

Hank turned to Parker. "Parker, thank you too. You are always you. You are exactly who we always expect you to be. You can always be trusted to say it like it is, whether we like it or not. As they were getting settled and the business going, I'm sure the girls needed someone like that. Thank you for being someone they could trust."

Cori watched Ava and Parker exchange looks. Ava smiled and shrugged. "It's all true."

"I guess," Parker said. But he seemed a little disappointed.

Hank finally turned to Noah. "And, Noah. Thank you. You

would give anyone the shirt off your back and the shoes off your feet and still feel like you hadn't done enough. I know you looked out for them, especially Brynn, and I know that you bent over backward to be sure they were safe and secure. Thank you."

Brynn opened her mouth as if to say something or ask a question, but then shut it again. Perhaps realizing that the man who could answer any questions wasn't here.

"And to all of you together," Hank said, addressing them all.

Oh, good, there was more. Everyone shifted on their chairs and a couple even leaned forward slightly.

"I hope that in the year that's passed and with everything I laid out in my trust and told each of you boys, that you've realized the most important thing. And that is, fathers are not always right."

Hank paused and let that sink in for a moment. Cori felt like she was holding her breath. That was maybe the most insightful of all the things Rudy had written. It applied not only to him, but to Evan, Parker, and Noah's fathers as well. Everyone here had a few "daddy issues". But then again, who didn't? Fathers, good or bad, present or absent, biological or not, affected their children.

"All of your fathers loved you. That I know," Hank went on. "They all did the best they could at the time they did it. But the bottom line is, you are not your fathers. You are not destined to do exactly what they did, nor are you destined to do the opposite of everything they did. You are destined to be *you*."

Cori blinked rapidly and felt Evan's hand tighten around hers. She knew it was a sign of support, but it was also because he needed *her* support too. She smiled up at him. His eyes looked a little shiny too.

"Learn what you can from us, kids. But then, go out and... find *your* bliss."

There was nearly a minute of absolute silence after Hank finished. He refolded the letter and tucked it back into his pocket. He stood, just letting them all think.

Finally, Parker broke the quiet. "You stole that line about finding your bliss from Rudy, huh?" he asked Hank.

Hank grinned. "I *gave* Rudy that line."

The dog yapped, coming up off of his haunches, his tail wagging excitedly over being talked about again. And that broke through the melancholy that had settled on the room. They all laughed.

"You helped him write that letter?" Cori asked, swiping at her eyes.

"Helped him?" Hank said. "Hell, he did probably eight drafts and read it to us every time."

"And Rudy—" Walter started.

That was too much for the dog and he jerked forward, heading for Walter.

Walter laughed as two big paws were planted on his lap. He rubbed the dog's head as he continued, "Rudy made Hank practice reading the final version out loud three times. Said he wanted to be sure Hank wouldn't break down crying."

Ben nodded with a smile. "He wanted to be sure he got everything in there. We all kind of helped him." He reached over and scratched Rudy's ear.

Cori smiled at the older men, her dog, then at her sisters, and finally at Evan. "But he got a lot of stuff wrong," she said. "None of us are leaving Bliss or going back to New York."

Evan shrugged. "But *we* got a few things right. And that's what really matters."

She sniffed and nodded.

Rudy barked and suddenly swung around as a group of people walked by the front windows. He started for the front door. Cori sighed and went after him, snagging his collar just as he got up on his back legs, his huge front paws on the door, barking his greeting to the passersby. It wasn't like he'd *graduated* from puppy school yet. And she wasn't sure he'd ever *not* be excited by and overly friendly with big groups of people. She hadn't known that side of her father, but more and more she believed that once he'd come to Bliss, he'd been like his name-sake—perpetually happy, wanting to be in the middle of things, and making people smile.

"And now, *my* check list is done," Hank said, pulling another piece of paper from his pocket.

"You really do have a checklist?" Noah asked. "From Rudy?"

The dog yapped at him.

"Oh yeah. You had yours in your head, but he made me write mine down," Hank said. He unfolded the paper and held it up.

Cori again felt her breath catch as she read it.

1. Make sure Cori is happy.
2. Make sure Ava is happy.
3. Make sure Brynn is happy.
4. Make sure Evan is happy.
5. Make sure Parker is happy.
6. Make sure Noah is happy.
7. Make sure Walter gets his prostate checked.
8. Make sure Ben gets a new hearing aid.
9. Make sure Roger has a huge birthday party.
10. Make sure they all know I love them.

There were little checkmarks by numbers one through nine. And Cori let the tear roll down her cheek even as she laughed, her heart full, as Walter checked off number ten.

MORE FROM ERIN NICHOLAS

Don't miss the rest of the Billionaires in Blue Jeans!

Diamonds and Dirt Roads
High Heels and Haystacks
Cashmere and Camo

And don't miss the Behind the Scenes and Bonus Scenes on Erin's website!

―――――

If you loved the Billionaires in Blue Jeans, check out Erin's other sexy, fun small town romance series, Sapphire Falls!

―――――

And next from Erin is a super sexy series set in the French Quarter of New Orleans! The Boys of the Big Easy series kicks off with
Going Down Easy!

GOING DOWN EASY!

I'm SO excited to take you to New Orleans in my new series! New Orleans is easily my favorite city to visit and I've been many times. I fall a little more in love on each trip. I always knew I'd set a series there eventually, but was waiting for the right characters and stories to come along. And now they have! I hope you'll come along on this adventure with me in the sexy, fun sultriness of the Big Easy! ~ xo, Erin

Going Down Easy

As far as flings go, single dad Gabe Trahan is pretty sure that Addison Sloan is his best bet. Once a month, Addison comes to New Orleans and then...*It. Is. On.* Until Addison returns to New York, it's just hot, happily-no-strings-attached sex. And beignets. And jazz. But lately for Gabe, it isn't *nearly* enough.

Sure, maybe Addison's gotten a bit hooked on Gabe. After all, who can resist a guy who's so sexy, so charming, and so...available? But maybe he's *too* available for her right now. Addison's just moved to New Orleans, and relationships are definitely off the table. Besides, guys always bail when they learn her secret: she's a single mom.

Only Gabe's not running. Worse, he's *thrilled.* But Addison never signed up for ever-after romance, and Gabe won't settle for anything less. Now it's a battle of wills—and when it comes to the woman he's falling for, Gabe isn't above playing a little dirty.

Get Going Down Easy today!
  Read on for a sneak peek!

ENJOY THIS EXCERPT!

It was still amazing to Gabe Trahan how well Addison Sloan's ass fit in his hands. It was as if it had been made specifically for him to cup and squeeze as he pressed her close while he kissed her. Or when he was dancing with her. Or when he was thrusting deep and hard.

His body stirred at the thought of doing just that as she pushed her fingers into his hair and arched against him as if he hadn't just given her two—count 'em, two—orgasms upstairs before she'd gotten dressed for work. But they were standing on the sidewalk in front of his tavern, and her cab was waiting. This was supposed to be a goodbye kiss, not a get-her-hot-and-ready kiss.

The problem was, not only did her ass fit his hands perfectly, but the rest of her fit against the rest of him pretty damned well too, and it was extremely difficult to stop fitting against her once he started.

Addison pulled back a minute later, breathing fast, her pupils dilated. "I have to go."

Yeah, he knew that. It was the second Monday of the month. That meant she was headed across town to the architectural firm where she was consulting on a once-a-month basis, to do whatever she needed to do there, and then she'd head to the airport to fly back to New York, and it would be another month until he'd see her again.

He leaned in, putting his nose against her neck, inhaling her scent. It was his favorite thing about her. And considering he knew every inch of her intimately, that was saying something. This woman had a lot of really nice inches.

"I know," he said. "Just give me a minute."

She sighed, her fingers curling into his scalp. The sound was almost wistful. "Shit," she said softly. "This goodbye thing was supposed to get easier."

Yeah, he would have thought so too. In fact, he would have expected that by the sixth weekend with her, he would have been over her. Especially considering they didn't really have a relationship. They had sex. And beignets. And jazz.

When she was in town, they stayed up all night Saturday night having the hottest sex of his life. Sundays they woke up late and spent the day in the French Quarter, eating and shopping and people watching. Then Sunday night, they burned up his sheets all over again. He loved showing her the classic New Orleans stuff—the café au laits and po'boys, the jazz bands on the street corners, the riverboats and the French market. She was addicted to it all. She couldn't seem to get enough. And seeing it all through her eyes was like rediscovering it for himself.

But they didn't talk about anything too personal, and they didn't communicate at all in between her trips to New Orleans. All he knew was that she was a restoration architect from New York who had been consulting with a local firm on a big project in the Garden District. She came to town once a month on Friday morning; showed up at Trahan's, the tavern Gabe owned and operated with his brother, Logan, on Saturday night; spent the rest of the weekend with him; and then went to the architecture firm again on Monday before heading back to New York Monday night.

When they were together, they talked about the food, music, and people around them at the moment. Occasionally they dipped into their interests and hobbies, their work, their friends to some extent, but nothing else. They kept it all in the moment, in the present, no talk of their pasts or their futures.

He had no idea if she had siblings, what her favorite color was, when her birthday was, or what kind of car she drove. But he knew that she loved sex against the wall, that she had a particular fascination with his abs, that jazz music made her horny, and that the sounds she made when he sucked on her nipples were the hottest things he'd ever heard.

And that was enough.

Or at least that should be enough.

She was a fling. A once-a-month diversion—that he thought about far too often in the time between her trips to New Orleans. A very fun way to spend thirty-six hours or so every once in a while.

She didn't even live in New Orleans. They barely knew one another. He had no desire to go to New York City.

And yet, it was definitely getting harder and harder to say goodbye to her.

Hell, after the first night she'd come to Trahan's with her friend and local architect Elena LeBlanc, and Addison had ended up in his bed for the weekend, he hadn't expected to see her again. But the next month, almost to the day, she'd been sitting on the stool at the end of the bar. And he'd been shocked by how happy he was to see her.

"Quit your job and come waitress at the bar," he told her now, pulling back and looking into her big brown eyes.

She laughed lightly. "You mean, quit my job and spend my days giving you blow jobs behind the bar while you serve drinks?"

It would have been playful and funny if he didn't suddenly want that with an intensity that freaked him out. "Hell yeah," he growled, lowering his head for another kiss.

It was, as always, long and hot and not nearly enough.

He started to back her up against the side of the building when her cell phone started ringing.

She pulled back and dragged in a deep breath. She stared up at him. "Damn, you're good at that."

"We're good at that." This was like nothing he'd ever felt before.

Addison continued to watch him as she dug her phone from her purse and lifted it to her ear. "Addison Sloan." She paused. "Yes, that's fine. I'll be there in twenty minutes." She disconnected and smiled at him. "I have to go."

He took a deep breath and stepped back, shoving a hand through his hair. "I know." Fuck, he should be relieved that she'd gotten the call and had to get in the cab. That was how he would have felt with any other woman. But no, he felt irrationally irritated that she was being called away.

He took another step back. Maybe if he couldn't smell her, he'd snap out of ...whatever this was.

It was not okay that he wanted her to stay and that he wanted to see more of her. If she did live in New Orleans, he would have called this off a long time ago. It didn't matter what her favorite color was or when her birthday was. He knew the important things—she was a New York City workaholic who, obviously, traveled extensively for her job. She wasn't what he was looking for.

"So I'll . . .see you," she said, suddenly acting awkward.

Gabe tried with everything in him to seem nonchalant about that. No, damn it, to be nonchalant about it. "Yep, see ya." He never asked when. He never confirmed that she'd be back the next month. He always bit his tongue before asking any of that.

"Thanks for . . ." She glanced up at the window to the apartment above the bar. "Everything," she finished with a naughty smile that made him want to put her up against the wall of the building, taxi driver be damned.

"You're very welcome." He couldn't help the half smile that curled his lips. God, this woman was the best hot-good-time he'd ever had. "And thank you."

Her cheeks got a little pink, but she laughed and moved toward the cab. "My pleasure."

Yeah, it had been. Heat rocked through him as he watched her open the car door, slip inside, wave to him through the window, and then pull away, headed for the offices of Monroe & LeBlanc, the best restoration architects in town.

Gabe took a big breath and worked on pulling himself together. He'd never been messed up over a woman, and he wasn't about to start now with one who could never be anything more than the best lay he'd ever had.

So what if her laugh made warmth spread through his chest? It also made his dick hard, and that was all that mattered. So what if watching her eat beignets made him want to pull her into his lap and hug her? It also made him want to hike up her skirt before pulling her into his lap so he could slide his hand up her inner thigh. And that was what he should focus on. So what if he really fucking wanted to know when her birthday was? He also wanted to know if she'd let him blindfold her in bed, and that was what he should be thinking about.

He yanked open the door to the tavern and stomped inside, pissed that he was upset that she had left. Of course she'd left. She fucking lived in New York City. He was her New Orleans fuck buddy. That was it. And it was really, really good. Why couldn't he just be happy with that?

"Good morning, Sunshine."

Gabe came up short when he realized that he wasn't alone in the bar.

"I assume Addison just left," Logan said from where he was

perched at the bar, a cup of coffee to one side and paperwork spread out in front of him.

Gabe glared at his brother and headed around the corner of the bar and straight for the coffeepot. "What the hell are you doing here so early?" Gabe was the primary bookkeeper for the business. Not the big tax and employee payroll type stuff. Their accountant, Reagan, took care of that. Gabe went over the weekend receipts and got the deposit ready for the bank on Monday mornings. He took care of inventory and ordering and paying the basic bills, while Logan was the one who dealt with repairs and maintenance on the building and appliances. They both handled issues with the employees, customers, and vendors, and, truth be told, it just depended on the day and the issue which of them was best at it.

"We have that meeting at one," Logan told him. "I'm getting some of the stuff together that they want to see."

"Meeting?" Gabe asked, turning with his cup of coffee and taking a long pull of the strong, dark brew. One thing he could say for his little brother—he made good coffee.

"With the architects?" Logan said. "The restoration? Remember?"

Of course he remembered. Well, he remembered that they were meeting with architects about restoring their building at some point.

"That's today?"

"Yeah. In about three hours," Logan told him with an eye roll. "Did she fuck you stupid or what?"

Gabe frowned. "Watch it." Even though, yeah, it kind of felt that way. He couldn't seem to focus on anything but Addison this morning. Still, he hated hearing Logan put it like that.

But he should be grateful to his brother for pointing out what this thing with Addison should be. Fucking. A fling. Orgasm central. Hot, no-strings-attached-and-thank-the-good-Lord-for-it sex. Something that he'd be getting over any fucking day now.

Instead, he found himself wondering if he should send flowers over to the office where she was today. That would be okay. It wasn't like he was sending flowers to her home or something. That would be more personal. And he wouldn't write anything sweet or romantic on the card. These would be thanks-for-the-two-blow-jobs flowers. Or you-do-cowgirl-better-than-anyone-I've-ever-met flowers.

"Hey, you okay?" Logan asked.

Gabe realized he'd zoned out. Thinking about sending Addison flowers. And not your-ass-fits-perfectly-in-my-hands flowers. More like I-already-miss-you flowers.

He could not send her I-already-miss-you flowers. Damn, he needed to get his shit together.

"Yeah, I'm fine."

Logan gave him a yeah-right look. "Damn, I knew I should have waited on her and Elena that first night," he said.

Gabe felt his hand curl into a fist and had to work to relax it. It was ridiculous to be jealous over the idea of his brother being the one to serve Addison that first night. And the insinuation that it would be Logan kissing her goodbye on the front sidewalk on Monday mornings if he had made her that first bourbon sour.

But the idea of someone else flirting with her, touching her, kissing her, making her laugh, watching her eat beignets, wrapping his arms around her as they stopped to listen to a band on the corner of Royal and Saint Ann . . .he definitely wanted to punch something.

If that wasn't a huge red flag, he didn't know what was. Dammit, he was a fucking mess.

"Shut the hell up," Gabe told his brother. "I forgot the meeting, but it's fine. What do we need to get together?"

Logan gave him a knowing grin but dropped the subject of Addison. At least for now. "I've got photos of the inside and outside from Grandma," Logan said, pushing an envelope across the bar. "I'm putting together a list of things that have been done over the years, the stuff that's original like the bar, the stair and balcony railings, the interior doors, the flooring in the back rooms. We also need to list the things that have been replaced and updated. The windows, the flooring out here, the exterior doors. That kind of stuff."

Gabe nodded as he leafed through the photos in the envelope.

The building that housed the tavern and the living quarters upstairs had been in the Trahan family for five generations. It was one of the first buildings built in the French Quarter after the fire of 1794 and, obviously, required a lot of routine maintenance. The basic structure was in good shape, but some of the unique characteristics of the Creole-style building needed a special touch to restore it to its original glory—something that was extremely important to Gabe and Logan's grandmother Adele. She was eighty-eight and had been nagging them to do the restoration for about three years. She'd gotten to the point where she was now claiming that she'd haunt the place if they didn't get it done before she died.

Gabe didn't want that. He knew Adele would be an irritating spirit, unlike the three fairly good-natured ghosts that already, supposedly, occupied the building. He wasn't sure he totally bought the stories, but they'd been passed down through the family for years, and he had heard some strange noises and had found things out of place for no reason. He'd never seen anything. And he was very okay with that. There was no reason to add a potential fourth haunting.

Now they finally had the funds to do a true restoration of the building, and they'd been courted by two of the best restoration firms in the city. They'd decided to go with Monroe & LeBlanc. Not just because Addison had been consulting with them on another project and had mentioned to Gabe, more than once, that the firm would do an amazing job on the tavern—though her opinion probably had far more weight than it should, everything considered—but because Gabe and Logan both sincerely liked and trusted Elena LeBlanc, one of the partners. She was a regular at Trahan's, and they considered her a friend. Plus, she'd brought Addison into the bar that first night and, hell, no matter how much he wished he wasn't completely whipped, Gabe couldn't deny that he was grateful to Elena for the introduction.

"So can you make up that list?" Logan asked. "I've got this about done."

"A list of the things that have been replaced rather than repaired and restored over the years?" Gabe asked. "Sure. Reagan probably has a lot of it, right? We would have needed to report that stuff for taxes and stuff?"

Logan sat up a little straighter. "I hadn't thought of that. Yeah, she would. I'll get that from her."

Gabe lifted a brow. "You're going to do that list, too?"

Logan studied the page in front of him. "Well, like you said, she probably already has those records. It won't be hard to pull those out."

Gabe leaned back against the counter behind him and watched his brother try to pretend to be cool about talking to Reagan. "Right, so I can easily get that from her," he said.

"Don't you have receipts and stuff to do this morning?" Logan asked.

He did. But he would always take time to harass his little brother. "That can wait. Reagan might need a little time to pull everything together for us. I should call her right away."

Logan already had his phone out. "I've got it."

Gabe smirked and lifted his cup. Logan was a player. He loved flirting—and more—with the local girls and tourists alike who came into the tavern. He never spent a night alone unless he wanted to. He was cool and charming and could get a girl to giggle and blush faster than any guy Gabe knew. But when he was around Reagan, he stumbled over his words, fumbled paperwork, said stupidly inappropriate things, and generally acted like a doofus. Clearly, his little brother had a thing for the sweet accountant. But Logan wasn't making any headway. Logan couldn't seem to keep his foot out of his mouth, and if it were Gabe, he'd be hiding out whenever Reagan came around. But Logan seemed to think every time was going to be the time he managed to get his act together and charm her, so he kept trying. And Gabe couldn't deny that he enjoyed the show.

Cooper needs a sibling.

The thought seemed to come out of nowhere, but it was nothing new, really. Gabe and Logan were close, and while no one drove him crazier than Logan, there was also no one he'd rather have at his back. His son needed someone like that—someone who could tease him but who would also take care of him.

"Hey, don't forget you're picking Cooper up tonight from day care," Gabe said.

"Yep, got it. What are you doing again?"

"Helping a couple of guys from the group bring some new tables to the community center."

"The group" was the single parents support group Gabe attended regularly. They'd decided to donate new tables to the community center that allowed them to meet weekly for free.

The support group was like a second family, and Gabe had appreciated their support over the past three years he'd been attending. His mom and brother helped with Cooper, and he couldn't imagine doing it without them, but the group made up of other single parents had given him a true "village."

"Oh, will Dana be there?" Logan asked.

Gabe rolled his eyes. Logan had gone from excited over talking to Reagan to interested in what another woman was doing tonight. Typical.

"I keep telling you, she's not your type," Gabe said.

That was an understatement. The uptight single mom who'd lost her hero husband in Afghanistan was not the type to fool around with a playboy bartender who thought responsible babysitting meant no one bled. Of course, Logan only ever babysat Cooper, and Cooper's only chance at bleeding was getting a paper cut from one of the pages in his books. Still, Logan would give the organized supermom a heart attack if he were around her kids. Or she'd kill him. Either way, Logan needed to stay away from Dana. Which Logan knew in the back of his mind. But it didn't stop him from flirting at every family picnic. Dana's cool reception to that flirting hadn't slowed him down either.

"No," Gabe said. "Just me, Caleb, and Austin."

Gabe loved hearing the female side of single parenting. Women just had a different take on things. But he couldn't deny that he felt a bond with the other guys who were also doing it alone.

"But you'll see her Thursday at the meeting, right?" Logan asked.

Gabe sighed. "Yeah."

"Tell her hi from me."

Logan gave Gabe a grin that he'd seen a million times directed at women across the bar. But Gabe didn't have breasts, and he did not find Logan charming.

"How about I just say, 'Logan, this is never going to happen,' right now and save us all some time?"

"She doesn't say it's never going to happen," Logan said. "She says, 'I don't think so.'"

"That's not the same thing?"

"Of course not."

He should just let it go, Gabe knew, but he couldn't help asking, "Why?"

"If someone asks if you'd like Brussels sprouts for dinner, what would you say?"

"Hell no."

"Exactly."

Gabe shook his head. "I don't get it."

"When you don't want something, you know it. And it's easy to say no to it. When you're not sure, or when you do want something but you don't want to let on, you say things like 'I don't think so.'" Logan sat back with a grin. "Dana has never said no to me."

"Not even a variation?" Gabe asked, not sure Logan was right.

Logan's grin dropped. "If she had, I would have backed off."

Yeah, okay, that was fair. They'd seen enough women getting unwanted attention and guys who didn't know how to take a hint to respect that no meant no. "I'll tell her hi for you," Gabe said.

"Thanks." And the grin was back.

Gabe finished off his coffee and mentally reviewed how to rearrange his day for the meeting he'd blown off. If that was three hours from now, it would put them at about eleven and . . .

Suddenly it hit him. Addison would probably still be at the office at eleven. She always caught the last plane out of New Orleans on Mondays, working all day at the firm when she was there.

He would get to see her again before she left.

His heart thudded far harder than was warranted even by the fact that she'd given him the best blow job in the history of blow jobs. A hard thud that probably meant he liked her for more than her blow jobs. A lot more.

He grinned, thinking about her surprise when she saw him walk into Monroe & LeBlanc. She was always the one to make the appearance at the tavern, on her own time line and terms, so he was the one to turn, see her, and feel his heart thump in a very not-just-a-fling way. Now it would be her turn. Maybe her reaction to seeing him unexpectedly would tell them both more about how she felt.

Gabe's grin dropped away immediately. Did he want to know more about how she felt? What did he want her to feel, exactly? And why would it matter? She fricking lived in New York. Even if she were head over heels, it wouldn't matter. He was not in the market for a long-distance relationship.

Even if what he had going with Addison felt like he was already in one.

Okay, he hadn't been interested in going out with—or even fooling around with—any other women since meeting her. Okay, he thought about her way more often than he should. And okay, he really fucking wanted to send her flowers. But he did not want to be involved with a woman who lived more than a thousand miles away and was in town only once a month.

It could only be a fling with the miles and time between them. They couldn't get more serious than that. Because with his business and his son, he couldn't make regular trips to New York, and he wouldn't introduce Cooper to a woman he'd see only every thirty days at most. Addison didn't even know he had a son. Because that part of Gabe's life wasn't a part of whatever he and Addison were doing. Hell, nothing about his life was really a part of whatever he and Addison were doing.

Besides, Cooper was only five. If he got attached to Addison but didn't have her in his life on a regular basis, it would be confusing.

And frankly, if Addison was only in town for a little more than forty-eight hours each time, Gabe wasn't sure how much of that time he wanted to share with anyone else. Even Cooper. Which probably made Gabe a bad father and an asshole. So it was better not to go there.

"Reagan didn't answer," Logan said a moment later. "So you might need to start putting together a list, after all."

Gabe nodded. That was good. He needed something to do. Something other than thinking about Addison and how she might react to seeing him at the architecture offices and how he wanted her to react to seeing him.

"Did you leave Reagan a message?" Gabe asked.

Logan ducked his head. "Yeah." He looked almost ...embarrassed.

Gabe grinned. "What did you say?" He knew Logan had put his foot in his mouth.

"Doesn't matter."

Oh, yes, it did. But Gabe would just ask Reagan. She really didn't understand why Logan acted like a dipshit around her. She thought he was like that with all women. Which was hilarious considering Logan was a well-known charmer and ladies' man.

"Okay, I'll get the list done," he said, pushing away from the counter and heading for the back office. He'd get right on it.

As soon as he sent Addison some flowers. Without analyzing why he was sending them. And he was only writing, See you soon, Gabe on the card. Nothing frilly, nothing romantic, and nothing about blow jobs.

Get Going Down Easy today!

And look for *Taking It Easy* and *Nice and Easy*,
coming soon!
Keep track of the whole series right here!

ABOUT THE AUTHOR

Erin Nicholas is the New York Times and USA Today bestselling author of over thirty sexy contemporary romances. Her stories have been described as toe-curling, enchanting, steamy and fun. She loves to write about reluctant heroes, imperfect heroines and happily ever afters. She lives in the Midwest with her husband who only wants to read the sex scenes in her books, her kids who will never read the sex scenes in her books, and family and friends who say they're shocked by the sex scenes in her books (yeah, right!).

Never miss any news from Erin!
Sign up for her newsletter today!
Find ALL of her books right here!
www.erinnicholas.com

And find Erin at
www.ErinNicholas.com,
on Twitter and on Facebook

Join her SUPER FAN page on Facebook for insider peeks, exclusive giveaways, chats and more!

Made in the USA
Monee, IL
17 November 2020

48007691R10184